JUMP CUT

A novel by Helen Grant

Jump Cut
Helen Grant

Published by Fledgling Press, 2023
Cover Design: Graeme Clarke
graeme@graemeclarke.co.uk

ISBN 9781912280643
www.fledglingpress.co.uk

Printed and bound by:
Print on Demand Worldwide, Peterborough

For Iona

Chapter One – September

I am sitting on the bed in my mourning dress, looking at the wall and listening to the clock ticking. The wall is painted pale green and at the edge of my line of vision there is the gilded edge of a mirror. I could look at the mirror if I turned my head, but I don't. I keep sitting there, not moving.

The weather is fitful today. The sun comes out briefly and the air is full of dust motes. I watch them moving on sluggish, invisible tides.

There is a distant creak as someone steps onto the landing, and then the brittle sound of heels on the polished floorboards. They approach the door. A moment's silence, then a tentative knock.

"Theda?"

I say nothing.

"Theda?" The voice is a little louder this time. "We have to go soon." A pause. "Can I come in?"

She doesn't wait for me to say 'yes'. I hear the rattle as the doorknob turns and then she comes into the bedroom.

"You're ready," she says, with artificial brightness. She's relieved, I suppose, that I'm not lying on the floor in my dressing gown, weeping.

I don't move my head, don't turn at the sound of her voice, so she crosses the room and stands right in front of me. The pale green wall is blocked from sight by a black crepe bodice.

"Darling," she says. "We have to go."

She leans forward, and perfectly-coiffed blonde waves dip into my view as she looks at what I am holding in my hands: my wedding photo, in its silver frame, me and Max standing outside the church door.

It was April, but we were lucky with the weather. We had sunshine all day, and the photograph has a crystal clarity. I am wearing a gauzy dress with a lace overlay and carrying a bouquet of peonies and roses. My dark hair is swept up into a studiedly careless style, with tendrils curling into my neck. And Max... Max is wearing the traditional morning suit but nobody would even look at that, because he's so *handsome*. He has brilliantly blue eyes and high cheekbones and golden hair, and because he is smiling you can see that his teeth are beautiful too, white and even. He is just marvellously good-looking.

Was marvellously good-looking.

Max is dead.

It hits me again, the way it keeps on hitting me, it will never stop hitting me.

Max is dead.

Celia puts her perfectly-manicured fingers over mine and prises them gently away from the photo frame. I tighten my grip for a moment, then let her do it.

What does it matter? I think.

She says, "The car is waiting. We shouldn't be late."

She's right, of course. Celia is holding it together wonderfully, considering she is Max's sister, and this must be hideous for her. Perhaps organising things and shepherding people about is what helps her do that. Supporting the bereaved wife, who has fallen to pieces completely.

She puts the wedding photo carefully on the dressing-table, and then she puts a hand under my elbow, encouraging me to get up.

The bed – our marital bed – creaks as I stand up. I look down at myself. My black silk dress is crumpled and it is a little loose around the waist and bodice. Even though Max has been dead less than a fortnight, I haven't been eating much. I am also wearing horrible black opaque tights and low-heeled black patent shoes.

I look like a crow, I think.

I let Celia lead me out of the room. I stand on the landing like a black-clad doll while she closes the bedroom door.

6

The click is resonant in the silence. Then she takes me downstairs. She walks next to me, holding my arm, as if she thinks I might fall otherwise, or perhaps throw myself down the whole flight.

There are several vehicles waiting outside on the gravel. One of them is a hearse. I glance at that, and then look away. Max is in there. My *husband* is in there. I can't remember what they dressed him in. Probably someone asked me what he would have wanted. Everything's a blur.

Celia's husband Simon opens the door of the second car for me, and I climb inside. The seats are leather, and cold, and the interior has a sterile smell of air freshener. There is a driver in a sober suit. It is a big car, with enough room for three in the back, so Simon sits on one side of me and Celia sits on the other.

"Theda," says Simon, kindly. He is a big man, with a large square face, and his expression is so sympathetic that I have to look down, at my hands clasped together in my black silk lap.

Trees slide past the car windows, and then the open road, and eventually we come to the church. It is the very same church where Max and I were married, a little over three years ago. It was spring then, and now it is autumn, so the trees and bushes in the churchyard and the climbing plants on the walls have an overgrown, tired look.

The car stops, and Celia puts her hand over mine. We wait for the undertaker to open the back of the hearse, and for the pallbearers to take up the coffin. Then we follow it into the church. As we approach the doorway with its ancient and weathered stone arch, I remember standing here as a bride. My parents were dead by then, so Max's father escorted me down the aisle. He looked like a very much older version of Max, grey and a little lined but still good-looking, with a full head of hair. I remember thinking that that was what Max would look like when he became old – but he never did become old.

We step into the church. Some, but not all, of the same faces are there, but they look drawn now, the colour leached out of them by the black clothes everyone is wearing. It's strange, I think, how the church looks the same but so different. It is full of flowers again, but all of them are white. At the wedding, we had shades of pink and white.

Then I look down, because the sight of so many sympathetic faces is more than I can bear, and ahead of me is the oak casket carrying all the hopes and dreams I once had. Instead, I look at the shiny black toes of my shoes moving across the ancient flagstones.

The pallbearers put the coffin onto the catafalque and we slide into a pew near the front. I don't really follow anything after that. Someone else does the eulogy. Nobody expects the widow to do that – to stumble through the dead person's virtues, the key events of their life, while trying not to break down completely. Nobody wants to watch her standing there crying, trying to get herself under control when really life has gone right off the rails and nothing is alright at all. Once or twice, the eulogist manages to raise a laugh. I think people are relieved, or perhaps it makes them feel as though Max is still with us, the fact that something about him can still make us chuckle. Celia and Simon don't join in, though; around me there is a capsule of silent grief.

Afterwards, we file out, and the priest clasps both of my hands in his, trying to offer some comfort, as though promises of the hereafter can be the same as having a warm and breathing person lying next to you at night. There are other faces, too, here and at the wake, which is at home, offering condolences or practical help or clumsily-expressed hopes for future happiness. I endure them all for as long as I can. Then I excuse myself and go upstairs to my bedroom, leaving Celia and Simon in charge. I lock the door, take off my shiny black shoes and lie down on the bed in my black silk dress, curling into a foetal position.

Max is dead, I say to myself, daring it not to be true. *Max is dead.*

Chapter Two – April

Seven months is not long enough to get over it. It is long enough to know that there is no pregnancy – nothing of Max for me to carry with me into the future. It is long enough, too, to start thinking about what might fill my life for a while, and help me to look forwards, instead of back at the past. Something to fix my mind on – to keep the bad thoughts out.

I have survived the winter: the long dark days, the silent emptiness of Christmas. Celia and Simon tried to make me go to them, but I wouldn't. I lied, and said I was spending it with old friends of mine, people they didn't know. I think they were relieved.

But now, there is spring in the air, and I am driving north, with no makeup on, and my hair tied back in a sensible ponytail. I am driving Max's car, which is a Mercedes, and bigger and faster than mine. There are two suitcases in the boot, and a box of books and papers on the back seat. My phone is on the passenger seat, but I don't really expect it to ring. Who would call me? I've pushed everyone away.

Around the tangled knot which is Birmingham, the traffic is very heavy and I make slow progress. After Manchester it begins to become lighter, and by the time I pass Carlisle, there are not many other cars on the road. The sun is low in the sky.

A little further on lies the border. There is a huge blue and white sign reading *Welcome to Scotland*, and underneath: *Fàilte gu Alba*. I stare at it for a moment and then it is gone, behind me. I am in Scotland. The motorway curves slightly to the west here and I am driving towards the sunset. Max and I never went to Scotland together. We went to France and Italy and Switzerland, but never Scotland. Perhaps that's why it feels like a good place to – forget? No; not to forget. Never to forget. To start over.

The satnav has been silent for a long time, but as I approach Glasgow it starts to issue orders in its toneless voice. That dead intonation is strange, like having someone there with me but not having them there at the same time. I'm used to that; I carry Max round with me, wherever I go. I follow the instructions, indicating carefully and observing the speed limit. The big car purrs along, comfortably.

Eventually I turn onto another motorway, heading north again. I stop at a services near Stirling, and have a cup of tea and a sandwich I don't fancy very much. Then I fill up the tank, and while I'm standing at the pump I can feel the bite in the air; it's quite a few degrees colder here than in the south of England.

Not long after leaving the services, I pass an illuminated castle on a rocky outcrop. It stands out because there are no lights along the road here. Then it, too, is behind me, and I'm barrelling into the darkness. Driving away from my old life, into the unknown.

I would miss my turn altogether in the dark, if the satnav didn't announce it. I pass through a tiny village, without so much as a shop or a pub, and then I'm onto a long stretch of A-road. It snakes along under canopies of trees, eerily underlit by the headlights, and over stone-walled bridges with black water sparkling beneath. Once, something with glittering eyes scurries away from the lights, into the undergrowth.

On the edge of a small town I turn down an even smaller road, one without a white line down it and with overhanging bushes on either side. It occurs to me that I could stop and check one of the maps in the glove box. But the satnav can't be wrong; it keeps telling me confidently where to go. I keep driving.

Eventually I take a right, down a turning that is more a track than a road; in places there is grass growing in the middle. I brake, gazing ahead into the dark, but after a few moments the satnav urges me onwards. There are one or two faint lights up ahead, so the road does go *somewhere*.

As I get nearer to the lights, I see that I am approaching a small stone-built house. Briefly I wonder whether I am going to end up on someone's drive, apologising to some furious person while I attempt to turn a large Mercedes in a small space. But then I see that the road simply passes close by it, and then dips sharply away.

The car's suspension bounces on a simply enormous pothole and for a moment I'm so busy worrying about the back axles that I don't brake. Then I see glossy black water, and I do.

The road just – stops. Ahead of me is a river, and the road just leads down into it and vanishes.

I put the handbrake on, open the door and get out. My eyes are not deceiving me. The road really does lead into a river. The beams of the headlights just about show me the opposite bank, where the road apparently resumes: I can see tyre tracks in the mud.

I feel the first spots of rain on my face and decide to get back into the car. The satnav is still telling me plaintively to proceed. I look behind me, and apart from the faint lights of that house, everything is a dark abyss. Not ideal for reversing. Then I look forward again and spot a sign almost overgrown with foliage; it stands out because it is made of white metal, with black lettering. It says: Ford.

So I am *supposed* to drive through the river? I'm still doubtful about that, so I get out of the car again, and take another look, shivering.

It doesn't seem to be that deep. In places, you can see little patches of stones sticking up out of the water. I pick up a stick, and go right down to the edge, where I poke it in. Only a few inches. I look back at the Mercedes. I don't think the water would come any higher than halfway up the wheels. I bite my lip and go back to the car.

I slide behind the wheel, and I am still pondering the

11

question when I see lights in the rear-view mirror. Another car is coming down the lane. That decides me; if someone else is going to cross the ford, so can I. Also, I'm in their way. I put the car in gear and touch the accelerator gently.

The car bounces a little again as the ground levels out, and then I drive slowly into the water. The wash from the wheels makes a rushing sound and I have to admit there's something exciting about doing this. It feels wrong, and sort of daring.

A flicker in the rear-view mirror catches my eye and I see that the car behind hasn't followed me. It's turned in at the house.

Oh–

There's a gentle bump as the Mercedes goes over something on the riverbed, and for a moment my attention swaps to that. Rain splatters on the windscreen, so I put the wipers on. I look ahead and my confidence falters a little bit.

Just before the far bank, the water looks a little deeper and it is moving much more quickly. In the dark and the rain it looks black and viscous, almost syrupy. Still, I can see the tyre marks emerging from the river, so I know it is possible to cross.

I press the accelerator a little harder, thinking that I can take the deeper part at a rush – momentum will carry me through. The car leaps forward and for a couple of seconds I think I'm going to make it; I see myself scrambling up the further bank with an interesting story to tell people afterwards.

And then I feel the current hit the car, and in spite of its size and weight, the nose slips to the left slightly. I rev, trying to urge it up the bank. For a moment the front wheels throw up mud, and then the Mercedes settles back into the river.

I sit there for a moment, dumbfounded. It's not possible to go forward now; I can see that. I won't get up the bank. After a couple of seconds of blind panic, it occurs to me to put the car in reverse and try to back out of the water. So I try that, but it won't shift. I'm stuck.

I am not an expert on cars, but I'm pretty sure getting water in the engine is a disaster, so I turn it off. Instantly, the sound of rain pelting the car is audible, even over the sound of the running water. If it keeps raining, as it shows every sign of doing, the water level is going to rise. I think that would be a very bad thing.

I wonder what the hell I am going to do.

Chapter Three

I have enough sense not to open the driver's door, which is on the upriver side. Even while the water is relatively low, I suspect it would flow right into the car. I take the keys out of the ignition and climb over to the passenger side. I put my mobile phone in my pocket. Then I open the door and get out.

Instantly I am up to my ankles in water so cold it nearly takes my breath away. I stifle a shriek.

I don't think the car would move, not yet, not even with this current, but I dare not hang around on the downstream side, just in case it does. I don't want to think about what will happen if I fall over, either. So I wade very slowly and carefully back across the river, towards the lights of the house. The water really isn't deep – so far, anyway – but the stones are slippery in places. I have my arms out for balance but my hands are curled into fists. A gust of wind tugs a lock of hair loose and instantly it is plastered to the side of my face.

I stagger onto the gritty track with a great sense of relief, and glance back at the car. This feels like a fairly big catastrophe, but I don't cry or anything. I cried enough after Max died. Instead, I wipe sopping strands of hair out of my eyes, pull my sodden jacket close around me, and march towards the house.

While I have been floundering about in the river, the owner of the house has parked a tatty-looking Range Rover outside it and seemingly gone inside. The door is shut and all the curtains are closed, but there is a light on over the lintel, shedding a little circle of comfort.

I look at the house for a moment. It would be a long walk to anywhere else, so I hope they won't mind me knocking. So I squelch up the path to the door, and knock very firmly.

I'm just beginning to think there won't be any reply when the door opens. It's a man, tall and wavy-haired, clad in ancient corduroys and a woolly jumper. The jumper has a hole in the elbow, I see. He is holding a sandwich in one hand and I see him swallowing before he attempts to speak.

"I'm really sorry," I say, shivering. "I'm–"

"–stuck in the ford," he finishes. "Did you not see me flashing you not to go in?"

"No," I say. I'm sure my teeth are about to start chattering. "I thought you were coming down after me and wanted me to get a move on."

He shakes his head. "You'd get across it in a tractor, and in good weather, a four-by-four, but not in a thing like that."

"The satnav–"

"It's always the satnav." He puts the sandwich down unceremoniously on a battered chair in the hallway and reaches for a coat from a row of pegs. "Do you want me to haul it out?"

I gape at him. I had been hoping to stand somewhere warm and dry while I called the rescue service. I didn't expect anyone to pull the car out themselves.

"Can you?"

"Aye, I can. We should get on with it, though. The rain's set in, and it won't get any easier." He is shrugging the coat on; it's a long waxed thing, the sort of coat you only ever see in country magazines. Then he looks at me, takes another coat from the pegs and holds it out. "I think you'll need this."

The coat is also waxed and probably of an even greater antiquity than the one he is wearing. Additionally, it smells of dog, or possibly horse. I put it on anyway. Then I give one last yearning look at the warm dry interior of the house before he shuts the door and we trudge off to look at the car.

He snorts a bit at the sight of it, wedged at a slight angle, with the water foaming at the upriver side. Then he stumps off into the dark and comes back a few minutes later driving a *tractor*. I watch him manoeuvring it from the safety of the bank and I am quite relieved when he goes to take the handbrake off the Mercedes so he can pull it out of the water; I am a little afraid of that running water and my feet are already like blocks of ice.

Then I wince as Max's car, his pride and joy, is hauled backwards across the stones. Even above the sound of the river and the hiss of the rain I can hear the scrapes and grinding noises.

I stand back as the tractor passes, dragging it along behind. Eventually it stands on level ground, in front of the house, looking very sorry for itself. The man gets down from the tractor, unhitches the two vehicles, then takes the tractor off somewhere around the back of the building. He does all this with a kind of concise practicality, as though he hauls cars out of the ford every day of the week.

Perhaps he does, I think.

I'm still standing there with rain dripping off my hood when he comes back.

"Come in," he says briefly, tilting his head towards the house, so I follow him, reasoning that if he were an axe murderer or something, he wouldn't have rescued my car. Besides, I'm so cold I think I'll die if I don't warm up a bit.

I'm taking off the malodorous coat when I hear a scratching noise. The man looks at me.

"You mind dogs?"

I shake my head. He opens a door and a black and white collie runs out, all lolling tongue and inquisitive eyes.

"Jess," he says, though I'm not sure whether he's addressing me or the dog.

I follow man and dog into a stone-flagged kitchen where the heat seems to come from an antiquated range. There is a worn pine table which is covered with dirty dishes at one end, and books at the other. A lot of the books seem to be old ones, with cloth or leather bindings. I can't pick out the names on the spines.

I sit on a hard kitchen chair, as close to the range as I dare.

"Thank you," I say, realising I haven't said this yet. "I don't know what I would have done."

"You're not the first," he says. "Easier to get it out of the river now, before the rain, than tomorrow."

"All the same."

I rub my hands together, trying to get life back into my fingers. Then I look up and he's holding out a very generous glass of whisky.

I shake my head. "I'm driving."

"Not tonight, you're not," he says. "Better get it checked over first thing tomorrow. Assuming it even starts."

He puts the whisky down right in front of me.

"Where are you headed? Must be somewhere local, if you've come down here. I'll drive you."

"I couldn't possibly ask you to do that. I'll get a taxi."

"No taxis out here at this time of night, unless you've pre-booked." The corner of his mouth twitches. "It's not London."

"I'm not *from* London," I say.

He shrugs. "Like I said, I'll drive you. Where do you want to go?"

I hesitate. "It's not a town. It's an estate. It's called Garthside."

A pause.

"Ah," he says.

"Do you know it?"

"I know *of* it. I haven't been in there, though. Don't know anyone who has." He thinks about it, and then he grins. The grin is genuinely warm, and it makes me look down at the glass that has miraculously found its way into my hands. "It's good to have an excuse to see it."

"They say it was pretty amazing in its day," I offer. "The house, I mean. But I've only seen old photos of it."

"I've heard that too. Hard to imagine it's still in good

17

repair. You should drink that, you know. It's an eighteen-year-old malt. It's a sin to waste it."

I take a sip. "It's good."

"Aye, it is. So what brings you to Garthside?"

I pause for a moment before saying, "Mary Arden."

"Ah, so you're a doctor – a specialist?"

"No, a writer."

"I see," he says, and then, "So she's agreed to see you, has she?"

"Yes."

"You're sure about that?"

"Of course I am," I say, slightly nettled. "I wouldn't have come otherwise."

"She doesn't see many folk," he says, mildly. There's a silence, and just before it gets awkward, he says, "It'll take a little while to get to Garthside by road, but as the crow flies, we're pretty much neighbours."

"That's..." I can't think of an adjective, so my voice tails off.

"You're staying a day or two?"

"Longer," I say. "I'm hoping to write a book."

"And you're staying *at* Garthside?"

"Mm-hmm."

He's leaning against the table, appraising me, and I sort of wish he wouldn't.

Then he says, "I haven't introduced myself. I'm Angus Fraser."

So I have to give my name too. "Theda Blake. I mean – Garrick. Theda Garrick."

His eyebrows go up. "Recently married?"

This is really *too* nosy of him, so it kind of serves him right when I say, "Recently widowed." Then I'm sorry, because his expression shows that he can see he's dropped a huge clanger.

"Oh God, I'm so sorry."

"It's okay. I mean, you weren't to know." I look away.

18

"I don't expect you to understand, but I can't bear people calling me Mrs Blake. It makes me..."

He waits for me to finish the sentence. When I don't, he says, "I'm very sorry."

The dog, who has been eyeing me during the conversation, chooses this moment to sidle up to me, so I occupy myself with her, not looking at Angus. After a while, I say, "This trip was a chance to get away. And I know I've been incredibly lucky to get Mary Arden to agree to see me."

"You have," he says.

"It's something else to think about," I say, and then, "That's a bit sad, isn't it?" I'm aiming for a light tone, but it's hard to stop my voice breaking.

"No, it isn't. It's sensible." After a moment, he says, "That's an unusual name – Theda."

It's a relief to be on safe ground. "It's after Theda Bara. You know, the silent era film actor."

He shakes his head.

"My dad was a huge film fan. Theda Bara was a star in the '20s. I don't think she ever did any movies with sound." I manage a smile. "I guess I should be thankful he didn't call me Joan or Norma or something."

"Lassie," he suggests, absolutely straight-faced and I can't help myself; I give a great shout of laughter. It's as well I've finished the whisky, or I'd have spat it all over the kitchen.

When I've finished laughing, he nods at the kitchen clock, which is just as battered-looking as everything else.

"It's late. Will they still want you arriving at this time of night?"

I nod, serious again. "I told them I was driving up from the south of England. I said I'd stay in a hotel somewhere, but they said not to worry. She, Mary Arden I mean, has staff round the clock. They said they'd let me in whenever it was."

He thinks about that. "Well," he says at last, "If there's any misunderstanding, I can drive you back to the town. There's a big hotel there."

"I don't think there will be."

"Alright. Do you want anything out of your car?"

"If it's no trouble, I've got two suitcases and a box of papers. I'd rather take those now than have to think how to get them, if the car has to go in."

"It's no trouble," he says. "Jess – bed." The dog walks off obediently to a basket in the corner, and settles down.

I put down the empty glass and stand up. There is a little pool under my chair and my feet are still cold, but I feel a lot better than I did before.

We go outside.

Chapter Four

The back of the Range Rover swallows my two cases and the box of books and papers, and I climb in beside Angus. Like the coat, the vehicle has a smell of dog, distinct though not offensive. There's a dog cage at the back, but I strongly suspect Jess rides shotgun on shorter journeys.

We set off, back up the lane, and I wonder how I ever thought this was really the right route. Rain is pattering down and through the sweep of the windscreen wipers I can pick out the overhanging trees. The Range Rover bumps over ruts and potholes, so that the trees seem to dance in the beams of the headlights.

We don't talk much. I am a little preoccupied; it has occurred to me that I am not going to make a very professional first impression, turning up soaked to the skin and very possibly smelling of whisky. Angus seems to be lost in his own thoughts. It seems to me also that you probably have to concentrate, driving along these roads. They are narrow, and there are some very sharp bends.

I glance over at him, just the once. He's very angular, with a rather long face and sharp cheekbones. Not as good-looking as Max. *Nobody* is as good-looking as Max was. I wonder if I will ever stop comparing people. A cloud settles over me and I think silently about Max for the rest of the way.

The turning up to Garthside is so abrupt that I would have missed it if I'd been by myself. It turns back on itself, too, so that it is very hard to see, if approached from this direction. It simply looks like a dark hollow between two stretches of hedge, though as the Range Rover turns in, I see two lichenous gateposts mostly hidden under wet foliage. A few metres further on there is a sign reading: GARTHSIDE HOUSE. STRICTLY PRIVATE PROPERTY.

I remember reading once that the trespass laws are different in Scotland. People can't stop you going where you like, as long as you don't do any damage. But I guess they can put up signs, to discourage you.

"I'd have missed this," I say. "If I'd been driving myself."

"It doesn't advertise itself," says Angus. He pauses. "There are some strange tales about the place around here."

I raise my eyebrows, but he doesn't elaborate.

The drive up to Garthside House seems to take a long time, and I wonder how big this estate actually is. We pass what I think are great rhododendron bushes, the leaves shiny with rain. Then at last I glimpse light up ahead and a minute or so after that, we see it, as the drive widens out into a large, gravelled area.

Angus brakes, and both of us stare at it.

"Wow," I manage to say.

Imagine a big house in Scotland and you think of some huge, grim stone castle, hundreds of years old. This isn't like that at all. It's sprawling, far wider than it is high, and it's in the very distinctive style known as Art Deco, popular in the 1920s and '30s. It has large windows divided by slender frames into small panes, a flat roof and bold geometric features covered in white stucco, so that the effect is that of a vast wedding cake. It has been carefully lit to accentuate these features.

I have seen old photographs of Garthside House before, but none of them really did it justice. It's stunning, magnificent in fact, and probably completely unsuitable for the Scottish climate.

We sit and look at it for a minute or two, long enough for an irregularity to snag my eye. Most of the lights are yellow, but far away on the upper left-hand side of the building, one window briefly flashes a bluish colour.

Someone is watching TV, I think. They must have one hell of a big flat screen.

The Range Rover begins to roll forward again. I, who

seem to feel so little since Max died, experience a twinge of nervousness. A lot depends on first impressions, and I'm turning up late and dishevelled. There's more to it than that, though. The house is magnificent but there is the sense of something being a little off, a little out of kilter – and not just because the place seems so unexpected in its setting. I look up at that white stucco façade and I have an unaccountable urge to stay in the car with Angus. I swallow. It's no use feeling like that. He's helped me enough already. He doesn't owe me anything. I don't really *know* him.

The car stops outside the front door, and pushing down my reluctance I open the door and get out. I go to get my suitcases from the boot, but Angus is there before me.

"You really don't have to," I tell him, but he shrugs. I guess he's getting a look at the place, anyway – seeing the reality behind that cryptic reference to *strange tales*. I take the box of books and papers, folding the cardboard flaps over to try to stop them getting rained on.

I ring the bell, juggling awkwardly with the box. Then I wait. Nothing. The rain patters down on my head and shoulders as I wonder whether the doorbell even functions; the place looks so antique that perhaps it doesn't. Feeling self-conscious, I press the bell again. The moments stretch out – perhaps it has even been minutes now – and still nobody opens up. Eventually I raise my hand to knock instead, and an instant before my fist strikes the door, it opens.

It's not Mary Arden herself standing there – obviously not. It's a woman of about fifty, perhaps a well-preserved sixty, in a neat dark suit. Her dark hair is sleeked back into a neat chignon and her grey eyes are framed by heavy spectacles. It's not an actual uniform she's wearing, but everything about her screams staff. I don't think she's a relative; I bet she's the housekeeper.

She looks at me and I can see a question forming in her

eyes, so I say, "Hello, I'm Theda Garrick. I'm very sorry I'm so late."

"Ms Garrick," she says. "Of course. Welcome." She pronounces it *Mz*, carefully avoiding either Miss or Mrs, although she can't know any of my circumstances.

"Do come in," she says, and then, to Angus, "You may leave those bags just inside the door."

I think she thinks he is a taxi driver and I wonder how to explain that he isn't, but Angus just puts the suitcases down where she indicated.

"Bye," he says to me and starts off back towards the Range Rover. Then he thinks of something and turns back. "If the garage want to know where the car is, tell them Garthside Ford."

"Thank you," I say into the wind and rain. I feel I ought to say more, but he is gone, so I turn back to the woman in the doorway.

"I'm afraid I'm rather wet," I tell her apologetically. "I followed the satnav and got stuck in the ford. I'll probably drip all over the floor."

"Don't you worry about that," she says. "Get yourself inside and let's shut this door. I'm Mrs Harris, the housekeeper."

So I was right about that. I thought she was a bit terse with Angus, but now she seems very friendly.

"I'll get someone to take your bags up," she says. "The box, too, if you'd like to leave it on this table. And I'll get you a towel. Would you like some tea?"

"Oh, yes please."

She opens a set of double doors and leads me into a sitting-room where there is a fire burning, although it is April. I am very grateful to see it, although I suspect I shall actually steam if I stand in front of it. Then she goes off to see to the tea.

I am left alone in the room. It is in keeping with the Art Deco exterior; the fireplace looks original to me. The walls are painted a very pale green, the colour they call Eau de Nil, I think, and there are chairs and a sofa in a slightly darker shade, the sides made of some dark polished wood. The door I came in by is mirrored by a door at the other end, and on each side of both there is a beautifully stylised peacock design. If it were not for me, damp and sniffing and very definitely a twenty-first century woman, the room could be right out of 1930. It is undoubtedly gorgeous and it also gives me a faint sense of unreality – of something artificially preserved.

There is a delicate scent on the air: something with top notes of orange or peach, and a warm oriental base. It is faint but distinctive – an older woman's perfume. I didn't smell it on Mrs Harris, so it must belong to someone else, who has either left the room recently or spends a lot of time here.

I step closer to the fire and warm my hands and feet, shivering a little.

I am here, I think. *Garthside House.*

Chapter Five

The tea arrives, extraordinarily, in a tea-set that seems to match the vintage of the house and even the colour of the room. The delicate green cup has a triangular silvered handle. There is a green plate, too, with shortbread petticoat tails tasting faintly of peppermint. I help myself rather liberally to those, since it is a long time since I last ate, and I have two cups of tea.

Mrs Harris tactfully leaves me alone while I am doing this, but then she comes back to take me up to my room.

"Mrs Harris," I say, "This is a little embarrassing but... my car is still over by the ford. I don't even know if it will start again."

"Don't worry, Ms Garrick. I'll have someone pick it up and take it to the garage for you. Garthside Ford, wasn't it?"

I nod. "I'm so sorry to be a nuisance–"

"That's perfectly alright, Ms Garrick," she says, firmly. Seemingly the matter is closed; she indicates for me to follow her. As I do, I think how strange it must be to live like this all the time, having people to sort out all the difficult, inconvenient things for you. I also hope that she won't send it anywhere too expensive, but I don't dare ask.

We go through the hallway again and I notice that in the intervening time my two cases and the box have disappeared. Whoever moved them did it very quietly; I didn't hear a thing.

I follow her up a sweeping staircase that starts at one side of the hall and curves round. The balustrade has a beautiful but archaic design of stylised flowers – lilies, I think. I run my hand along the highly polished rail at the top as we go up. In truth, I am not really comfortable with Mrs Harris. The whole idea of someone having staff is too alien, and I'm not quite sure how to behave. Does Mrs Harris expect me to chat with her, or would that just be annoying, or gauche? It seems rude to say nothing, though.

"Have you worked here a long time?" I ask her.

"Oh, more than twenty years," she says, turning to me with a smile.

"Wow." That seems like a safe response. There are loads of other things I'd love to ask her, but can't, like *Have you got a life of your own? And what can you possibly do here all day, with just one old lady to look after?*

"Miss Arden is an excellent employer," she says.

"That's good."

"Yes, it is."

"The house is really beautiful."

"Thank you," she says, as though it's hers. Perhaps, to a certain extent, it is. Mary Arden can't possibly get around it very much.

At the top of the stairs, we turn right.

"I've put you in one of the bedrooms along here," says Mrs Harris. "That way, you won't be disturbed by anyone else going about the house during the night." She glances at me. "Miss Arden has staff in attendance twenty-four hours a day."

I nod. I guess if you are a hundred and four and incredibly rich, you have whatever you like.

Almost at the far end of the landing, she opens a door and stands back to let me go in first. The room is stunning in an old-fashioned way, like the rest of the house. It is pink and pearl coloured, with a lot of walnut, and looks like the sort of place a film star would sleep in, which shouldn't be a surprise, really. The bed is enormous, and has a big padded headboard in the shape of a shell. I stare at it, imagining myself lying there like a child in an adult-sized bed, small and frail-looking.

Mrs Harris shows me the ensuite, which is cream and green. Even the soap has a kind of Art Deco look to it. What was charming at the beginning is starting to weird me out a little bit: it's like I've actually stepped back in time. I'm quite glad when I see that she is preparing to go. I'm tired; I guess I'll be more appreciative tomorrow.

"I'll brief you on Miss Arden's schedule in the morning," she says. "I expect you'd like to retire for the evening. When would you like breakfast?"

"At eight?" I hazard.

"Perfect," she says. She pauses for a moment in the doorway. "I hope you will have a successful stay here, Ms Garrick."

"Thank you," I say, and watch her close the door.

A successful stay, I think. I wonder what she meant by that. What's an unsuccessful stay – one where Mary Arden has you thrown out? But perhaps she didn't mean anything at all. She has a formal way of speaking; perhaps that's all it was.

My suitcases are both here, and the box of papers is sitting on a little walnut escritoire. I go over and look into the box. Thankfully very little rain seems to have got in. I wipe a few drops off the front of the topmost book, but that's about all.

While I'm standing there with the book in my hands, I listen. I am pretty sure Mrs Harris has gone downstairs, but I'd like to be sure. Silence. All the same, I put the book down, go over to the door, and very quietly turn the key in the lock. Staff are probably a nice thing to have if you can afford them, but I don't fancy anyone walking in while I'm in the bath or something.

After that, I take my shoes off, because I am leaving wet marks on the pink carpet, even after drying myself in front of the fire. I start a bath running and while the water is thundering into the big cream-coloured tub I unpack my stuff. In spite of the age of the house and its decor, everything seems to be very clean. I pull out drawers in the walnut units and the interiors are carefully lined with paper and scented with sachets. The big wardrobe has plenty of hangers. The only thing the staff have missed is the top of the wardrobe; I climb onto a chair in my stockinged feet to see whether my cases would fit up there, and find there is a thick layer of dust on it. I climb down, brushing my hands together to get it off my fingers.

The bath is full. I turn the taps and the sudden silence is striking. The water ripples lazily and is still. I unpack my washbag in front of the big mirror. It's an extraordinary thing, that mirror: it has a fan of glass panels at either side of the main one, so when I move, the gesture is repeated multiple times. I try not to examine myself too carefully in its gleaming depths; the rain and wind have done a lot of damage and I wasn't looking particularly glamorous to start with, since I didn't even put make up on this morning. There didn't seem any point, as there often seems little point in such gestures these days. It would all have rubbed off before I even got to Carlisle, anyway. Tomorrow morning I will have to make an extra effort – and not just for Mrs Harris, either. I can't imagine meeting someone like Mary Arden, someone who once epitomised glamour, looking like a drowned rat.

There are little cupboards either side of the sink, so I think I will stow the washbag in one of those. So I open the right hand one, and there, right at the back of the shelf, is a little pot of face cream. I take it out, thinking that perhaps this is a helpful offering for guests. But it's been opened, and used. The marks of someone else's fingertips are visible in the cream. *They must have had other guests*, I think. *Or at any rate, one guest.*

I remember Angus saying 'She doesn't see many folk.' Evidently, though, she has seen someone.

I screw the lid back on, and put it back on the shelf. I suppose it doesn't matter who else Mary Arden has seen – as long as she talks to *me*.

Then I climb into the big bath, intending to have a long welcome soak.

Alas, it's not as glorious as I was hoping. The water is hot enough, but the tub is so long that I can barely touch the end of it with outstretched toes; if I lie down there is a definite risk of slipping under the water altogether. So I sit bolt upright while I wash, and then I sit for a little while with my arms around my knees, and think that it is possible to have *too much* luxury; if I fell asleep in a bath this big I'd probably drown.

Chapter Six

The next morning, I am downstairs at five to eight, my hair tamed into a neat up-do and a respectable but not overt amount of makeup on. I've chosen a quiet but smartly casual outfit of skirt, shirt and cardigan because I have no idea who I am going to meet down there, and I want to present a professional front. I can't imagine Mary Arden will be breakfasting at this hour, but you never know. Older people often seem to get up pretty early.

In fact, I am the only one. Breakfast is served in a bright room with windows that run almost up to the ceiling. It's so light and cheerful that the sense of something a little awry fades away; it's more like being in a very well lit museum.

The woman who is setting out the things asks me what I'd like, and since it's on offer, I agree to the cooked breakfast. I notice she has a southern English accent, like mine. So they don't recruit locally – or perhaps she is a recent incomer. The breakfast, when it arrives, is enormous, and includes some slabs of square sausage and potato scones. I work my way through this, looking around me with interest. There is a huge decorative panel on the wall; it looks a bit like a stylised fountain. I wonder how they keep everything like this, so old-fashioned but so new-looking. Some things must have been modernised over the years – there was plenty of hot water last night, after all, and I doubt you'd get that from a 1930s heating system. And there is the flat screen TV at the other end of the house.

I spear a piece of potato scone with my fork. A cooked breakfast, just for me. A room fit for a Hollywood film star. Someone to sort out the problem with my car. I feel as though I should pinch myself to check I'm awake. But they suggested staying here when we were exchanging letters. I could have stayed in a hotel – it would have been expensive, if I was here a long time, but I could have done it. Or a rented apartment. But they offered me this. It's amazingly generous. I guess Mary Arden has decided it is finally time to tell her story before it is too late and that is why she has offered to let me stay here, for as long as it takes.

I have cleaned the plate and am just finishing my second cup of tea when Mrs Harris appears, looking immaculate again. It's impossible to imagine her doing *human* things like sleeping or sitting in the bath.

She says, "Good morning, Ms Garrick. I hope you slept well?"

"Like a log." This is true – I was so worn out from the driving and the dip in the ford and the whisky that I doubt a bomb falling could have woken me.

"Excellent. If you're ready, we will go into the morning room and go through Miss Arden's schedule and some other details."

I follow her through into the room where I had the tea yesterday, the one with the beautiful peacock designs on the walls. We perch on two chairs, both sitting very upright: I because I am nervous, and she because she doesn't do anything as unprofessional as lounging.

"First of all, Ms Garrick, to set your mind at rest, your car has been collected from Garthside Ford and is at the garage. Is there anything you needed out of it? No?" She waves off my thanks. "That's perfectly alright. Now, regarding Miss Arden's schedule..."

This is the bit I've been waiting for.

"Given her age, Miss Arden can generally give you about an hour a day. Longer than that would be exhausting for her, and probably unproductive for you."

An hour. I suppose I shouldn't be surprised. Mary Arden is really ancient, after all. It will take a long, long time to gather enough information for a book from an hour a day, though. Plus that leaves twenty-three hours a day of kicking my heels at Garthside House... Well – it's not as though I have anything to get back for. Getting away from the silent home that Max and I shared was what I needed.

"The best time of day would be between three and four. Miss Arden is usually at her most rested and alert in the afternoons."

She's looking at me over the top of her spectacles.

"That's absolutely fine," I say. "Perfect."

"There are various books, papers and memorabilia that she is happy to share with you, so you may wish to spend some of your time on those."

"That would be amazing."

"When your car has been repaired, you may like to explore the surrounding area. In the meantime, the grounds are at your disposal, and they are very extensive. Please, feel free to go wherever you like." She pauses. "As regards Garthside House, you are welcome to use this room and the other rooms on the ground floor. All the rooms on the east side of the house – that is where your bedroom is – are also open. We only ask that you respect Miss Arden's privacy and stay entirely out of the upper west wing." Her gaze holds mine, unwavering.

"Of course," I say.

"All being well, Miss Arden will meet you this afternoon at three, in this room. You may record the interviews if you wish, but on audio only. Miss Arden does not wish to be filmed, nor has she given her permission for it. If you wish to have photographs to accompany the interviews, Miss Arden will be happy to supply them and to grant permission for their use at no cost. Is there anything you would like to ask me?"

I hesitate, because there are about a thousand things, but I am not sure whether I dare ask some of them.

"I should call her Miss Arden, right?"

"Yes."

"And is there anything else I should know? I mean..." I stop short, because I am not sure what I *do* mean, just that it's a little odd discussing the preparations for meeting someone when I don't even know what she looks like now.

"Well, Miss Arden's eyesight and hearing are good considering her age," says Mrs Harris. "She is short-sighted, so don't sit too far away from her. Her hearing is better on the left hand side, so it might be as well to sit to the left. But I will ensure the chairs are arranged in that way. And although she is a hundred and four, and tires easily, you should not assume that she will miss anything. She is as sharp as a tack."

I guess she sees an expression of trepidation cross my face, because all of a sudden she unbends.

"Don't worry, Ms Garrick. I am sure that Miss Arden will like you very, very much. Just be yourself."

She gives me a genuinely sunny smile and I find myself smiling back. I think soon I might suggest she calls me Theda. I could be living here for a while, after all, and it will be weird if everyone calls me Ms Garrick all the time.

"I must get on," she says after that. "And I expect you'd like to look around. I suggest lunch at one?"

I agree, and we both get up. It's on the way out of the morning room that I think to enquire, tentatively, about WiFi.

"Ah," she says. "There is no WiFi. Miss Arden doesn't approve of it."

Perhaps I should have anticipated that – all the contact we had was by actual letter. It's still a surprise. But never mind; I have the data on my phone. So I thank Mrs Harris and we part in the hallway. It is a quarter past nine, and until one o'clock, my time is my own.

Chapter Seven

I could go upstairs and start looking over my notes. I could do that, but I don't. I spent the whole of yesterday cooped up in the car and now I want some fresh air. So I go upstairs to my room and fetch my coat, because it's April in Scotland and I'll probably freeze to death otherwise.

As I head back towards the head of the stairs, the double doors to the west wing are directly ahead of me. They are opaque doors, decorated with a variation of the lily design on the balustrade, so you can't see what's on the other side. Heavy and ornate, they remind me of the doors to a church – or a mausoleum.

It's amazing how being told you mayn't go somewhere makes you intensely curious about it. I wouldn't dream of peeking, though. I'm very well aware how lucky I am to be here, staying in Mary Arden's actual home. So many people have asked to interview her over the years, and always been turned down flat. There have in fact been other books about her in the past, but they were always filled with conjectures. Suppositions. Guesses. I'll be the first person to get the whole truth.

Why is that so important to me? I've asked myself that many times. A book about film, even a best-selling book, won't mend my broken life. I'll still be a woman with a dead husband. A woman who's too ashamed to build bridges with the friends she pushed away. But I think my father would have been proud of me. He loved films so much. He named me, his only child, for a film star. I might never have heard of Mary Arden or Pola Negri or Louise Brooks if it weren't for all his stories about the silver screen. And if one day I hold my book about Mary Arden in my hands, maybe I'll have found my way back to the person I was before.

I turn away from the double doors and descend the

staircase, cross the hallway and open the tall front door. The sunshine is dazzling, the air distinctly fresh. I breathe in, and it tastes clean and damp. The rain from last night is evaporating; mist hangs over the treetops. I step outdoors.

Last night, I saw the great wedding-cake confection that is the house lit up with spotlights that flattered its bold lines and towering features. By daylight, things look very different. It is still impressive, but you can see the struggle to maintain it in the face of the Scottish weather. The white stucco, though relatively new-looking, has damp green stains creeping up it like rot, and there is a descending stain where a gutter has overflowed. Having a flat roof seems nothing short of insane when you get this much rain, but perhaps there is a slope that cannot be seen from below, allowing it to drain away.

In front of the house there is the clear gravelled area where Angus parked the Range Rover. That whole experience seems oddly unreal now. He was incredibly kind, though, and it occurs to me that I should thank him. I should have taken a number, although perhaps he might have taken that the wrong way. At any rate, I should find some way to get in touch.

Beyond that area, I can see a stretch of drive which leads away and disappears under a heavy canopy of trees, some of them conifers, so even now, when the spring foliage has not appeared, there is an impression of dense green. I remember it being a long way from the road; I don't think I shall be walking into town.

Everywhere else, up to the edge of the woods, is garden, and all of it in a sorry state. It's not just the time of year – it looks as though the garden has been left to run wild. Everywhere, there are the browning remains of rioting plants and bushes, proper horticultural specimens mixed with gigantic weeds. There is a narrow terrace along the front of the house, and from there I can make out some of the features that are now buried under heaps of mouldering vegetation: paths, walls and a dried-up fountain. You can see that once it must have been a very grand garden, but it has suffered years of neglect.

Funny, I think. *I wonder why they let it go like this.* It's a contrast to the interior of the house, which is very highly maintained. Automatically, I glance up at the west wing, where the house's most important occupant resides. Doesn't she care that all this devastation is down here? But Mrs Harris did say she was short-sighted. Perhaps she has no interest in maintaining what she can't see.

I gaze down at a big stone planter, in which some pitiful plant has shrivelled into brittle brown stalks. The other thing, of course, is that maintaining these gardens would mean a whole bunch of local people working here, a lot of the time. Someone who valued their privacy might not want that.

I watch as a large brown spider picks its way out from amongst the brown stalks and scuttles away down the side of the planter. Then I keep walking, along the terrace and past the ground floor windows. At the corner of the house I turn and keep following the wall. Once you get to the back of the building, you can see some sturdy-looking outbuildings – functional structures, hidden away where they can't spoil the carefully-designed architecture of the main house. There is also an overgrown track, leading off into the woods.

I stop for a moment, to consider. Then I get my phone out and open a mapping app. There seems to be a pretty big blank spot around Garthside House, but by swapping to the satellite view and doing a bit of judicious zooming in and out, I can work out where I am. I can also see where the ford is. Angus was right; by road it's a fairly long way, doglegging across the countryside, but in fact it's very close. I could walk there quite easily.

Why not? I think. *If I'm going to say thank you, there's no time like the present.*

The track is gritty under my shoes as I start off down it.

In places it is muddy, too. There's no sign it gets any regular use. I walk for a bit, listening to the birds singing and the soft sigh of the wind through the trees. As the woods close in, I feel alone, but it isn't bothersome. Perhaps I may find peace of some kind here. I listen to the rhythmic crunch of my footsteps.

Max, I think, because he always fills the empty spaces, but that word doesn't have quite the same power to hurt me here. The pain is less sharp in a new place. A new time.

The track curves and now some way ahead of me I can see a gate blocking my path. Beyond that, the woods seem to end and fields begin. It is a tall gate, and as I approach it, I begin to think that perhaps my walk will be curtailed. It's too high to climb over, and on either side of it is galvanised steel fencing of the same height.

I go up to the gate, and sure enough, it's padlocked. This seems like overkill; I can't imagine many people wanting to walk through here. But I seem to remember that the very tall fences have something to do with keeping deer in or out. Should I turn round and go back? I look through the gate, at the fields beyond, and the land sloping away, presumably towards the river, and the ford. It's annoying getting this far and having to give up. Perhaps I might walk along the fence for a bit and see if there's a gap anywhere, or a gate I can open. It's April, after all, so things aren't too overgrown.

It's not too difficult to make my way along beside the fence, and sure enough, after about thirty metres I find a place where a tree has come down and taken a fence panel with it. It's easy to hop over the tangled remains and into the field. There's nothing growing here, it's just short coarse grass, so I set off right across the middle of the field, heading downhill. After five minutes I can see the river, and in fifteen minutes I'm standing on the bank. I walk upstream a little way, and now I can see the track that runs down to the ford.

The river is very high – that's the first thing I see when

I get there. You wouldn't think the water level would go up that much after one night of rain, but it has. I can't see the banks of stones anymore, and on this side of the river, the deepest part, there is a torrent of fast-flowing water. I had vaguely thought it might be possible to get across if there was a place where the channel was narrow, but it's clearly right out of the question.

Thank God he got the car out last night, I think, looking at the murky waters boiling past. Then I look across the river, to the spot where the house can just about be seen. My car has indeed gone, picked up, as Mrs Harris said it had been. There's no sign of life from the house, and I can't get across. Still, I know how to get here now. I'll come back some other time. I turn away, and walk back up the hill.

Chapter Eight

It's ten to three and I'm in the bathroom, checking myself in the mirror. Not a hair out of place; no lipstick on the teeth. I eye myself in the glass, trying to impart confidence.

Then I go into the bedroom and collect up my things. Notepad, pen, spare pen in case the first one runs out. Phone for recording the interview; app definitely working. Five to three. I leave the room and go downstairs.

Why should I be nervous? The worst thing in the world has already happened to me. But I am, as I descend the stairs. Anxiety fizzes in my stomach and my fingers are tight around my things: my pens, my phone. I try not to let it master me; I cross the hall and tap lightly on the morning room door, not giving myself time to think about it, and then I open it and go inside.

Mary Arden is sitting in one of the armchairs, carefully propped up with cushions as though she were as valuable and fragile as a Fabergé egg. The first thing I think as I look at her is that I would have recognised her, wherever I had seen her, under whatever circumstances. The last published photographs of her are from the 1960s, and it is nearly ninety years since the role that made her career, but still I would have known her. She is dreadfully wrinkled, as seamed as an old walnut, but the glorious bone structure is still visible, as though that beautiful skull has risen to the surface as she has aged. Her hair is dead white, of course, and very fine, and she wears it falling in ripples over one eye, the way she always has done. She is wearing a salmon-pink dress with a black trim and a matching bolero jacket. The legs that protrude from the skirt are stick-thin, the feet shod in flat black shoes, and the hand that clasps the head of a walking stick is as gnarled as a root.

"Hello, Miss Arden," I say. "Thank you so much for seeing me."

"Come here," she says, with the air of someone who is used to having their every command obeyed.

I walk closer and stand in front of her, not liking to sit down until asked. I force myself not to fidget.

She closes her eyes for a moment, as though the whole experience is tiring her.

"Sit down," she says. "It makes me feel exhausted, just to look at you standing over me like that."

Just as Mrs Harris said there would be, there is a chair placed to her left, so I sit down on that, right on the edge. I am quite close to her now, so I can see every detail: the pulse that beats in the withered throat, the sunken chest underneath the salmon-pink crepe. Her eyes are blue, but the whites are a little yellow with age.

She studies me for a long time. "You're quite pretty," she announces, "But you don't look well. Too thin, too drawn."

It's hard to know what to say to this, so I don't say anything.

"So you've come to interview me, and you want to know about that film, *The Simulacrum*."

"I would absolutely—"

"Don't worry," she interrupts. "I'll talk about it. I'm a hundred and four – if I don't talk now, I never will." She looks around. "Nurse?"

I hadn't realised there was anyone else in the room with us, but now I see there is a woman in a white uniform, sitting quietly at the back of the room. She gets up, and comes over.

"Yes, Miss Arden?"

"I want you to wait outside."

"I really shouldn't, Miss Arden—"

"You have to. This is a private conversation. You can wait in the hall. I'm sure this young lady will let you know if I have a heart attack or anything."

41

"Yes, Miss Arden."

"Not that I'm planning to," she growls. She watches as the woman leaves the room, closing the door quietly behind her. "Now," she says. "Tell me your name. I've forgotten what it was."

"Theda Garrick," I say.

"Like the actress," she comments.

"Yes. My father was a big fan of the movies."

"Funny choice though. Fancy calling a baby Theda! Theda Bara was known for playing vamps."

"I suppose so," I say neutrally.

She looks at me for a moment. "You can disagree with me, you know. It will be very dull talking if you agree with absolutely everything I say."

I look her in the eye, holding her gaze. "Alright," I say. "But I've always thought Theda was a pretty name. Better than a lot of the others from back then."

"Like Mary, you mean?"

"No... I meant, like Norma or Joan."

My mind skips back suddenly to sitting in Angus' kitchen, and him saying *Lassie*, and me laughing and laughing. I suppose I was giddy with tiredness and cold.

"Hmph," she says. "Nothing wrong with either of those names. Good, plain, straightforward names."

"I guess I just don't find them pretty," I say, taking her at her word about not agreeing with everything.

"Ha!" Her eyes glitter. It seems to me that she likes to be crossed. She's very old, and very rich; I suppose everyone agrees with her most of the time. All the same, I am wary, in case there are limits to her tolerance for being contradicted.

"So, Theda Garrick," she says. "Plenty of people have asked to interview me over the years. You're the first I've seen. I suppose I was intrigued. Tell me why you want to know about *The Simulacrum*."

"I'd like to write a book – about you and your debut

film." I think she must know this; I made it very clear in my letters, that I wanted permission for a book.

"Why? I don't suppose anyone has even heard of it, these days."

"I think they have. I mean, I suppose it's not a household name or anything, but it's a legend amongst film fans."

"I still say: why? None of them have seen it. Nobody has."

"That's the point," I say, and the enthusiasm spills over into my voice. "It's intriguing. It's like *London After Midnight*. The fact that nobody's seen it, that there aren't any copies of it, makes it fascinating. People would give an arm and a leg to see it."

"They can't, though, if there are no copies."

"No, but reading about it, imagining it – reconstructing it in their heads... I think people would want to do that."

"Do you?"

"Yes."

She considers. "You've told me why people would want to read a book about it. You still haven't told me why *you're* so interested in it. A young woman like you must have more in her life than ancient films. I'm sure you must. A man friend... or a husband."

Instantly I feel the colour rise into my face at this. The assumptions. The horribly antiquated way of looking at things. But mostly the hurt, because she has touched me on the one point guaranteed to cause the most pain. *Max.* How can I possibly tell her about *that* – about the terrible, burning need to bury myself in something, *anything*, so long as it isn't the horror of his death? That agony is a hard little knot inside me, one I can't unravel for anyone.

I'm silent for a long time; even someone so old and so indulged by everyone around her must realise something is wrong.

I struggle with myself, because I know that if I lose my cool I may blow this chance, however much Mary Arden

43

thinks she likes sparring with people. I look up and she is studying me with her beady old eyes, like a bird of prey. I think she knows perfectly well she has upset me, and she doesn't care. It's all a game to her.

I say, carefully, "I'm not prepared to discuss my private life. I'm here to talk about the film."

One side of her wrinkled mouth puckers wryly. "You think so, do you?"

I stare back at her.

"Well," she says, "I'm old, and I'm bored. I'm not going to have any more love affairs. If I want to ask you about yours, I shall." She puts up a hand. "Before you say anything, you might consider that you want me to tell you an awful lot of things. You want me to tell you all about *The Simulacrum*. Why it got made, why it was never shown. It's old news, and I'm tired, but I will tell you. But – if I do, I don't expect you to sit there like a clam shell, with all your pearls shut up inside."

I open my mouth to say something, though I'm not entirely sure what, but she is already banging her stick on the floor, and calling for the nurse to come back in. The woman materialises so fast that I suspect she was hovering outside the door.

"You can take me back upstairs," Mary Arden says to the nurse, and to me, she says, "We're done for today."

We've only had about fifteen minutes, if that, and I haven't even switched the recording app on.

"You'll get your hour tomorrow," she says to me, as the nurse helps her out of the chair. "If you're prepared for a little give and take. You can think about it this evening."

And that's it. I'm dismissed.

Chapter Nine

That night I toss and turn, finding it hard to sleep. It was strange having dinner on my own after lunch and breakfast on my own; it made me think that perhaps I didn't consider carefully enough what it would be like staying here by myself. Too much solitude, too much time to think. A lively hotel dining room would have been better; it would have taken me out of myself, as I'm desperate for this whole project to do.

I spent a long time reclining awkwardly in the enormous bath this evening. I had a couple of books lying on one of the bathroom cabinets and I could have done some more reading around *The Simulacrum* but... My mind kept going back to the meeting with Mary Arden. It still does, in fact.

Mary Arden is a very spoilt old woman. A *bored* spoilt old woman. I've seen that much already – not that you could really expect anything else. She's extremely rich but too old to do very much at all. In spite of what she says about give and take, having someone to listen to her reminiscences is probably the most interesting thing that's happened to her in ages. It's hard to imagine her forgoing that, if I stuck to my guns and said I wouldn't talk about my private life.

On the other hand, there must be other researchers who'd be prepared to tell her absolutely anything, just to be the one to interview her. Supposing she said she'd talk to one of them instead? I think about that. Even a delay, while she played me off against someone else, could be disastrous at this stage. I mean, at a hundred and four, her card is marked.

What are you afraid of? I ask myself. *You don't have to tell her the truth.*

That, I think, would be impossible – to have her picking over my life with Max with her greedy old talons. If it's love stories she wants to hear, I could start long before Max, with the messy first love affair and the horrendously sensible boyfriend who was the reaction to all the drama with the first one. Hell, I could embellish absolutely everything with salacious details. I'm a writer, after all, even if I write non-fiction. A few anecdotes of interestingly pervy behaviour would probably be enough to get the history of *The Simulacrum* out of her.

Anyway, you're overthinking this, I tell myself. *She'll probably have forgotten the entire conversation by tomorrow.*

I turn over, and punch the pillows, trying to get comfortable. Usually a hot bath makes me drowsy, but tonight I'm really unsettled. The outside spotlights have been turned off and the curtains are tightly closed, so there's no light to disturb me, and I'm neither too hot nor too cold. I just don't feel sleepy.

Perhaps it's too quiet, I think. Max and I lived in a house with no close neighbours, so it was fairly quiet there too, but you could still hear the main road in the distance. There's nothing like that here.

In the silence, I hear the crisp sound of a door closing somewhere in the house. Mrs Harris going to bed, perhaps. It's late, after all. I close my eyes and try to think soothing thoughts. And maybe I succeed in drifting off, because the next sound seems to rouse me, as if from a reverie.

A gentle slapping sound – that's what it was. I lie in the big pink bed, blinking, and suddenly my mind fits an action to the sound: the sound of the double doors that lead to the upper west wing slapping back into place. Someone has come in or out. A change of shift, maybe. My eyes are sliding closed again, when I hear something else. A long creak, as though someone has put their weight down on the floorboards.

I lie there listening. Now my eyes are wide open, staring into the dark. Creak. Silence. A long, long pause and then another creak.

A cold feeling slithers through me. I think: *it's coming closer.*

Why does that bother me? Simply that I can't work out what's going on out there. Surely the staff, if it's one of them, would move briskly? Would they even come into this part of the house?

Did I lock the door? I ask myself. I think about that. I'm fairly sure I did. I know I *meant* to – not because I think there's any reason to be nervous, but simply because I don't want anyone walking in, which I think they might do, in a place full of staff. I'm ninety-nine per cent certain I locked it.

But not one hundred per cent.

I listen to those stealthy creaks, which keep coming closer to my door. I put back the bedclothes as silently as I can, and slip out of bed, my heart hammering in my chest. The carpet is soft under my bare feet. I move cautiously towards the door, holding my hands out in front of me, feeling my way in the dark because I don't want to put the light on – I don't want to draw attention to the fact that I am here and awake.

My outstretched hands touch the door panels and move down over them, trembling just a little as they seek the door handle and the key sticking out of the lock. My fingers close on the key and with infinite care and slowness I try to turn it. It won't budge, so I guess the door is already locked, but I grasp the handle and try it.

The door is locked. There is the tiniest rattle from the handle as I let it go. I hold my breath. Outside, there is nothing. Then another quiet creak and a gentle impact, very close by. I don't move. I stand there in the dark in my nightdress and listen. It sounds to me as though whoever it may be is feeling their way in the dark, going hand-over-hand along the wall.

The sounds come right up to the door. There is a silence, so absolute that I am afraid the thumping of my heart must

47

be audible. Then I hear the door handle move back and forth, very gently.

This is the moment when I should say something – issue a verbal challenge from inside, asking the person out there what the hell they think they are doing. I don't. I listen, straining my ears.

Such a tiny sound: a wheeze, or a sigh. Then whoever it is moves on, feeling their way down the corridor.

I creep back to bed, but sleep is now out of the question. I get under the covers and lie there, every nerve screaming at me, my body as taut as a clenched fist. There may be a reasonable explanation why someone just tried my door in the middle of the night, but I can't think of one.

A little later, I hear the same noises again, coming furtively back down the hallway, passing my door, going back towards the staircase. Then the slap of the double doors at the other side of the stair head, and after that, silence.

This time I switch on the bedside light. Then I make myself get up and go to the door. I steel myself for a moment, and then I unlock it. Outside, the corridor is very dark. I look left, shivering; nothing. No matter how long I stare, and listen, there is only quiet, empty darkness. I look right, towards the head of the stairs and those double doors. They are not quite shut. When they swung to and fro, with the passing of whoever it was, one of them stuck. There is a gap of perhaps six inches. Through that gap, I see the faint flicker of a distant light, bluish and tremulous.

I realise I have been holding my breath. Very carefully, I close the door, lock it, and go back to bed.

Chapter Ten

The next day, I wake up with a stiff neck from tension and think I must have dreamed it – all of it. The conversation with Mary Arden, the unnerving experience during the night. None of it feels entirely real. When I go down to breakfast, I shoot a wary glance towards the double doors leading into the upper west wing but they are completely closed. The house feels quietly serene.

After yesterday's rain, I suspect there is no point in going down to the ford. The river will still be too high. Over my solitary lunch, Mrs Harris comes to check whether there is anything I need, so I ask her about my car and she says she will find out.

Then it's five to three and I am on my way to see Mary Arden again. This time, when I get to the morning room, the nurse is already sitting outside. I go in, and there is Mary, in a powder blue ensemble with navy trim this time, her eyes glittering. She looks about as harmless as a gila monster. I remind myself, though, that she is only an over-indulged old lady.

"Theda Garrick," she says. "Sit down. A little nearer – I want to see you properly."

She waits for me to sit down, watching me all the time.

"Have you thought about our conversation yesterday?" she says.

"Yes," I say truthfully.

"Aha, I thought you might. You've got an hour of my time today. Mind you don't waste it."

"I won't."

"And you'll answer anything I ask?"

"Within reason," I say levelly. I have no intention of telling her *everything*.

"Ha!"

I put my mobile phone down on the coffee table and press the screen a couple of times.

"It's recording," I say. "Audio only. No video, as you requested."

"Good," she says. "You won't want to be filmed when you're a hundred and four, either. I'd like people to remember me the way I was when I was as young and pretty as you."

"If that's what you want," I say, "we could choose a photograph from your early career for the front cover of the book."

"First things first," she retorts. "You'd better hear the story, before you decide what you want to put on the cover of the book."

"Of course."

She looks at me for a moment, thoughtfully. "I wonder where we should start? With the director, Lillian Velderkaust, I suppose. How far do you want me to go back?"

"Assume I don't know anything," I say.

Her finely-traced eyebrows go up. "I hope you *do*."

"Yes, I've read all about Lillian Velderkaust. But the readers of the book might not have."

"Hmmm. Very well, then." She sits back a little in her chair and looks up at the ceiling for a few moments, collecting her thoughts. Then she exhales through her nostrils and begins to talk.

"Lillian Velderkaust was a family friend. I suppose you know that. It wasn't likely I'd have got involved with her in any other way, being very young in 1930. She was born in the late 1800s. You can look the date up for yourself. I don't remember it.

"By the time *The Simulacrum* was made, she'd have been around forty, I suppose. Small, skinny woman, but full of energy. Very thick dark hair, with a streak of white in it. A real smoker's complexion – she smoked about forty a day for years. And bitten nails. Disgusting. She wasn't always like that, though. I mean, even at that age, and living that way, you could see she was the remains of a beautiful woman. Have you seen photographs of her when she was younger?"

I shake my head.

She shrugs. "Anyhow, Lillian's parents were well-off, and pretty indulgent for the times. Her father's family was European. I don't know what sort of name Velderkaust is – German or Dutch or something. Her mother was American, though, and that was where most of the money came from. They had several houses and one of them was close to ours. That was how we got to know them. My parents weren't anything like as well-off, but the Velderkausts didn't care about that. I suppose you'd call them Bohemians. My father was an artist, so they thought he was interesting. This was all before I was born.

"Lillian must have been born about the same time as cinema was. The first commercial showing of a film, that was in 1895 – did you know that? The Lumière brothers, in Paris. By 1914, when war broke out, there were regular cinemas all over the place, showing serials and newsreels and so on. All silent, of course. Lillian was nuts about it. Adored film. Went as often as she could. She decided really early on that she wanted to be a film director one day. You have to realise that this was a crazy idea for a woman, back then. There were a few female directors, but they were very much in the minority – not just then, but for years after. She was determined, though. Got herself a job at one of the early studios, as a typist or stenographer or something, and started working her way up. Learning the ropes."

She pauses and looks at me. "As I say, all this was before I was born. If you want to know the ins and outs of it, you'll have to read about it."

"I have," I say. "She moved onto editing screenplays and went on from there. But there *were* female directors. Alice Guy-Blaché, women like that."

"That may be true," she says, somewhat severely, "But it was hard. They didn't get the recognition the men did. Alice whatever her name is, she isn't a household name like Cecil B. DeMille, is she?"

I'm tempted to point out that Cecil B. DeMille probably isn't a household name anymore, but I hold my tongue, not wanting to get into an argument about a side topic.

"Anyway," Mary Arden resumes, with the air of someone who has carried her point, "there she was, completely immersed in the world of film, and as happy as a sandboy. But from what I've heard, her parents weren't quite as happy. This was 1914, after all. Women mostly got married, *if* they got married, around the age of twenty-one. And here she was, in her middle twenties, and no sign of any interest. I dare say they weren't quite as Bohemian as they thought they were, or they'd have left her to it.

"A big part of it was that she was so serious about making it in film. It was a man's world and she had to compete on their terms. It was no use being fluffy or temperamental. Professional, that was what she had to be. No sleeping with the leading man or anything." She snorts. "She didn't dress like a vamp, either. Strictly business. Kept them all at arm's length.

"And then – she met Hugh Mason."

She pauses.

"You know who Hugh Mason was?"

I nod. "Yes, of course."

"Did you ever see a photograph of him – before, I mean?"

I shake my head.

"There's one in all those boxes you're going to look through. A studio portrait of Hugh, in uniform. You'll see why she fell for him," she says. "Hugh Mason was one of the most beautiful human beings I've ever seen."

Chapter Eleven

I have my pad on my lap, so I make a note to look for the photograph of Hugh Mason, not that I'm likely to forget. I didn't know there was one in existence from that time, pre-1918. If Mary Arden would let me put *that* in the book, what a scoop that would be!

There is a long silence after Mary tells me about the photograph. She closes her eyes, sliding into reminiscence, and when she has still not opened them a couple of minutes later, I wonder whether she has fallen asleep. I am beginning to fidget when she speaks, still not opening her eyes.

"Has it happened to you?"

I look at her guardedly, and she opens her eyes.

"Someone so irresistible that you just fell," she says.

For a moment, it flashes through my head that I could just lie. I could claim never to have been in love – to have spent my life thus far buried in my work, quietly drinking tea and feeding my house plants in my spare time. I think I *will* do this, because I don't want Mary Arden in my head, malicious old creature that she is. But then my mouth opens and I say:

"Yes."

I say it quietly, and the moment it's out I wish the word back. Perhaps she won't have heard it, with her one-hundred-and-four-year-old ears–

But she smiles and I know she *did* hear it.

"So," she says, "Where is he now? Or what's the matter with him? You wouldn't be up here, in Scotland, for an unspecified length of time, if he was at home, waiting for you."

When I don't reply, she prods further.

"Already married, is he?"

This is so far from the mark that it provokes me into replying.

"He's dead," I tell her flatly. I hope that this will shut her up. And for a moment, it does.

She sits in her chair, her gnarled old hands clasped on the head of her walking stick, and looks at me.

Then she says, "How?"

The barefaced, brazen, heartless cheek of it takes my breath away. My fingers tighten on my notebook as I consider standing up and simply walking out of the room. I keep myself under control with difficulty; I am practically vibrating with pain and anger.

"An accident," I say. I glare at her, daring her to ask me *what sort of accident?*

She doesn't. After a pause, she says, "Boyfriend, was he?"

"Husband," I say, almost choking on the word. I want to tell her to shut up, that I am not discussing any of this, but I can't get the words out.

"How old are you, Theda Garrick?" she asks me, her yellowing eyes fixing me as though she is a bird of prey, and I a mouse.

"Twenty... seven," I say through gritted teeth.

"Young, for a widow."

I sit and stare at her. This is only the second time we have ever met, and I cannot believe she is doing this, that she has managed to get under my skin in such a short time. And it was going so well – she was starting to tell me about Hugh Mason...

"Please," I grind out, "Can we get back to Lillian Velderkaust?"

She smiles, and I see what are certainly false teeth, because nobody of that age has such white and regular dentition.

"In good time," she says. "I'm interested in this topic. Love... It can be so... destructive, can't it? Here you are,

54

aged twenty-seven, thinking that your whole life is over. And yet, if you live as long as I have, it is only a quarter done."

"I don't think my life is over," I say stonily. "Love isn't the only thing to live for."

"Isn't it? What else is there?"

"There's work. There are projects like this one, which I'd like to–"

"Work," she repeats. "That's a dull *raison d'etre* for someone of twenty-seven, don't you think?"

Enough. "This isn't 1930," I retort sharply. "Women don't have to get married."

"Ah," she says, "But you did, didn't you?"

"Yes," I say. "I did."

And it comes back to me, very vividly, the remembrance of standing outside the church door together, me in my diaphanous wedding gown, Max in his morning suit, and the church bells ringing. Max smiling down at me. The new wedding ring on my finger. The sunshine. Happiness.

I can't help it. I let the notepad drop and put my head in my hands. I don't want to cry in front of her. I don't. She's a miserable sadistic old bitch, trying to squeeze me dry like a lemon, to suck out the bitter juice. I'm not here to *do* this. But most of all, what I feel about Max is too complex, too broken to be spread out in front of a virtual stranger for them to pick over with morbid glee, like glittering shards of glass, something too smashed for anyone to tell what it once was.

It's no use, though. I do cry. The hot tears well up in my eyes however hard I will them not to, and spill over and run down my face. I wipe my eyes with my hand and that just seems to make it worse. I sob, and choke, and the tears are salt on my lips.

Mary Arden just sits there while I am doing this. Is she satisfied? I don't know.

I think about leaving, about getting out of the room, and

then I think about the audio tape, which is still running. I pick my phone up with trembling hands and stop the recording, the recording that has several minutes of me sobbing on it. The spare pen rolls away across the table and drops onto the floor as I scrabble for it. Escape – that's all I can think about.

When I'm on my feet she says, "You haven't had your hour."

"I don't care," I tell her. "I'm done for today."

"As you wish," she says, just as if she hasn't said anything amiss. "We can go on tomorrow."

I've already turned to go when she adds, "One thing."

There's sufficient command in her voice that it checks me, in spite of everything.

"His name," she says. "Your husband. What was his name?"

I hesitate, and she waits.

"Max," I say. "My husband's name was Max."

Chapter Twelve

Thank God, I don't meet anyone in the hall or on the stairs. Even the nurse is not at her post. I go back to my pink bedroom, lock the door and curl up on the bed. Then I cry for a long time. It's a shapeless pain, this crying over Max. The sensation that someone has tried to prise the lid off it is worse than anything. If I could talk to anyone, it wouldn't be Mary Arden. If I could ever do it, it wouldn't be now.

Eventually the tears stop, or at any rate, they harden into a deadly numbness, like a grim amber with my emotions buried inside. I try, hard, to think it through rationally.

Can I really do this? Can I really buy the information for the book by telling Mary Arden about Max?

No, no, no is what my instinct is screaming at me. She's too good at provoking, at winkling out information I didn't intend to give her. I thought I could fob her off with tales of old love affairs, but already she's found out I'm a widow. It's a pitiable thing, to be a widow at twenty-seven, and I can't bear her pity, or her prurient interest. And I am afraid – afraid I will tell her everything about it, when it's too terrible even for me to look at.

I could just go. I could find out from Mrs Harris where they've taken Max's car, and I could call them and beg them to hurry up. Then when it comes, I could pack my bags and my box of papers, get behind the wheel and just drive away. I imagine that, the road unfurling before me and my foot on the accelerator.

That would be running away, argues the rational side of my personality. *You can't run away forever. Max's death is going to follow you wherever you go, and the sooner you learn to live with it, the better.*

I roll onto my other side, biting my lip.

You came up here to see something through, says that rational voice, relentlessly. *To draw a line under the past.*

But I didn't know I'd have to talk about Max, I counter silently. *How can I do that?* And my face screws up into a sob again.

The answer comes pat: *You can't avoid talking about Max. You know that. People will always ask. And you had better find a way to do it.*

I wish...

I wish I had a friend I could call right now, someone I could ask what I ought to do, because I don't know – I don't trust myself anymore. I can't tell whether staying will brace me up, make me look things in the face and talk about them without flinching, or whether it will send me screaming over the edge of some dark abyss. But there is nobody to call. I did have friends, university friends like Ellie and Sam, former colleagues like Susie. I drove them all away. I have a lot of bridges to build before I could ever ask them for advice now. So it's down to me. I have to decide.

First things first: Max's car is the important thing, because I can't go anywhere without that, even if I want to. I go into the bathroom and repair the damage done by the crying fit as best I can, touching up my makeup and brushing my hair. When I'm sure you can't tell I've been howling my eyes out, I leave the room in search of Mrs Harris.

The house is unnaturally quiet. I suppose all the staff are in the west wing, tending to the malicious bundle of bones that is Mary Arden. The double doors are, as usual, carefully closed. I stand and look at them for a moment, wondering whether Mrs Harris is on the other side somewhere. While I am hesitating, I hear the click of heels crossing the parquet floor down below. I go to the head of the stairs, and look down.

Mrs Harris is at the bottom, looking up at me. I wonder

whether she noticed that I came to the head of the stairs from the west side?

It doesn't matter if she did. You didn't open those doors or anything.

"Ms Garrick," she says. "Were you looking for me?"

"I was," I say, starting down the staircase with a slightly guilty feeling. Now is not the moment to ask her to call me Theda.

When I get to the bottom, I say, "I was just wondering whether there is any news of my car?"

"Ah," she says. "Yes, there is, and it's not good news, I'm afraid. I telephoned the garage this morning, and they said the engine is hydrolocked."

"Hydrolocked? I'm not sure what that means."

"Well, I'm not a technical expert either," she says, "But I gather it's what happens when you get water in the engine."

"Is that serious?"

"I'm afraid it is, and probably expensive."

"Oh *no*."

How can I possibly have been so stupid as to try to drive through that ford? I can't see the insurers paying for this – not in a million years. I did the damage myself, after all.

I could almost start crying again. With an effort, I control myself.

"Did they say how much?"

She shakes her head ruefully. "They're still assessing the damage."

Still? I imagine dozens of mechanics crawling all over Max's car for hours, and the labour costs *that* is racking up. They'll probably think someone who drives a car like that is loaded, too, and won't care what the bill comes to. And I'm really *not* loaded – there's the house, of course, but that's all. Max was the one with the well-paid job. This is a catastrophe.

"Ms Garrick?"

Mrs Harris's voice recalls me to myself.

"I'm sorry," I say. "I'm just a bit stunned. I can't believe I did that much damage."

"Please," she says, "Don't distress yourself. I've spoken to Miss Arden about the situation." She pauses delicately. "As you know, she is very affluent. As you incurred the damage while attempting to reach the house, she is prepared to meet the costs of repairing the car for you."

I stare at her. "I don't understand..."

"Miss Arden will pay the car repair bill," she says, firmly.

My jaw drops. "That's amazingly... But Mrs Harris, it could be thousands–"

"Really," she says, "Don't worry about it for one moment."

She smiles at me. "I think she is enjoying your sessions. She gets very little entertainment, you know."

"I'm glad," I manage to say.

We look at each other for a moment. Then she says, "Well, I must be getting on – see you later, Ms Garrick."

"Please," I say, as she is turning to go, "Tell her thank you from me."

"I will."

She trots away across the hallway and disappears through a door. I watch her go and then I go outside, into the tangle of a garden, because I want to clear my head.

I go down some steps that have brambles curling across them and follow the crumbling remains of a path, my face resolutely turned away from the house. Since Max died, everything has felt weird and unreal. Coming here has made that worse, not better; I feel as though I am losing touch with reality. The things I heard in the night, the stealthy patting along the walls, the fumbling at the door – were those real? As for the sessions with Mary Arden... Mrs Harris seems to think they are some kind of gentle diversion. For me, they are like some horribly brutal therapy I didn't sign up for. The original point of them, to write something about Mary

Arden and *The Simulacrum*, seems like someone else's ambition, not mine.

I stop and look at a cascade of browning stalks that covers what appears to have been a fountain. I think about Max's car. When it's repaired, however long that takes, I could go. Except... By picking up the tab, Mary Arden has guaranteed I'll stay. It would be absolutely, grossly ungrateful to leave after she's done that. Not to mention the fact that she's doing it because I'm here to interview her, and if I decide to go, maybe that won't count anymore. I could be left with a terrifyingly huge bill to pay.

I sit down on the fountain's rim, on the one small spot not covered in decaying vegetation. The stone is cold, even through the fabric of my skirt.

She's checkmated me, I think.

Chapter Thirteen

I don't like to stay here, where I imagine that anyone in the house, Mary Arden perhaps, if she likes to sit by the window, might look down and see me. Inside feels no better; the sense of being stuck in the 1930s is suffocating. I haven't managed to thank Angus Fraser for hauling the car out of the ford, so I think I might as well walk down there again. Perhaps the water level will have dropped a bit, or he might be out and about; I might be able to wave from the far bank. If I'm honest with myself, his kitchen and collie dog and pile of old books feel like some sort of haven compared to here. And it would be nice to have a conversation without feeling as though the other person is trying to gouge out my emotional innards.

I feel an ill-defined reluctance to advertise where I am going, so this time I go around the house the other way, moving with a studied air of nonchalance. Once past the outbuildings, I slip off into the woods, through the broken fence, and across the fields to the ford.

At the edge of the water, it's muddy, and the river is still fairly high. I stand and scan the opposite bank, the place where the track leads up out of the water, and the house beyond it. There is no sign of life over there. I can't see the Range Rover, either. The river flows on between the two banks, but otherwise everything is still.

I find myself a large stone that is reasonably dry and sit on that, with my face to the river. It's remarkably soothing, just watching the water and listening to it rushing over the stones. In places there are thick hanks of bright green water weed, flowing like hair, and I watch them undulating in the current. Once, a fish jumps right out of the water. It could be good, being here, if it weren't for Garthside House and Mary Arden.

"Theda Garrick!"

A voice pierces my reverie and I look up. Angus is on the other bank, Jess at his heels. The ancient Range Rover is parked up outside the house.

I get up and wave.

"Hi!"

He looks at the water, which is only an inch deep in places on his side but much deeper on mine. Then he makes his way towards me, keeping to the shallow bits, where the stones are almost out of the water. Jess stays on the bank, contributing the occasional bark; I do not think she likes it when Angus goes into the water. He has to stop when he gets to the edge of the deep bit, though. Nobody could walk through that at the moment.

"Hi," he says back. "How are you getting on at Garthside House?"

I come as far down the bank as I dare before answering that, though I know I am far too far from Garthside for there to be any chance of anyone hearing. I still feel self-conscious and somehow oddly disloyal. I say, "It's a bit..." and tilt my hand back and forth to indicate doubt.

I guess my concern shows because he glances up, behind me.

"What's she like, the old lady?"

It makes me uneasy, calling back and forth across the river.

"A bit strange," I say, trying to keep my voice down. "I'm sorry about the other evening."

He shrugs. "In what way?"

"Mrs Harris thought you were a taxi driver."

"That's not your fault."

"Well... She sort of hurried me in, and I didn't say thank you properly. I thought I ought to come down. I'd have brought you a bottle of something, but I can't get out to the shops while the car is being mended. I promise to bring you one later."

"You're welcome," he says, "But what's wrong with the car?"

"It's hydrolocked, whatever that means."

"Really? That's bad. I thought it'd be okay, as long as it got a once-over."

I shake my head.

"That's bad luck," he says. "Insurance?"

"I'm going to check," I say, "But I don't think it's covered. I mean, I did the damage myself. I just drove right into the ford."

"Shit."

"Yes," I agree, and then I hesitate, wondering whether to tell him about Mary Arden's offer to foot the bill. It seems so implausibly generous I can hardly believe it myself.

"What will you do?" he asks me, his head on one side. "Write it off?"

"No... Miss Arden said she'd pick up the bill."

"She did?"

I nod.

"Wow," he says. "You've only been there a couple of days. You must have made a hell of a first impression."

"I'm not sure it's that," I say, thinking of those beady old eyes drinking in my misery.

"It's a shame the river's so high," he says. "This sounds like an interesting story."

"I'll come back," I tell him. "When I've got that bottle I promised you."

"Don't bother with the bottle. Just come back anyway."

"Alright." I smile at him. "And thanks for pulling the car out of the ford, *and* for running me round to Garthside House."

"Welcome."

He grins at me for a moment, then turns to pick his way back to the far bank, where Jess is waiting.

I go carefully up my bank, trying not to get too muddy. When I get to the top, Angus is at the other side. He doesn't look back. I hear him whistle to Jess, and the pair of them walk back to the house.

I look at my shoes. Yuck. Then I start back across the field, to the break in the fence, and the wood, and Garthside House.

Chapter Fourteen

That evening, it rains again. I have my lonely dinner with a book for company – a book about film, naturally, because that's all I brought with me. I dearly wish I had a novel right now. Rain runs down the windows and somewhere I hear it splattering off the roof. A broken gutter or something.

When I got back to Garthside House, I took off my filthy shoes and carried them upstairs with me. Then I did my best to clean them with tissues and water from the bathroom tap. It wasn't terrifically successful. I left them on the bath mat, because it was the only place they wouldn't leak muddy water onto the floor.

When I get back to my room after dinner, the bed has been turned down and my shoes have gone – presumably for cleaning. Nothing on the escritoire has been disturbed though: the books and papers are still littered about on it. It's very clear that any organisation (or lack of it) of mine will be respected, although I still feel very conscious that anyone could walk in at any time.

Then I think about the person I heard trying the door last night – or thought I heard. Why didn't I ask Mrs Harris about it? I'm not even sure myself. Perhaps I imagined the whole thing, though a little nagging feeling tells me I didn't. In the end I lock the door again that night, though I am slightly embarrassed about doing it.

I lie awake in the dark for a long time, thinking about the day, and about Max's car, and how different things would look if I hadn't driven into the ford. There is silence in the corridor outside; nobody goes in or out of the upper west wing at all. Eventually I fall asleep, my arms around the spare pillow for comfort.

The next day, at a minute to three, I stand outside the

morning room with my notepad and pens and phone and say to myself that I will *not* let Mary Arden get under my skin. Then I open the door, before I have time to think about it too much.

There she is, in the same chair, but wearing a mustard-coloured crepe ensemble that doesn't do her any favours at all. That is the first thing I notice. The second is the wooden box sitting on the floor at her feet. I see that, and in spite of my trepidation I feel a flash of excitement. If that's full of things to do with *The Simulacrum*...

"Good afternoon, Theda Garrick," she says, tilting her head back to look at me in a distinctly combative way.

"Good afternoon, Miss Arden." I close the door behind me, juggling the notepad and other things. I sit down, lay them out on the table, and before I turn the recording app on, I say, "Miss Arden, the situation with my car – what you've offered to do – it's incredibly kind–"

She cuts me off with a wave of her hand.

"Don't talk about it. It's not interesting."

"Even so–"

She is shaking her head. "I have too much money and too little time. Don't let's spend it talking about car repairs. Where were we? Something about Hugh Mason..."

I sit dumbfounded for a moment, but then I pick up my phone and turn the app on.

"The photograph of him, the studio portrait, it's in that box," she says. "I had Harris look. There are other boxes, and I'll have them sent to your room, or you can look through them down here if you prefer."

"That would be amazing!"

I can't help myself – it's too tempting. I reach for the box, and the next instant she presses the rubber ferrule on the end of her walking stick down firmly on the centre of the lid.

"Not so fast."

Her eyes glitter maliciously.

"First, I want to hear how you met your husband Max. Then, you can look through the box."

"You–"

I catch myself just in time.

"Bitch?" she finishes scornfully. "Oho, yes, but I'm the bitch with all the money *and* the information you want."

I stare at her in disbelief. Then, extraordinarily, I burst out laughing. I simply can't help it. She's so ludicrously *brazen.*

"Alright," I say in the end, when I can speak properly. "I'll tell you." I'm amazed to find that saying this doesn't hurt, not even a little bit. She's so insanely nosy, so off-the-scale blunt, that I can't take her seriously. Perhaps it might even be good to talk about it, in a way.

She sits back and waits, though I notice the end of the walking stick doesn't leave the lid of the box.

"Well," I say slowly, "We weren't meant to meet at all, that was the thing. I was at my friend Ellie's wedding... and Max was at something else."

"Go on."

"It was about four years ago. Four and a half. Ellie's from Herefordshire, so she had the wedding there. The service was in a beautiful old church, one of those ones with brasses on the floor and flags on the wall. She had the reception at a country house hotel. It was a very big place..."

It occurs to me that Mary Arden's idea of *a very big place* is probably different from mine.

"Big enough, anyway, for more than one event. They had one of those notices in the reception area, directing people left or right, for the Martin wedding (that was ours) or the other one.

"Ellie asked me to be one of her bridesmaids. There were three of us and..." I laugh a little bit, remembering. "She went a bit bridezilla. Honestly, we looked like a trio of fairies. We had these floor-length chiffon dresses in very, very pale pink, with beaded bodices and little tiny straps,

68

and for the bit in the church we had matching boleros made out of fluffy faux fur. She was very fussy about the shoes because we were different heights and she wanted us to be about the same. Luckily I'm fairly tall, so I got away with kitten heels, but one of the others had to wear stilettos. Are you sure you want to hear all this?"

She nods. "I'll tell you if I'm getting bored."

I'm sure you will, I think.

"We even had matching earrings and necklaces, which she gave us before the ceremony. Oh, and matching *nail polish*. She gave us that a few days beforehand, so nobody would turn up with dark crimson talons or anything.

"I guess I'm being a bit mean. I wasn't that bad about *my* wedding – at least I don't *think* I was – but you want to get things right. I mean, you hope you're only going to do it once."

The moment those words are out of my mouth it occurs to me that a widow of twenty-seven might reasonably expect to do it more than once. I falter, but then I try to put down a shutter in my mind. *Don't think about that. Keep going.*

"We had our hair caught back and a cascade of ringlets down the back. It took *ages* to do those. The hair was done up with these hairpins with beads on the end, and the beads matched the ones on our bodices. It was insanely perfect, if you know what I mean."

She nods.

"And we all carried bouquets of roses in a contrasting colour, a darker shade of pink. I think she went for that because she couldn't be sure of getting the exact same shade of pink as the dresses.

"Anyway, the ceremony was beautiful and then there were a few photos, and after that we went to the hotel. You don't want me to describe all the speeches and what we had for dinner, do you? I'm not honestly sure I can remember."

"No," she says, waving her hand dismissively.

"After dinner there was music, and eventually it started

to get a bit... Well, everyone had had a few. They were letting their hair down, having a bit of fun...

"This one guy kept pestering me. I danced with him once, because it seemed rude not to, and after that he seemed to think he'd scored. He kept following me around. He stank of booze so I don't think it was my amazing charms or anything. And it was a bit awkward because I didn't want to tell him to – to eff off in case it caused a scene, which you don't really want at your friend's wedding. So I said I had to use the ladies' and bolted off.

"I went into the ladies' and spent absolutely ages touching up my makeup and combing the ringlets very carefully and really hoping that this guy would have forgotten all about me by the time I came out. But when I put my head out, there he was, cruising up and down in front of the double doors like a shark. An *inebriated* shark. Waiting for me. So it was try to go back in and get pounced on again, or go somewhere else for a bit.

"I waited until he was looking the other way, and then I slipped out and headed down the corridor. I took the first turning I came to, just to get out of sight. Right down at the end, there was a fire door and someone had propped it open, which I guess you're not supposed to do, but it was very warm indoors. It occurred to me that perhaps I could go out through that, go right round the building and get back into the wedding reception via the French windows. With a bit of luck, the guy who'd been bothering me would keep waiting outside the other doors, and I could enjoy myself in peace.

"So I went down the corridor, and out through the fire door, and then I took a right around the corner of the building. I found myself in a sort of little garden with a pond full of koi carp in it and next to the pond was Max. He was gazing into the water, but when I came around the corner he looked up.

"He said, 'My God, an angel.'

"I said, 'I'm a bridesmaid.'

"And he said, 'The bridesmaids were all wearing turquoise. I can remember that quite clearly.'

"'I don't think I'm one of yours,' I said.

"You asked me if I've ever met anyone so irresistible that I just fell. I'm not sure I believe in love at first sight. I mean, how can you know what someone is really like, from looking at them? You don't, do you? But I felt *something*, right away.

"Looking at Max was like looking at the sun. He was blindingly gorgeous. He had this very thick blond hair, and blue eyes, and his face was just... I don't know, *perfect*. He was a bit older than me, but not too old. I looked at him and just wanted him, straight away, though I didn't think I had a cat in hell's chance. There was no way someone who looked like that wasn't already taken.

"He looked amused at what I'd said. 'Like football teams,' he said, and I laughed. Then he said, 'Are you lost?'

"I said, 'No, I came outside because someone was hassling me. I thought maybe I could go around the building and get back through the French windows on the other side.'

"He said, 'I don't think there's any escape round that way. I've tried, and you'd have to go through a very muddy shrubbery. I'm not sure you're dressed for that.'

"'Oh crap,' I said.

"For a moment we just stood there, looking at each other. Then he said, 'There's another option. Don't go back to *your* wedding. Come to mine instead.'

"'Are *you* getting married?'

"'No, I mean, the wedding I'm attending.'

"I gaped at him. 'I can't do that.'

"'Why not? They're all too drunk to notice – even the bride.'

"And still I might not have gone, because I wasn't sure if he was being serious and it would have been *so* embarrassing if he wasn't, but I glanced back through the open fire door and there was my drunken suitor, lurching down the corridor. So I said, 'Alright then, but we'd better go now, because here comes trouble.'

"He glanced through the doorway and raised his eyebrows. 'Come on then,' he said, and offered me his arm.

"So I took it, and we went off the *other* way around the building, to the *other* wedding, which was in full swing. He was right about everyone being drunk; nobody seemed to notice anything odd about me at all, though I was distinctly overdressed for an ordinary guest.

"We went up to the bar and got a glass of champagne each, and I started to relax a bit. It was funny, after all, crashing someone else's wedding dressed as a bridesmaid.

"'I'm Max Blake,' said Max, and I said, 'Theda Garrick.'

"'Like the actor?' he asked, and that was a surprise because most people comment about the Theda bit.

"'Supposedly a distant relative,' I said. 'I'm not sure I believe it, though.'

"Max was really charming – he could keep a conversation going so easily. I kept looking at him over the top of my champagne flute with this feeling of unreality because I couldn't believe he was on his own and he was talking to *me*.

"After a while, the wedding felt too rowdy for holding a conversation, so we went off to another bar where it was quieter. We just talked and talked. In the end, I started to feel a tiny bit worried about whether Ellie or the others would notice I'd gone, so Max said he'd walk me back to the other party. The drunk bloke had gone, which was a relief.

"He didn't come in. He left me at the door, but he said, 'I'll call you, Theda,' and he leaned over and kissed me on the cheek. I went back into the reception in a sort of dream.

"A couple of days later he did call me. And that was that. The story of Max and Theda."

Chapter Fifteen

"That is *not* the story of Max and Theda – not by half," says Mary Arden. "But it'll do. You can look at the photograph. When–" she adds, still pressing the lid of the box closed with the walking stick, "you have answered one last question."

I sigh inwardly. "Alright."

"Why had Max left the wedding he was at?"

I think about that. "I don't know. I've never thought about it – I just assumed he felt the same as I did, that he wanted to get away for a bit, or maybe he just wanted some air."

"Hum," she says. "Well, I suppose that will do."

She lifts the walking stick off the box and puts it down next to her. "Go on, then. Open it."

Gracious, I think. I lean over and lift the box onto my lap. It's quite heavy, and looks handmade. The lid is fastened with two tarnished hooks and eyes, which I undo carefully. Then I open it.

There is a thick stack of papers inside but right on top is the photograph. This is the first time I've ever laid eyes on Hugh Mason as he was in 1914, but I'd have known it was him from the description – he really *was* a beautiful human being. I stare at him.

The photograph is in sepia, on a piece of board about the size of a quarto. The background – which is only dimly seen – appears to be panelling. In front of it stands Hugh, visible to about mid-thigh. He is wearing a military uniform. He has on a woollen jacket with four pockets, the breast pockets each showing a bright metal button, and the sleeves having a trim in some lighter stuff. Over this he has a belt and a diagonal strap, the sort of thing I think they call a Sam Browne belt. He has a shirt and tie of some dark material. In his right hand he is holding something of which only a part is visible – a swagger stick, I suppose. He is wearing a service cap and his eyes gaze out to meet the viewer from under its peak.

Those are the facts of his appearance. What is harder to describe is the effect of looking at that face. He is handsome – very handsome – and I should know the power of good looks, because I was married to one of the best-looking men I've ever met. He has great dark eyes, a straight nose, fine cheekbones and a perfectly-modelled mouth. And these do not seem to be accidents of mere appearance; the charm of his face is in the intelligent, quizzical look in his eyes, the way his gaze seems to challenge mine even over the distance of a century. His looks are full of energy; this is a man who means to live life to the full.

How different things might have been if he had had those qualities for a lifetime, I think to myself, looking down at that sepia face.

This may be the only photograph of Hugh Mason in existence. I am dying to look through the rest of the box; if this is in here, what other treasures might there be? I hardly dare to hope for an actual still from *The Simulacrum* – but if anyone had one, it would be Mary Arden.

"Handsome, wasn't he?" says Mary Arden. "A face for anyone to fall in love with."

"Yes," I say.

"Handsomer than your Max?"

She *has* to do that, doesn't she? She just has to twist the knife in every single way.

I look her squarely in the eye and say, "Alright, yes. He was handsomer than Max."

I hope that she will let it rest there. Of course, she doesn't.

"Would you have done what Lillian did, then? Given your soul for a man with a face like that?"

"Impossible to say," I tell her neutrally. "Nobody

could do the things Lillian did. There was only one Lillian Velderkaust."

"Ha," she remarks.

I could keep staring at the photograph of Hugh all day, but I don't. I shut the box carefully, and set it down on the floor again. There will be plenty of time to go through it later. Then I sit up straight, my shoulders back, and do my best to stare Mary Arden down.

"Right then," I say. "I want to hear how Lillian met Hugh Mason."

"You do, do you? But I've already shown you the photograph of Hugh."

"That's not enough. And I haven't had my hour."

She laughs briefly – a short bark of a laugh with not much humour in it.

"Very well. But this is extremely second-hand, you understand. All these things happened in 1914, a full year before I was even born. Anything I tell you is simply hearsay, things I gleaned from listening to Lillian talking about it. And that would have been years later, so who's to say any of it really happened like that?"

I shrug. "Nobody can contradict it, either. I'd like to hear what you have to tell."

"Well, then," she says. "They met in 1914, some months before the war began. It was at a dinner party; I don't know whose house it was. I can't tell you all the people who were there, either, because I heard about it from Lillian, and she only had eyes for Hugh.

"The hostess had put her next to Hugh, perhaps because she had heard that Lillian had a reputation as a bluestocking and Hugh would be forced to converse with her niece – or perhaps it was her goddaughter – on his other side. In this, she had gravely misjudged Hugh. In spite of his time, he wasn't a man who was afraid of a woman with opinions.

"Lillian, for her part, was a little suspicious of Hugh to start with. He was so very good-looking that she thought he was probably a cad, or at any rate, used to getting a little more out of women than was good for either of them.

"I see from your face that you think these are old-fashioned views. Well, they are, but those were the times, you see.

"Hugh was fascinated to discover that Lillian was working in film – or at any rate, trying to make her way in it. He agreed with some of her views. She felt that it didn't have to be a mass-market, low brow sort of medium; at its best, it could be an art form, and she was interested in seeing how far she could go with it. Of course, at this stage she was still learning, and hadn't made any films of her own. But Hugh didn't pooh-pooh that, nor did he try to patronise her. He was genuinely interested, and that way he won her over."

I find myself leaning forward, fascinated; even after a century the story is engrossing.

Mary Arden continues, "Their hostess must have been gnashing her teeth over it, because her niece had to spend most of the evening talking to the man on her other side, who for some reason was of no use as a marital prospect at all.

"Anyway, Hugh and Lillian got on like a house on fire, and they could probably have spent the entire evening talking about films if left to themselves. However, the conversation amongst the other guests was largely about the probability of war, and eventually it became a lively enough debate that it sucked Hugh and Lillian in as well.

"I say *lively* – heated was perhaps nearer the mark, in some departments. The table was divided between those who thought the whole thing was horribly ominous, and those who thought it was a fuss about nothing, and would, as they said, 'be over by Christmas' if it happened at all."

I grimace a little at that. *Over by Christmas.* If they'd known...

Mary Arden sweeps on. "Of course, there was a lot of

discussion about who would volunteer, with those who were far too old to consider it being very enthusiastic about pushing the younger ones forward. I think they imagined heroic cavalry charges and things like that. At that stage, nobody really knew what the reality would be like.

"Of course, Lillian wasn't in love with Hugh by the end of the evening; it takes a little longer than that. But the seeds were sown, and she already liked him enough to find the talk of going off and fighting a little uncomfortable. She said she remembered one thing from that evening later on – something Hugh said. Someone asked him, 'What about you, Mason? Would you sign up?' in a challenging sort of way, and he said, 'Yes,' very quietly, and then he added, 'But I don't think I'd come home the same man I am now.'

"Of course, he couldn't have known. Nobody knew what it would be like.

"Anyway, that evening was the beginning of the affair between them. Hugh called on her after that; it was all above board, not like the way you young people carry on today. I think if the war hadn't started, they'd have married, perhaps a year or so later. But it did start, of course, and Hugh joined up, just as he'd said he would. He asked Lillian to marry him before he went, and she said yes. It would have been around that time that the photograph was taken; it was something to remember him by, while he was away.

"So Lillian became his fiancée, and shortly after that, Hugh went off to war."

Chapter Sixteen

After my meeting with Mary Arden, I take the box upstairs with me, to look through at my leisure. I hug it to me, greedily, imagining the finished book, with Hugh Mason's photograph taking up a whole page. Or the front cover, under the title *The Simulacrum – the Making of the World's Most Famous Lost Film*, or something like that.

When I get upstairs, my shoes, the ones I unsuccessfully tried to clean, are waiting for me, looking almost new. You'd think I'd never been down to the ford in them.

I put the box down next to the walnut escritoire and open the lid. There is a faint smell, of dust and old documents. The photograph of Hugh Mason is still on the top, so I take that out and prop it up on the desk. Then I start looking through the other things. I do this slowly, relishing the experience. There are other photographs, most of them of Mary Arden in her younger day, posing in settings which look very artificial to modern eyes, but no others of Hugh. There are cinema tickets, and some folded newspapers which probably contain reviews of Lillian's or Mary's films – I will have to look through those later. I even find a single lobby card for *The Wild Lady*, made eighteen months after *The Simulacrum*. It has Mary Arden on it, in all her teenage beauty, her hands clasped and her eyes upturned in a thoroughly melodramatic manner. I rummage through the box, but there are no other cards or stills. There are receipts and letters – most of them dull.

At the very bottom, I find two sheets of a screenplay. They are still attached to each other with a rusty-looking clip. The top one is the title page; it reads:

The Simulacrum

by Lillian Velderkaust

The second is the beginning of the opening scene. I run

my eyes down it. There is nothing sensational here; it is seemingly the parting of two lovers at a railway station. What there is, is finished before it has barely begun; I turn the page but there is nothing more. This is just a tiny piece torn from the front of the script.

There are other boxes. That was what Mary Arden said. So the rest of the script *might* be in one of those. My heart is actually racing at the thought of it. Of course, most film historians know broadly speaking what the content of *The Simulacrum* was, but having a full script, scene by scene...

For now, though, I have mined all the treasures in this particular box. I push back the heavy curtains as far as they will go to admit the maximum daylight, and then I lay out the photograph of Hugh, and the fragment of script, and photograph them carefully. If Mary Arden changes her mind and tries to whisk all these things away, I want a record of them, even if it's only for my own use.

Then I put all the things back in the box. They are too precious to be left out – even to be exposed to the light for too long. Last of all, I replace the photograph of Hugh Mason. He gazes up at me from under the peak of his service cap. Handsome Hugh. I shut the box carefully, and latch the lid.

Late that night, I hear it again.

I have actually fallen asleep this time and I jerk awake, disorientated. When I closed the curtains this evening, I did not pull them all the way across, and a thin bar of moonlight bisects the room. I lie in the bed, blinking into the darkness. The door is locked again – I know it is; I remember doing it.

What woke me up? A sound from outside, a night bird's cry perhaps? Then I hear the slow creaks, the stealthy taps as someone feels their way along the wall outside my door, and suddenly my mouth is dry. This time, they are heading *towards* the upper west wing. Whoever it may be is returning there – they have already felt their way past my door once, as I lay there innocently sleeping with my arms around one of the pink pillows.

I clench my fists, digging my nails into my palms, and say to myself: *There is no reason to be afraid. Who can it be, after all?*

Images of the people I have seen in the house flit through my head: Mrs Harris, the woman who brings my meals, the nurses occasionally glimpsed. There might be a driver, or a handyman, but I have never seen either one. There is Mary Arden herself, though it can hardly be her. None of them are threatening. Yet it is unnerving how whoever it is feels their way along in the dark, not doing the obvious thing and switching on the lights. The way they tried the door so furtively, but never said a word.

Get up, I tell myself, though every nerve is screaming at me not to. *Go and see. Don't be a coward.*

I hesitate, and then I throw back the covers, reach for my robe and pull it around me as I go over to the door. As my fingers close around the key, I hear that familiar slapping sound. The doors to the upper west wing.

I open the door swiftly then, and peer out cautiously. The double doors seem to be closed; there is no light leaking from them into the dark. I know that is what I heard, though.

Swiftly, I glance the other way. Nobody. I don't give myself time to think about it; I step out into the corridor. There is just enough moonlight filtering through the windows that I can find my way. Barefoot, I am almost silent as I slip down the hallway, passing the head of the stairs with a quick glance down into the dark pit of the stairwell to make sure nobody is coming up. I see nothing. I wait and listen, and hear nothing either. Then I am standing in front of the double doors, my heart thumping.

I'm not going in, I say to myself. *Mrs Harris told me not to, and I'm not. I'm just going to look.*

I put my hands very lightly on the left hand door,

and push. It opens just a little, just a crack. I think I hear something then – a distant creak, a gentle bump. A cold thrill goes through me at the sound. Steeling myself, I push the door open a little further, and now I can see a slice of corridor, the mirror image of this one, stretching away into the west wing. At the end of the corridor there is a right turn, and someone is in the process of making the turn. I have only the most indistinct impression of them before they vanish around the corner – a staccato movement. Then they are gone. The blue-grey light I have seen before flickers again from that side, and then everything is dark.

I take my hands off the door and let it swing back into position. I stand there for a little while, feeling disturbed, although I could not say why. Then I pad my way back to my room.

I am on the threshold when the double doors open behind me. Brilliant yellow light spills out, washing up to my very feet; someone has put a light on. With a sinking feeling I glance back.

Mrs Harris. Does the woman never sleep?

"Ms Garrick," she says, a question in her tone.

I straighten up and smile at her, all innocence. "Hello, Mrs Harris. You'll think me ridiculous, but I couldn't sleep and I was wondering whether to go down and get a glass of milk."

"Let me fetch you one," she says. "I'll bring it up to your room."

"Thank you so much," I say. "I'm sorry for the trouble."

"It's no trouble at all," she says, and she smiles back, but I notice she watches me, as I go back into my bedroom.

Chapter Seventeen

"I don't know what you want me to tell you about my life with Max," I say to Mary Arden. "It was perfectly happy, and ordinary."

"Nevertheless," she says, severely. Today she is bilious-looking in peppermint green.

"But *why?*" I ask her. I have become bolder. She doesn't mince her words, after all. "It can't possibly be interesting compared to being a movie star."

"It is to me," she says. "I never married, after all."

"But..." I give up. I could give her a lecture about a woman's life not being defined by marriage, but I would be wasting my time. I'm not convinced she even thinks it's interesting – she simply likes to watch me writhing around like a bug on a pin. "What do you want to know?"

"Tell me about the first time he took you out."

"Alright." I shrug. "He didn't live *that* far from me, which was lucky, really – wedding guests could come from absolutely anywhere, couldn't they? So he drove over and we went to this riverside restaurant. I'd never been there before, though it was nearer me than him."

"What did you wear?"

"What did I wear? Let me see... A sleeveless navy dress, with a jacket over the top, because it was spring, and not all that warm."

"Hmph. Safe choice."

"I suppose," I say, noncommittally. I don't want to let her get a rise out of me this time.

"And what was the restaurant like?"

"It was beautiful. It was right *on* the river, with all the outside seating on this kind of wooden jetty thing, with a canopy overhead. They had those outdoor heaters, so it was warm enough. But the nicest thing of all was the lighting.

They had strings of lights everywhere, and lights on the water too, floating ones. It was honestly... I mean, people say things are like a fairy tale but this really was.

"Don't ask me what I ate, because I can't remember. We sat right next to the river's edge, and I remember looking at the water flowing past some of the time, how dark it was, and glossy, with the coloured lights moving gently on the surface. The rest of the time I looked at Max.

"It felt so unreal, being there with him. He was good-looking enough to make you feel like losing your head but he was also incredibly *nice* to me. He was interested, really interested – he asked me loads of questions.

"I remember I ended up telling him all about my parents and how difficult it had been after they died. They had me fairly late on so they were older parents to begin with, and then my mum got cancer. She lived to see me get my degree, and then she died. My dad had a heart attack about eighteen months later but I always felt it wasn't just a physical thing; he was heartbroken about Mum going. They were always really close and I think after she went, he just didn't really have much appetite for life anymore.

"I guess all of it was a bit heavy for a first date, but that didn't seem to matter. It didn't put Max off. He said he wanted to know everything about me."

I sigh, remembering.

"I told him about my job, too. I was working for a publisher back then – I'd been an intern first, and used up the bit of money my parents left me, and then I got an actual paid job. So I told him all about that too, and he just listened. It was kind of a luxury having someone that interested, and being able to talk about myself. Does that sound horribly egotistical? I'd been on my own for a while and I was just lonely, I suppose.

"And I asked him things too, obviously. He had his own startup, and it was going pretty well, but it ate up a lot of his time, so he hadn't met anyone. I remember looking at him across the table, and thinking *How is it possible he hasn't met anyone, however busy he is? Surely every single person he passes by on the street falls in love with him.* But he hadn't.

"So we talked all evening and by the end we were already talking about other things we were going to do together – we weren't even pretending we were going to see how it went or maybe call each other in a week.

"That evening – it was absolutely a dream come true," I finish, sadly.

"Hum," says Mary Arden, which might mean anything, but to which she manages to give an ironic overtone. "So did you sleep with him?"

"That is none of your business," I say indignantly. "But actually, no." I glare at her. "And I am not discussing that any further with you."

"Suit yourself," she says. "I think it sounds like a very dull evening."

"I warned you," I say, keeping my temper. "Perfectly happy, but ordinary, that's what I said." I clear my throat. "Now, tell me about Lillian and Hugh."

Chapter Eighteen

"Well," she says, "Hugh joined up fairly early on, that's my understanding. 1914, or early 1915, the year I came into the world. At the beginning of the war, people thought it would be over quickly. If he'd known it would last four years, would he still have signed up? I am sure he would have. I also think he might have actually married Lillian before he went. They'd only known each other a matter of months, but difficult times have a way of concentrating the mind. And Lillian was always a person who knew what she wanted."

I nod, not wanting to interrupt.

"Anyway, off he went, looking very handsome no doubt in his uniform. You've seen the photograph. After he'd gone, Lillian threw herself into her work. You might not think there was much call for film-makers during World War One, but there was. A lot of people wanted a bit of escapism – thrillers, fantastical stories, things like that. Then there were the war films and the actual newsreels. And of course there was the outright propaganda – depicting the German soldiers as rampaging barbarians, or showing the shelling of historic buildings.

"Footage from the Front was sometimes supplemented with work done in the studio, because of the obvious difficulties of working on the battlefield. So Lillian was involved in that. She also worked on domestic projects, the sort of thing the company probably thought was more suitable for a woman – films about cooking creatively during food shortages, that sort of thing."

I roll my eyes a bit at this, but Mary Arden continues, oblivious.

"She preferred the battlefield recreations, because they offered a bigger dramatic scope. It's an interesting problem, to try to demonstrate what war is like in a silent film, with no sounds of bullets or explosions. Even the supposed newsreel material had an element of propaganda too, because you couldn't show anything too distressing. It would have been detrimental to the war effort.

"And obviously she and Hugh wrote to each other. Some of those letters are in the other boxes, the ones I mean to send up to you."

This piece of information, so casually delivered, makes me want to faint. Actual letters between Lillian and Hugh! With an effort I keep silence, encouraging her to go on.

"You may wonder how I ended up with them," she says. "Well, she gave me them to read. When we started working on *The Simulacrum* all those years later, she wanted me to understand what it had been like – not just the circumstances of war, but how it had been between him and her.

"I can't remember the wording exactly verbatim. You can look through them yourself if you want that. Lillian wrote and told him about the film work she was doing and how much she was missing him and just longing for him to come home. Hugh tried to write back cheerfully – he sent her one letter all about the chaffinches and larks still flitting about the French countryside in spite of the trenches and the fighting going on. That was very characteristic of him, to find beauty and familiarity, even somewhere like that. The alternative, I suppose, was to describe how actually awful it was, how loud and filthy and dangerous. He couldn't bring himself to do that. Perhaps he thought it would be easier to forget afterwards, if he didn't."

She glances away, her gaze distant. After a moment she resumes.

"I remember in one letter he mentioned briefly that someone had been shot by a sniper while standing next to him. 'Poor Smith' he called him, and then he said that it had been instantaneous, which was merciful. But imagine the reality of that situation. One moment, he is standing there next to this person Smith – perhaps even speaking to him. The next, he is blinking the man's blood out of his eyes. Maybe he has the man's brains all over his woollen uniform. And, you know, it could have been him. If the sniper had aimed to the right a little...

"I think what he said to Lillian that night at the dinner party was true. Whatever had happened, he wouldn't have come home the same man.

"Of course, he did come home a few times. He got a week or ten days' leave about once every twelve months. That included travel time, back from the Front, so it was never really enough. Lillian used to get particularly anxious about him when she knew he was scheduled to come home, in case something happened to him at the last moment and he never made it back. She had an almost superstitious fear about that."

I bite my lip. I can understand that.

"But he did keep making it home," she says, "through 1915 and 1916. In 1917 he was injured slightly – a shrapnel wound to the leg – and spent some time in a hospital away from the Front. There were no antibiotics back then, so whether you survived an injury was down to good hygiene and luck. He did survive it though; it wasn't serious, and it didn't get infected. He took some leave and then he had to go again.

"Lillian told me once that when he came back to England in 1917 he was different. He still had his marvellous good looks, although he was gaunt and a little haggard. He was tired, though, and he'd developed a chain-smoking habit, though he'd hardly smoked a thing before the war – a cigar after dinner was about his limit. He would keep smoking all the time – his clothes reeked of it – and his hands would tremble slightly. Three years of war, that was a long time to be living on your nerves like that."

"I bet," I say under my breath, but she doesn't seem to hear.

87

"Of course, there were men who survived the whole of World War One without serious injury, improbable though it sounds, considering what any individual soldier was likely to face. But if you'd been in the game since the beginning, by this time whatever battle experience you'd gained was likely to be offset by exhaustion. So much for it all being over by Christmas.

"Anyway, he was home for his week and then he went off again. Lillian went to the station to say goodbye. She kept up a cheerful appearance although she felt sick inside; he seemed so worn and tired that she couldn't imagine how he would keep fighting. He kissed her goodbye but she felt as though he had gone back already. He moved like a man in a dream.

"She went home tight-lipped, and shut herself up to grieve. Her last glimpse of his face haunted her – it was so pale and set. She had a presentiment that she would never see it again.

"When she went back to work, everything felt hollow. Nothing that glorified the struggle felt right. Even the thrillers and fantasies that distracted people seemed horribly empty. Instead, she wanted to create something that would seize people by the lapels, and force them to confront the horror of what was happening.

"Meanwhile 1917 slid into 1918, and in the coldest, most miserable time of year, the letters from Hugh stopped coming."

Chapter Nineteen

It is an infuriating aspect of my conversations with Mary Arden that she always decides where to break the story. An hour – that is what I am supposed to get. In practice, she talks until she gets tired, or bored, and then she stops. It's usually at a place guaranteed to leave me desperate to find out what happened next. I suppose that's the idea – she's like some kind of very elderly Scheherazade. I'm not charmed, though; I'm ready to scream with frustration.

I part from her graciously, because she has something I want. *I can last out until tomorrow*, I think. But when I am having breakfast the next morning, Mrs Harris comes in to see me, and tells me that regretfully, Mary Arden cannot see me today.

"She's meeting her lawyer," she says. "Those meetings always exhaust her."

I look at Mrs Harris for a moment. I have decided not to ask her to call me Theda. I don't feel comfortable enough around her, somehow, even though she is perfectly polite.

"Alright," I say, smiling blandly. "I'll work, or walk around the gardens."

I don't say *walk down to Garthside Ford* because that is my business, and not hers. But that is entirely where I mean to go. It's been dry since the last time I went, so hopefully my shoes won't give me away this time.

Meanwhile, I spend the morning going over my recordings and transcribing them, and looking at the photograph of Hugh Mason under a magnifying glass to see whether I can work out what regiment he belonged to from the badge on his cap or anything like that. Looking at the lobby card and the other things, I wonder whether Mary will agree to let me take them away with me, if I promise to return them later. I have a feeling she won't, just to be difficult, so I take some more photographs in the strong midday light.

Lunch is a lonely affair again, and then I put on a jacket and go out, ostensibly to walk around the grounds. As I come out of the front door, I hear the sound of a car approaching, and I wait to see who it is; the days here are quiet enough to make this an actual diversion. So I stand by an overgrown fountain in the brown remains of the garden and watch as a large and expensive Jaguar purrs its way out from under the trees and up the drive. It stops in front of the house, and a man gets out – an older man, bearded, dark-suited, a little robust in build.

The lawyer, I think, watching him retrieve a leather document case from the back seat of the car. Well, there was no reason to think Mrs Harris was telling an untruth. He goes up to the front door and rings, and clearly someone has opened to him because although I can't see them from here, he steps inside, nodding.

There's no reason to linger after that, so I circle the house and set off through the wood. As I climb over the remains of the fence, I wonder what this spot will be like in June, or August when the undergrowth is tall. Impassable perhaps, but I should be gone by then.

When I get down to the ford, there is a surprise. A wide plank is lying there on the grass. I go to the river's edge, and look at the water. After a couple of dry days, the level has dropped. The plank would *probably* reach across the deepest, fastest bit. I'd still risk wet feet crossing the shallows, but it could be done. I think.

I look at the plank. It's definitely there on purpose. There is no other structure it could have come from – there is a bit of fence on one side of the ford but it's only wire. Then I look across the river, at the house. The tatty Range Rover is outside, but Angus is not to be seen. So there's no help to be had. I have to decide whether to do this or not by myself.

Well, I think, looking down into the water, which is

fast-flowing but not all that deep, *hopefully I won't drown, whatever happens.*

Hopefully.

I pick up one end of the plank, and drag it to the water's edge. After a little thought, I upend it with some difficulty, so that I can drop it across the gap. Down it goes and for a moment I think it won't work, that it will be dragged away by the current, but it isn't. The far end lands in the very shallow water, and now I have a narrow, unsteady-looking bridge. I put a foot on it, and it seems firm enough, but it's kind of unnerving seeing the water shooting along underneath. There's nothing for it, though – it's cross by the plank or give up and go back to Garthside House, so I step right onto the plank. Then I take a deep breath and run across the rest. I almost make it – almost – but running makes it bounce a little and at the last moment I lose my footing. I don't fall into the deepest bit – thank God – but I get both feet wet, up to the ankles. After that, I wade cheerfully across, not even bothering to see where's shallowest, slosh damply up to Angus' door, and knock loudly.

It takes him a while to answer, so I am biting my lip and wondering whether I have braved the plank for nothing, when the door opens.

"Theda." He grins, pleased to see me.

"I fell in the river," I blurt out.

"So you did," he says, looking at my feet. "You'd better come in and dry off."

I hear a click of claws as Jess comes out of the kitchen to investigate.

"Jess, *bed.*"

We follow her into the kitchen, which is only slightly less messy than last time, and comfortably warm. The dirty dishes are in the sink; the table is covered with books and papers. A battered-looking laptop is half-buried under them.

"Monthly accounts," says Angus succinctly, and starts gathering up the papers, making a bit of space.

"Oh, if I'm interrupting–"

"No," he says, shaking his head. "I'm looking for an excuse to stop for a bit. It's deadly."

I sit down on one of the kitchen chairs and look ruefully at my shoes. "I'm leaking water on your floor again."

He glances at the puddle. "Yes, you are. Are you sure you're not a selkie?"

"A what?"

"A selkie." He grins again. "A seal woman."

I laugh, a little uncertainly. "I don't think so."

We look at each other. "Tea?" he suggests. "Or coffee? It's a bit early for the other stuff."

"Tea would be nice." I watch him start hunting for a clean cup, and teabags. Jess huffs and sighs on her bed. I say, "This is sort of a relief. This feels like the sanest place I've been all week."

He looks at me, eyebrows raised. "You said the old lady was strange."

"She's not just strange. She's a *monster*."

"Didn't you say she offered to pay for your car repairs?"

"She did. And I'm grateful, I really am. Only..."

"Only...?" he prompts.

"Well, now I have to stay. No matter what she says or does."

For a moment, as he holds the kettle under the cold water tap, Angus doesn't say anything. Once the kettle's on, he leans against the stove and looks at me.

"Is it that bad – what she says and does?"

I look down, at my hands clasped in my lap. "She asks me about Max."

"Max was–"

"My husband, yes."

He thinks about this. "And if you tell her to mind her own business...?"

"Then she won't talk to me about *The Simulacrum*, which is why I'm here."

There's a long silence. Then he says, "Aye, she sounds like a monster alright."

I watch him washing two cups up. "I don't know what to do. I suppose if the car is that badly damaged I could write it off, though they might have started work on it by now."

"That's a lot of money to lose."

"I know. But honestly, that's not the worst thing that's happened to me this last year. Sorry," I add. "That sounds a bit self-pitying."

"True though," he says. He sets out the cups and puts a teabag in each. "Do you *want* to write the car off and go?"

"I don't *think* so. But..." I hesitate. "I guess I'm afraid."

"Of what she's going to ask you?"

"More of what I'm going to tell her. She has this way of winkling things out of you..." I look away again. "I don't like talking about Max's – about his accident."

"Has she asked you about that?"

"Not yet. But I think she's going to."

For a minute or two Angus occupies himself making tea. He fetches milk from the fridge and picks up an ancient sugar bowl to peer inside. When he has put all these things down on the table, he sits down.

"Are you asking for advice? Because I'm not sure anyone else can tell you what to do about this. Me, I'd be inclined to tell the old besom to stuff her book, but it depends how much you want to write it."

I don't know what a besom is, but I think I can guess. None of this is funny at all, but I can't help it; the corner of my mouth twitches.

"Quite a lot," I say. I help myself to tea. "The whole place is strange, really. Mrs Harris – she's the one who thought you were a taxi driver – is always prowling around the house at ungodly hours. And..." I hesitate. This is going to sound improbable in broad daylight, here in the warm kitchen. "Well, someone comes along the corridor at night sometimes, stealthily, like they're feeling their way or something."

"Drunk?" suggests Angus.

"I suppose... I can't think who it would be, though. Mary Arden has nurses there all the time, round the clock, but if one of them were drunk on duty Mrs Harris would be bound to notice."

"Maybe it's Mrs Harris," he says.

I shake my head. "I don't think it is. I mean, she'd put the lights on, wouldn't she?" I pause. "Whoever it is tries the door, too."

"Your door?"

"Yes. It was locked the first time, because I felt weird about sleeping in a strange place without locking it, but now I've been locking it every night."

Angus looks grim. "I don't like the sound of that. I think I've changed my mind about giving advice. Maybe you should go, or at least stay somewhere else."

"I know." I sigh. "The thing is, this is such a unique chance. So many people have tried to see Mary Arden over the years and she's always said no. I don't know why she said yes to me, but she did. And she's a hundred and four. There's no time left to talk to her – it has to be now."

"You could stay in a hotel, you know."

"I could, but without the car it would be a problem getting there and back every day. I mean, she doesn't exactly live on a bus route – it's in the middle of nowhere."

"Does her story need telling that much?"

I think about that. "I think I need to tell it. I've felt so... I don't know... lost, since Max..."

Died. I don't say that, because I hate to say it.

"It's given me... meaning, if that makes sense."

"I suppose it does."

"Angus? What are the stories about the house?"

"Oh, the usual. Ghosts. Things that go bump in the night. The staff up at Garthside don't mix with the locals, and they don't recruit from the town." He shrugs. "A bit of mystery and people start talking. You know how it is."

I shiver, in spite of the warmth. "Well, it's nice to come down here, where things feel a bit more normal. Just to get away for a bit."

He reaches for my cup, to get me a refill. "You can come whenever you like, you know."

"Thanks." I run a finger along the edge of the table, feeling the grain of the wood. "Angus... I'm not... I mean, Max – it was only September. I'm not looking to start anything yet."

He glances at me. "I didn't think you came down here for *that*. I thought it was the single malt you were after."

I laugh. "Yes, that and the dog's company."

After that, things feel more comfortable. I dry my shoes against the stove and have more tea and ask Angus things about his work. His father owns the land on which the house stands, but Angus has a lot of ideas about what they should be doing with it, and it doesn't sound as if they always agree. Old Mr Fraser sounds like a peppery character and we laugh over some of Angus' anecdotes. Eventually it starts to get towards evening, and so he walks down to the ford with me and puts one foot on the plank while I cross, so it won't upend me into the water.

Before I go, he says, quite seriously: "Keep locking your door, Theda."

"Don't worry, I will."

"And come back, when you feel the need to see Jess."

I grin. "I'll do that too."

I walk along the plank, this time without falling in, and hop onto the opposite bank. Then I give him a last wave and set off across the field towards Garthside House.

I am not looking to start anything, I tell myself.

Chapter Twenty

The next day, as I am gathering up my things to go downstairs and meet Mary Arden, I think I hear a car engine. I cannot see the drive from my window but I pause and listen, thinking that I can hear a distant rumble. Perhaps the lawyer is back again – if so, that will mean more agonising delays.

It's not the lawyer, though, unless he has more than one car. As I descend the stairs I can see through the front window that there is a vehicle parked on the drive outside. From here I cannot see exactly what it is, but it's an eye-watering shade of electric blue and has a huge spoiler on the back. It is very hard to imagine whose it is, but my curiosity is not to be satisfied; I have to go into the morning room or I will be late for my meeting.

There is a shock waiting for me: Mary Arden is not alone. Seated very close to her, on her hearing side, is a man, leaning towards her in a confidential pose. He is wearing a suit and he has his face turned away from me, so all I see at first is thick brown hair. At the sound of the door closing, however, he turns to look at me and I have a first impression of very vivid blue eyes set in a face that is not unpleasant, though not handsome, and decorated with some very carefully cultivated stubble.

Mary Arden, I see, is looking at me, screwing up her eyes behind her spectacles; her gaze slides from me to him and back again. I suspect she is assessing my reaction.

Then the man is on his feet, holding out his hand to me.

"Richard Foster," he says, his handshake crushingly firm. "I'm a relative of Mary's – a sort of nephew, only rather further off."

"Theda Garrick."

I stand there juggling my phone and notepad and

wondering how to react to this: is my meeting with Mary on or off?

"Aunt Mary was just telling me about you," he says. "I'm sorry to interfere with your meeting. I'll go off and find Harris and see about a late lunch. I can talk to Aunt Mary later."

I look at Mary Arden doubtfully, wondering what she thinks about this; if this is someone she doesn't see very often, won't she want to spend time with him right away? Not to mention the fact that crossing people is her pet habit, and here she has a perfect opportunity to frustrate me. But Mary waves her wrinkled hand dismissively.

"Yes, be off with you, Richard. You make the place look untidy. Go and park that monstrous vehicle of yours around the back of the house, too. I can't bear to look at it. Cars should be black or white."

"That's a dreadfully old-fashioned view, Aunt Mary."

"I *am* old-fashioned. Go."

So he does go, though once he has his back turned to Mary Arden he gives me a blatant wink, to which I dare not react. I hear the door close behind me and then I go and sit, somewhat awkwardly, in the seat he has just vacated.

"What do you think of Richard?" she asks me.

"I can't give an opinion. I've only just met him."

"Hmmm. Not as handsome as your husband was, I suppose."

"No," I say stiffly.

She studies me for a moment. "Well, I don't have all day. Where were we?"

I switch on the recording app. "Hugh had stopped writing to Lillian." I am sure she remembers this.

"Ah, yes." She closes her eyes for a moment.

I eye her warily. Can it be that she is actually going to talk to me today without exacting some painful reminiscence in return? It seems so.

"Usually," she says, "Hugh wrote to Lillian once a week,

and it took about a week for the letters to reach her. Then suddenly... nothing.

"She didn't think the worst, not right away. It was wartime, after all – there were plenty of things that could have gone wrong with the mail. But the days crept by, and still there was nothing.

"If anything had happened to him, she wouldn't have been the one to get the telegram; it would have gone to his mother, who was a widow. Lillian was on good terms with Mrs Mason, so it was reasonable to think that she would have passed on any news. So perhaps no news was good news, but still Lillian felt uneasy. She couldn't telephone the old lady either, because Mrs Mason didn't have a house telephone. It was 1918, remember, and not everybody did. It felt cold-blooded to send a telegram asking, so instead she decided to write a letter, and if that produced nothing, to go down to Mrs Mason's in person.

"So she wrote, and she got no reply, and there was still nothing from Hugh. He had never gone long without writing and the days were stretching out. On her first free day, she took a train down to where Mrs Mason lived. Surrey, I think."

I gaze at Mary Arden, fascinated and horrified by this story. I know where it's going but somehow the details make it more real. More hideous.

"The first thing she saw when she got there was that the blinds had been drawn down," says Mary Arden. "She said that she stood there, outside the house, and she felt cold. The blinds were drawn down for a death, you see. She didn't cry. She stood there for a while, looking, and then she steeled herself and went to knock on the door.

"It took a long time for anyone to answer, and when the door opened, it was an older woman, a domestic servant employed by Mrs Mason.

"Lillian said she had come to see Mrs Mason and the woman told her that Mrs Mason was dead. The blinds were drawn down for her, you see. She had had a stroke some days before, and died. And at that Lillian said she had to hang onto the door frame because she was almost faint with relief, thinking that at least the blinds hadn't been put down for Hugh. The woman thought she was shocked at the news, so she asked her to come inside and sit down for a few moments, which Lillian did.

"Anyway, I suppose this particular woman had never met Lillian before, otherwise she would have known who she was and how she stood in relation to Hugh, and she might have been more careful about what she said – or perhaps she was just stupid and unimaginative. She told Lillian that Mrs Mason's stroke had been brought on by bad news – a telegram saying that her son, Hugh, had been reported missing, presumed dead. I think perhaps she even fetched the telegram, for Lillian to see."

Mary Arden looks at me then, to see how I will react to this tale of bereavement, and I press my lips together, determined not to show any emotion. At last she resumes.

"Lillian said she cried out, 'He's dead – oh God, he's dead!' and she pressed her hands over her mouth, as though she were trying to hold back the screams that wanted to come out. But the woman looked at her in a sort of bewildered way, and then she said, 'No, he isn't, Ma'am. The other one came after, saying he was just injured. But Missis never saw it, because she was too ill, and then she died.'

"So Lillian made her fetch the other telegram too, and she read that feverishly. Sure enough, it said that Hugh had been found with grave injuries and was being evacuated to a hospital in England. So she did not know whether to laugh for joy that he was alive after all, or cry her heart out because he was injured, and quite likely to die; they didn't send men back to England for slight injuries. It did not occur to her at the time to wonder why it was that they had first thought him dead, and then taken some time to find him alive."

She shakes her head.

"The woman, at last realising her tactlessness, offered tea. Lillian could not remember afterwards whether she had accepted any, and could not remember leaving the house or making her way back to the station. There were soldiers on the train, on their way back to the Front, and she tried not to cry in front of them.

"She sat in a corner of the carriage, twisting her engagement ring on her finger, praying that Hugh would survive, that he would recover, and that they would marry as she had promised him."

Chapter Twenty-One

Mary Arden stops, and closes her eyes. She has on a cream bouclé suit today and in it she looks like an Egyptian mummy. I wait for her to say something more.

Don't stop now, I think. I don't say a word out loud though.

After a little while she opens her eyes again and looks at me, her gaze bright and malicious.

"I am tired," she announces. "Perhaps I should stop there."

"Please go on," I say, as quietly and humbly as I can.

"You haven't told me a single interesting thing today," she remarks.

"I know. I mean, I will. But would you go on just a little longer?" I say.

She looks at me over the top of her glasses. "Hmmm. Well, answer me one question, and then I will."

"Alright."

"Do you think Richard is attractive?"

"No." The word is out before I have time to consider whether it is tactful or not.

She laughs wheezily, like an old bellows full of dust.

"Too fast," she says. "I don't believe you." After she has laughed herself to a full stop, however, she says, "Now, where was I?"

"Lillian was on the train," I prompt her.

"Ah, yes. Well, she knew where Hugh was now. It was a place in East Anglia, not impossible to reach. The next day she wrote to them, asking for confirmation, and whether she could come and see him. A couple of days later, she received a reply from the matron. It was a starchy letter, Lillian said, but kindly all the same. The matron said that Hugh was indeed there, but she did not advise Lillian to visit him; he was too ill to see her. She added that Lillian should prepare herself for difficult news and treasure her memories of Hugh, rather than looking forward."

Mary Arden pauses and looks at me. "Well, what would you have done?"

I think about it, but not for long. "I'd have gone anyway."

She nods. "And so she did. But she wasn't certain that they would let her in, given that she wasn't a member of his family – yet. So when she got there, she said she was his cousin, Alice. She knew Alice a little – well enough at any rate to know that she would never have gone to visit Hugh: she was a selfish little thing, silly and squeamish. So there was very little chance the staff would know she *wasn't* Alice. The nurse who took her to see him asked her if she knew what to expect, but it was obvious that she had her mind on other things; they were run off their feet there. So Lillian just nodded, and followed her down the passage.

"The hospital was one of those grand old houses. They had to requisition those in the Second World War, but this was a voluntary thing, with Lady somebody presiding over it like a queen bee."

I nod, imagining it very clearly.

"Anyway, they came to the end of the passage and the nurse knocked briskly on a door. Then she opened it a little way and said, 'Mr Mason's cousin has come to visit, nurse.' The nurse who came out looked almost too young for her uniform, and she shot Lillian a look as she passed her. Lillian held her gaze for a moment and something in the quality of it sent a cold feeling through her. There was sympathy in it but also, she thought, fear.

She paused for a moment with her hand on the doorknob, and then she went into the room.

"She told me that the room was cool and shadowy. It was the early afternoon when she arrived, and the winter sunlight was at its very brightest, but the shutters were partially closed. As her eyes adjusted to the gloom, she could see that it was an elegant, though rather shabby room. Much of the original furniture had been moved out to make space for a metal army bedstead and other items, but there was rather pretty wooden panelling painted white, and a high ceiling with decorative plasterwork. Of the bed's occupant she could see little from where she stood, other than a glimpse of white strips of bandage. There was a kind of cage over the end of the bed, holding the blankets away from the body."

I swallow, but I do not say a word.

"Lillian took off her gloves and her hat and put them down on a wooden console near the door. She was conscious of doing this to consume time, to put off the moment when she went forward to look at Hugh. As she had entered the room, her heels had sounded crisply on the floorboards, but he had not stirred.

"'Hugh,' she said softly, and waited. 'It's not your cousin. It's me, Lillian.'

"There was no reaction. The man in the bed was motionless.

"Lillian swallowed. She said to herself: *Perhaps he cannot hear me. The shelling – his eardrums–*

"'Hugh,' she said again, and then she walked over to the side of the bed and looked down at him. Her heart was beating very fast. It took her a little time to make sense of what she was seeing. The dressings were very clean and white, so that for a moment they preserved the illusion that everything was in order, everything in its place. Then the eye began to pick out what was not there anymore. Where an arm should have lain on the smooth white sheet, and a hand and fingers, there was nothing. Her gaze travelled up to the stub over which the gauze had been folded and pinned with excruciating neatness. The face was bandaged so that very little could be seen of it, but there was a flatness where the nose should have protruded, and faint depressions over the eye sockets. With trembling hands she lifted the cover from the cage over the end of the bed and saw that he would never walk again.

"She could smell something, too, in spite of the sharp scent of antiseptic. It became worse when she lifted the covers, so that she fumbled her handkerchief out of her pocket and pressed it over her nose.

"*Gangrene*, she thought, and fought back nausea. She let the cover drop. She stood there looking and looking, and there was nothing familiar, nothing she recognised in this body.

"*They are wrong. This is not Hugh*, she said to herself. *It is a mistake.*"

As Mary Arden relates this, I feel a sudden and terrible pang of empathy. I remember – oh so well – the desire to believe that what has happened did not happen; that horror and tragedy can be *unmade*. I struggle to keep my expression neutral. Thankfully, Mary Arden has not noticed; she is too wrapped up in the story she is telling.

"She felt a great wave of overwhelming relief," she says. "And she began to think how she could prove this – how she could show them that this was not her fiancé at all but some stranger, wrongly identified as him. On a chair by the bed there was a little pile of belongings, and she began to sort through them. Cases of mistaken identity were not unknown; friends exchanged items, even identity tags, before they went over the top. There was a battered cigarette case containing Hugh's brand of cigarettes, and that might have meant nothing, because everyone smoked them, and she couldn't say for certain whether the case was his or not. A pocket knife too, with nothing to say whose it was. But then she picked up a small packet of papers carefully tied with string, and when she opened it she saw her own face looking up at her: a tiny sepia photograph, the corners dog-eared.

"Then she knew. Hugh would never have given that photograph to anyone else. It was him in the bed. The shock had a numbing effect, like plunging into icy water; she couldn't feel anything yet, couldn't think. She put out a hand to touch him but there was nowhere to lay it.

"'Hugh,' she said again, and there was no reply."

Chapter Twenty-Two

Mary Arden sits back in her chair with a sigh, and closes her eyes. "Go away," she says. "I've decided I don't want to talk any more today."

"Okay," I say. I've had enough for one day too. I think I'd like to go outside into the grounds, look at the forest and the distant hills and breathe in the fresh cool air. Clear my head.

I switch off the recording app, gather up my things, and get to my feet.

"Thank you," I say, hesitate, and then, "Do you want me to get the nurse for you?"

But she just waves me away with one skinny claw, not opening her eyes to watch me leave.

I drop my things in my room and then I go outside. It is a clear day, and bright. The shiny blue monster has gone, spirited away to some discreet area behind the house. There is no sign of its owner, either, thank goodness, so I am able to wander amongst the drooping plants and weathered stonework in peace. It is good to feel the wind on my face, to see a bird skimming overhead.

Eventually I go inside but I cannot face working so instead I have a long hot bath in the Art Deco bathroom. I sit in the big cream-coloured tub and think about Mary Arden and Hugh Mason and the book I am supposed to be writing. I think about Max, too, though I don't want to. Beautiful things, broken... I ask myself if I should even be writing this book, whether the whole terrible tale wouldn't be better off resting in obscurity.

I say to myself: *Other people would give anything to interview Mary Arden. She's a hundred and four. This is the last chance to talk to her. When she dies, all those memories will be gone. You have to.*

I know this is true. I know I shouldn't waste the chance. With a sigh I reach for my bath towel. Dinner will be ready shortly – another lonely dinner with only my working notes for company, if I can face taking them down with me.

But when I get downstairs, my hair still damp and my skin glowing, I find that I am not having dinner alone. I open the door to the high-ceilinged room where my meals are always served, and there is Richard, already sitting at the table. It's too late to retreat; he is already getting to his feet in a display of old-fashioned courtesy: rising when a lady enters the room.

"Theda," he says, smiling.

I hesitate. "I'm sorry..." I begin, meaning, *I'm sorry, but what are you doing here?* but he takes it at face value.

"Don't be. Come and sit down."

I can't think of any reason not to, but the invitation makes me slightly uneasy, all the same. He waits until I'm sitting opposite him before he takes his own seat again. There is wine on the table – something I have not seen before, nor asked for – and he is halfway through what looks like a duck breast salad, a starter by the size of the plate.

The woman who usually brings the dinner comes in at that precise moment and asks me whether I'd like some of the duck, and when I turn back, Richard has taken the opportunity to fill my glass with red wine. I don't say anything about that, but I pour myself a tumbler of water from the carafe as well.

"So," says Richard cheerfully, skewering a piece of duck breast with his fork, "You've come to interview Aunt Mary for a book?"

"Yes."

"She says you want to know about that film, *The Simulacrum*. Rather old news now, isn't it?"

"The film is old, yes. But people never get tired of a mystery."

"I guess they don't. It's tantalising, isn't it? Knowing

107

there was a film by such a famous director, such a personal one, and nobody's seen it."

I think about the fragment of script I found, and the hope of finding more, but I keep that to myself.

"I'm hoping Miss Arden will give me some details of the film – an outline, maybe."

"Well, she might," he comments. He picks up his wine glass and takes a long swallow. "You've done well to get this far. She's never seen anyone else. Plenty have written asking, but she always says no."

"I know. It's a privilege."

"You could call it that," he says. He looks at me, his expression friendly but his blue eyes shrewd. "What do you think of Aunt Mary?"

"I don't know how to answer that. She's..." I think about it, about what I can say that will be tactful. "Intelligent. All there. Quite strong-willed."

"Yes, she is, isn't she? I notice you don't say *sweet* or *fluffy*."

I pick up my wine glass. "I suppose you can be however you like when you're a hundred and four."

"And as rich as Croesus. Don't forget that." He puts the last piece of duck into his mouth, his eyes still on me.

"I haven't," I say levelly. "She's been very generous."

"That's when you have to watch her," he says.

I take a mouthful of wine while I think about that. Then I say, "What about you? Are you and Miss Arden close?"

"I'm her only relative."

"Ah."

"*Ah*, she says. That's very succinct." He pushes the plate away. "One day in the not-too-distant future, all this will be mine. Unless Aunt Mary decides to leave it all to a cats' home, that is."

"Is that why you're here?" I ask him, meeting his eyes. "So she doesn't leave it all to a cats' home?"

"Of course not," he says drily. "I'm here out of pure family feeling."

"Shouldn't you be in the west wing, then, having dinner with Aunt Mary?"

"I'd love to, but she won't have me. She eats very little in the evenings, and she goes to bed early. I was banished down here, to have dinner with you, which I must say is preferable."

"Considering she's a hundred and four, I'm not sure that's much of a compliment."

He laughs at that. The door opens and the woman arrives carrying a plateful of the duck for me. She sets it down, and then she says, "Would you like me to bring your main course now, Mr Foster, or will you wait until Ms Garrick has hers?"

"I'll wait," he says, and watches her leave the room. Then he helps himself to another rather large glass of the red wine. He tops mine up too, though I've hardly drunk anything. Richard Foster seems friendly enough, but I'm not sure I fancy getting inebriated with him just yet.

"It's a beautiful house," I say, staying on safe ground.

"If you like Art Deco."

"I guess I do. The room they've given me is like a film star's room."

"In the east wing, I suppose."

I just smile at that. "Will you live here?" I ask him. "After – I mean–"

He shakes his head. "Live out here? No way. I'll sell it. The gardens are a mess, but the house is decently maintained. And someone might get a kick out of knowing it belonged to Mary Arden, the famous film star." He pauses. "You needn't tell her that, by the way. I'm sure she must know on some level that I wouldn't want to live out here, but there's no need to spell it out."

"I wouldn't dream of saying anything. We don't talk about things like that, anyway."

"So what *do* you talk about? *The Simulacrum?* Just that?"

"No," I say. "She asks me about myself."

"Really? What kinds of things?"

"Just ordinary things." I shrug. "She says she finds it interesting, because she never married, herself."

"Ah – so you're married, then."

Is it my imagination, or does he look very slightly disappointed?

"I was," I say shortly.

"Didn't work out?" he says, sympathetically.

"He died." I look down at the duck, which is suddenly unappetising, red juice leaking out onto the plate.

"Oh God. I'm sorry."

I force myself to look at him. "Don't worry. But don't let's talk about it, okay?"

"Okay," he says hastily. After that he makes a determined change of direction and we talk about a variety of things – his job, which has a grandiose title but is seemingly flexible enough that he can come to Garthside House for days at a time; the news; the latest films. The main course arrives, and more wine, and I wonder whether to ask Richard how long he plans to stay, and whether he intends to have dinner at the same time I do every night. That would be pointed though, so in the end I say nothing. I can't decide what I think of him. I told Mary Arden I didn't find him attractive and I'm not sure that's entirely true. But there's something about him that slips away from my grasp.

I turn down the pudding and even coffee and escape upstairs, and when I get to the top I lean over the balustrade a little way and look down, feeling slightly shamefaced. There is nobody on the stairs or in the hall. The house is very quiet; I could be quite alone. As usual, I go back to my room and lock the door from the inside.

*

I wake some time later with a start. The room is pitch dark, and it is unbreached, because the door is locked. But someone is trying the handle. I lie there for a moment, holding my breath, and there it is again: a rattle as it moves back and forth. It's not like last time; whoever is doing it isn't even trying to be subtle. When it doesn't open at the first attempt, they try harder. The door trembles in its frame.

I put on the lamp and get out of bed, reaching for my robe. When I have tied it around myself with grim firmness, I go over to the door.

"Who is that?" I say loudly, without opening it.

Silence. Then the assault on the handle begins again.

"Who's there?"

My heart is thumping. I try very hard to persuade myself that I am angry, not afraid.

"Richard?"

Silence falls again, and this time it stretches on and on. I put my ear to the wooden panel and listen, and I *think* I hear someone moving away, but I am not sure.

I go back and sit on the edge of the bed, still listening. There is nothing more. After a while, I get back under the covers and lie there stiffly, unable to relax. A long time passes, and eventually I drift off to sleep again without turning out the light. There are no more disturbances; I sleep through until dawn.

Chapter Twenty-Three

"Tell me how you became engaged," says Mary Arden. "Did it take him long to ask you?"

Today she is resplendent in an unseasonal dress of white fabric with a large print of bright red poppies. It makes her look as though she is covered in bloody handprints.

I have the unpleasant feeling that as I relate these incidents from my past to Mary Arden I am populating my memories with her presence – that from now on she will always be there in the background, a wizened and malicious spectator.

"You're assuming *he* asked *me*," I say. "It doesn't have to be that way nowadays, you know. But actually, he did ask me, and it was months after we met. Not even a year."

"I suppose you expect me to say how romantic that was," she remarks. "If you ask me, it was precipitous."

I didn't ask her, so I say nothing to this.

"Go on," she says, sounding bored. "Did you know it was coming, or was it all a big surprise?"

"I didn't know it was coming. I loved Max so much – I adored him. So of course I'd thought about it. Who wouldn't? But I didn't think it would happen so soon.

"On the actual day he asked me, I wasn't thinking about it at all – it wasn't anywhere in my head. I was still working for a publisher back then, and the whole office was gearing up for a huge presentation that evening. We had half a dozen new titles coming out and we were going to present them to an audience of journalists and book bloggers. So the whole place was mayhem. Some of the authors were going to be there, so people had to meet them and look after them. The meeting room had to be rearranged and promotional materials collated and laid out on all the seats. There were some last minute problems – one of the book samples had been printed in the wrong page order, things like that. I was run off my feet, and when Max phoned I nearly didn't take the call.

"I was walking around the meeting room with my arms full of folders and my phone between my shoulder and my ear. Max said, 'Theda' and it took me a minute to react. I was just going, *mmm-hmmm*, because my mind was on other things. Then I realised it was him so I put the folders down and said, 'Max.'

"He said, 'Listen. You have to bunk off work, right now.'

"I said, 'What? Max, I can't do that.'

"He said, 'Yes you can. If you leave now, you can get home, get changed, and I'll pick you up at six-thirty. Come on, Theda. Live dangerously for once.'

"I glanced around me and there were a couple of other people in the room, so I went into a smaller meeting room, next to it, and shut the door. Then I put down the files and said, 'Look, Max, I'm sorry, I really can't get away.'

"'Why not?' he said cheerfully.

"'Because there's a huge meeting on this evening. We've all been working on it for months.'

"'Can't they manage without you?' he said. 'You said you've *all* been working on it. Can't someone else cover?'

"'Max... I can't.'

"'You can. It's... Theda, it's important. I want to ask you something.'

"I didn't know what to say to that. All of my sudden my heart was just thudding and I felt hot all over. I thought: *does he mean what I think he means?* I could hear people moving about in the room next door, and someone said, 'Where's Theda?' so I knew it wouldn't be long before they tracked me down.

"When I didn't reply, Max said, 'Please. Please, Theda. Just come.'

"And I had to decide. I looked at the pile of files and said, 'Alright. I'll come.' Just then there was a knock on the door, so I said, 'I have to go. See you at six thirty,' and hung up.

"The person who'd knocked was my boss, Elise. She said, 'What are you doing in here, Theda? There are a thousand things to do.'

"I said, 'I had to take a call. I'm really sorry, but I have to leave. It's a family emergency.'

"She said, 'But Theda, we have a launch presentation in ninety minutes.'

"'I know,' I said. 'I'm sorry.' And I more or less ran out of there."

"So you lied to your employer, then," says Mary Arden.

I stare at her. How can she unerringly find the worst way of putting things?

She waves a skinny claw at me. "No matter. Go on."

I continue to look at her for several seconds but then I resume the story.

"On the way home I had a text from Max: *Are you out of there?*

"*Yes*, I texted back. *Where are we going?*

"*Surprise. Wear your red dress.*

"I smiled to myself at that. Wherever we were going, it had to be somewhere nice. So I texted back, *Okay x* and after that there was no reply.

"So I got home and had a super quick shower. I put the dress on, and put my hair up, and I was just putting the finishing touch to my makeup when the front door bell went, and there was Max. He said..."

I stop, because the memory is so vivid in my head. It makes me feel like crying.

"He said?" repeats Mary Arden, craning forward like an elderly vulture.

I pull myself together. "He said, 'You look beautiful.'"

"Humph," she says, sitting back. She is so irritating that I stop wanting to cry.

"He'd ordered a car, so neither of us had to drive. We

went to that riverside restaurant, the one where we'd had our first date. Max had booked out the entire section by the water, so we'd have the place to ourselves. He'd planned the whole thing. It was absolutely perfect. We went and sat down by the river, and the waiter came out with a bottle of champagne. And after he'd gone, and we were alone, Max proposed."

I look away, anywhere but at her avid old face.

"He said, 'Theda, will you marry me?' and I said, 'Yes.' Well, actually I said, 'Oh my God – yes.'"

"Did he have a ring already?" asks Mary Arden, with every appearance of genuine interest.

I nod. "A huge solitaire diamond, set in platinum."

Her gaze falls to my left hand, which is naked.

I rub my hands together, self-consciously. "I don't wear it often now. It's... it's not practical. I have to take it off whenever I wash my hands and I'm afraid I'll leave it on the side of a washbasin somewhere."

"And your wedding band, that isn't practical either?"

I grit my teeth. "I don't wear that for the same reason I don't use my married name. I don't like people asking. I can't stand their bloody pity."

Chapter Twenty-Four

"Bloody pity," says Mary Arden. "Nobody wants it. You don't, and neither did Lillian."

We are back on the events of 1918, which is a relief.

"She knew," she says. "That Hugh would die, I mean. He might have recovered from those injuries, dire though they were. But the smell of gangrene... Lillian knew what that meant. Well, I told you there were no antibiotics in 1918. The treatments were debriding of the wounds and antiseptics. If those didn't work..."

Mary Arden's gaze is unfocussed, far away; she is imagining Lillian and Hugh in the dim room of the mansion house, slivers of sunlight slanting through the gap between the shutters to reveal the peeling paint. "You know," she says, "Lillian lived a long time; she was in her nineties when she died. She outlived Hugh by many decades. But there was never anyone else, nothing serious."

She is silent for a moment, as though even her cynical old heart is moved by this thought. Then she continues.

"That first afternoon, she stayed for an hour, and when she left she told him she would come back, though there was no indication that he heard or understood her, or was even aware of her presence. She went out into the passage, and as she hurried away she was distantly aware of the young nurse going back into the room she had just vacated.

"It was a busy place; nobody took any notice of her. There were nurses bustling about and porters wheeling people in and out, and voices – sometimes conversing ordinarily, sometimes groaning with pain. Lillian went out of the nearest door, into the gardens, and leaned against a wall. She took out a cigarette – she rarely smoked at that time, but later it became an ingrained habit – and lit it with hands that trembled. She shook out the match, took a deep drag and tried to think about what she had seen, about her situation and Hugh's.

"Part of her still didn't want to believe it. She wanted to think that there had been an error – a case of mistaken identity. Someone else was sitting up there in that darkened room, his face blown away, the air thick with the smell of infection. Hugh, her Hugh, was still out there somewhere, at the Front, or perhaps dead, but not so dreadfully wounded."

I look at my hands, feeling the sting of empathy again.

"She thought about the matron advising her not to come. It made her think of that horrible fairy tale, Bluebeard, about the woman whose husband tells her she may open every door in his mansion except one. Of course she cannot help opening it and there is unimaginable horror behind it. But who can resist opening that door?

"And she felt a kind of numbness and helplessness too, because she hadn't yet let go of all the things they had planned to do together when the war ended. Marrying, travelling, working, having children. Her mind kept trying to think of ways in which they could find their way back to those plans – if he overcame the infection, if he learned to live with his injuries. None of these ideas could get past that terrible scent of corruption.

"After a while someone brought out a wounded man in a wheelchair to take the sun, so Lillian put out her cigarette and went back inside. She found the matron, represented herself as Alice Mason, and asked to be notified if there was any change, explaining that Hugh's mother had died. She left her own home address. Then she turned away and walked back to the railway station."

Mary Arden pauses for a moment, lost in the past, and I wait silently for what will come next, not wanting to interrupt her train of thought. The papery eyelids slide down over her eyes and she is so still that I wonder whether she is drifting off to sleep. She inhales delicately, lets out a long sigh, and opens her eyes.

117

"She never saw him alive again," she says. "The gangrene took him off, of course, and it happened pretty quickly. He never showed any sign of knowing that she was there when she visited, but you wonder if he did know, somehow. If he'd held on, just long enough to say goodbye." She shrugs. "Well, who can say?

"A very few days later, after that first visit, she went back again, to discover that her journey had crossed with a letter telling her Hugh had died. The nursing staff were sympathetic but brusque – their concern was with the urgent needs of the wounded, after all, and besides, everyone had seen tragedy in their own circle. Having lost someone, that was hardly unique."

She shakes her head.

"Someone showed Lillian into the room where Hugh had lain. The shutters had been put back and the sun streamed in, making it almost unbearably bright. The bed was empty, with just an uncovered mattress. The nurse gave her Hugh's possessions. 'Miss Mason', she called her, still thinking she was Hugh's cousin, and Lillian did not disabuse her. She laid a hand on the bare mattress. The stink of disinfectant was in her nostrils.

"'He never suffered, Miss,' said the nurse. 'Never woke up at all.'

"'Thank you,' said Lillian, her voice breaking. Then she turned and left.

"I think she broke down for a while after that. Lillian told me all about her life, but that part was very hazy. She descended into a pit of grief and loss that lasted months."

Mary Arden looks at me then, a slyness in her rheumy old eyes, to see how I will react – I, who have also loved and lost. I keep my face still, and wait for her to give up and go on.

"The worst of it was," she says, "the War was almost over. Before the end of that year, they were all celebrating Armistice Day. The streets were full of people partying –

the only ones who weren't were people like Lillian, who had lost someone at the last. It seemed to drive a wedge between her and other people, because she couldn't feel the way they did – she couldn't celebrate. For a while she didn't see many of her friends, though she did keep in touch with my parents. My mother had lost a younger brother, you see, only a month or so after Hugh died. He was killed outright. A shell landed in the trench where he was standing and blew him to pieces. So there was no lingering death from gangrene for him, but it was a loss, and I think Lillian felt a kind of bond with my mother because of that.

"My mother used to say that it took a long time for her to accept Edward's death, because there was very little for them to send home. She never saw his dead body or anything. She used to think sometimes that he would come home one day – just come walking through the front door and chuck his cap onto the little table there, and hug her."

I nod. I know that feeling. There were days when I thought Max would come back, that he wasn't really gone. His death, the funeral – those things seemed so much less real than Max's life.

"Well," says Mary Arden, ploughing on, "I think Lillian had difficulties accepting what had happened too. But she didn't take it the same way. For my mother, there was a kind of strange sad unreality about Edward's death. But when it came to Hugh's death, Lillian just wanted God, or Fate, or whatever there was, to take it back. To give her Hugh back. And that, I think, was what was behind it all."

Chapter Twenty-Five

I sleep heavily that night and get down to breakfast early the next day. I eat by myself and while I am pouring myself another cup of very strong, very sweet tea, it occurs to me that Richard may have left. This is a relief, really. He seemed friendly enough, but there was a cynical tone to the way he spoke, and his habit of topping up my wine glass without being asked was annoying. His employers, too, may be reasonably relaxed about allowing him time off to see his elderly relative, but they cannot be endlessly elastic about it.

I help myself to another piece of toast and look out of the big windows. It is a dry, sunny day, and I am very tempted to go and see Angus again. I told him I wasn't looking to start anything, and I'm really not; if I keep going down there, however, I may give the entirely opposite impression. But he feels sane and sensible in a way that nobody in this house does. It's not healthy, just talking to Mary Arden and occasionally to Mrs Harris. The story of Lillian Velderkaust and Hugh Mason is fascinating but disturbing, and as for the way Mary Arden picks over my life, like a gloating old cannibal sucking the marrow out of human bones, it makes me positively shudder. No; an hour or two in that warm untidy kitchen, with Jess the dog snoring in the corner, is just what I need.

Crossing the hallway on the way to fetch my coat, I run into Mrs Harris.

"Good morning. Ms Garrick," she says. "How are you today?"

"I'm fine, thank you."

"I do hope you're not finding it too dull here," she says, "since Miss Arden can only see you for an hour or so a day. Are you managing to amuse yourself?"

"Just about." I laugh awkwardly. "I go for walks and... things."

"It's a fine morning for walking," she says. "Where do you like to go?"

"Oh... not far," I say, vaguely. "The grounds are very interesting."

"Really? Goodness me."

"Mrs Harris?" I say, seeing that she is preparing to bustle on to her next task.

"Yes?"

"Is there any news of my car?"

"They're still working on it, that's my understanding. I can telephone them to check, if you like. The damage was quite severe."

"No... that's alright," I say, although I can't help being disappointed.

"If you wish to go anywhere – into the town, for example – someone can drive you."

"Thanks," I say doubtfully. I'd rather be in control of my own movements, though I may eventually get desperate enough to take her up on the offer.

"Anyway," she says, "I must get on. Enjoy your walk."

"Thank you." I watch her walking off and then I run upstairs to my room.

I tidy myself up a bit, fetch my coat and change my shoes, and descend the stairs again. The hallway is silent and deserted as I let myself out and close the door behind me. The air is crisp with a very light breeze; crows coast past, crying harshly. I step down into the garden and begin to make my way along the front of the house, planning to turn at the corner and make my way into the woods, and then the fields leading down to the ford.

A door slams behind me, and I hear footsteps. I resist the temptation to turn my head, but I amend my direction, making instead for a lichenous statue standing in a patch of dry stalks, as though it is so thrilling that it has to be examined.

"Theda," says a voice that I recognise as Richard's. "Wait up."

My heart sinks, but by the time I turn to face him I have plastered a polite expression onto my face.

"Where are you going? I thought I'd come too. Nothing like a bit of fresh air."

"Nowhere in particular," I say. "Just taking a turn around the grounds."

"Would you like some company?"

I pause. "Um... not really. It's kind of my thinking time."

"Oh." He looks at me. "Well, just for a few minutes, then. I don't want to interfere with your thinking, but I'm desperate to stretch my legs."

I begin walking again and he falls in beside me. Clearly, there is no getting rid of him.

"How are the interviews going?" he asks me, pushing back his thick brown hair.

"Not much different from how they were yesterday evening," I say. Then I relent. "We're up to the point where Lillian Velderkaust finds out what has happened to her fiancé Hugh."

"Intriguing," he says, and I have the impression he knows nothing about it at all. He sees the look on my face and says, "No, really."

"For film fans, it is," I say. "It's a very poignant moment – understanding the motivation behind the film. So much pain."

"It fascinates you, doesn't it?"

"I suppose it does. The fact that the film is lost, too... It only really exists in her head now, so it depends how much of it I can winkle out."

"That's why she agreed to talk to you. You really care about it."

"I suppose the others did, too."

"Not enough. It was a commercial project. The most sought-after lost film ever, the famous director's missing masterpiece, etcetera."

I pause and look at him. "Are you just inferring that? I thought none of them ever came here."

"They didn't," he says promptly. "They just didn't impress Aunt Mary the way you did."

His vivid blue eyes are wide and ingenuous-looking.

"You're flattering me," I say drily.

"Well, why not? You're probably the most interesting thing about this particular visit to Aunt Mary."

"Probably?" I repeat. I'm both amused and irritated. "There's not much competition, unless you're interested in Art Deco architecture."

"I meant, definitely the most interesting thing." He looks at me mischievously.

I suppress a sigh and start walking again, and he keeps pace with me.

"It's beautiful, isn't it?" he says.

"You mean the garden?" I say, raising my eyebrows.

"I mean all this. Nature." He gestures vaguely towards the distant hills. "Look at those blackbirds."

"Those are crows," I say severely. I can't help it; the corners of my mouth twitch, and he sees this, and laughs.

So we stroll on, through the decaying remains of the ornamental gardens. Richard's company is not unpleasant and anyway, I couldn't get rid of him without being rude. But I suspect I shall not see Angus today, after all.

Chapter Twenty-Six

I set my mobile phone to record audio and put it down on the table with an audible click. It has the desired effect: Mary Arden opens her eyes. I do not believe she was really asleep; I think she was waiting for me to be ready before she went on with her narrative. I do not think she can be bothered with niceties.

"So, Theda Garrick," she says, "Did you enjoy your walk this morning?"

"It was alright," I say noncommittally, wondering how she knew about it, but deciding not to give her the satisfaction of asking.

"Take care," she says. "He's a real charmer, that Richard. He'll charm the pants right off you." And she laughs wheezily, clutching the head of her cane so that the rubber tip beats on the floor.

"Thank you for the warning," I say neutrally. I sit straight in my chair, pen and pad at the ready, willing her to stop amusing herself and get on with it.

Eventually she laughs herself to a standstill. "You're no fun," she says, dismissively. "Very pretty, but no fun at all."

"I suppose I should thank you for that, or for the complimentary part of it, anyway."

"Don't bother. Now, where were we?"

"Lillian had been back to the nursing home – and found that Hugh had died."

"Ah, yes. Well, when she left she took Hugh's belongings with her, which she was allowed to do because of course, the nursing home thought she was a member of the family. Amongst them was the tiny photograph of Lillian herself, that Hugh had had with him right up to his death."

Mary Arden pauses. For the first time since I began interviewing her, I detect hesitation in her manner.

"That photograph..." she says.

"Yes?" I prompt.

"Well, she mightn't have kept it, since it was of herself, except Hugh had been carrying it when he died. So she had it near her and looked at it often. And..." She pauses. "After a while, she became convinced that the photograph had changed."

"Changed?" I can't make sense of that.

"That there was something new in it," she says. "She herself looked no different than before. But at her right shoulder, there was a mark. A blur, a white mist – well, that was what it looked like, she said.

"Without seeing the photograph, it's impossible to say. Hugh had been carrying it around with him – it was dog-eared, and it could perfectly easily have been damaged in some other way. Scratched or scuffed, or maybe it got damp. Perhaps the mark had been there all along, a flaw in the film or some actual object moving too fast to be captured. Or," she adds, "It might have been Lillian's imagination, and there was nothing there at all. The fact was, she thought she could see something. She thought it was–"

She breaks off, and I am the one who says it.

"Hugh."

The word hangs there between us for a moment. Then she nods.

"I know what you're thinking," she says. "But there were plenty of respectable people who believed in it – spirit photography, I mean. The Sherlock Holmes writer, Doyle, he was one of them. He published a book about it in the '20s. Lillian wasn't the only one, not by a long chalk. There were a lot of families who'd lost someone, who wanted to believe that they weren't really gone forever." She snorts. "There were plenty of cheats and swindlers too, who were very happy to fake photographs to take in the gullible."

I bet, I think, and then: *Poor Lillian.*

"Lillian wasn't stupid," says Mary Arden, as if reading

my thoughts. "She knew that just because she wanted something to be true, that didn't make it true. So she set out to find the truth for herself. She tracked down spirit photographers, showed them the photograph of herself, and got them to take others. Of course, nearly all of them told her the photograph she had with the blur or whatever it was, was genuine. Some were more eager than others to take new pictures, and the most eager usually attached a high price. She got through a lot of money that way, and the results were very mixed. One photograph showed a soldier in uniform alright, transparent as a sheet of glass, reaching for Lillian in a very touching manner, and with the face a convenient blur. But she knew it wasn't him. Whoever had posed for it was heavyset, and Hugh was athletic, but much leaner.

"She laughed when she told me about that one. The photographer tried to bluff his way through it, she said. First he claimed it really was Hugh, and that the camera had a distorting effect on the spirit world. Then he said it was someone other than Hugh, some other person who was significant in her life. But Lillian said she hadn't lost anyone else. The photographer got his pay; she never quibbled about that. But she tore up the photograph and dropped the pieces in his lap."

Good for her, I think.

"Sometimes, the results seemed genuine, or at least, no fakery could be detected," says Mary Arden. "Most of those were frustratingly vague in form, though: a soft haze, a blur, something that might have been an outstretched arm. And one – just one – where the faint pattern of light and dark patches that appeared behind Lillian's shoulder might have been an out-of-focus face – Hugh's face."

She shakes her head. "It was never enough to satisfy her, of course. Enough to draw her in, to keep her searching. In a way, perhaps it was her obsession with the spirit world that kept her going. She said that she felt as though she were in a great unlit room, always feeling for Hugh's hand in the darkness.

"It was at about this time that her career began to gain a little traction. A silent film she had worked on during the War, some escapist piece of nonsense, became unexpectedly popular and she began to pick up other projects. So there were these two things in her life – her film work and the spirit photography – and it was only a matter of time before they overlapped."

Suddenly I see where this is going, and I sit back with my mouth open.

Mary Arden continues, "In 1922 she was making a silent film, one of those sentimental dramas which typified her early work, before she got famous enough to have a free hand in what she did... I don't recall what it was called. She was setting up some shot with the main actor in it and when she looked through the viewfinder, the focus required adjusting. For a moment she perceived his face as a blur, a pattern of dark and light that reminded her instantly of that single spirit photograph that might have shown Hugh's face.

"Lillian stepped back from the camera for a moment, feeling a stab of shock. Then her professional side took over again. She adjusted the focus and the face that might have been Hugh's sharpened into that of a living actor, with only a passing resemblance to the dead man. She proceeded with the scene, going through the motions automatically, but her mind was ablaze with a new idea. If the spirit of a person could be captured in a photograph, why not on film? Why shouldn't they move, and breathe, and gesture?"

Because it's impossible, I think, but I don't say so aloud.

"Of course, films were still silent in 1922," says Mary Arden. "Did Lillian know sound was coming? I think so. Work had already been done on creating films with sound – the photographophone, for example, and later, Phonofilm. So perhaps she even dreamed of hearing Hugh speak to her.

But mostly she imagined seeing him again – she *hungered* for it. To give him life again. To see his face, to tell him all the things she had not been able to say, and to see that he understood. That was what she wanted.

"How to achieve that? How to fund it? She had no idea at that point. Even if she had known how to produce a result, no studio would have been prepared to indulge in experiments in spiritualism. But Lillian told me she knew she would find a way. It might take her years – decades... In fact, it did take the best part of a decade. But she would do it."

Mary Arden sighs and leans back in her armchair, her hands like gnarled roots on her lap. She closes her eyes.

I wait. The audio recording is still running. I don't want to prompt her. I'm afraid to say or do anything to break the spell. The things she has told me are extraordinary. They will make a sensational book – the great director, searching for a way to recreate her dead fiancé on film. The moments spool out like film running through a projector, but in every frame there is only Mary Arden, unmoving.

I think that her weight of years has caught up with her; she has gone to sleep. I clear my throat, wondering if I should tiptoe out. Instantly, her eyes open.

"That's enough from me," she says, and her eyes glitter maliciously. "Now it's your turn to talk."

Chapter Twenty-Seven

My turn. I ask myself twenty times a day whether it is worth dragging out all my old history for the benefit of Mary Arden, in exchange for the information she gives me in snippets. But she won't go on without it, and I have nothing to go home to.

She is watching me. "Tell me," she says, "about your wedding."

I prepare myself to tell her about the church and the flowers and my gown and the bridesmaids' dresses, but she says, "No."

I stop with my mouth open, staring at her, and she says, "Tell me what was *wrong* with your wedding day."

I feel the heat rush into my face. All of a sudden my palms are perspiring and there is a strange cold tight feeling in my throat. "What?" I say, stupidly.

"Tell me what was wrong with your wedding day. I'm not interested in hearing whether the bridesmaids wore teal or turquoise or what flowers you had in the church. Tell me what was *wrong*."

I look at her, and the seconds ooze past like treacle. Then I clear my throat. "Nothing was wrong. It was an absolutely perfect day."

"Poppycock," she says. "Nothing is absolutely perfect."

"I don't know what you want from me," I say sullenly. "I was going to tell you about my wedding, like you asked."

"But that's not interesting, is it? Your special day." Her lip curls. "What interests me is what didn't go into the wedding album. The fly in the ointment. That's what I want to know about."

For a while I sit there in silence, thinking. Then I say, "The table flowers. I told the hotel we wanted shades of pink – I *agreed* pink arrangements. But a wire got crossed somewhere, or they got us mixed up with someone else, and when we got to the hotel everything was yellow and orange. And I–"

"No," says Mary Arden, shaking her head. "That's not what I want."

"Well, what do you want?" I can't help the edge creeping into my voice.

"I want to know the first thing you thought of, when I asked you what was wrong with your wedding day. I saw it, you know. Your reaction. I saw the blood come into your face. Tell me what did that."

"I don't know what you mean."

"Yes, you do." She waits for me to say something. "I want to know," she says. "You can think about it, if you like. Come back and tell me tomorrow instead."

"Why?" I say through gritted teeth. "Why do you want to know?"

"Because the perfect wedding is unutterably boring. Because I am old and have never had a wedding myself. But mainly because you don't want to tell me."

"There's nothing to tell."

Silence.

"Nothing important."

Mary Arden sits back in her chair again, lets her head rest against the back of it, and closes her eyes. The expression on her face is one of great boredom.

"Look," I say, "Why do we have to keep talking about me? Can't we just talk about *The Simulacrum*? You've heard how I met Max, and how we got engaged, and all that. It can't possibly be that interesting. Not to you. You've met movie stars, and travelled all over the world. Can't we just talk about you?"

I babble on, and once or twice when my voice goes up to a higher pitch she opens her eyes briefly and looks at me. But she says nothing. She's done talking, unless I do what she wants. Eventually I run out of things to say. I sit there, on the edge of my chair, my hands grasping each other in my lap.

Somewhere close by, a clock is ticking. I realise that the audio recording is still running, so I pick up my phone and turn it off.

I say, "Alright."

Those wicked old eyes open in a flash.

"I had a row with Max."

There it is, out in the open. I've never told anyone this before.

"It was on the morning of the wedding. I know what you're going to say, that the bridegroom is not supposed to see the bride before the ceremony on the day of the wedding..."

"Did you want to see him?"

"No." I'm surprised when that pops out. "I like those old traditions."

"So why did you?"

"Because... Because we were living together anyway so he'd have had to move out the night before, and... well, Max wanted to." I shrug nervously.

"Why?"

Her eyes are unblinking.

"He – well, he wanted to make sure everything was right, I guess. I mean, it was a big wedding. Everyone we knew was there. And Max... Max was a perfectionist."

"So he wanted to check you over, did he? What if he hadn't liked the dress? What would he have done then, hey?"

"That wasn't going to happen."

"Why not?"

I take a deep breath. "Max helped me choose it. And before you start, there was absolutely nothing wrong with that. We had a certain look in mind for the wedding – we agreed it between us. And it's the twenty first century, for God's sake, not 1950. There's no earthly reason why you can't choose the most expensive dress of your entire life between you."

"That's true," she says coolly. "So the row wasn't about the dress?"

"No."

"What was it about, then?"

I sigh, glancing away from her. "It was about a necklace. My parents are both dead – they died before I even got engaged to Max, so they never saw our wedding day. And I wanted to feel like they were there in some way, so I decided to wear the same necklace my mother wore for *her* wedding. It was a double string of pearls with a heart shaped diamond on the clasp – classic. You could have worn it with anything.

"But that morning Max gave me a present. It was a necklace and earrings, with diamonds set into gold. When I opened it, I just didn't think. I said something like, 'Oh Max, these are gorgeous, but I'm going to wear my mother's necklace.'

"At first he didn't seem that worked up about it. He said, 'But look how well these go with your dress', and he took the necklace out of the box and undid the clasp so he could put it round my neck.

"I said, 'It's really beautiful, Max – I love it. But I could wear it after the wedding. I just really want to wear something of Mum's today.'

"I guess there was a bit more discussion after that, but I was pretty clear in my own mind. I undid Max's necklace really carefully and put it back in the box. I didn't put the other necklace on right away. I felt that would be kind of..."

"Provocative?" suggests Mary Arden.

"Tactless," I say. I bite my lip. "We didn't talk about it again after that. Max just whispered, 'wear mine', and then he went off to get dressed himself. The bridesmaids arrived and they were getting into their dresses and checking each other's hair. We had a glass of champagne each. There was a lot of laughing. I kept my mum's necklace on but I put on Max's earrings because they sort of matched.

"Then, a little while before we had to leave for the church, I left the other two in our room, doing their makeup, and I went down the hall to use the bathroom before we left. I came out, and as I was going to go back to the bedroom, Max looked out of the spare room. He grabbed me by the wrist and pulled me in and shut the door.

"He had a face like thunder and I was just bewildered. I didn't know what the matter was. He said..."

I swallow. "He said, 'What the fuck, Theda? I told you to wear my necklace.' He sounded so angry that I jumped and tried to pull away, and that was when he grabbed at the necklace I was wearing, and it broke. The pearls went all over the floor, bouncing under the furniture. I just stood there. I put my hand up to my neck and said, 'Mum's necklace.' I thought I was going to burst into tears. I knew we only had a few minutes before we had to leave for the church. There was no way I could collect up all the pearls and thread them together again. There was no time to do anything – not to think about what he'd just done or anything else. I was just so shocked.

"As for Max, the fit of temper was gone as quick as it had come. He couldn't stop apologising. 'Don't cry, don't cry,' he kept saying. He put his arms around me and kissed the side of my neck, and he seemed like my Max again, his kind, normal self. He was just so sweet that I wondered if the whole thing had been some kind of weird figment of the imagination, but the pearls were still rolling around the floor underfoot.

"After the other two had gone downstairs, Max came to the bedroom with me and found the box with his necklace in and put it around my neck. I stood in front of the mirror and he stood behind me, smiling. He said, 'It looks beautiful, doesn't it?' and I nodded. And he kissed me again and said, 'I'm sorry about your mother's necklace. We'll get it restrung after the wedding. And I'm sorry I swore. I'm keyed up. This is a big day.'

"And so I forgave him. I knew we were both nervous, that people aren't always themselves when they're under pressure. He'd never been temperamental, and I didn't think he'd ever do it again. And, you know... I loved him. I loved Max so much."

For perhaps half a minute there is silence between us, Mary Arden and me.

Then she says, "And did he? Have the necklace restrung?"

I lean forward, putting my head in my hands. I don't look at her.

"Yes," I say. "He did."

Chapter Twenty-Eight

I don't feel up to having dinner with Richard tonight. The conversation with Mary Arden has sickened me – it's made me think about things I wanted to forget. I sit on my bed, hugging myself, remembering. It was true what I told her – Max did get the necklace restrung. It looked exactly the same afterwards. I've never worn it, though.

I touch my collarbone with my fingertips. After the wedding, when I was undressing in the hotel room, I saw that there was a mark on my neck, where the clasp of the necklace had cut into it just before it broke. The mark was small enough that nobody would have noticed it, or thought anything of it if they did. But it was there.

Reluctantly, I go downstairs, because I must eat. I learnt that from my early days of widowhood: you have to keep eating, and sleeping, and all those other things because looking after yourself is the only way you will get through it. So I repair my makeup and drag a brush through my hair and then I go down to the dining room.

Richard is there already, looking relaxed. He has a couple of books with him, one of them open on the table, but he looks up when he hears me come in.

Books, I think. *I wouldn't have thought–*

"Theda. I'd started to think you were skipping dinner." He stares at me as I sit down. "You look pale. Is Aunt Mary giving you a hard time?"

I force myself to smile. "Not really. I'm just a little tired." I nod at the books. "What are you reading?"

He shows me the spine of the one lying open. "*The Hound of the Baskervilles*. It's Aunt Mary's. She doesn't have anything recent." He picks up the other volume. "This one, I haven't tried yet."

I peer at it. "*Moonfleet*. I love that book. I read it years ago."

He shrugs. "Borrow it, if you like. I can't read two at once."

I take it from him. "I'd love to. I brought some film books with me, but I didn't think to bring anything to read in my spare time."

"Can't you get something from the library?" He checks himself. "No, of course, Aunt Mary doesn't like people going in that part of the house, does she?" He skewers something idly with a fork. "The library used to be downstairs, but she had it moved upstairs when she lost her mobility. Shame for you. If you want anything particular, I can look for you, if you like. It would have be something old, though."

"That's okay. This will do." I put the book down. "It must be a pain for her, coming downstairs to meet me every day."

It occurs to me that I have never seen them bringing her down. There must be a lift somewhere else in the house.

"She really wants to see you," says Richard.

"Mmm," I say noncommittally. *Wants to amuse herself torturing me, more like.*

After that, we talk about books and films of books and places we have both been. Richard is easy company this evening – almost *too* easy. Is he playing me? I have a glass of wine, but only one. I look at Richard across the table, assessing.

I think: *You are not Max, and never could be.*

This time, it is not a stealthy fumbling at the door that awakes me. It is a thump, loud and violent and not very far away.

My heart is thudding. I sit up and reach for my phone, my fingers skittering across the polished surface of the bedside table until they finally close on it. I look at the time. 01:03.

The screen fades to darkness and I look towards the door. There is not so much as a sliver of light around it; the corridor outside is unlit. I slide out of bed and pick my way gingerly across the room in the dark. Carefully, very carefully, I try the door. Of course, it is locked. I lean in and listen, holding my breath because the ragged sound of my own breathing is too loud.

There is silence, and yet – I *know* there is someone outside, in the dark hallway. Only the wooden panel separates us. There is a prickling sensation at the back of my neck.

And then – I hear a sound, wordless and incoherent, a sob or a groan, but textured with a strange metallic grittiness, an insect-like seething that makes me think of a worn and ancient recording. It is close by, close enough that I freeze behind the door, a cold dread curdling in my stomach. My hands are perspiring; I dare not let go of the door handle.

I wait, and wait, and the sound never comes again. The silence stretches out into minutes, and then I hear the soft noise of the double doors slapping gently closed.

I make myself open the door, as quietly as I can. I can't go back to bed – I have to know who it is who wanders these corridors when everyone else is asleep, because one night I may forget to lock my door. One night–

I squash the thought, and step outside. It is cold out here – unnaturally cold after the warmth of my room. The air seems to crystallise around me, raising the tiny hairs on my arms. At the head of the stairs I pause and peer over the balustrade. Nothing moves. The darkness seems to pulse with emptiness. I go to the double doors. I push one of them gently, and when it yields, I don't just look, I step through. I am in the upper west wing, where I am expressly forbidden to go.

At the end of the corridor I see it again: that blue-grey

light, flickering eerily like cold fire. And I see a figure within it. A man. He has his back to me; I cannot see his face, only his close-cropped dark hair. The blue light washes over him, dyeing him the same cold colour as itself. At this distance it bleaches out much of the detail and yet it seems to me that he is wearing formal clothes. A military uniform.

I can make no sense of this but the *wrongness* of it throbs through my veins and shivers through my rapid breathing. The thought that he might turn and look back at me fills me with a creeping sense of dread. My hands curl into fists.

Don't let him turn round.

The blue light surges to a painful intensity. Involuntarily I blink, and the man has gone. As the light fades, the darkness closes in, encasing me.

I swallow. Did I see what I thought I saw? It seems so unlikely, so impossible... I put my hands out in front of me and take a few halting steps further down the hallway, and then I stop, disoriented. The darkness is absolute. I find myself afraid of what my hands might touch if I went any further. I imagine a silent shape there in the dark. Fabric. A face.

I am standing there hesitating, when I hear the distinct sound of a door opening, and a faint light flares.

"Hello?" says a voice. Mrs Harris.

Panic. She sounds close; too close for me to get back through the double doors and into my room before she sees me. My head turns from side to side, looking for an escape route.

Then a door opens and Richard drags me inside. It happens so quickly that there is no time to react; he places a finger on my lips to silence me as he shuts the door. A second later, I hear a *click* and the hallway lights come on. I see them through the crack around the door.

"Hello?" says Mrs Harris again. Her footsteps advance along the hall. Then she says, quietly, cautiously, "Ms Garrick?"

I have a confused impression of an untidy bedroom – the green satin coverlet pushed to the end of the bed, clothes strewn on the floor, a single lamp burning – but most of my attention is directed at Richard. I signal him frantically with my eyes, begging him not to give me away.

I hear the slap of the double doors; she has gone through them, into the east wing. There is silence for perhaps a minute. Richard stands with his head cocked to one side, listening, and I press my hand to my mouth in an agony of suspense.

The doors slap again.

"Ms Garrick?" There is an edge to the voice this time.

Richard pushes me gently away, silently indicating the ensuite. He waits for me to go inside and then he opens the bedroom door. He takes his time about it, fumbling with the handle as though fuddled with interrupted sleep.

Behind the bathroom door, I look at myself in the large mirror and see infinite Thedas reflected, the frame of another mirror surrounding me. My eyes are large and full of alarm.

"Mrs Harris," says Richard, in a theatrically sleepy voice that makes me wince.

"Mr Foster," I hear her say. "I'm terribly sorry – did I disturb you?"

"That's alright," he says generously. "What's the problem?"

"There's no problem. Ms Garrick's door is open though, and I wanted to be sure she hadn't wandered into this wing – by accident."

"Oh. And she isn't in there, in her room, I mean?"

"No."

"Oh well," he says vaguely. "She can't have gone far."

The seconds slide past greasily.

Then Mrs Harris says, "Are you quite sure you haven't seen her?"

"Absolutely," says Richard, and I hear the door hinges

creak as it opens to its full extent. "Look – you can see for yourself I'm quite alone."

"I'm sorry, Mr Foster. I didn't mean to imply–"

"That's perfectly alright," he says. "Can't fault you for thinking she might have fallen under the old Foster charm. But – alas, no."

"I'm so sorry to have disturbed you," says Mrs Harris, who sounds as though she can't get away fast enough now. A moment later, I hear the bedroom door close. I realise I have been holding my breath and let it out in a long gasp.

The door opens and Richard appears. I see now that he is dressed for sleep in a baggy t-shirt and boxer shorts; his legs and feet are bare. And here am I, in a nightdress and not very much else. Hastily, I cross my arms over my chest, a movement that makes the corner of his mouth twitch upwards.

"So," he says, "Was it that? The old Foster charm?"

"Um..."

I am wondering what on earth I am going to tell him when he steps closer and I just have time to think *that's a bit too close* before his arms are around me and he's kissing me. His tongue is exploring my mouth, with quite a bit of enthusiasm.

With a struggle I manage to work my arms free and push him away.

"Stop it."

"Come on, Theda..."

"I mean it. Keep your bloody distance."

He shrugs. "You're in my room at two thirty in the morning. What am I supposed to think?"

"You pulled me in."

"You were in the corridor outside, in your nightdress. Seems to me you were looking for *something*."

"Not that." I glower at him.

"Really? What, then?" He leans against the door frame.

"Since I've lied to Harris on your behalf, I'd kind of like to know."

"I..." I think about it. "I heard something in the corridor outside my room. It's not the first time. So I came out to see what it was. Who it was, I mean."

"And did you see?"

"Sort of."

He waits.

"I only saw from the other end of the corridor. I thought it was a man, in a uniform. I know that's going to sound nuts."

"Not really. I expect whoever you saw was just one of the staff."

"It wasn't that sort of uniform."

"Well, what other sort of uniform could it be? I don't think the Royal Marines are trying to creep into Aunt Mary's bedroom."

"Thank you for that," I say stiffly. "Look, I should get back to my room. Can you just look out and see if Mrs Harris has gone? I don't know what will happen if she catches me in here."

"Sure." He goes over to the door, opens it a crack, and then fully. "The coast is clear."

"Thanks."

"Theda?"

I pause, hugging myself against the cool air that raises goose bumps on my bare arms. "Yes?"

"If you did fall for the Foster charm, well... I wouldn't blame you, you know."

"No chance," I say, as icily as I can.

"Never say never," says Richard.

I stalk off down the corridor to the double doors, but it is not until I am pushing them open with infinite care that I hear his door close behind me.

Chapter Twenty-Nine

The next morning, I go down to breakfast in slight trepidation, thinking that it will be awkward. But there is no sign of Richard so I breakfast alone. I push a poached egg around my plate, feeling slightly repelled by the viscous yolk clinging to the tines of the fork. The tea is somewhat better – hot, strong and sweet. I dawdle over it for a while, wondering if Richard will come down; it might be better to clear the air, though I can't think what I would say. But the clock ticks and the long hand moves down to the bottom of the clockface, and he does not appear. Perhaps his feelings are hurt at my failure to succumb to his charms, or perhaps this is his idea of being tactful.

I think about last night, and about what I saw: the flickering blue light, the dark-haired man with his face turned away from me, the uniform. The memory is hazy this morning; disturbing though it is, it has a dream-like quality that makes me doubt myself.

I think: *I will ask Richard again. There must be some explanation.*

But he does not appear, and at last I ball up my napkin and get up from the table. The hallway is empty. Mrs Harris is clearly occupied elsewhere, so I am able to go upstairs and get my coat and shoes on without being seen. I let myself out and go down the steps.

It's a fine fresh morning with blue skies, and the ground is dry, so I suspect the river will be low. I slip around the side of the house and set off through the woods. Spring comes late here compared to the south of England; the first cautious buds are appearing. I come to the hole in the fence and climb through. Then I walk down across the fields, while a buzzard hovers high above my head.

At the river's edge the plank is carefully set out of reach

of the water, awaiting my return. I drop it over the deepest part again. The river is very low today; I'll hardly have to get my feet wet. I glance behind me, at the fields that curve up and away towards the woods. There is no-one to be seen. I run across the plank, splash through the inch of running water that flows over the stones, and walk up to Angus' house. The Range Rover is there, which is a hopeful sign.

He answers on the second knock. He has his coat on, a tatty old waxed thing, but the grin says he's pleased to see me. Jess comes pattering at his heels.

"Theda."

"Are you going out?"

"I was, but it can wait."

He stands back to let me in, and we go through to the kitchen, where Jess gets back onto her bed with a resigned air.

"Tea?"

"Yes, please. If I'm really not holding you up."

I'm relying on him not saying, *well, actually I have to go in two minutes*, because I need to talk to someone who does not belong to Garthside House. I sit on one of the uncomfortable kitchen chairs and watch him going through the pantomime of trying to find a clean cup.

"What's new at Garthside?" he asks.

I run a finger along the grain of the table. "Mary Arden is still making me pay for every bit of information with details about myself."

"Oh? What was it this time?"

"My wedding."

He is quiet for a moment, rinsing a cup under the tap. When he is drying it with a cloth, he says, "Are you sure you want to go on with it?"

I look at my hands. "I don't know. I guess so. I mean, what else would I do?"

"Run away to sea? Join the circus?" He shakes his head. "Something."

"The thing is... She's just getting to the interesting bit. We've talked about what happened to Hugh Mason, you know, the guy the film was about, and the background to why Lillian Velderkaust made it. She has to get onto the actual film soon." I look up at him. "And she's hinted that she might have a copy of the film – or part of it, anyway. If that's true, it would be amazing. Nobody's seen it since 1931."

"Do you believe her?" he says. "Seems to me it's a great way to keep you interested, saying that."

"I don't know. Maybe. But if she doesn't have a copy, then nobody does."

"I guess that's true." He finishes making the tea and hands it to me.

"Thanks, Angus."

He lounges against the stove, and for a few moments there is silence.

"A relative of Mary Arden's is visiting," I say, making conversation. "A sort of nephew, only not quite."

"A nephew? I can't work out how old that would make him."

"About as old as me, I guess."

"Oh," he says. "Well, that must liven things up, I suppose."

"Sort of. I'm not entirely sure what to think of him, though. He's her only relative, and he says he's going to inherit everything unless she decides to leave it to a cats' home... which is why he keeps visiting."

"Bighearted of him. Did he actually tell you that?"

"Yes. Over dinner. Not dinner like that," I add hastily. "He can't eat with Mary Arden because she goes to bed early. So he eats downstairs with me."

"It must be good to have company," says Angus mildly.

"I'd call it a mixed blessing. He fancies himself quite a bit."

Angus grins at that. "Mind yourself. He sounds like a dodgy character."

When he says that, I think of last night, and Richard sliding his arms around me and kissing me. I try not to react, but I guess something is visible in my face, which is suddenly hot, because Angus's eyebrows go up a bit. He says nothing about it, though, and nor do I, because I don't feel I can say, *Well, something happened, but I didn't want it to.*

I think: *Damn it, why did I mention Richard?*

For a moment there is silence. Angus has made himself a cup of tea too, and he turns away to put more sugar in it. In the corner, Jess whines softly.

I look at his back, at his broad shoulders and the hair curling into the nape of his neck, the spare way he moves. The memory of Richard kissing me is large in my mind, the sensation of his lips on mine is so vivid I can almost feel it, but it is not Richard I am thinking of. Angus is a little taller than Richard, and he would have to stoop if he were to–

I try so hard to squash the thought. Only seven months a widow.

No, I say to myself. *No, no.*

My hand, the one not holding the cup, curls into a ball, so tight that the nails cut into the flesh.

Angus finishes stirring his tea and turns back to me, too quickly, and he sees it in my face. He sees *something* in my face.

We stare at each other.

"Theda," he says, "Are you alright? You look..."

I feel myself trembling. I put down my tea, slopping some of it onto the table, and struggle to my feet.

"I have to go," I blurt out.

"You do?"

"I'm sorry – I'm sorry–" In my haste I don't see that the edge of my coat has caught on the chair back, and when I pull away there is a moment of resistance and over it goes with a clatter.

"Shit," I say, and realise I am nearly sobbing. I pick up the chair, aware of Angus putting down his own tea cup and Jess suddenly on her feet, alert to the noise, and I say "Sorry" again and run for the door.

"Theda?"

Angus follows me, and Jess follows me too, thinking it's a game, jumping up and getting tangled in my feet so that I stumble over her, still trying to fight my way out. I get to the front door and turn the handle and push, push with all my might, forgetting that it opens inward; you have to pull. Angus is on my heels and when this happens, when I mess up opening the front door, he almost runs into me. I turn and his face is inches from mine. His hand hovers over my shoulder.

And I can't do it. I can't push him away. I can't run.

I can't.

I pull him to me, and kiss him.

Chapter Thirty

For one moment Angus freezes, startled, and then he kisses me back. His hands, hovering over me, settle on my shoulders, clasping me, pulling me closer. His mouth moves over mine. And I cling to him, my hands making fists with handfuls of his woollen sweater in them. The luxury of touching, of being touched, overwhelms me; it burns through me with savage brilliance. I want Angus so badly – here, now.

I push him away.

He stares at me, aroused, confused. "Theda..." he begins, and then stops, not knowing what to say.

"Oh God," I say, and then, uselessly, "I'm sorry."

"What for?" he says. "For kissing me, or for stopping?"

"I don't know." I put my hands over my face. "This is wrong. *I'm* wrong."

"You're not wrong, Theda. You just–"

"I am!" I nearly scream it at him. "Max is only seven months dead! Max is *dead*. He's dead. And I – I–"

But I don't finish because there are no words about what happened, about what left me alone, without Max. Thinking about it, *really* thinking about it, makes me feel as though I am cracking apart, as though great fault lines are appearing inside me. I shake with it, rigid with misery and horror, curling in on myself like the victim of some grisly conflagration.

I turn to the door, meaning to find the trick of it, to open it and escape, but I'm so close to it that there's no space to pull it towards me.

"Theda," says Angus gently, and when I don't reply he says it again: "Theda."

I shake my head. "I have to – I have to go."

"Come back into the kitchen. You can't go back to Garthside like this. Come back in for a minute."

I let him lead me back there, because he is right, back at Garthside there are Mrs Harris and Richard with their inquisitive eyes, and also because I cannot resist his kindness, although it makes me want to cry.

I sit on the hard chair again, and Angus says, "I'll make some more tea," as though that's the cure-all, or perhaps because neither of us really knows what else to say. Jess pads about, unsettled, because she knows something is wrong, and eventually Angus says, "bed" to her.

After a while I am able to say, "I'm sorry" in a level voice. I look Angus in the face, trying to make myself sound sensible. "I shouldn't have done that."

"Don't be," he says, also sounding serious. "It wasn't... unpleasant."

I laugh at that, in an unsteady, choking sort of way. "I'm glad."

"Look, Theda..." He hesitates. "However long – seven months or – or seven years – is up to you. Nobody's counting. But you shouldn't feel bad about it." He pauses again. "I'm not sure I should say any more, because I kind of have a stake in this. But you don't have to feel sorry."

In the ensuing silence I hear the ticking of the kitchen clock, and Jess's gentle snuffles from the corner.

"Angus," I say at last, "Can we forget that ever happened?"

He thinks about that. "I don't think I could *forget* that, exactly. But I won't... Well, we can agree it didn't mean anything."

I look down at my cup of tea instead of at him. I am not sure it didn't mean anything. But I say, "Yes, let's do that."

"You know," he says, "You can still come down here, any time you want. Don't feel you have to stay away."

"Alright."

"I mean it."

148

"I know."

I hear him exhale. I don't look up, because I know that I want to get up, and go over to him and kiss him again.

Seven months, I say to myself. Inside me there is a horrible tangle of feelings that I cannot unravel: pain, guilt, loneliness and yes, desire. I should not feel the last one. It has not been long enough. So I stare into my tea as though I shall read some fascinating fate in the leaves.

"Theda," says Angus eventually, "Tell me to mind my own business if you want, but Mary Arden, these interviews with her, they're not doing you any good. She's raking over stuff that you don't need to be dwelling on. It's not surprising you feel... I don't know, confused."

"She's a bitch," I say, quite levelly, and now I do look at him. "But I'm so close, Angus."

He shakes his head. "At least tell me there haven't been any more night time disturbances." He looks at me, noting my silence. "There haven't, have there?"

I sigh.

"Theda–"

"I keep my door locked," I say. The memory of last night flashes across my mind again, but this time I have myself under control. I quash it.

"So it's still happening."

I nod.

"I don't like it," he says, crossing his arms.

"Well, neither do I. But I do lock my door."

He thinks about this for a bit. "If it gets too much," he says, "If you don't feel safe... Call me, okay? I'll come and get you – take you to a hotel or something."

"I don't have your number."

"I'll give it to you." He pauses. "I'm not saying you can't look after yourself or anything like that."

"I know."

"You still haven't got your car back though, have you?"

I shake my head.

"So if you want to leave Garthside at short notice... I'm not far away, is all I'm saying."

"Thank you."

He drinks some of his tea, thoughtfully.

"It's not just an excuse to give you my number."

"I'm sure it isn't," I say gravely. I drain my own cup to the dregs and set it down. "I should get back to Garthside. They'll be wondering where I've gone." I rub at my eye with the heel of my hand. "Do I look alright – normal, I mean?"

Angus studies me carefully for rather longer than is necessary. "I'm not sure about *normal*..."

"Wretch."

He laughs. "Come on, I'll walk you to the ford."

When we get there, he holds the end of the plank with his foot to keep it steady. He says, "You will come back?"

I look up at him.

"Yes," I say, meaning it. "I will. Soon."

Chapter Thirty-One

At lunch, there is still no Richard. I am drinking my coffee when Mrs Harris comes in, all smiles and briskness as usual.

"Ms Garrick," she says. "How was lunch?"

"Very nice," I tell her. "Quiet."

"Ah," she says. "Mr Foster has gone back to Edinburgh."

I smile blandly. "Busy man."

"Yes, indeed." She folds her hands. "Ms Garrick, I trust you are sleeping perfectly well?"

I put down my coffee cup, sit back and look at her.

"Very well," I tell her.

"Because," she says, "I happened to be in the upstairs east wing very late last night, and I couldn't help noticing that your door was open."

"Really?" I say.

"I took the liberty of going to close it," she says, "And I saw that you were not inside."

"No," I say. "Come to think of it, I wouldn't have been."

She waits, so I add, "I went to get a slice of bread from the kitchen. I had an upset stomach and I thought that might settle it."

"How strange," she remarks. "I thought perhaps it might have been something like that, so I went down to the kitchen, but there was nobody there, and I didn't pass you on the stairs either."

"I got lost," I say. "I didn't find the kitchen at all." I pick up my napkin, and fold it carefully, smoothing the folds with my fingers. "I wandered around and then I gave up and went back to bed." I look up at her. "I suppose I missed you."

"I suppose you did," she says. She clears her throat. "You did remember what I said, that the upper west wing is entirely private?"

"Of course." We look at each other. "Mrs Harris," I say, "I woke up because someone tried the door of my room."

I am watching her face, and I see her react, briefly, before she conceals it under her usual smooth expression. What was that I saw? Alarm? *Fear*? I feel a prickle of unease.

"It's happened before," I say, thinking that I'd better exclude Richard from the equation. "Several times."

"Garthside House is nearly ninety years old," she says. "It has all sorts of creaks and rattles. If you aren't used to hearing them, you might think..."

"It wasn't just a creak or a rattle," I say. "I heard the handle moving."

She says nothing. She just looks at me.

"Mrs Harris, who is it who wanders up and down the corridors after dark?"

She licks her lips. "Perhaps you have heard me," she offers. "Sometimes I check the unused rooms for weather damage. I might have tried your door by mistake."

I think about that male figure, stepping into the flickering blue light that comes, I suppose, from Mary Arden's television. I think about Mrs Harris coming from that same direction *after* I have seen this. And I know that she is lying.

"You keep such late hours," I say, holding her gaze.

"I've never needed a lot of sleep," she says. "Ms Garrick, I take it you lock your door at night?"

"Yes, I do."

"Well, that's very good. If I, or anyone else on the staff, should try the door by accident, we won't walk in on you. I should keep doing that, if I were you."

"I most certainly shall."

We eye each other, the air heavy with unspoken words. At last Mrs Harris says, "Well, I must be getting on," as though we have been doing nothing more interesting than making idle small talk. We give each other false smiles, and she leaves the room, closing the door behind her.

I look at the door for a few seconds after she has gone.

Then I realise I have been holding my breath, and I let it out in a long sigh.

After lunch, I meet Mary Arden again. She is wearing lilac today, a colour which is subtle and pretty and does not do her any favours at all; it makes her faded skin look grey.

While I am sitting down and setting out the phone on the table, she says, "Richard has gone. Scared him off, did you?"

"No," I say composedly.

"You haven't much luck in love, have you?" she says, gloatingly.

"Shut up," I say before I can stop myself. She is not offended – far from it, she bursts into peals of creaky old laughter.

"Well," she says, when she has finished, "You can tell me about your beau again today – how he showed the cloven hoof for the first time."

"No," I say. "You tell me about Lillian Velderkaust first. What has spirit photography got to do with *The Simulacrum*?" I put my head up, my chin out.

She lets my demand hang there in the air for a while, so that she won't seem like a soft touch. Then she says, "Oh, as you will. But I'm only telling this tale once, so you can hear it all in the proper order, and in my own good time."

And I have to be content with that. I wait for her to talk.

"There is a story," she says, "Probably not a true one, but popular nevertheless, that when the Lumière brothers showed a film of a steam train arriving at a station, there was panic in the audience, because people thought they were going to be run down. That was the 1890s."

I nod. I've heard this story.

"Richard tells me that nowadays they can recreate dead actors with computers." She waves a skinny claw dismissively. "Don't ask me how. I've no interest in modern

153

films at all – never watch them. But they can do it. People who are long dead can move and talk again. The line between real and artificial, between science and magic – it's a thin one. Maybe there *is* no line.

"1922, that was so much closer to the birth of moving pictures. Imagine the wonder of it! People were working all the time to expand the limits of what was possible – colour movies, synchronised sound. So why shouldn't they have explored that other frontier, the world beyond the veil?"

"You mean, beyond death?" I say.

"I do." She looks at me for a moment, and then shakes her head. "You don't believe in such things." It's a statement, not a question.

"I think we can be haunted by the past," I tell her. God knows, that's true; it can sit on your shoulder like a demon, whispering into your ear. "But as for the spirits of the dead... No, not really."

"You wouldn't want your Max to come back, one last time?"

Always when I least expect it. I force myself to hold her gaze, controlling the sudden cold effervescence in my stomach. "I wouldn't torture myself thinking about something that can't happen."

"Really? You give up too easily," she says. "Lillian didn't."

I don't rise to the bait. I sit there silently and wait for her to go on.

"She explored everything," she says. "She began with the spirit photographs, the few that couldn't be debunked. What had the photographer done to obtain them? Had they seen the phenomena with their own eyes, or only through the medium of the camera? Could the conditions be recreated? The thing she was most interested in was how the spirits had been summoned, but it was hard to get a specific reply about that."

That seems dismally predictable to me. The thought that

Lillian Velderkaust was prepared to entertain these ideas is both fascinating and sad.

"The only thing she could glean was that the spirits seemed attracted to the familiar," Mary Arden continues. "To people they had known." She shrugs. "And that wasn't helpful, so far as she could see. Who else would go looking for them, if not the people who'd known them?"

Those were people who wanted to believe, I think.

"She experimented too," says Mary Arden. "After a day's filming she would run the camera for a while, to see if it would pick anything up. She'd film things that had belonged to Hugh. Sometimes she got someone else to film *her*. Afterwards she'd study the footage for signs that Hugh was there. She never found anything.

"During the '20s, her career really took off. She moved away from the sentimental dramas and produced more sophisticated work. The budgets got bigger and sometimes she filmed on location too, creating that authenticity the critics loved so much. And all the time she kept looking for the answer.

"Then in the late '20s both her parents died and left everything to her. That made it much easier, of course, because she could fund her research. She sought out anyone she thought might be able to help her. Some of them were genuinely trying to study the paranormal. Others were just cranks, or were actually out to fleece the unwary.

"She went to Damascus and Cluj and a lot of other places I don't recall. She met Russian and Hungarian psychics and defrocked Roman Catholic priests, Kirlian photographers and schismatic physicists. She stepped through beaded curtains into the cluttered domains of fortune tellers, and sat up all night by campfires, listening to traditional tales of ghosts and revenants, the flickering flames illuminating a face that became more deeply graven with disappointment as the years went by."

"Why didn't she give up?" I ask.

155

Mary Arden looks at me scornfully. "It was not in her nature to give up. What had happened to Hugh, it didn't just grieve her; it *outraged* her. The unfairness of it. The desecration. She couldn't let it lie. The more difficult the struggle, the more determined she became to find an answer. From time to time she found clues, traces that encouraged her to go on. Just enough to hint that she might succeed one day.

"I suppose you will say that she might have found someone else, and if that had happened, she might have moved on. But in the years after World War One, there were many more young women than young men. And she never found anyone to match up to Hugh."

She falls silent for a moment, contemplating this. Outside, the sun comes out from behind the clouds and sunshine streams through the window, illuminating every sag and wrinkle on her ancient face with savage clarity. So terribly old, this last link with Lillian Velderkaust and her lost love. I wonder where the story of Lillian's search for some way to reconnect with Hugh is going to end. It's well known that *The Simulacrum* was a kind of biopic of Hugh, so perhaps she finally concluded that the best thing she could do was memorialise his life.

But then Mary Arden astounds me.

"Lillian never told anyone where she found the answer," she says. "Not even me, and she told me everything else, because she wanted me to understand. And so–"

"Wait," I say. "*She found the answer?*"

"Well, self-evidently she did," says Mary Arden. "Otherwise there would have been no film."

I stare at her. "I don't understand."

"You will," she says. "Or at least, I can tell you how it worked in practice. I don't know what Lillian had to *do*, nor the cost."

"The cost?"

"Oh yes. There was a cost; of course there was." She

shakes her head. "She wouldn't tell me what it was, either. But I know she spent a long time thinking about it. In the end, though, she was never *not* going to do it; she'd spent too long looking for a way."

She sits back, folding her hands, and looking for all the world like a great crinkled lizard in a lilac suit.

"And now," she says, "You can tell me some more about Max."

Chapter Thirty-Two

I sit and look at her for a moment. I am desperate to know more about what she just told me. How can Lillian Velderkaust possibly have found an *answer*? This can't be true; someone must have hoodwinked her. But how can it be that there would be no film otherwise? I really, really want to take Mary Arden by the collar of her lilac suit and shake her until she tells me the rest of the story. I know that won't work, though.

"You can hear it all in the proper order, and in my own good time," she said. I grind my teeth.

"Come," she says, coaxingly. "Tell me how it went on. How long did it take before he lost his temper again?"

This spurs me into speaking, reluctantly. "It wasn't like that. The morning of the wedding, we were both keyed up. That was why Max... It's a big day. You want it to be perfect. And the rest of it was," I tell her. "Everything went exactly as we'd planned it. It was a really happy day."

"If you say so," says Mary Arden. "And where did you go on honeymoon, exactly?"

"Iceland."

"Iceland," she repeats. "And whose idea was that? His, I suppose."

"We chose it together," I tell her, with dignity.

"Hmmm. You don't like sunshine, then?"

"I do like sunshine. But I don't have to go to a hot place every single time I go away."

"No, you don't," she says. She tilts her head, and in the sunlight I can see her scalp shining through her carefully-coiffed hair. "So he behaved himself on the honeymoon, then?"

"I don't know what you're getting at," I say stiffly.

"Oh well," she says dismissively. "So you came home

from this trip to Iceland. What then? You settled into your little love nest, I suppose."

"Not so very little," I say, not without some pride. "Max's business was doing really well. It's an older place, with a little bit of land around it. Max never liked the newer ones. Even the top of the range houses were squashed into too little land, he said. Like battery hens. So we bought this place and had it done up. It has big gardens, mature ones, with lots of big bushes and trees. It's beautiful really."

"No neighbours overlooking it, then," she remarks.

"No. Isn't that everyone's dream? A bit of privacy."

She grunts. "Go on."

"Well, I don't know what else to tell you. We had the bathroom and kitchen replaced, and the whole place pretty much redecorated..."

"His business *was* doing well, then."

"Yes. It was." I sigh.

She considers. "I surmise that this house is not near London, though."

"No. It's in Gloucestershire. Max had a home office so he didn't have to commute every day. It was–"

"I know," she says acidly. "It was perfect." She rolls her eyes, and the whites show yellow, like old ivory. Then she says, "So what about you? You used to work in publishing, didn't you? I thought most of the publishers were in London."

"A lot of them are."

"A lot of them, including yours?"

"Well, yes. But I wasn't working for them anymore by that time." I shrug. "They'd had a reshuffle, and some redundancies, and one of them was me."

"Ah." She puts a gnarled finger to her lips. "Well, I suppose that can't have been entirely unexpected. I mean, you were the person who'd abandoned ship in the middle of one of the most important events of the year, weren't you?"

I frown. "That wasn't it. I'm sure it wasn't."

159

"It can't have helped," she observes. "It looks unreliable, doing something like that."

"Well," I say staunchly, "It was for the best anyway. I couldn't have stayed in that job forever."

"You certainly couldn't – not living in Gloucestershire. So, what did you do instead? Or did you simply minister to Max's every need?"

"Do you have to be so sarcastic?" I say.

"I wasn't."

"Since you ask, no, I wasn't just looking after Max. I'd always wanted to write, and now I had the time and the space. I mean, this is self-evident, because I am here right now with the intention of writing a book."

"Yes, you are," she says, thoughtfully. "But you didn't write to me until after your husband died, did you?"

"No, but this book is one of a number of projects," I tell her.

"So what were the others? They weren't about film, were they? I had Harris check, before we agreed to see you. You haven't published anything about film or the cinema."

"No," I say levelly, and then: "Why did you agree to see me, considering that, and not anyone else?"

She waves a claw, airily. "Whimsy. Pure whimsy. And the fact that I will be dead soon, and someone needs to hear it."

Not soon enough, I think to myself grimly. But the story needs to be told, she is right about that, so I keep my annoyance to myself.

"I did think I might try writing fiction," I say.

"Oh?" she says, without much interest, but then she waits for me to go on.

"I had an idea," I tell her. "For a suspense novel. Kind of Gothic, I suppose. About a woman who buys a house – a newbuild, nothing spooky – and it turns out it was built on the site of an older one. And a lot of weird stuff starts happening, and she can't work out whether it's the house

160

or her fiancé." I smile to myself, a little sadly. "I quite liked that idea."

"But you didn't write that?"

"Well, I started it, but it didn't work out. I didn't finish it in the end."

"How far did you get?" she asks.

"Oh, about fifty thousand words." Actually, it was 52,237.

Mary Arden reflects. "That's quite a lot, isn't it? How much is a novel?"

"Ninety thousand, maybe. Or a hundred thousand."

"So you wrote about half? And then you gave up. That's surprising, really. You'd already made quite an investment of time."

"Yes, but it wasn't working." I'm squirming just a little now.

"Why not?" she says, inevitably.

"Well, I guess the idea was a bit of a cliché. The haunted house in a lonely place. The possible gaslighting."

She shrugs. "A lot of people read things *for* the clichés. People didn't stop writing books about women marrying rich aristocrats after Jane Austen did it, did they?"

"No, I suppose not." I hesitate. "But I guess my style wasn't great, either. Maybe that type of fiction wasn't really my thing."

"And why did you come to that way of thinking, after writing half the book?"

"Well..." I say, and stop.

She waits.

"I gave the book to someone to read," I admit in the end. "A lot of writers do it. Beta readers, they call them. And after that... Well, I decided it probably wasn't worth going on with."

"And who did you give the book to?" she wants to know.

"Is it important? It wasn't good enough."

"I think it is."

"Just... a beta reader."

She holds my gaze, sternly. "Who was it?"

"Okay," I say angrily. "It was Max. Happy now? Max read the book and didn't think it was any good."

She opens her mouth to make one of her horrible retorts and I pre-empt her.

"He thought I could do better. He *believed* in me as a writer. He thought I could do something truly great. A literary novel. That was why he didn't think I should go on with it. He really believed in me."

She folds her arms.

"And did you write it, this great literary novel?" she asks.

"I tried." I sigh. "But..." I spread out my hands in a gesture of defeat.

"It wasn't good enough," she says.

I shake my head.

"It was never good enough."

Chapter Thirty-Three

After the interview, I go upstairs with my pen and pad and phone, feeling irritable and close to tears.

Why does she always have to twist everything? I think. There is a cold, dragging feeling in my stomach. I go into my room and drop all my things on the pink satin coverlet. Then I sit down next to them and put my head in my hands.

In my head, I see those yellow eyes rolling upwards, the skinny hands sketching callous gestures in the air, the wrinkled lips pursing and grimacing.

Lie to her, I say to myself. But I know it's no good. Somehow she manages to winkle things out of me. She always finds the angle – she drags me unwillingly into places I don't want to go.

I glance around me at the room, at the books and papers piled up on the escritoire. There are no photographs of Max – I know that, because I didn't bring any, not wanting to marinate myself in that particular pain. But now I want to look at one. I grope for my mobile phone, go online and look at one of his professional profiles. There he is, smiling up at me. Blue-eyed, golden, handsome. Perfect. That is what I want to show Mary Arden, the world, *myself*. The perfect husband. The perfect marriage. The perfect life.

For the thousandth time, I consider walking away from these discussions, from the relentless gouging at the most tender parts of me. But I'm so close, and I can't stop now – not when she's given me this intriguing, impossible, fascinating snippet. *Lillian found the answer*. I have to know what that means. I *have* to.

That evening I am reckless. I accept wine with my dinner, and drink several glasses of it while I pick at my chicken Florentine. The woman who brings my food is in a hurry, not in a chatty mood at all, so I eat alone with the copy of *Moonfleet* open on the tablecloth next to me. By the time I get to the pudding I have had too much wine to concentrate. I find myself reading the same page over and over, so I shut the book, forgo coffee and make my way upstairs.

I have a hot bath, after which I can hardly keep my eyes open. Digging around in things I don't want to think about, trying to keep my cool in front of Mary Arden: these things are exhausting. *Early night*, I decide. It's not as though there is anything to stay up for. So I clean my teeth desultorily and get into bed. Some slight thing, some nagging doubt, some unticked box, is floating around in the back of my mind, but with the tiredness and the wine, it never coalesces into anything concrete. I slide easily down into a deep sleep.

Some time later, I jerk into wakefulness, knowing precisely what it was that was bothering me. I didn't lock the door.

The reason this comes to me with lightning quickness is that the door is opening. The sound that woke me was the latch sliding back as the door handle was depressed, a crisp little *click*.

The coverlet makes a soft slithering sound as I start up, and instantly I freeze. My heart is thudding; I am afraid some sound has escaped me, some gasp or sigh. I look towards the door but it is dark inside and out, and all I can make out is a faint rectangle, barely lighter than the surrounding blackness. There is someone there, although they are nothing more than a denser patch in the texture of the darkness.

I cannot say why, but I *know* this is not Mrs Harris checking the doors or one of the nurses or cooks or even Richard come back again from Edinburgh. This is something else altogether, something that raises the tiny hairs on my bare arms. Something that makes me very keen indeed to be silent and still, not to give myself away.

This faceless, almost formless person in the dark, will

they move on, taking silence to mean that the room is uninhabited? No. I hear the tiny rattle as the door handle is released, and then the sounds of fabric rubbing together and feet moving softly over the carpet tell me that they are inside the room with me.

Fear has slid so fast up the scale that it sings in my ears like a high note. Spots dance in front of my eyes. The bedside lamp is only an arm's length away. I could turn it on and shed brilliant light on the scene, but I don't. I can think of no better protection than being unseen, unheard. My ears, my eyes strain in the darkness.

The tread is stealthy, surreptitious. I think: *maybe I could outrun this person, maybe I could move faster than they can*. But the thought of making for the door and running into their open arms in the dark makes cold horror wash over me. I hold my breath and listen. I bite my own fist in the dark, afraid that I will cry out. I think about my phone somewhere in the room, perhaps on the bedside table, perhaps on the escritoire.

Useless, I think. Even if I could lay my hand directly on it, even if I tried to call someone – Angus, or Mrs Harris on the landline – the person in the room with me is much, much closer than they are. Whatever they want, they could have it long before help ever arrived. And what, I ask myself, would I see when the tiny screen illuminated – what would be looming over me in the darkness, dreadfully underlit?

I left my shoes lying on the floor to the right of the bed and now I hear the unseen person stumble on them. I know that they are only a short distance away now, almost close enough to stretch out in the blackness and touch the bed. To touch me.

I cannot help it. I have to get away. I grip the coverlet to stop it slithering off me again with that audible sibilance that will pinpoint my presence, and I slide across the mattress. It's useless trying to be silent. Before my bare foot has even touched the floor on the other side of the bed, I've signalled my whereabouts to the intruder. With appalling speed they swoop at the place I have just left, the hollow still warm from my sleeping body. The patting sounds I hear as I crouch on the carpet on the other side, the stealthy fumbling, that is the unseen person checking every inch of the bed for an occupant.

I can't stay here, pressed trembling against the side of the bed. It cannot be long before it occurs to them to come around here. Panic unfurls inside me but I know a sudden movement, a blundering into the furniture in the dark, will give me away instantly. So I creep with cringing slowness across the floor, my outstretched hands testing the way. In the pitch black, with the ominous rustling behind me sending adrenaline zinging through my veins, I cannot orient myself. I cross what seems like an impossibly wide stretch of carpet before my hands touch something. The leg of the escritoire. There is a narrow space between it and the corner of the room, and into this space I squeeze myself, unable to think of a better hiding-place. I draw in my limbs like a spider, curling in on myself, ducking my head. And then I wait.

The patting and rustling stop. For a moment there is silence. Then I hear something I cannot quite identify: a fragment of speech, grainy and distorted. A single vowel, stretched out into a sigh. And then – nothing.

I crouch beside the escritoire for a long time, until I am shivering in my nightdress, but I hear nothing else. No more sounds of someone feeling across the bed. No more sounds of someone moving about the room. No sounds of anyone leaving. A faint cold draft tells me that the door is open but I have not heard footsteps receding up the corridor.

I listen, and listen, and I *think* I am alone. The thought of turning on a light and seeing someone in the room, perhaps right at my elbow, is too awful to contemplate. But I cannot stay here all night. I am aching with cold; the temperature in the room has plummeted. So I unfold myself and stand up, chafing my stiff limbs with icy hands, and feel my way carefully back to the bed. A gentle *click* and soft yellow light from the bedside lamp fills the room. I see that I am indeed alone, but that the door is standing wide open. Outside, all is dark.

I do not have it in me to go out into the corridor and look for the intruder. Instead, I go over and close the door, lean against it and lock it. Then I go around the entire room, checking behind the curtains, peering into the bathroom, even opening the wardrobe, making sure that there is nobody hiding anywhere. I look at the bed. The cover has slid most of the way off, and the pillows are disarranged. Did I do that myself? I do not think I did. I did not imagine that horrible furtive patting.

I do not want to climb back in, but I must. There is nowhere else to sleep. So I straighten the bedclothes first, and plump up the pillows, trying not to think of the unseen hands that have been all over them. Then I climb back into bed.

I lie there for a while, my ears straining for the sound of anyone outside, or for the merest touch on the door handle. And at some point I suppose I slide into sleep, because when I wake it is morning. The daylight is filtering in through a slim crack in the curtains, and the bedside light is still on.

Chapter Thirty-Four

This time, I am determined to have it out with Mrs Harris. There is no sign of her when I go down to breakfast, so when the woman brings my tea I ask her if she knows where Mrs Harris is.

"If not, I can always go and look for her," I say.

The woman glances at me, a slight tension in her manner. "I'll find her for you," she says.

"Thank you so much."

I am helping myself to more toast when Mrs Harris appears, sleek in another dark suit and discreet pearls that glow dully.

"Good morning, Ms Garrick. I understand you wanted to see me?"

I put down my knife. "Yes, Mrs Harris." I eye her, and then I get straight to it. "I wanted to tell you that the person I have heard moving around the corridor actually entered my room last night."

There is a silence as we contemplate each other.

"Ms Garrick," she says at last, "Are you quite sure you didn't dream…? "

"Quite sure," I say firmly. "I woke up as the door was being opened. I heard the latch click. And they came right into the room, and felt all over the bed to see if there was anyone in it."

"Did they touch you?" she asks, and her voice is faint and brittle.

"No." I shake my head. "I slid out the other side before they could do that."

I see her swallow. "Did you see who it was?" she asks.

"No, I didn't. It was pitch dark – after whatever time the landing lights are put out, and before sunrise."

I am watching her very closely, and it seems to me that she relaxes very slightly when I say that.

"Mrs Harris," I say, "Who was it?"

The moments stretch out.

At last, she says, "Ms Garrick, I hesitate to say this, but since you press me... Louise, who served your dinner last night, says that you consumed rather a lot of wine."

I lean back in my chair and stare at her.

"And? I wasn't so drunk that I was seeing things. And anyway, I *didn't* see anything. I heard it, and felt it."

"Perhaps you were mistaken," she says quietly.

"I really wasn't." I can feel myself getting angry, and make an effort to keep my voice calm. "Yes, I did have some wine with my meal last night. But the only effect of that was that I forgot to lock my door. And quite honestly, Mrs Harris, I shouldn't have to do that. I should be able to sleep the night without people coming into the room."

"Of course," she says.

"Mrs Harris, someone *did* enter my room."

We stare at each other. I am determined not to back down, and I guess she sees that in the set of my jaw, the fact that I do not drop my gaze. At last she says, "I can only imagine that one of the other staff may have entered your room by accident, thinking it was theirs, and then realised their mistake and left."

"The staff?" I repeat. "Do any of the live-in staff have rooms in the upper east wing?" As I ask this, I am fairly sure I know what the answer will be – that they don't. I have never seen anyone else living in my part of the house, only people cleaning it, and that in the daytime.

"Well," she says, "I don't believe so." She folds her hands. "But it is the only possible explanation."

I could scream with frustration, but I can see I am not going to get any further with this line of enquiry.

Instead, I say, "And what about my car? Is there any news about that?"

"Ah," she says. "I telephoned the garage yesterday, as a matter of fact. The vehicle is still not ready, unfortunately. The damage was very severe, you know."

My mind skips back briefly to the night I drove into the ford. There was water pouring into the car. And Angus had to drag it back out of the river, causing God knows what kind of damage to the underneath of it. It's not implausible, what Mrs Harris is saying. And yet...

I open my mouth to say that I want the garage's telephone number, so that I can call them myself, and find out what is going on with it. But then I think about what she said when the car first went in for repairs. *Probably expensive.* Mary Arden is a malicious old ratbag, but she has offered to pay for those repairs. Do I want to interfere? Do I even want to *know* the exact extent to which I have indebted myself to her?

I shut my mouth again.

Mrs Harris watches me. She says, "Don't worry, Ms Garrick. I'm sure the car will be ready by the time you need to leave."

I think: *Why does she make that sound like an incredibly remote possibility?*

She adds, "As regards the other matter, I can only apologise for whatever occurred, and suggest, as before, that you take care to lock your door at night. I will speak to the staff and see whether I can get to the bottom of it. However, what is locked cannot be opened. That simple precaution should ensure no further issues."

I feel as though I am the one being admonished.

"Yes, Mrs Harris," I say.

There is a long silence and then she says, briskly, "Well, I must be getting on. Enjoy the rest of your breakfast, Ms Garrick."

"Thank you," I say flatly.

I watch her leave, and then I look down at my plate. The remains of the toast look leathery and unappetising. I ball up my napkin, get up from the table and abandon breakfast altogether.

On the way out through the hall, I glance towards the front door. Bright sunshine slants through the windows. A fine morning for a walk – probably. I shan't be going on one. The only place I can think of to go is the house by the ford. I told Angus yesterday I would come back soon, but now would be *too* soon.

And when would be the right time? I ask myself, as I turn my back on the door and start up the stairs. There is no answer to that, except *not now*. I think about kissing Angus, about the way I fell on him like a starving woman. Warmth comes into my face and I step up my pace until I am almost running up the flight.

Not now.

I spend the morning in my room, going over my notes.

Chapter Thirty-Five

By three o'clock I am in a state of almost unbearable impatience. I try hard to conceal this from Mary Arden, resplendent today in an unflattering shade of sunflower yellow, because I suspect she would refuse to talk at all if she knew how keen I am. My hand trembles a little as I set my phone down on the table to record the session.

"Where was I?" says Mary Arden, as though she doesn't know perfectly well.

I pretend to think about it. "Lillian had found the answer, I think. You were just about to tell me what it was."

She smiles unpleasantly at this, and lets the silence stretch out for a while before she replies.

"Yes, I suppose I was."

I wait, and after a moment she sighs. Perhaps she was hoping I would beg.

"Well, I don't pretend to understand how or why this would work. Nor, as I said, do I know where or from whom she learned what to do. But I can tell you that the principle was this: that the circumstances into which the departed were to be recalled were to be as true to life – to their life – as possible. The familiarity principle, you might say. That was one thing that she learned from the spirit photographers that turned out to be absolutely true.

"I can't tell you *why* that would work. Perhaps the idea was that the spirit would recognise its former circumstances. Or possibly, having completed its activities on the earthly plain, it could only ever re-enact the events of the past."

She looks at me over the top of her spectacles, assessing how I am reacting to this information.

What *do* I think of it? I'm bemused. She is talking about things that are speculative, if not outright fantastical, as though they were facts. It's fascinating having this insight into Lillian Velderkaust's mind, but I still don't see how this relates to the production of an actual film. I wonder whether this is some kind of delusion, whether the clockwork of that one-hundred-and-four-year-old brain is finally running down. I also wonder whether she is deliberately spinning a yarn.

She is waiting for me to respond, so after a moment I say, "I don't really understand."

Mary Arden rolls her eyes. "You are terribly dense sometimes. She had to recreate a significant part of Hugh's life, that is what I am saying."

"I see."

"With the significant characters."

"In that case," I say slowly, "Where do you come in? You were a tiny child when Hugh died. You never even met him."

She smiles as though I have finally said something intelligent. "You've seen photographs of me from the '30s, haven't you?"

I nod.

"What about Lillian Velderkaust? Have you seen any of her when she was a young woman?"

I shake my head. The ones I have seen are all later; the commonest shots are of Lillian as a mature woman, her face lined and her hair streaked with white, sometimes with a cigarette clamped between her teeth.

"We were very alike," says Mary Arden. "But actually, I was not her first choice."

"Who was that?" I ask her.

"An actress calling herself Salome Safir, although I'm fairly sure that *wasn't* her real name. Big break for her, working with Lillian Velderkaust, although I suspect she didn't know what she'd signed up for. Perhaps, if she'd really done the film, she'd be sitting here instead of me, in the big house in the country, with people running around whenever she clicked her fingers. But just before filming began, Salome died very suddenly, from an overdose of veronal."

I make a mental note to check this; I've never heard of Salome Safir.

"Not long after that, this would have been late in 1929, Lillian came to our house. She accepted a glass of sherry and sat down to talk with my parents, but after a while she said: 'Is Mary here?'

"My parents were a little surprised, but my mother called me downstairs. I was just 15 then, and had finished school; in 1929 you didn't have to stay on until you were 16. I was sulking because I wanted my hair cut short and done in Marcel waves, and my parents wouldn't let me, so I hadn't come down when I heard a visitor arrive, and when I did, it was with a very bad grace. I came into the room without smiling, with my chin up. And Lillian said, 'Stop.'

"I stopped without thinking, and she said, 'I knew it. She's perfect.' And she stood up and came over to me. She walked right around me, just looking. Then she said, 'Say something.'

"I said, 'What would you like me to say?'

"And she clasped her hands together – like this – and said, 'I want her. For *The Simulacrum.*'"

"Wow," I say, but Mary Arden ignores me.

"None of us understood at first. My father said, 'You mean, as an extra?'

"She said, 'No. For the lead.'

"I just stared at her. I couldn't quite take in what she was suggesting. I was fifteen, and I had absolutely no acting experience except for the school play. As for my parents, they had never even thought of anything like this. They weren't particularly hidebound for the time but I'm not sure they considered film acting as a respectable sort of career. So they saw it as a bit of a joke, and as for me – well, I was stunned. I didn't really think she could be serious. Not that I wouldn't have jumped at the idea, because I was mad about

174

films – I'd been to the Regal lots of times with my parents. But I couldn't imagine being up there on the screen, in black and white. The idea was alluring enough in theory but when I thought about trying to act I was terrified."

The corner of my mouth lifts at that. It seems a strange reminiscence for someone who went on to become such a famous screen actor.

"Still," says Mary Arden, "you'll have gathered by now that Lillian wasn't the sort of person to give up, once she had an idea in her head. She wasn't going to let the whole thing founder because Salome Safir had taken an overdose. She nagged and cajoled and persuaded, and when my parents said (somewhat doubtfully) that they didn't think it would work, she said she'd give them time to sleep on it; she wouldn't take no for an answer. She promised she'd chaperone me too. Everything would be above board.

"Lillian worked on me as well. She flattered me. I admit that. She told me I was a great natural beauty and that I would be wasted working as a clerk or a shop girl. She was thrilled I hadn't cut my hair, because of the wartime scenes. And she said it wouldn't be difficult; it wasn't like stage acting, where you had to memorise huge pieces of text, because it didn't have to be filmed in one go.

"So she worked on my parents, and she worked on me, and in the end you can imagine how it went. Lillian," she says grimly, "nearly always got her own way."

I can believe this. Lillian Velderkaust's strength of personality was legendary.

"I remember the day she sent for me," says Mary Arden. "It was winter then, not long after Christmas, and it was already becoming dark. The lights were still up but the celebrations were all done. There was no snow – simply endless, dreary rain. A big black car drew up outside the house, gleaming with wet, the headlamps reflected in the puddles on the road. Lillian hadn't come; she had just sent the driver.

"I suffered my parents to kiss and fuss over me. I was a little afraid that if I crossed them in anything they would change their minds and not let me go. Then I picked up my bag and went to the car. The driver opened the door for me and I got in and we drove away. I didn't look back.

"I remember too that that first evening at her house she took me over to a huge mirror, one of those fan-style Art Deco mirrors that looks like a stylised sea-shell. There was an open fire in that room, as there often were back then, and the flames were reflected in it. We stood side by side and she made me look at myself and at her.

"She said, 'For the film, when we are on set, you will be me. You will be Lillian Velderkaust – whether the camera is running or not. You must *believe* it.'

"I said, 'Yes, Miss Velderkaust,' and she said, 'Call me Lillian when we are at home. But not on set. When we are on set, *you* are Lillian. Do you understand?'

"And I said, 'Yes... Lillian.' I didn't quite understand the reasoning behind it, but I was a little afraid of her."

I bet, I think. Some of the directors of the period were legendarily domineering, and Lillian Velderkaust was clearly no different. Mary Arden's first hand memories of her are absolutely fascinating. I am dying for her to get to the bit about how Lillian *found the answer*, though that has to be impossible in the literal sense.

Mary Arden continues, "After dinner she gave me the script to read. She said, 'We will shoot the film in short sequences. You won't have to remember a great deal of this at once, but what you deliver must be absolutely word perfect. Not a word transposed or replaced.' And she asked me again if I understood.

"I nodded, and took the script from her. To be truthful, I was daunted. When she was persuading me to take the part, she had concentrated on all the marvellous things about it – the opportunity to start a wonderful career, the extraordinary good fortune of being filmed by a director

176

with an established reputation. She'd flattered me so much that I had started imagining myself up there with the greats, with Mary Pickford and Greta Garbo, an enormous, beautiful face on the silver screen."

And of course, that really did happen. The ancient woman sitting by me, telling a story from nearly ninety years ago, is at least as famous as either of those actors. And all because of this strange idea of Lillian Velderkaust's – this *delusion* or whatever it was.

"Now I was beginning to be afraid of the task I had taken on," continues Mary Arden. "After Lillian had gone, I even cried a little. It was not that I regretted agreeing, exactly, but everything was so strange. I read the script through and that seemed peculiar too. I had no experience of movie scripts, of course, but even so it seemed oddly undramatic in places, as though Lillian had simply written down the real things that people had said. And she wanted me to deliver all of it perfectly – that simply made me dreadfully afraid of making a mistake.

"But, you know, I was fifteen, going on sixteen. I had my poor little *amour-propre*; I wanted to hold up my head amongst the adults. I couldn't imagine saying to Lillian, *I don't think I want to do this anymore*, and suffering the humiliation of being delivered home again in that big black car. So after a while I dried my eyes, and before I went to bed I spent a good hour studying the script, determined to be word perfect."

Chapter Thirty-Six

Mary Arden has been talking for a while, and of course she wants her pound of flesh in return. After she has got to the point where she was sitting in her room in Lillian's house, reading the script, she sits back in her chair, folds her hands in her lap, and looks directly at me. Suddenly she's all briskness and sharpness.

She says, "I've talked enough. Now you tell me something."

It is so terribly frustrating, the way she can turn off the tap like that, stop in the middle of her reminiscences and demand I tell her something in return. She still hasn't told me the thing I really want to know – in what sense did Lillian Velderkaust *find the answer*? I would scream if I thought it would do any good. Instead, I reach out and pick up my phone, and switch off the audio recording app. The *click* as I set the phone back down on the table sounds very loud in the silence.

I say, "What do you want to know?"

"Did he hit you?"

"What? *No*."

"Did he throw things?"

"No." I shake my head.

"Was he cruel... in bed?"

And just like that, I snap. "That's it," I say. I get to my feet, grabbing for my mobile phone, my notebook, my pen. "I've had it with you and your horrible, prurient questions. We're done for today."

She grins at that, the miserable bitch.

"No, we're not."

I don't dignify that with a reply. I stride towards the door and my hand is actually on the door handle when she says, "I have a reel of the film."

I'm so angry with her that I consider going anyway. But I pause there with my fingers on the handle, and I know then that I am lost. I let go.

"I want to see it," I say.

"And so you shall. But talk first."

"Why?" I burst out. "What does it matter to you? Why do you care whether Max was the perfect husband or an utter bastard? You didn't know him, and you don't know me, even if you think you do. And he's *dead*."

She shakes her head, regretfully. "Talk."

"I'll lie," I tell her.

"No, you won't. I can tell when you're lying."

"What are you, a witch?"

It's no use. Whatever I say, however rude I am, it just bounces off her, like pebbles off plate armour. She laughs at me, seeming genuinely amused.

I pace up and down, approaching the chair where I sat before and then retreating, like an animal that does not trust itself.

"Stop pacing," she says. "You're not going to solve anything and you're making my eyes hurt."

"Good," I say savagely.

"Sit," she says, as if I'm a dog.

Reluctantly, I drag myself over to the chair and sit down again. I put my things down next to me in a little heap, so that I can grab them and run if I really have to. I push back the strands of hair that have fallen over my face.

"I want to see the reel of film."

"Later."

"Now. You could be lying about it. In fact, you probably are."

"I'm not. I'll ask Harris to fetch it as soon as we've talked, if you like."

As soon as we've talked. I look down at my hands; I look out of the window. There is a long silence.

"Alright," I say.

She waits.

"I don't know what to tell you. Max wasn't perfect, okay? He had the occasional fit of temper, like he did before the wedding. It was usually when he was stressed about something. He didn't hit me."

"But he did do something?"

"He... well, he didn't do anything intentionally. He grabbed me a bit too hard once or twice. And..."

"And...?"

"And he shoved me, once. He was tired and ratty and he caught me off balance. It was an accident, really. I fell over. But," I say, "most of the time he wasn't like that. You're just pushing me to tell you the bad things. Most of the time he was wonderful – kind, thoughtful."

"Especially after he'd lost his temper, I'm guessing."

I look at her levelly. "You only want to hear one side."

"How many sides are there, when a man is shoving his wife around? The thing I don't understand is why you're defending him."

That stops me in my tracks. I take a deep breath. "Because he's dead," I tell her. "Okay? Haven't you ever heard of not speaking ill of the dead? Whatever his faults, it's all over now."

"Hmmm." She studies me for a few moments. "And your family, what did they think of Max? Did they like him?"

This feels like firmer ground. I spread out my hands. "Well, my parents were dead before we got married, of course. I don't have any siblings. I have a few relatives but I'm not all that close to them. Not so close that they'd give me an opinion about whether they liked my husband or not."

"And your friends? What about them?"

"Envious. When they met him, they couldn't believe their eyes. Max could be really charming, you know."

"I bet he could." She considers. "Did you socialise a lot with them, your friends?"

"Yes," I say easily.

"Right up until... the end?"

"Well, in the last year before Max... before he died, I suppose I didn't see as much of them," I say awkwardly. "I mean, I'd moved out of London, stopped working at my old place, and we were doing up the house."

And Max didn't like them. I don't say that and I try not to *think* it, because Mary Arden has this way of reading my mind.

She looks at me for a long time. Then she says, "Tell me about them – your friends."

"Well... my three best friends are Ellie and Samira, who I met at university, and Susie. I used to work with her. Ellie was the one whose wedding I met Max at. The one who went a bit bridezilla. She has a baby now. Sam's doing a PhD in zoology. And Susie – well, she's the wild card you have in every bunch. You can hear her laughing half a mile away."

I grin while I'm saying that, remembering.

"Hmmm," says Mary Arden. "Tell me about Ellie's baby."

"There isn't much to tell," I say. "I mean, She's a girl. Her name's Lucy. I've seen photos of her but–"

"Ah, so you haven't met her?"

"No, not yet." I shift uncomfortably.

"What about Samira? And Susie? When did you last see them?"

"I don't know," I say defensively. I feel as though I'm being cross-questioned; heat is coming into my face. "Not that long ago."

"At the funeral?"

"They... weren't at the funeral. It was a really bad time for me. A lot of it... I just can't remember. I was on anti-depressants for a while too. I definitely wasn't up to phoning round everyone and telling them what had happened." My hands twist together in my lap. I hate feeling as if I'm

181

making excuses. "You can't possibly understand that," I tell her. "You've probably never loved anyone in your whole long selfish life."

"You think?"

"Yes."

She makes a noise – a grunt, a chuckle – that I can't identify. Then she says, "So you have very little family, and very few friends, and your husband is dead. I wonder if anyone would even notice if you never went back to your life down there in England?"

A cold sensation runs through me, like a knife blade sliding under my ribs.

"Of course they would..." I start to say.

And then I think of the box I carried out of my office on my last day, now stowed in a corner of the spare room, unopened for months, even years perhaps. I think of my wedding day, and Max's father giving me away because my parents were no longer around. And I think of the calls from my friends, the ones that came up *Sam* and *Susie* and *Ellie* on my mobile phone just before I pressed the red button to reject them. Calls I never returned, because I had no words for anyone. I do not like thinking about these things.

"I don't think," says Mary Arden, "that there is a Theda-shaped hole in anyone's life, is there?"

I stare and stare at her, but I cannot disagree.

After a while it seems she has got bored of tormenting me. She tells me to go outside and fetch the nurse, and then she tells the woman with the bored insouciance of someone who is used to ordering people about, to go and find Mrs Harris.

The reel, I think. *In two minutes, or five, I will have it in my hands.*

And that is what I cling to.

Chapter Thirty-Seven

Mrs Harris appears, bland and smiling as ever. She seems unsurprised by Mary Arden's order to go and fetch the reel of film – "you know the one."

"Yes, Miss Arden," she says. Her gaze moves over me neutrally, professionally, as though I am a piece of the furniture.

She is gone less time than I expect. I imagined her having to go upstairs, to the furthest part of the west wing, and rummage in some neglected cupboard. But she is away such a short time that I suspect the pair of them planned this – that Mary Arden would use the promise of the reel to bait me into revealing more about my sorry past.

This thought passes through my brain with infinitesimal swiftness. And then I am on my feet. I cannot help it. I stare at what Mrs Harris is carrying in both hands, holding it as carefully as if it were a newborn.

It is a circular metal container, clearly very old – nearly ninety years old, in fact, if Mary Arden is to be believed. Tiny specks of rust cluster around the ridges on its surface. There is a sticker across the front of it, yellowed and peeling, and when Mrs Harris sets the cannister down on the coffee table with reverent care, I see that it says *The Simulacrum, 1930* on it, in an old-fashioned hand.

My head is buzzing. Mrs Harris steps back, and I sink down to my knees in front of the coffee table, my hands hovering over the cannister as though I dare not even touch it. As though it will vanish in a puff of smoke if I so much as lay a finger on it.

This is gold. In film historians' terms, it's the Holy Grail, like finding a copy of *London After Midnight* or something.

I gaze at it, while images bloom inside my head of the book cover with a glossy still from the movie on it, of British Film Institute screenings, of me being interviewed for television by experts who can hardly believe what I've pulled off.

My hands settle, light as butterflies, on the cannister, caressing it. The metal is cold, a little rough in places. I grip the edges, preparing to twist.

"Don't open it," says Mary Arden, sharply.

I glance at her.

"I can't answer for the condition if you do," she continues. "The film is very old and very delicate. A film restorer might be able to do something with it."

"You said–" I begin through gritted teeth.

"I said I had a reel of film," she finishes. "I didn't say you could watch it, as it is." She shrugs. "You can't have imagined you'd be able to watch it here and now anyway, not without the proper facilities."

"No," I snap back. "But for all I know, this is a cannister full of dust."

"Well," she says complacently, "If we continue to get along, I will permit you to take the reel with you when you leave Garthside. You can get it professionally assessed, and restored if it needs to be, and indeed if it can be."

"If," I say crossly.

She leans back in her chair, as though the conversation is wearing her out, and her papery eyelids slide down over her eyes.

"I don't think it will be too much longer," she says, and her voice is thoughtful, dreamy. "I think we might meet twice more, or perhaps three times. By then, I will have told you everything I can about *The Simulacrum*, and you will have told me everything I need to know about yourself. There can't be that much more to tell, can there?"

"No," I say firmly. "There's nothing important left to say."

Her eyes open again – blue rimmed with yellow. She looks at me steadily and I stare back at her, my gaze level.

"Go," she says at last, with the manner of someone who

is used to being obeyed. "I am worn out with talking. And you had better leave that can of film here. It should go back into storage for the time being. It's highly flammable."

I get to my feet. I am determined that come what may, when I leave Garthside House I will have that cannister with me – and any others she is keeping back.

"Fine," I say, and she does not reply. Before I turn to go, her eyes are closed again, and as I leave the room, the nurse outside gets to her feet.

I go upstairs, because there is nowhere else to go except the ruined gardens, and try to think.

Don't open it, she said, and I suppose she was right. I have no way to watch it now and exposing it to the air might simply damage it. If it is genuinely 1930s film stock, much depends on how it has been stored. There might be something salvageable in there, or there might be nothing but acidic powder. Come to that, it might not be a reel of *The Simulacrum* that's in there at all – it could be any old film, cunningly labelled with that name.

I know all of these things and yet something tells me that this is the real deal, that something can be rescued, that this is only part of what Mary Arden has, squirrelled away in the upper west wing, where nobody is allowed to go. It's more than *wanting* to believe it; it's an utter conviction. My hands curl into fists. I want it. I want the rest of it.

Downstairs, the nurse will be helping Mary Arden into a wheelchair so that she can take her back up to her room. How many more times will she have to do that, before it ends forever? A hundred? Fifty? Seven? Perhaps it doesn't matter what I tell her. Pretty soon, she'll be gone, taking whatever fragments of memory she retains with her. Hell, the story she's been telling me is so bizarre nobody's going to believe it anyway. But a copy of the actual film...

Will I tell her everything, in exchange for that cannister and any others?

I bite my lip.

Chapter Thirty-Eight

At 1 a.m. my phone vibrates gently on the bedside table – just enough sound to wake a light sleeper. I'm already awake though. I've slept a little, fitfully, but the thought of what I mean to do has made it impossible to do more than that.

I don't switch on the bedside lamp. Instead, the light from my phone shows me the heavy curtains closed against the night, and the expanse of carpet between me and the door. The room has a strange greyish look in the dark. I get out of bed very carefully, and belt my robe around me. I don't put anything on my feet. Bare feet on carpet – that is the best way to move around silently. Then I go over to the door, put my ear against the wooden panel, and listen.

Silence. I wait until I am really sure and then very carefully I open the door. Outside, the hallway is dark. It is late enough now that the main lights have been switched off. I step outside and draw the door closed behind me.

If I am caught, I say to myself, *I shall say–*

What? Possible excuses flit through my head: *I thought I smelled burning, I was sleepwalking...* None of them are convincing. I resolve not to get caught.

I put my phone in my pocket and stand on the landing until my eyes adjust naturally to the darkness. I can make out the double doors that lead to the upper west wing because of the moonlight filtering in through the windows opposite the head of the stairs. As I pass those stairs, I steel myself and lean right over the bannisters, looking down into the deep gloom and listening for footsteps; I could still justify my presence here if I were seen, just about. Downstairs everything is perfectly dark and silent. No Mrs Harris prowling around. The silence is so complete that my ears ring.

The double doors look heavy and somehow ominous, but they yield easily to my push. On the other side, the corridor is a black pit.

I step inside, keeping a light pressure on the doors so that they won't slap closed. They settle softly back into place and suddenly the moonlight is gone. Velvety blackness engulfs me.

I freeze, fumbling for the phone in my pocket. But then there is a faint blue-grey flash at the end of the corridor, enough to show me that I am alone. I imagine Mary Arden propped in front of her enormous flat screen TV, fast asleep – the sound turned down, the characters in some vintage film or chat show or cookery programme gesticulating away to themselves while she snores, her old mouth sagging open.

I stare at that flickering light for a moment. So far as I can tell, there is no other floor above this one, although there are probably attics. I can't believe they'd have stored the film up there. They know it's a fire hazard. So if there are any more reels, they are down here somewhere, and I intend to find them. Before I tell that old horror anything else about my life, I want to know whether it's worth doing it. My soul for a piece of hers.

I stay close to the wall, feeling my way along, trying not to think about the other person I have heard doing that very thing. There are periodic brighter flashes from the other end of the corridor and I keep looking that way, full of simmering unease. If the next flash should show me someone creeping along the wall towards me–

I squash the thought. *No. I am alone.*

The first door on the left leads into the room that Richard occupied while he was here. To check, or not to check? I don't take time to think; I open the door and slip inside. Once the door is closed, I put on the light with a great sense of relief.

The last time I was in here, I was preoccupied with escaping Mrs Harris – and Richard. I had an impression of untidiness, but that was about all. It doesn't take long to see that there is nowhere in here that anything much could be stored. The bed has been carefully made up and everything looks orderly. The copy of *The Hound of the Baskervilles* lies on the bedside table, with a strip of paper hanging out of it as a bookmark.

I leave the room, not forgetting to switch off the light, and continue my furtive progress down the corridor. The next door leads to another bedroom, all done out in pale blue and clearly unoccupied for a long time. The air is cold in here and there is a faint musty smell. I half-heartedly open the large wardrobe, but there is nothing inside except a handful of wire coat hangers.

The room after that is one that would delight me, if circumstances were different: the library. Either this is a double-sized room or they knocked two into one when they converted it, but it's huge. Big windows show me reflected in their black depths, books at my back, but during the daytime the view is probably superb. Every inch of wall is lined with bookshelves, the contents mostly vintage volumes in old-fashioned bindings. There is nowhere anything else could be stored. There is no time to browse; I glance around, then switch out the light and move on.

I am getting close to the end of the corridor. Much further and I will be level with the corner and visible from Mary Arden's room, if anyone is sitting up with her. There is one last door on this side. It is made of polished wood like the others, but when I touch the handle it swings open easily to reveal a second door inside. This one is smooth and white and it has a key pad for security.

I look at that, and then I *know*. She has the whole film and it's in here. It has to be. What else would she be keeping in temperature-controlled storage?

I'd like to see it, though. Who wouldn't? So I step close to the door and try a few combinations in the key pad. There's always the chance whoever uses this door has gone for something easy, like *0000* or *1234*. I try those and neither of them works, so then I try *9999* and the little red light flips to green.

It was as easy as that. My heart thumping, I press down the door handle. And then my luck runs out.

It isn't even a sound that tells me there's someone behind me. It's just a change in the quality of that pulsing bluish light. I let go of the door handle. Wild ideas run through my head – possible excuses I can give for trespassing here. I turn slowly and shock shrills through me, brisk as a blade.

He's so close. Almost close enough to touch.

Silhouetted against that eerie blue flickering, he would be nothing but a dark shape, but the tiny green light on the security door begins to blink. With every flash of light his face is lit up, and it is a face I recognise.

My breath seems to coagulate in my throat. I back up against the inner door, my eyes widening and widening until I think they must burst out of their sockets. A small sound escapes me – not a scream, something like air escaping from a punctured balloon. All over my brain klaxons are going off, because my eyes are telling me what they are seeing and my head refuses to believe it.

Time's up. The green flash reverts to a red glow which barely illuminates more than those perfectly-moulded lips, parting to say – what? Nothing I want to hear.

I sense a movement towards me, but it's too late; I twist away, panic-stricken, and lunge away down the corridor on unsteady legs. The double doors seem a million miles away. I run for them, my bare feet making soft thuds on the carpet and I don't care, I have to get *away*, I have to put space between me and him. When I get there I stare at them, my mind blank with panic – do I push them or pull them? And then I turn and look back and he is still there. He is working his way towards me and I see the contours of him against the distant light: the hip length tunic, the trousers that are wide at the thigh, tapering into booted calves. The uniform.

I manage to open the doors. I bolt for my room, where at the last moment I force myself not to slam the door – I close it quietly and turn the key in the lock with trembling hands. Then I lean against the wooden panels and listen. There is a lump in my throat, and my eyes are stinging with tears of sheer fright. I wait for the slap of the double doors to tell me that the man in uniform has followed me, that he is heading straight for the spot where I am standing now, the two of us separated by an inch or two of wood, nothing more.

Silence.

Time oozes past and I hear nothing outside the door. I could open it. I could look. I've done that before, after all. But I don't. My nerves are shot to pieces. I can't imagine opening the door and seeing him standing there in the dark, inches away, silent, his intentions unknown and ominous. I don't want to see Hugh Mason.

Chapter Thirty-Nine

I wake very early, before it is properly light, and find myself lying across the doorway. I hear a pattering sound; rain on the windows. From the feeling of the carpet under my face I suspect I have the texture of it imprinted on my cheek. When I sit up, everything feels stiff. My phone is lying on the floor next to me; I pick it up and get slowly to my feet. Then I stagger over to the bed and sit down, rubbing my face.

No matter how long I sit, or rub, shivering now, I cannot make sense of it. It is not possible that I saw Hugh Mason a few hours ago, and yet I did. I was not dreaming. I can remember very clearly going into the bedrooms in the west wing and opening that last door, the one with the security door behind it. Then I turned and he was there. But he cannot have been there. He has been dead for a century. Round and round my head it goes, and there is no possible answer to it.

I think: *Those other nights, when I heard someone outside, when someone tried the door. Was that him too?* And then I think: *The night someone got in–*

I press my hands to my mouth, thinking of the unseen person running their hands over the pillow where my head had been, just a few moments before.

After a while I make myself get up and run a bath, thinking that hot water against my skin will make me feel alright, make me feel that everything is normal. I have to get myself to the point where I can go downstairs and have breakfast, and talk to the woman serving it, or to Mrs Harris, as if nothing has happened at all. Right now I think it would show on my face that things are *not* alright.

While the water is thundering into the tub, I open Mary Arden's box of papers and force myself to look at the picture of Hugh Mason. I stare and stare at it. It was him.

I put the photograph back in the box, cover it with other papers, and close the lid. I go and climb into the bath, and think about what to do, in a fragmented sort of way.

I could leave. I have the problem of the car and the potential bill, but I could just go. If I called Angus, he'd come and get me. If I told him *why* I wanted to leave, he'd probably think I was off my head, but I think he'd still come.

And then what? I think. I have no other plans, just the idea of writing this book. And I'm so close. I've seen that reel of film. I'm certain she has the rest of them in that refrigerated room in the west wing. She's said herself that we're nearly at the end of what we can tell each other. If I can tough it out...

I try to be rational, although it seems insane to be applying reason to this situation. There's nothing to say that this... I can't say the word, even to myself. *This relic of Hugh Mason*, I decide. There's nothing to say that it is dangerous. All the times that the door was locked, he never managed to get in. As long as I remember to lock it, there's nothing to worry about. Is there?

I think about Mrs Harris. I'm pretty sure she knows. There was the way she seemed to relax a little, when I told her that I hadn't seen whoever had come into my room that night. If she knows, there can't be any risk, surely?

I put my head in my hands. I can't believe I'm even having these conversations with myself. The one thing that I cling to is the idea of finishing what I came here to do. If I can prise the rest of the story out of Mary Arden, if I can persuade her to let me take some or all of the film with me...

Just a little longer, I tell myself.

At breakfast, the woman serving the food looks at me a little strangely. I sketch a quick taut smile and pour myself a big cup of tea, heaping in the sugar. I haven't put any makeup on, I realise, and then I wonder if I brushed my hair. My mind keeps reverting to what I saw last night, that face illuminated by those tiny green flashes. The reality and the impossibility of it. Those things fill my head, crowding everything else out.

All of a sudden I make up my mind to go and see Angus after breakfast. I don't care how it looks – whether he thinks I'm messing him about after what happened last time. I need to be with someone who isn't part of this bizarre place, just for a little while.

So after I have choked down some toast and drunk a lot more tea, I do what I can with my hairbrush and my makeup bag, put on a coat and the stoutest shoes I have, and let myself out of the house. The rain is coming down hard. There are puddles on the terrace and water is running off the drooping black remains of plants. The river will be high, I realise. Well – perhaps I can shout until Angus hears me and comes over.

I look up at the facade, visible through a haze of rain. It doesn't look magnificent any more. It looks deceitful, brooding. Wind claws at me. I hold onto my hood with my hand and scurry around the corner.

Once I'm away from the house, striding through the woods, the ground becomes hopelessly muddy. My shoes and legs are quickly splattered. In places it's hard to keep my footing; the mud sucks at my heels. It also shows me that I am not the only one who comes through these woods: there are tyre tracks, from something heavy by the look of them. In places they have filled with water. I become more watchful after that, listening for the sound of a vehicle over the hissing of the rain, but I see nothing.

Eventually I come to the tall gates at the boundary of Garthside. I turn to follow the line of the fence but I already have a sinking feeling in my stomach. I can see how the tyre tracks also turn, penetrating as far as they can into the remains of last year's undergrowth. There are other shapes in the mud too. Footmarks. Workers have been here, and they have mended the fence.

I keep going, stepping high over rotting wet plants, until I can touch the fence, hooking my fingers through the metal links. I look up, but I can see it is impossible to climb it. The holes are too small for me to insert the toe of my shoe. I flex my shoulders, trying to shake the mesh, and it barely moves. It would take something a lot stronger than I am to pull this down. The field on the other side, and the river, and Angus, might as well be on the planet Mars.

I stand for a while and look at the coarse grass, at the falling rain and the wind that tears at the faded blades. Then I turn away, and trudge back to Garthside House.

Chapter Forty

I am late for the first time today.

After I got back indoors and changed out of my sodden clothes, I sat for a long time with my phone in my hands and wondered whether to call Angus. Why didn't I? For a while, I heard a droning and thumping that was someone vacuuming the carpet right outside my bedroom door. When that stopped, it was replaced with a silence that was even less conducive to private conversation; it seemed to have an expectant, listening quality to it. I told myself I was imagining that, but still I didn't phone.

I picked at lunch, and after that time seemed to slip away from me. I looked through the papers in the box again and re-read that tiny fragment of script. Perhaps it was true what Mary Arden said, that the script sounded more like banal everyday chat than drama, but it isn't really possible to tell from so short a sample. The photograph of Hugh Mason I slid between some other papers, hiding it. At last I glanced at my watch and saw that it was five past three.

So now here I am, feeling flustered and horribly dishevelled as I push open the door, praying that the old witch won't summarily decide not to talk to me today.

"You're late, Theda Garrick," are the very first words that pass her lips, which are outlined in an unsuitable shade of lurid orange, matching today's ensemble.

"I'm so sorry. I–"

"Oh, never mind. I'm not interested in your excuses. Sit."

I do sit, and I set out my things – notebook, pen, phone – with hands that tremble just a little. I drop the pen on the floor and have to feel about under the coffee table for it.

Mary Arden watches this, her orange lips pursed spitefully. In her neatly tailored orange bouclé suit and matching patent shoes, she manages to make me feel like an urchin. She folds her hands on her lap and I see that her nails are painted the same fiery shade – a piece of towering vanity, because someone will have to remove that polish if she wears another colour tomorrow, which she surely will. I don't suppose for one moment she does it herself.

"Ready?" she says.

"Yes."

"Very well then. Today I will tell you about the actual filming of *The Simulacrum*."

"That's–"

"But first," she interrupts, "You will talk to me."

I swallow. "There's nothing else to tell. My life has been utterly boring compared to yours. Really it has. Can't we talk about the filming?"

She is shaking her head.

I try flagrant flattery. "But you have so many fans. Honestly, people will be *dying* to read this book. Isn't that more–?"

"No," she says. She stretches out one gnarled hand and admires the orange fingernails. Then her rheumy blue gaze flicks to me. "You look terrible today," she remarks. "If this Max of yours was so handsome, I can't think how you netted him, not if you looked like this."

Perversely, this piece of rudeness braces me up. I say, "I'd look better if I could get a decent night's sleep, without people rattling around the corridors in the night."

The look she gives me then is very sharp, but after a pause she simply says, "All old houses have their creaks and groans. Now," she adds, "Tell me where you got that scar on your arm."

Coming out of nowhere, the question catches me off balance, but instinctively I grasp the cuff of my cardigan and pull it down over my wrist.

"Well?" she says.

"I don't know."

"I think you do."

"I don't. I really don't. I had an accident – I can't remember it clearly."

"Why not?"

"Because I was concussed." This is perfectly true. "It's quite common to have memory loss after concussion," I tell her. "One of my friends was once in a car accident and–"

"I don't want to hear about that," she says dismissively. "I want to hear about *your* accident."

I look away. I don't want to talk about it.

"What kind of accident was it?" she persists.

I clasp my hands together, rubbing my fingers over each other. "A fall," I say reluctantly.

"A fall? So where was this fall? From a horse? From a wall?"

"Stairs," I say, very quietly.

"Speak up, I can't hear you."

"STAIRS." I glare at her. "I fell down stairs."

"Careless. And you cut your arm in the fall?"

"I must have done." I hesitate. "There's a wrought iron thing, a kind of sculpture, at the turn in the stairs, and I think I did it on that."

She considers this. "You must have taken quite a tumble. Where did you end up? There, at the turn in the stairs?"

I look down, at my hands. "At the bottom."

"My goodness," she comments. "You certainly did fall with some force, then. And you don't remember it?"

"No," I say firmly.

"And can you remember what happened *before* you fell?" she wants to know.

"Not right before."

"Well, what *can* you remember?"

I look at her, and all of a sudden there's a pricking in my eyes. I press my lips tightly together, feeling the strange sensation in my throat that precedes tears.

"You must remember something," she coaxes.

197

I nod, and then I swallow, forcing the feeling back. "I was happy."

She waits. I know she isn't going to let this go; she wants to know. And to be honest it's almost a relief to tell someone. Almost.

"The thing is," I say, "We weren't trying. I couldn't take the pill because I got apocalyptic migraines. But we were using other things, so I wasn't expecting it to happen..."

"You were *pregnant*?" she says.

I nod again. "Yes. And even though it wasn't planned, I was just so... happy. I thought... this is going to bring us both closer together. A baby..." I close my eyes, remembering, and unbidden a tear slides out from under one of the closed lids. "I can recall thinking how surprised Max was going to be, and how pleased. I knew we'd manage, because I wasn't working anyway, and we were still getting by. We were upstairs in the bedroom – I do remember that. Max had just got home from work and was changing his clothes, and I said... I said, *Max, I've got something to tell you.* He turned towards me, with a question on his face." I pause. "That's the last thing I remember." I shake my head. "I was so happy."

It's true; I can't remember anything clearly after that. But there is something – something just beyond my grasp. It's not even a foggy sort of memory; it's more of an echo of something. Shouting. The light behind Max. I am afraid to think about it too much, in case it takes some more solid shape.

"But you don't have a child, do you?" says Mary Arden. She almost sounds bored.

"No, I don't," I say in a small voice. "I lost it." I press my fingers together, as though I want to hold my own hand, to comfort myself.

She considers. "So, you fell down the stairs – two flights, if there was a turn in the middle. You cut yourself on the

198

way down. And then what? What do you remember after that?"

"I remember being on the floor, looking up. There's a light above the stairwell, all the way up at the top, and I remember staring at that. I wanted to let my eyes slide shut and float up to that light and just keep going, out through the roof and away. But then I saw Max's face. He was leaning over me, and he looked... horrified, distraught. And then there were other faces – paramedics – asking me questions. Max said, 'You have to do something. You have to help her.' He sounded almost angry with them, as if they were spending too long thinking about it. I tried to say, *I'm pregnant*, but I couldn't make the words come out; they were only in my head. And later, in the hospital, I found out I wasn't, not anymore."

Mary Arden looks at me with something close to sympathy for once – or at least, as much of that emotion as she can manage.

"And how did Max react to that news?" she asks.

"He put a brave face on it," I say.

"I'm sure he did," she says tartly. "And what do you think caused the fall?"

I look at her for a long time, not saying anything.

"You must have some idea," she says. "What did Max say?"

"Max said... He said I must have slipped on the rug on the upstairs landing and fallen down the stairs."

"You 'must have'? So he didn't see it happen, then?"

I don't answer that. "The rug was rumpled," I tell her in the end. "You could see how it could happen." I look away, out of the window. "He was very kind with me afterwards. He said we'd try again, later on. When I'd recovered, and when it was a better time. He said that it was sort of for the best, really; we'd wait until his business was more secure, until we were sure we could afford a baby. He kissed me; he kept kissing me. He said he was so sorry this had happened; he said he loved me so much. So very, very much."

And I can't help it. I shudder.

Chapter Forty-One

Mary Arden looks at me for a while, not unsympathetically.

"Poor Theda," she says, as though we were talking about a third person.

I wipe my eye with the heel of my hand, and say nothing.

"What did the paramedics, the doctors, say? Did they ask how you came to fall down the stairs? What did you tell them?"

I shake my head. "The same. I couldn't remember. Max said he heard me scream. He was in the bedroom, changing his shirt, he said. And the rug was rumpled up. You could see how I could have tripped."

"And nobody questioned it? Nobody thought it could have been something other than an accident?"

"One doctor," I say. "He asked me if... if I'd been happy about being pregnant."

I can't help it then; I cry, really cry, until my nose is running and I am fumbling uselessly for a tissue.

Mary Arden reaches into her handbag and passes me a handkerchief with *M.A.* embroidered on the corner. She watches me blow my nose.

"I was, you know," I tell her. "I was very happy."

"And how was Max?" she asks.

"Oh... He was the picture of the caring husband. He wouldn't leave me alone at first, not for a moment, until the doctors absolutely ordered him away. He – he wanted to know if I remembered what had happened."

"But you didn't?"

"I said not." I bow my head. "He asked the doctors if I'd recover my memory and they said, maybe, but possibly not. It was a severe concussion. I was unconscious for a while."

"Well," says Mary Arden briskly. "That sounds very convenient for Max."

I don't answer that. We sit for a while in silence, listening to the rain pattering against the window panes. There is nothing more I want to tell her about that day. Nothing I want to tell myself. There's no reason I can't have another baby in the future – that's what they told me. But I'd have to trust someone again. I'd have to feel safe with them.

Mary Arden leans forward with some effort, and pats my hand with one bejewelled claw.

"We needn't go on today," she says.

"No," I say, and something blazes up in me. "I want to go on." I shake back the hair that has fallen over my face, and look her in the eyes. "You've dragged a lot of horrible, painful shit out of me, stuff I never wanted to think about again. So you can bloody well return the compliment."

She gives me a slow, tigerish smile.

At last she says: "Very well. Where were we?"

I don't have to consult my notes. "You were at Lillian's house, learning the script." I wipe my eyes again, and then I pick up my phone and start the audio recording.

Mary Arden sits back with a sigh. "Yes, I recall. Well, that wasn't the only thing I had to do. The next day, Lillian brought in a hairdresser. That was the first thing. I sat in a chair while the pair of them walked around me, picking up the ends of my hair and discussing what to do with it as though I wasn't even there. The hairdresser had some ideas of her own; she asked a few questions at the beginning, about when the film was supposed to be set, and so on. But Lillian cut her off pretty quickly. She didn't want someone else's interpretation; she wanted it to be just so, the way she intended. She specified a particular length, not very much shorter than it was already. And she also wanted a very specific colour."

She holds up a hand. "You will say, no doubt, that the exact colour was unimportant, because the film was to be shot in black and white. Well, that may be so, but to Lillian it was critical. She showed the woman a lock of hair, all

202

done up in a black ribbon, and said she wanted her to match that, exactly."

"Whose hair was it? Do you know?"

"Hers, of course. From a long time ago, though. Lillian greyed early, and by 1930 her hair was already shot through with white. This was *young* hair.

"She said to the hairdresser: 'Don't think near enough is good enough. It must blend in exactly.'"

"The woman didn't argue. Lillian Velderkaust was a forceful personality. You did what she wanted, or you got out. So she just nodded, and said, 'Yes, Miss Velderkaust.' She did a good job, too, though it took her a long time.

"I just sat there while she worked, reading the script through again and again. The more I read it, the odder it seemed. But then I thought to myself, what do I know about scripts? Perhaps this will sound perfectly natural when it's performed. I bit my nails, though, until Lillian came in and slapped my hand for it.

"When the hairdresser was finished, Lillian seemed very happy with her work. It wasn't a radical change from my normal colour – as I say, we were very like, me and Lillian. It was just a little darker, I would say. But still, it was curious to look at myself in the mirror and see that rich new colour. My parents wouldn't let me have a Marcel wave, and here I was with an expensive dye job."

I digest this. I understand what Mary Arden said before, about the familiarity principle, but I can't see what it can possibly have *done* except feed Lillian Velderkaust's delusion.

Mary Arden continues, "After it was done, Lillian paid the woman very handsomely and sent her off; she said she'd call her back if anything needed adjusting. She also said she'd give her double the money to keep the whole thing to herself. No gossiping. And of course the hairdresser agreed, because who wouldn't?

"Then she got a makeup artist in. She was very fussy

203

about that – she sent the first one away because she tried to talk Lillian into doing something different from what she wanted. The second one was prepared to do whatever Lillian asked. She'd experiment, and Lillian would come and look at it critically.

"All the time they were doing these things, I had the script on my lap, and when they weren't holding up my chin to examine my features I was reading, doing my best to memorise the words. I was very anxious about that, but in spite of being preoccupied with it, I was very puzzled about the whole set-up. Lillian was fussing over every aspect of my appearance, down to the minutest detail, but all the time this was going on, there was never any mention of the rest of the cast."

This makes me sit up a little. Everyone knows that Mary Arden was in *The Simulacrum* but nobody knows who the rest of the cast were.

"The script had lines for *Hugh*," says Mary Arden. "So that was pretty clearly going to be someone playing the part of Hugh Mason. But who? I never saw any male actor, right up to the beginning of filming. Lillian would sit with me sometimes and read Hugh's lines for me, so that I could get the responses right, but I didn't see anyone else.

"Once, I screwed up my courage and asked her outright who was going to take the role of Hugh. She looked up from her script and said, 'Hugh, of course.' After that, I didn't like to ask her again. The way she said it gave me the creeps, but I said to myself that it must be the same as me playing the role of Lillian; whoever it was had to look like Hugh, and imagine themselves right into the part. They had to *be* Hugh for the duration of filming. Perhaps that was why Lillian didn't want us to meet beforehand; because it would spoil the illusion if I saw him eating his lunch or reading the paper or something."

I nod. That makes sense, though those words, *Hugh, of*

course, send a little prickle of unease through me. What did Lillian think she was creating?

"Lillian got a costumier in as well, and she was just as particular about that," says Mary Arden. "I was measured, and she brought in some clothing for them to copy. The things had been worn – I could see that – and Lillian wanted exact copies, but new-looking. They were in an old-fashioned style, too. By 1930 hemlines had gone up. Women still wore hats, but they were smaller. These things were back from the wartime period. I didn't fancy wearing them; I was a teenager, after all, and I didn't want to look like my mother. But I didn't dare say anything.

"They put me in a suit of some kind of dark stuff, with my hair done up under a big hat, and my face carefully made up, and Lillian came and walked all around me, just looking. She made this little hiss under her breath, like steam escaping from a kettle. The costumier was standing there with a little cushion full of pins, ready to make adjustments, but Lillian waved her away. She said, 'Perfect', that one word. She had an expression on her face I can't quite describe: a sort of awe, as though she couldn't quite believe what she'd achieved, but mixed with fear. It frightened her, or else she was afraid of what she was planning to do."

I am horribly fascinated by this. But I dare not interrupt, dare not ask questions, because I know Mary Arden is determined to tell this story in her own time, in her own way.

"Then she said, 'Speak', so I said, 'What do you want me to say?' and she suggested some line from the script, something banal like *Write as soon as you can*. I think that was it.

"'Write as soon as you can,' I said, and she gave a little shriek.

"'No, absolutely not. The emphasis is all wrong,' she said. 'The stress should be on *can*, not *soon*. I thought we'd gone through all this.'

"'Write as soon as you *can*,' I repeated. I watched her pacing up and down; she was making me nervous, and I was afraid I would forget my lines altogether.

"'Better,' she said. 'But I wonder if we should have got an elocutionist?' She wasn't really talking to me – more to herself. I dared not say anything. I just stood there and waited.

"In the end she decided to train me herself; it was her ear that needed pleasing, after all. I took off the hat and the dress, washed off the makeup and brushed out my hair. Then we sat down together and she went over the script, line by line. Some of the lines I spoke pretty well; others she made me repeat, over and over. She absolutely drilled me – that day, and the next, and the next. Every word, every tiny emphasis, had to be right.

"I thought there was something more to it than that, though. There was a brittle nerviness in her manner; it seemed to me that by being so exacting she was putting off the moment when we would begin filming. The committing step, the reality of letting the camera roll, was perhaps too vast a thing – viewed comfortably in the future but looming too large in the present.

"I had been nervous myself to begin with, and Lillian's edginess infected me, making it worse. I could not imagine how angry she would be if I made a mistake. So I asked her if I might go home for a night, to see my parents. That seemed to decide her; she turned on me rather sharply and said, 'Of course not. We begin filming tomorrow.'"

Mary Arden closes her eyes for a moment, remembering, and as she falls silent, her face relaxing, I can see again that beautiful bone structure under the papery skin. From the palimpsest of her face, the former loveliness has not quite been erased.

Then she opens her eyes again, and the watchful malice that is never far away flows back into her features.

She says: "And we did. The next day, we began filming."

Chapter Forty-Two

"The following afternoon, the gleaming black car took us both to the set. Lillian sat beside me but she said very little to me. She fidgeted, crossing and re-crossing her legs, the upper foot jiggling nervously. After a while she took out a cigarette case and a silver lighter and lit a cigarette; she smoked it for several minutes until I began to cough. Then she shot me a glance, wound down the window a little and threw it out.

"The few seconds when the window was open let in the biting cold. A few snowflakes whirled on the air, pale flecks against the gloom. It was not yet evening but it was already getting dark, the sky bruised and lurid. I wondered why Lillian had left it so late to go to the studio; there was hardly any day left. It seemed all the odder when we arrived, because we saw several cars coming out. People were leaving for the night."

Makes sense, I think to myself: if you wanted to film in absolute secrecy, it would be much easier at night when the studios were mostly empty. All the same, I feel it again: that slight stirring of unease.

"Lillian leaned forward and told the driver where to pull in. She also told him he wouldn't be wanted for a number of hours, and suggested a place he could go to eat, somewhere away from the studio, in the next town. I stood next to her on the tarmacadam, shivering in spite of my winter coat, and only half-listening.

"After the car had gone, we went inside and I had my hair and makeup done, which took a considerable time. Then the costumier helped me into the first of my outfits – the one intended for the opening scene.

"While they were making me up and dressing me and all the rest, I didn't see Lillian at all. To this day I don't know what she was doing during that time, to make what came afterwards happen. But just as the costumier was putting the finishing touches to my outfit, the door opened and in she came.

"She was deathly pale, and her eyes were very wide, as though she were seeing something neither of us could see – something compelling and terrible." Mary Arden pauses for a moment, remembering. Then she resumes: "I heard the costumier give a little gasp. Neither of us dared say anything. Lillian swayed a little as she crossed the room towards us, and I saw her put out a hand to steady herself on the back of a chair. Her lips twitched, and for a moment I thought she was about to burst into hysterics, though whether crying or laughing, I couldn't have said.

"Then she mastered herself. She said, 'Is she ready?' and the costumier said, 'Yes, ma'am.'

"Lillian came right up to me and put her hands on my shoulders. She looked me in the face, and I could see that she still had that little tic at the corner of her mouth.

"She said, 'You must be strong. Professional. Whatever happens, whatever you see. Do you understand?'

"I nodded, swallowing, but I didn't understand – not really. The way Lillian was behaving and the way she looked, those things made me fearful, but I didn't know what I was afraid of. I was determined to see it through, though. If nothing else, I was too much in awe of Lillian to try to back out now.

"So I followed her out of the dressing room, me in my hat with my long skirts swishing around my ankles, and her in her modern dress, which was quite a bit shorter, so that I felt ludicrously like her mother.

"I'd seen the set before, because Lillian had showed me round while they were still working on it," says Mary Arden. "It was still a surprise how complete it looked. The first scene, as I've told you before, took place in a railway station, in the waiting room, and within the confines of the set they had recreated something that was utterly lifelike, even down to the posters on the walls, which looked terribly old-fashioned to my eyes. If you had seen this without seeing the edges of the set and all the apparatus around it, you would have believed in it utterly; you would have thought a train would rattle past at any moment.

"Lillian made me go and stand a little to the left of the centre of it. Then she went and had some discussion with the gaffer and they did something with the lighting. It took a while for Lillian to be satisfied, and she wouldn't let me move from where I was. When that was finished, she insisted that every extraneous person left the set altogether."

This I can believe. The secrecy surrounding *The Simulacrum* persists to this day.

Mary Arden goes on, "All this time, I was standing there reading and re-reading the posters on the walls. One of them I particularly remember; it ran *Your chums are fighting – why aren't YOU?* and there were silhouettes of soldiers lunging forward with fixed bayonets. I kept looking at that, and thinking about the pressure there must have been to sign up, and then Lillian said, 'Mary,' in a very quiet voice, and I looked round.

"She said, 'Remember, from now on, you are Lillian. I will call you Lillian, and you will respond as Lillian.'

"I said, 'Yes.' My throat felt dry.

"She gave a curt little nod, and then she went over to the side of the room and opened a door. And out of that door walked Hugh Mason."

Mary Arden falls silent, and I – I stare at her in disbelief. Her gnarled hands clasp in her lap and she rubs her fingers together, comforting herself.

"An actor playing Hugh Mason?" I say at last.

And Mary Arden says, "It *was* Hugh Mason. There was no mistaking those wonderful looks. With his dark eyes and hair he looked like a Greek god in an army uniform."

I open my mouth to say that this is not possible and then

I think of last night – of the moment I saw Hugh Mason's face by the winking green light of the door alarm. I *know* it was him. I don't know how it could have been, but it *was*. I am absolutely certain of it.

Mary Arden doesn't notice me react; her gaze is far away, reaching into 1930.

She says, "Lillian just melted away and went to stand by the camera operator. Hugh walked over to me at a measured pace, doffing his cap. I was frozen to the spot, staring at him. He looked – perfect. The sharp cheekbones, the beautifully-modelled mouth, the dark expressive eyes. In one hand he held his army cap; the other swung beside him as he walked. He wore polished leather boots, and his footsteps rang out briskly on the hard floor. He came nearer, and nearer, and I just gaped at him.

"A sense of unreality and the fear of angering Lillian kept me rooted to the spot. Otherwise I would have stepped back before he reached me. Because beautiful though he was, perfect though he looked, there was something absolutely wrong with Hugh."

I stare at Mary Arden as she shivers, remembering.

"There was nothing to *see*," she says. "He looked exactly as he did in the photographs Lillian had shown me. It was more the sense that there was an absence; some vital thing missing. Every movement seemed subtly rehearsed, every nuance of expression somehow false.

"Every ringing step he took across the space between us amplified the dread I felt. My eyes sought Lillian, but she was somewhere behind the big stage lights. I couldn't see anyone but Hugh as he closed in. His handsome face filled my vision. The feeling of *wrongness* was far, far worse when he was close. Even though each detail of his skin and hair and eyes was perfect, I knew it was a kind of shell."

Yes, I think. And then: *No. This is madness. This cannot be true.*

But Mary Arden is continuing. "He reached out and took

210

my hand, holding it as you would if you loved someone and you wanted that simple human contact as you spoke with them. I wanted to drag my fingers out of his grasp – I wanted to turn and run. Instead, I stayed where I was, unable to move an inch.

"He spoke the opening lines of the script – I don't know what it was; something banal like *It's ten to six; another ten minutes*. And I looked calmly up into that unearthly face and spoke my lines in reply.

"It was absolutely automatic. I was so full of terror that I couldn't have consciously recalled a word I was supposed to say, and yet out it all came, every phrase and gesture and nuance perfect. We spoke to each other and moved about the set as fluidly as if we had been clockwork figures travelling along their accustomed tracks. I was screaming inside, but outside I acted my part to perfection.

"At the end of that scene, Hugh had to kiss me, and as it progressed and the moment grew nearer, I felt as you might if you were lying on a train track, helplessly watching a locomotive approach. But I couldn't stop him, or myself. Part of me had turned to ice. He pulled me into an embrace and tilted my chin so that I had to look at him, at his eyes. They were large and dark and lustrous and dead, so dead. Every gesture he made was charmingly romantic and horrifyingly mechanical. Then his lips came down on mine, and oh God! I can't tell you what it was like. It was *wrong*. If you went to an abandoned graveyard and dug up a skull and pressed your lips to it, ran your tongue over its grinning teeth... It was like that. Hugh *looked* beautiful, but he was not *right*."

"Oh God," I say under my breath. Mary Arden doesn't react, lost in her own terrible story.

"I didn't hear Lillian shout 'Cut!' At the end of the scene, Hugh let me go," she says. Her voice is rimed with horror. "It took me a few moments to recover myself, to realise who I was again, and then I heard the sound of the door closing and he was gone. There was a waiting-room bench at the back of the set, and I went over and sank down onto it. I took off the big hat and put my head in my hands, digging my fingers into my carefully styled hair. I couldn't even cry; I was too shocked.

"I heard footsteps; Lillian had come over. She was as white as a sheet and there was a horrible, tremulous smile on her lips.

"'Brava,' she said. 'You were perfect.'

"I burst into tears. 'I can't do it again,' I said.

"'Yes, you can,' she said inexorably. She lit a cigarette and stood there looking at me. 'You're under contract,' she said. 'You can't get out of it. And why would you want to? A few hours of your life, that's all, and then I'll make you famous.'

"'What is he?' I said, and she said, 'He's Hugh Mason.'

"'He isn't. He isn't even *human*.' There were tears running down my face now, making streaks in the makeup.

"'Well, he's as much of Hugh as I can summon back,' she said. 'And only for as long as it takes to capture him on film.'

"'I won't do another day,' I said.

"'Yes, you will.'

"'You don't know what it's like.'

"'That may be, but I don't very much care. You'll do what you're contracted to do. I meant what I said. This will make a career for you. Don't be so ungrateful.'

"Then she turned on her heel and went off to talk to the camera operator about something, leaving a blue haze of smoke hanging on the air. I said to myself that I would not stand for this; that night I would wait until Lillian was asleep and let myself out of the house and go home. Even if I had to walk all night, I would go.

"It was no use, of course." She shakes her head. "Lillian locked me in my room that night. She didn't bother trying to conceal it. Immediately, I tried the windows and discovered

212

that those had been nailed shut. However much I tried, I couldn't prise the nails out. I looked for a nail file, for anything I could use to do it, and found Lillian had removed them all."

She sighs. "I looked at myself in the mirror and asked myself whether I could do anything to stop the filming. Could I cut off all my hair? No; there were no scissors, no knife, nothing in the room I could use. Perhaps I might have hurt myself somehow, scratched my face or something, but I strongly suspected that Lillian would simply make me stay until it healed up. In the end, there was nothing for it. I had to do what she said.

"The next day she took me back to the set again, and made sure that I was never left alone for a moment. I could have refused to act, I suppose, but I was afraid of Lillian as well as Hugh. I knew she would never let me off the hook as easily as that."

She looks at me. "You know they say that when the famous director Fritz Lang was making *M* he threw Peter Lorre downstairs to make him look suitably dishevelled? Lillian had that same kind of energy within her, and worse. I thought she'd have done *anything* to make me carry out my part. So I just had to get through it.

"The second day, when Hugh entered the set, I felt sick and faint before I even laid eyes on him. All the same, I went through my part flawlessly; the words and gestures seemed to come to me quite naturally. And I thanked God there was no bedroom scene; I couldn't have borne that. The original events had taken place during the Great War, of course, and Lillian hadn't given herself to him, though women sometimes did."

Mary Arden closes her eyes.

"And so it went on. Don't ask me how Lillian achieved what she did. I can't tell you. She told me many things about herself, but not that. It came at some personal cost, I do know that, because she was always pale and haggard, more as time went on. I don't know what she told the camera operator and the gaffer and all the rest of them either. Presumably she said it was an actor playing Hugh. They wouldn't have known otherwise, and perhaps they didn't have the same horrible dread of him that I did, because they never got that close; they didn't have to interact with him. They didn't have his arms around them, or his lips against theirs."

She pauses, and I have nothing to say. My rational mind tells me that this story cannot possibly be the literal truth, but if something like that happened to me, I don't think I could keep my sanity.

At last she goes on. "You may think there was some other explanation for this. That the original Hugh Mason hadn't really died, for example. Perhaps the story of her visit to the military hospital was all a lie, or it was a case of mistaken identity. Perhaps he really *was* injured, but not as badly as she had described. That wouldn't explain why she felt the need to make the film in 1930, of course. But anyway, I know none of those possibilities was true. This – thing – that appeared every day on set was genuinely the Hugh Mason of 1918. He looked no older than he had then, which of course he would have in real life, because this was 12 years later. But also I simply knew it.

"Towards the end of filming, it became clearer to me what he was. In one scene I had to look up at him, and for an instant I saw him, not in the peak of his male beauty, but as he was at the end: eyeless, noseless. Once, he put out a hand to touch me and there was only an empty sleeve. Sometimes the scent of gangrene would well up around him, thick and poisonous.

"How did I get through it? I can't tell you, after nearly ninety years. When you are young, you have a certain resilience, a certain belief in things that has not yet been shaken. Perhaps it was that. The whole experience was like an evil fever dream and I trusted that I would wake and forget it."

She smiles, but the smile is not for me, and there is no good humour in it. "Well, I did wake up, but I never forgot."

Chapter Forty-Three

There is silence between us for a while after Mary Arden has finished relating this extraordinary, horrible tale.

So this is Mary Arden's version of the *answer* that Lillian found. How will it fit into a book about the film? I don't know. How can it possibly be true? Even if it were, would anyone believe it? My book about a wildly intriguing film that was suppressed is rapidly turning into one about a paranormal experience that most people would consider utterly implausible. They'd think she'd played an elaborate practical joke on me – or else that I had given credence to her delusions. I grimace. And she has made me pay for every single instalment with the details of my own life.

I stick my chin out. "That's an astounding story, Miss Arden."

"It's not a story; it's the truth."

"There were rumours at the time that *The Simulacrum* contained shocking or obscene material, and that it was banned because of that," I point out.

Unperturbed, she nods. "Oh yes, there were rumours. Lillian put them about herself. She had to have a reason why she'd hired a studio and film crew and didn't produce something for general release at the end. And of course, she'd promised me she'd make my career. How better than to hint at my involvement in something too outrageous to be shown – especially at my tender age? People were falling over themselves to cast me: the young Jezebel of the silver screen."

"But it wasn't actually shocking at all," I say. "It sounds like a fairly banal biopic."

"People's real lives often sound banal," she remarks. "Every word of the script was based on real life; I thought I told you that?"

"Yes," I say. "But it wouldn't make for a dramatic story. Who would want to watch that?"

"That wasn't the point," says Mary Arden acerbically. "Everything had to be exactly as it happened, or as close as possible: every action, every word."

"But *why*?"

"Because Hugh's life, his *real* life, was over, and he could not do anything he hadn't already done." She waves a hand, dismissively. "Lillian could only summon him through the familiar, remember."

"Well, why..." I think about this, although I don't *want* to think about it, not as a logical sequence, because all of it sounds utterly batshit. "Why didn't Lillian play the role herself? Even if everything you say is true, why would she go to the trouble of making someone look exactly like she did, when she could have done it herself? People direct films and act in them too."

"Don't you think I asked her that? I *screamed* it at her. 'Do it yourself.'"

"What did she say?"

"She gave a sort of groan, and said, 'I can't.' And I said, 'Why not?' and she said something I didn't really understand, something along the lines of, *The heart that wishes must be the eyes that see.* That was all she'd say."

"And what does that mean?"

"I don't know exactly, though I've thought about it a lot. I think the eyes that see were hers, behind the camera. That she put something of herself into the film. Her soul, perhaps."

Her *soul*? I am fighting with the desire to put my head in my hands. There is a certain sort of weird logic to what Mary Arden is saying, but none of it can possibly be *true*.

"Okay," I say finally. "So she reproduced certain scenes from his life exactly as they happened – and you say this summoned him up. And Lillian filmed it. What for? What was the point? I mean, supposing this were true, it would just be going over old ground, wouldn't it? It wouldn't add anything. It wouldn't give her that life back."

Mary Arden shakes her head. "It would give her something new."

She leans forward, urgently; she is looking crazier by the minute. "The last time Hugh Mason walked off set, he vanished," she tells me. "That was on the last day of filming. He walked back to that door and went through it, and a moment later Lillian ran after him. He had already gone. She went through the doorway, and I heard her footsteps receding, but not his. Wherever he came from, he'd gone back there.

"Lillian came back onto the set with tears running down her face. I never thought I'd see that; she was so hard. But she did cry then, because he had gone. Then she wiped her eyes with the heel of her hand and said, 'It's a wrap.'

"I don't think she was even aware of me or anyone else at that moment. All she could think about was the film she had created. Hugh Mason would live again, and breathe again, whenever she wanted him to."

Mary Arden sits back, and looks at me.

"And now," she says, "It's your turn."

"What?" I say. "You must realise I can't use what you've just told me in my book. Summoning the dead? Publishers would laugh at me."

"Nevertheless," she says. "It's the truth." She snorts. "I don't care what you say in your book. Why should I care? I'm 104. I doubt I'll live to see it published. Tell them I'm completely insane if you like. Tell them I made the whole thing up. It's of no interest to me. Just tell me what I want to know, and you have my permission to print absolutely anything."

I think about this, and sigh.

"What do you want to know?"

"Tell me how Max died."

Silence.

218

"No," I say eventually.

She laughs, showing off her unfeasibly white false teeth. "I thought you would say that."

"Why did you even ask then, you old..." I stop myself, just in time.

"You can tell me tomorrow," she says airily.

"I'm not talking about it then, either." I reach for my phone to turn the audio recording off, and fumble it. It clatters back onto the table.

"I'll make it worth your while."

"What, with more of your fantastical stories about raising the dead? Forget it."

I'm on my feet now, gathering my things with shaking hands.

She says: "I've got the whole film."

I shake my head. "I don't believe you. This entire thing has been a waste of time. I can't believe I bore with you for so bloody long."

"I have got it. It's upstairs, in the cold store."

I pause. I have seen the cold store. I'd decided myself that she probably had the whole film in there. Now she's admitted it. But I am not going to talk to her about Max's death – not in a million years.

I'm halfway to the door when she says, "You can have the film. The whole thing. We can organise temperature-controlled transport and you can take the whole thing with you. It's yours."

I stop walking. Is it really possible she would do that? It wouldn't matter how unbelievable her story was, if I had an actual copy of the film.

She begins to speak rapidly, sensing that she has an opening, trying to talk me round before I decide to walk out again. "We don't have to talk here," she says. "There are too many people down here, at this time of day. The cook, the nurses changing shifts, and Harris of course. Anyone could be passing and might overhear the conversation. I understand that it must be deeply personal, that you wouldn't want anyone listening in... to satisfy their own prurient curiosity. You could come tomorrow evening, when only the night nurse is here, and Harris has gone to bed. Come to my own sitting room in the west wing. Anything you tell me, it will be completely private." She pauses. "Even supposing it weren't, who listens to the ramblings of an old woman? It might... help... to get it off your chest."

I look at her in silence.

"Think about it," she says. "You could come at – let's say eleven. Eleven tomorrow night. And the day after that, if you can organise the transport, you can go. What do you say?"

"I say you're a duplicitous old baggage," I tell her. "And don't forget I haven't even seen what's inside that one cannister you showed me. I might tell you all the most – the most traumatic things in my life, and you might give me a lot of cans full of rust."

"True, I suppose," she remarks, looking up at me. "And you might lie. Though I'll know if you do. I can always tell." She looks away, out of the window, as though the entire conversation has become unutterably boring. "Go and think about it," she says again. "We won't meet tomorrow afternoon. You can start looking into transport if you wish. And if you decide you want the film, come and see me at eleven."

I don't bother saying goodbye. I just walk out after that, closing the door behind me, and go up to my room. I drop my things onto the big pink satin bed and sink down onto the cover next to them. Then I stare up at the pearly Art Deco ceiling lights for a long time and try to decide what I am going to do.

I wish I could talk this over with someone.

Angus, I think. *If I could talk it over with Angus...*

I can't, though. I know that. I sigh, and roll over onto my side. Whatever happens, I'll be finished here within 48 hours. I can go. No more barbed conversations with Mary Arden. I won't see Richard again, because I'll have gone before he comes back. No more supercilious Harris. No more lunches and dinners alone, or walks in the decaying remains of the gardens. If my car isn't ready, I could ask Angus to come and get me. But will the film be staying here, or will it be coming with me?

After a bit, I sit up and pick up my phone. I text Angus:

Planning to leave here day after tomorrow. If my car's not fixed, would you give me a lift?

After a pause, I add:

I'm sorry about the other day. x

I tell myself I'd better put the phone down; there's no use hanging over it waiting for a reply. But one comes back, very quickly.

Don't be (sorry). Of course about the lift. Let me know.

Then I do put the phone down. I stand up, restless, and wander over to the escritoire where the box of books and papers is. The photograph of Hugh Mason is buried under most of the other papers, but I leaf through them until I've found it, and fish it out.

His handsome face stares up at me, telling me nothing. This was the face I saw in the night, and yet I am starting to doubt myself now – to doubt my own eyes. The fallout from Max's death, the broken nights, the afternoons spent sparring with the most poisonous old woman I've ever met... Is it possible these things conspired to make me hallucinate? That's what I'd think if someone else told me they had seen this man walking the corridors in the dark.

As for Mary Arden's story about the film...

I need to get away from Garthside, that much is very clear. I can no longer tell what is real and what is not real. If I stay here, I'll start believing every single thing Mary Arden tells me.

Chapter Forty-Four

That night I sleep through, undisturbed. The next morning I have breakfast alone, as usual, and then I get to work. I find Mrs Harris crossing the hallway with a big vase of purple irises.

"Mrs Harris," I say, with no preamble, "I'll be leaving tomorrow. What's the situation with my car?"

She sets down the vase on a console table and folds her hands.

"That is very fortuitous, Ms Garrick," she says. "The garage called me early this morning and said that your car will be ready tomorrow. May I say that we shall be very sorry to see you go? Your presence here has been quite the diversion. I haven't seen Miss Arden this animated in a very long time. I feel she has enjoyed your discussions very much."

"How lovely," I remark.

"Yes, it is," she says, apparently without irony. "Is there anything I can help you with? Would you like a hand with the packing?"

"No," I say hastily, and then: "Yes, actually there is. I may be taking some film cannisters with me tomorrow – with Miss Arden's agreement, of course. But I'll need to organise transport, temperature-controlled storage somewhere within travelling distance of my home, and insurance. Can you help with any of that?"

"All of it," she says smoothly. "I have done this a number of times before. I presume the film you are considering taking is *The Simulacrum*? Miss Arden has a number of other films of the same period, and she has occasionally sent them elsewhere for viewing or restoration work in the past. It's probably best you leave the entire thing to me – I'll ensure it's all done correctly, including the insurance." She pauses. "You say you may be taking them with you. Would you like me to book the transport, or shall I wait a little, until things are quite decided?"

I hesitate, and she adds, "Perhaps this afternoon?"

That decides me. "No, please do go ahead and book it." *I can always cancel it later*, I think to myself, traitorously.

"Very well, Ms Garrick. I'll book it for tomorrow, shall I?"

"Yes please."

After that, I go upstairs and start sorting through my things, stacking papers and folding shirts and cardigans. I wonder how Mrs Harris really feels about me leaving. I expect she'll be glad to see the back of me; it must be a nuisance planning in my daily interviews with Mary Arden, and having to haul her downstairs from the upper west wing each time. She's never really trusted me not to go into the west wing, either (with some justice, it has to be said). She'd be spitting feathers if she knew Mary Arden had invited me to go there tonight.

I finish with the clothes and go into the bathroom. I'll need some of these things – the toothbrush, for example – so I can't pack everything, but I can clear out the cupboards and put some things in my sponge bag. Anything to keep busy, really; anything to stop myself thinking about what I'm going to do. So I pack away an opened packet of ladies' razors and another one of interdental brushes and then I pick up something at the back of the shelf and find I'm holding that jar of face cream again. The one that isn't mine – it was here when I came.

I hold it in my hand, wondering what to do with it. Bin it? But it isn't mine and it's an expensive brand, by the look of it. So I simply put it back in the cupboard again.

So strange, I think. Someone has been here, and not all that long ago; it's a fairly recent product. But who knows? Perhaps Mrs Harris invites her friends to stay here, on the sly. If she *has* friends. I close the cupboard door.

*

At ten o'clock I am still not decided. I want that film – I know that. And I *could* lie to Mary Arden and hope she doesn't realise. Or tell her the truth.

I think about that. It might exorcise the great weight that lies over me, all the time – a weight I can't offload onto anyone else. She's 104, after all. If she decides she isn't keeping my private business to herself, what then? She can only talk about me to a handful of staff, who probably don't pay attention to a word she says anyway. I tell myself this, as I pace up and down my pink bedroom, rubbing my hands together. The minutes tick past.

At half past ten I say to myself that I am definitely not talking to her tonight. She's a prurient old ratbag poking her nose into my life out of sheer malice. I'll abandon the whole project if I have to; she hasn't told me anything I can put into print anyway. As for the film itself, she might not even have the whole thing, she might be lying, or it might have disintegrated by now, even in controlled storage. I might lay my soul bare for absolutely nothing.

Yes.

No.

Yes.

At one minute to eleven, I open the door of my room and look out into the corridor. No one is about and the lamps are all out; the only light on this side of the double doors comes from the room behind me.

I step outside. I am fully dressed, except I have taken off my shoes, so that I can move as silently as possible. Clumping down the corridor would be a sure-fire way of drawing attention to myself, if anyone else is up – Mrs Harris, for example. I know she's supposed to have turned in by now, but I don't trust her not to pop up with a suspicious expression.

I go down the corridor and carefully push open one of the double doors, so that I can peer through. There is no flickering blue light at the far end, but it's not completely dark tonight; someone has plugged in several night lights, providing a little illumination. Guiding the way. It's a relief; I can see at a glance that the corridor is deserted. I slip through the door and let it swing closed behind me. Then I straighten my back, and begin to walk to the other end, where Mary Arden's sitting room must be. If anyone sees me now, I had better look confident, as though I have a right to be here. Mary Arden has invited me, after all.

I pass Richard's room and the library and, shortly before I get to the end, the door to the temperature-controlled store room. My heart is thudding. Am I really going through with this? I think about the film. *Yes*, I say to myself.

I turn the corner, and hesitate. I've seen that bluish light emanating from here before, but tonight it isn't there. Presumably Mary Arden isn't watching her flat screen TV. I hope she's waiting for me in the sitting room, as she said she would. But where is that?

Ahead of me, a door stands open, and I can just glimpse bedroom furniture, that and walls done out in powder blue. There is a dressing table with a shell-shaped mirror, meant to reflect back some 1930s beauty à la Jean Harlow, someone in a satin dress, with Marcel waved hair and red lipstick; instead, it reflects rows of medicines: boxes, bottles, blister packs. The paraphernalia of very old age. That is clearly not a sitting room. Nor is the door marked *Screen*. That one's a surprise. Perhaps it isn't her TV whose light I've seen; I guess she has an actual home cinema in there. Well, she's fabulously rich; why not?

I guess I haven't been as quiet as I thought I was, because suddenly Mary Arden's voice cuts through the silence.

"Theda Garrick? Is that you?"

I pause. "Yes."

"Come in here," she says. Following her voice, I open a

door, and there she is, enthroned in a large high-backed chair. I'm used to seeing her in a succession of expensive designer outfits, but now she is resplendent in an extraordinary ankle length peach negligée and matching bed jacket trimmed with marabou. Her feet are encased in little slippers with the same fluffy trim. She is still fully made up, and has diamond earrings in. It is an ensemble entirely impractical for sleeping and I can't help staring.

"Come," says Mary Arden, impatiently, and I step inside. The room is large for a sitting room, and like the rest of the house it is decked out in 1930s Art Deco style. Everything is in shades of dark green and peach, like the negligée, which taken altogether gives rather an overpowering effect. As well as the armchair, I notice several sofas and a folding Japanese screen decorated with cranes and pine trees. It is quite a large screen, concealing the corner of the room.

I look at that screen for a moment. This is no time for niceties. I go over and look behind it. There is nothing there, simply a bare expanse of carpet and a plug socket.

Behind me, Mary Arden cackles. "Not very trusting, are you?" she says.

"No," I say shortly. I go over and perch on the edge of one of the sofas, close to her, where the scent of Chanel No. 5 is distinctly detectable.

"You needn't worry," she says. "We're quite alone. The night nurse is in her own room; she never comes unless I ring for her. So," she adds, "do you want the film?"

I hesitate, and then I nod.

"Speak up."

"Yes, I want the film."

"Then tell me," she says. "How did Max die?"

Chapter Forty-Five

"He fell," I say.

I twist my hands together in my lap.

"We were having some renovations done. The house was quite old – I told you that. Very pretty, very private, but quite old, so we had to get various bits of work done, and one of them was the windows in one of the upstairs bedrooms. The window looked out over a sunken paved area with potted shrubs and then lawn; it was a gorgeous view, so Max said we'd have a little balcony.

"The men took the old window out and they were going to come back the next day to start work on the balcony. They put some planks across the gap, so that there was no danger of anyone falling out by accident. It wasn't anyone's room. We thought about moving in later, once the balcony was in, but..."

My voice trails off. It never happened. We never moved into that room, because Max was dead.

It's no use faltering, though; Mary Arden will never let me off the hook. I squeeze my hands together and go on.

"I was downstairs when it happened. They don't know exactly *why* Max fell. They think maybe he didn't realise that the boards weren't meant to be leant on; they were there to warn you not to fall out. He fell straight into the sunken area, onto the paving stones, and broke his neck. There was nothing the ambulance men could do. He was dead before they got there. Simon – that's my brother-in-law – wanted to sue the company after. But it wouldn't have brought Max back."

While I have been speaking, Mary Arden has been sitting with her head thrown back and her eyes closed, as though she wants to drink in every last drop of my misery. But as I stop speaking, she opens her eyes, looks at me and says:

227

"Poppycock."

I gape at her.

"What?"

"Poppycock. Pure and simple," she says. "*I was downstairs when it happened*," she says, mimicking my voice. "*They don't know exactly why Max fell.*" She snorts. "I've never heard such a concoction in my life."

"Con–"

"Lies," she says. "All lies." She leans forward. "Tell me the truth. The truth, and you can have the film."

In the face of my dumbfounded silence she decides to try sugar instead of vinegar. Her voice drops into a soft, wheedling tone.

"You want the film, don't you, Theda Garrick? There's so little left in your life. Love went sour, but not before it had driven all your friends away. Poor Theda, all alone. If you take the film with you, at least you'll have something in your life, something that will make a name for you." She chuckles softly. "Fame is a cold thing, Theda Garrick, but it's very much better than nothing. And you don't want *nothing*, do you? You don't want to drive away from here with nothing to show for it, not after you've told me so much already. What a waste that would be! All that pain, for no reward. No, you don't want that."

She waits to see what effect her words have had.

"Tell me," she says, coaxingly. "Wouldn't it be good to get it all off your chest? It must be a terrible burden. And whom better to tell, than a one-hundred-and-four-year-old woman, who will soon be dead anyway? Whom nobody would believe if she tried to pass it on, because it would simply be the ramblings of someone too old to remember what day of the week it is?

"I know you loathe me, Theda. You think I'm cold and brutally insensitive and full of malice, and all of that is quite probably true. But all of that makes me the right person to tell. Would you really want to spill the beans to someone you *love*? What about that young man who towed your car out of the ford?" She shakes her head. "Oh yes, I know all about that. Very gallant. How do you think he'd react if you told him how your husband died?

"No," she says. "Better to tell me. You have to tell *someone*, if you're ever going to put it behind you. And I shall be dead soon.

"Tell me, Theda. Tell me the truth."

I stare at her, at this monster, this vampire, swaddled in peach chiffon and marabou, her ancient eyes glittering. She's right: I do loathe her. I hate her with a passion. The word *bitch* doesn't come close to describing what she is. But...

It would be a relief to loosen the hideous knot that has been inside me all these months, and tell someone what really happened. And she's right, I couldn't tell anyone else – certainly not Celia or Simon, not any of my friends (assuming I still have friends) and not Angus. No, not Angus.

So I look at Mary Arden and say, "Alright."

"It's true about the balcony," I say. "We really were having that installed, in one of the bedrooms, and the workman did fix planks across the gap to stop anyone falling out. There was a plastic sheet, too, in case it rained during the night. Max and I were the only ones in the house, so it wasn't risky. A – a child might have fallen out, but not two adults who knew it was a window. The workmen weren't really to blame, whatever Simon said.

"After I lost the baby, I kind of stopped caring about things." I look down, at my hands. "I didn't even care much about what Max did. You'll probably have worked out from what I've already told you, that he liked to be in control of everything. When we went out, like the night we got engaged, he told me what to wear. If I didn't comply, like with my mother's necklace on our wedding day, he got angry. And he didn't like any of my friends, so I stopped seeing them. I guess you'll say, *why didn't I get out?* But it's like that thing about the frog in the slowly boiling water. It gets hotter and hotter without you realising it, and when you do, it's too late. You've been scalded to death. Suddenly, there I was, in a house in the middle of the countryside, with no job and no friends. No one to confide in, and nowhere to go.

"The fall downstairs, I couldn't remember that very well afterwards. I guess a psychologist would say I didn't *want* to remember. But even knowing that, I couldn't make it all come back clearly. I thought I could remember Max shouting at me, but everything was hazy. Not being quite sure, that made it worse. Maybe I could have said something to someone – the doctor, perhaps, or I could have gone to the police. But I couldn't tell them anything that wasn't vague. Ifs or maybes. The same with Celia and Simon. What could I have said to them? 'I think Max pushed me downstairs'? Unless I could prove it, there would have been anger and disbelief and at the end of all of it, I'd have had to go home with Max again."

I shudder. "He was all sympathy at first, or so it seemed. *Poor Theda, never mind darling, we'll have another baby, when the time is right.* All that. But something had just snapped for me. I just shrank back into myself, into a place where Max couldn't go. I didn't care what he did, or what he said. I complied because it was easier and safer, but part of me went somewhere Max couldn't get at it. And he didn't like that.

"At first, it wasn't too bad. Maybe he'd frightened himself with what he'd done. If I'd been able to remember the fall downstairs, he might have been in serious trouble. It was just luck for him that I couldn't. But the sympathy started to run out pretty quickly. He started to get irritable, to complain that I was too apathetic, I wasn't *trying*. I wasn't *fucking trying*. It was shit for him too – he'd lost a baby as well – and I ought to have been able to put a braver face on it than that. He would work himself up, getting angrier and angrier until he didn't look handsome anymore; he looked like a devil. He would rant, and shout, and then eventually he'd run to the end of his energy and be syrupy-sweet, all *poor little Theda* again because he didn't quite dare touch me again after the fall, not yet. Someone would have smelled a rat. It was like living in an atmosphere of tropical storms, you never knew when a squall would break over your head.

"That wasn't the only thing. He said we ought to try again – for a baby. That was crazy – you're supposed to wait a few months at least, if you've lost one, and anyway, the whole row had happened before because he didn't want one now. It was just some perverse thing in him, or some need to control everything.

"I told him I didn't want to try. I wasn't ready. In fact, I didn't even want him touching me, though I didn't dare say that. But..."

My voice falters.

"He went ahead anyway."

I shake my head.

"The day Max died, he was supposedly working from home. He was in a vile mood. First thing in the morning he'd insisted we 'try' and then he was furious because he said he might as well have been..." I swallow. "...fucking a block of wood. And then he had some problem to do with work, they'd lost a client or something. It was like a storm front was coming over; the house was throbbing with his anger. I went upstairs, very quietly, hoping to stay out of his way.

"I could hear a flapping noise coming from the spare bedroom when I was passing it, and I guessed that the plastic sheeting the men had attached over the window had come loose. So I went in, to see whether I could fix it before Max saw it and started ranting about that too.

"I was right; the sheeting had come away at the bottom of the window. There was a breeze, and the wind was making it snap like a flag. I went over to see what I could do.

"I stood in the window, and reached for the end of the sheeting. It was just out of my grasp. I tried a couple of times to grab it and couldn't get it. So I leaned on the planks very slightly, not enough to put my whole weight on them, obviously, but I heard them give a little creak which made me step back very quickly.

"At that moment something – I don't know what it was, a sort of sixth sense – made me glance behind me. There was Max. He'd come into the room completely silently and he was just standing there. There was the most peculiar look on his face – it unnerved me. It was sort of sly, as though he were nursing some horrible secret.

"He said, 'You were going to jump, Theda.'

"'No, I wasn't,' I said, and my heart began to beat very fast. He'd said it with such conviction that for a moment I almost thought perhaps I *had* been going to. The creak the wood had made, and the drop to the sunken garden below, were suddenly very large in my mind. I tried to step away from the window, but Max was in the way.

"'Nobody would blame you,' he said. 'Nobody would be surprised. It was so tragic that you lost the baby, Theda. I think it sent you out of your mind.'

"'Max,' I said, in a pleading tone.

"He shook his head. 'You might as well do it, you know. Nobody wants you, nobody loves you. I don't love you. You're so dull and depressing to be around.'

"He put out a hand and gripped the topmost plank. 'Look, it isn't strong. It would break if you put any weight on it. One instant and that sad little life of yours would be over. You don't need to hurt anyone else. Nobody would even have to know it wasn't an accident.'

"He looked at me, and his gaze was almost hypnotic. 'Jump, Theda.'

"My throat was dry. I couldn't even force out the word *No*. Instead I shook my head, slowly. I knew where this was going. If I didn't jump, he'd push me out. I could see it in his eyes.

"My chances of fighting him off were not good. He was taller than me, heavier, and determined. All the same, I wasn't going to agree with him. I wasn't going to do it. If I fell from the window, it would be because he had pushed me, not because I had jumped. I kept shaking my head, even as I could see the colour creeping up his face – I could see his anger rising and rising.

"'Stupid, Theda,' he said, and lunged for me.

"I did the only thing I could think of. I dropped to the floor. Grappling with him would have been useless; down there I was harder to move. The lunge took him over my head and he grabbed the top plank again. It made a splintering sound, but it didn't break.

"In the instant he was off balance, I scrambled out from under his feet. My heart was thumping; my whole body seemed to be thrumming with electricity. I was on my feet in an instant. Max turned to face me, his features distorted with fury. And I..."

I make a choking sound in my throat.

"I pushed him. The planks broke and he fell. He had a shocked look on his face. I nearly fell out with him, but I grabbed one of the plastic sheets, and by some miracle it held, though for one sickening moment I thought it wouldn't. Max didn't even have time to yell. He hit the paving stones below with the most hideous sound, like a sack bursting open.

"Apparently some people have fallen from that height and survived. Max didn't. When I had steadied myself, I looked down, and I could see at once that he was dead. There was blood on the stones, a lot of it, and other stuff.

"I stood in the window, framed by the ragged ends of

233

the broken planks, and looked down at my dead husband's brains."

I lean forward, putting my head in my hands.

"I killed him," I say.

"What's that?" snaps Mary Arden. "Speak up."

She really is a bitch. I straighten up, put my hands down. I look her in the eyes, not crying now. Calm. The thing is out at last.

I say, "I killed Max."

Chapter Forty-Six

"Thank you, Theda," says Mary Arden crisply, as though I have done her a favour.

I stare at her, nonplussed.

And then she turns her head, away from me, and says in a loud voice, "Harris."

My heart seems to stop. Time has slowed to a crawl as I follow her gaze and see the person who is stepping from her hiding place behind the floor length curtains – the place I didn't think to look. Mrs Harris.

"Good evening, Ms Garrick," she says, politely. Then she turns to Mary Arden and holds up a mobile phone. "All done," she says crisply. "Judging by the tests beforehand, it should be a very clear recording."

"Oh God." I stare from her to Mary Arden, my eyes wide with horror.

"Don't be distressed," says Mrs Harris. "It sounds as if it was thoroughly deserved. I can't say I wouldn't have done the same myself in your position."

I don't know whether to cry or scream. All this time, I've kept my secret bottled up. And now I've told it to *two* people, one of whom has *recorded* it.

I feel suddenly weak. If I were on my feet I'd pass out. This is – this is–

"I think Ms Garrick is going to faint," says Mrs Harris. "Shall I fetch the brandy, Miss Arden?"

Mary Arden gives a grunt of disapproval. "Brandy indeed! The things *I've* seen without passing out. You might try slapping her."

"Don't," I say. I lean forward, trying to get the blood to my head, fighting down nausea.

I've told two of them. If I'd just told Mary Arden, it

would've been my word against hers, the ramblings of a hundred-and-four-year-old woman. But now...

Eventually I feel well enough to glance up. They are both looking at me, Mary Arden with bored disdain and Mrs Harris with a sort of polite sympathy which is somehow worse. I want to cry, but the time for crying is past. It's all over. I should have known there would be no escape. Max has won, like he always wins.

"Please," I say to them. "Can I have a little time? Just a little time?"

"For what?" says Mary Arden tartly.

"Until you call the police."

They glance at each other.

"Ms Garrick – Theda," says Mrs Harris, "We aren't going to call the police."

"You're not?"

"Well, I very much hope not."

"But..." I feel I'm missing something fundamental here. "Why did you record me?"

Mrs Harris glances at the phone. "Miss Arden felt we should have an insurance policy."

"An insurance...?" I shake my head. "I don't understand. What's going on?"

Mrs Harris looks at Mary Arden, who waves one of her skinny claws at her. *Proceed*, it says.

"Miss Arden has something she'd like you to do. The recording is just... a little encouragement to say yes. That's all."

Mary Arden has something she'd like you to do. She makes it sound so harmless, as though Mary Arden wants me to climb onto a chair and get something down from a high shelf. But nobody goes to the kind of trouble they've gone to, to get someone to do something harmless. All the afternoons I've sat downstairs with her, while she doled out little bits of her past and gradually, gradually wheedled my secret out of me. Whatever she wants me to do, it's going to be unpleasant. But if I say no...

I'm aware of them both watching me, waiting to see how I am going to react. I put off asking them what it is they want me to do. I know already that I'm not going to like it. Instead, I say: "Why me? Why did you bring me all the way here from the south of England to do *this*?"

"Because you're perfect," says Mary Arden. "You have a real appreciation of classic film. Not everyone has that. The enthusiasm you've displayed for *The Simulacrum* has been absolutely... touching."

That makes me want to snort. I don't believe Mary Arden knows the meaning of the word *touching*. But I say nothing.

"And," she says, "You don't have anything to go back to, do you? I meant what I said when I told you there wasn't a Theda-shaped hole in anyone's life. No husband, no job, no friends. There's the matter of that lovely old house in the country, of course, but houses are easily sold, and besides, I can't imagine you wanting to live there long term." She smiles unpleasantly. "Every time you walked past that sunken garden you'd remember your husband's brains spread all over it."

"Shut up," I say in a low voice.

"And finally," she adds, undeterred, "there is the matter of leverage. It's unfortunate we have to have that, but the stakes are too high, you know. If you fail to do what I ask, and do it properly, Harris will take the recording to the police." She studies her fingernails. "Of course, you could take your chances with that. Battered wife, abusive husband. You might get off with manslaughter, or self-defence. But we only have your word for it that the abuse took place. Max can't defend himself, can he?"

"No," I say. It's not as though any of this is news to me. I've gone over it in my head a thousand times.

My voice is steadier now. "How did you know? About

Max, I mean? You must have known, to go to all the effort of trying to get me to confess."

"I didn't know," says Mary Arden. "Not for certain. I got Harris to research you, and I thought there was a good chance." She considers. "To be quite frank, you weren't the first. I've tried before – you can't imagine that I *haven't*. It would be madness to leave something like this until I was 104 years old. But nobody else had quite the... leverage you do."

My mind skips to the pot of face cream I found forgotten at the back of the bathroom cabinet.

"You had *other* people here? You told them all the same things you told me?"

I can't imagine for a second that there wouldn't be books about it if she had.

She nods.

"And they didn't write about them?" I stare at her levelly. "What happened with those people?"

She meets my gaze. "Well, I suppose they must have agreed not to write anything, and just driven away. I'm sure that's what happened, aren't you?"

This seems highly improbable. A scoop like finding an entire copy of *The Simulacrum* in cold storage – something would have come out. I have a bad feeling about what became of those other people. But whatever Mary Arden and Mrs Harris have on me, I have nothing on them.

I shake back my hair. "So," I say heavily. "What do you want me to do?"

"I should have thought that was perfectly obvious," says Mary Arden. "I want you to look after *The Simulacrum*."

Chapter Forty-Seven

I stare at Mary Arden, dumbfounded.

Look after *The Simulacrum*? I'd give my hind legs to get my hands on that film. Why would they have gone to all the trouble of getting the dirt on me, just for that?

No, I think. *It can't just be that. There's something else going on here.*

I glance from Mary Arden to Mrs Harris and back again. Mary Arden sees me do it – confusion must be written all over my face. She smiles, and the smile is not pleasant.

"Harris," she says.

"Yes, Miss Arden?"

"Go and do whatever it is you have to do to that recording to make it safe."

"Upload it to Dropbox–"

"Don't blind me with jargon. Just go and do it."

"Yes, Miss Arden."

Mrs Harris gives me a bland smile on her way out – as though I haven't just wrenched out the secret that has been eating at the heart of me like a worm in an apple, and handed it to her.

The door closes behind her, and Mary Arden turns to me.

"Cheer up, Theda Garrick," she says. "I am a very rich woman, and you will be, too. I'll leave you everything you need to preserve and show the film after I've gone, which Lord knows, cannot be long now.

"I can see you are wondering why Harris and I bothered with the entire charade – encouraging you to confess what you did to the late, unlamented Max. Why didn't I just offer you the film, the money, the house?"

She raises her eyebrows. "The fact of the matter is, most young women of your age are not prepared to live on a remote estate in rural Scotland, regardless of what is on offer. I know this because I made the same offer to some of the previous... applicants, shall we call them? No; they wanted to get back to their lives in the city, where there are wine bars and boutique dress shops and I don't know what else–" She waves her hand. "Men, I suppose. There won't be any possibility of that; this is strictly a position for one person.

"That person has to be young too. An older person might agree to do it; comfort and security in later life is a wonderful thing, you know. But then in ten years' time, or twenty, there would be the same issue: who will look after the film? It's taken me so long to find you; I should not like to think of the same problem recurring so soon."

"So what you are suggesting..." I begin slowly.

"Is that you live here, at Garthside House, and enjoy the beautiful surroundings and the peace and quiet and my not inconsiderable fortune. In exchange for which, you will become *The Simulacrum*'s guardian for the rest of your life, and you will exert yourself as far as possible to find someone else to succeed you."

"But..." I shake my head. "When my book comes out–"

"There will be no book. There was never going to be a book, Theda; you must see that now? Nor are you going to take the film outside the estate, or show it to anyone else."

"You want me – you want me to literally just *look after* the film? And not publish *anything*?" I can't believe my ears.

She nods. "That is correct. And show the film, of course."

"To whom?"

"To nobody. Well, to yourself, that is all. Harris will show you how to handle it, and how to run the film. Once an evening is sufficient."

"Once an evening?" I stare at her.

"Yes."

"It's a *copy* of the film, then? Because to show it every

night, film stock from 1930... I mean, I wouldn't think that's even possible..."

She shrugs, a motion that might mean anything. "This film is... singular," she says. "You'll see."

I open my mouth to ask something else, but it seems that topic is closed; she breezes on without giving me time to speak.

"Apart from the showings, the rest of the time is yours, to use as you please," she informs me. "Rewrite that Gothic novel of yours, if you like. You'll have plenty of spare time, after all."

I put my head in my hands. "I don't understand. I don't see the point of this."

"You will, very shortly," she says. "And Theda, naturally I would prefer that this goes forward on a friendly basis, but if you should fail to agree, or if you try to abscond after I have died, or you do not show the film... Harris will take the recording to the police. Well, the last part of the recording. The bit where you confess to killing Max."

I put my head up. "What about Richard?" I say. "Couldn't you have asked him to do this? He's your own family, after all. He's *expecting* to inherit the house."

"I don't trust him," says Mary Arden. "He's a very accommodating relative while I'm alive and as rich as Croesus. After I'm dead, he'd simply sell Garthside and pocket the proceeds."

I can't argue with that. I've heard him say as much.

"Can I think about this?" I ask. "Can I have twenty four hours?"

Before the last words are out, she is shaking her head. "There really is no point, Theda. What is the choice, after all? Probable prison, or a comfortable if rather quiet life here. We both know which one you will choose. Besides, there are things we need to be getting on with. Selling your house, for example."

"Selling my *house*?"

"Well, of course," she says, impatiently. "It's no use to you if you're going to live here."

I see a chance in this to get away, just for a short while, just to get some advice about what the hell I am going to do. Legal advice, perhaps. Are lawyers bound by confidentiality, like priests? I don't know. I've never thought of confessing to anyone before today. Another thing to check out, if I can only get away...

"There are things I want in the house," I say, boldly. "I can't just sell it from here."

"Oh yes you can," is the riposte. "You can send someone in to collect the things you want, and have them delivered here. Cost is not a problem; we have more than enough money, you and I."

We. She's already talking about *we*. In her own mind, it's a done deal; I am caught, like a fly wound round with spider's silk. For me, it's more like a sensation of impending doom – I cannot believe that the jaws of the trap have already closed around me. There must be some way out of this. If I can just have some time to think–

A quiet knock on the door, and here is Mrs Harris again.

"It's done, Miss Arden."

"Good," says the old wretch. "Now you can go and get my wheelchair from my bedroom. And then we'll go through."

"Go through where?" I say.

"To the screening room," she says. There's a pause, and then she adds, "You want to see it, don't you? You've gone to so much trouble over it, after all – *The Simulacrum*."

Chapter Forty-Eight

Isn't there some saying about being careful what you wish for? I think about this as I watch Mrs Harris helping Mary Arden into her wheelchair, handling her as if she were Meissen china and not a malevolent old bundle of sticks wrapped up in peach chiffon.

In a few minutes I'm going to get a private screening of *The Simulacrum*, the entire film – something cinematologists would kill for. Something I was desperate for, myself. It was an obsession, a way of giving purpose to my life, a straw to grab at. A way not to think about the fact that *I killed Max*. Now I'm going to get what I was after, but it feels empty. None of this even feels real.

I think about Mrs Harris uploading my confession to some untraceable inbox. If I had kept my mouth shut – lied – anything–

If I had given up, the night I drove into the ford.

If I had chosen some other obsession, never come here at all.

But I can't go back, and right now I can't see any way out. I watch Mrs Harris with dull eyes, and then I follow her as she pushes Mary Arden to the door.

"Would you?" she says to me, nodding at the door, and I open it for them. I notice a new tone to her voice. I'm staff now, and can be ordered about. I hold the door until they are both through and then I shut it and follow them down the hall.

In other circumstances, I would be intrigued to enter the room marked *Screening*. It's just as expensively equipped as you'd expect. It's painted dark charcoal grey with wall-mounted sconces in the Art Deco style, in keeping with the rest of Garthside House. There are two matching padded chairs upholstered in blue velvet, with arm rests, facing a screen which takes up most of the far wall and runs right down to the floor. It is flanked with heavy curtains in the same blue velvet, which add to the old-fashioned look.

Mrs Harris positions Mary Arden next to the padded chairs and indicates that I should sit next to her. She fusses about her employer for a while, making sure that she is completely comfortable. Once, she shoots me a look, but I cannot read her expression.

"That's enough, Harris," says Mary Arden. "These old bones won't be comfortable whatever you do."

"Yes, Miss Arden."

Mrs Harris takes herself off to the back of the room and looking over my shoulder, I see her disappear through a door that is the same colour as the wall. I suppose she is going to the projection room.

Then I look at Mary Arden, nestling amongst her marabou feathers. "Don't look at me, look at the screen," she says out of the corner of her mouth.

So I settle back in my padded chair and put my hands on the arm rests. The lights in the wall sconces slowly dim until we are sitting in darkness. I gaze into it, the formlessness adding to the overwhelming sense of unreality. If it were not for the feeling of the blue velvet under my fingers, I would think I was dreaming.

A little time passes, and then Mrs Harris has done whatever she needs to do in the projection booth and light streams out, illuminating the screen. A second after that, the film begins.

There are no titles, no studio logo, no preamble. A flicker, and we are looking at an interior. I see a window frame, a bench, posters. One of them reads *Your chums are fighting – why aren't YOU?*

A waiting room, I think.

The film is shot in black and white, but there is a strange lurid blue tint to it. I think about the blue light I saw coming from Mary Arden's quarters at night – the same light I saw in the window high up in the west wing, the night I came to Garthside. This is what she was watching, not a programme on a flat screen TV.

A moment later, she appears onscreen: the fifteen-year-old Mary Arden, in the bloom of a youth that withered and died over the many years between then and now. She wears a large hat and a suit that comes down almost to her ankles, a dated look even in 1930, but somehow she carries it; you can see a hint of the quality that made her such a huge star later on. The camera lingers on her: her hair and makeup have been done very carefully so that she really does resemble the photographs I have seen of Lillian Velderkaust.

In spite of myself, I sit forward, fascinated. These are someone's memories after all, brought vividly to life.

Young Mary's chin comes up; she is reacting to something. The camera begins to pan away from her, towards whatever she is looking at.

Now, I think, *I shall finally see the truth of it*. It will be an actor made up to look like Hugh Mason, for certain – what else can it be?

I see him. A man in an old-fashioned woollen uniform, his lower legs encased in boots, his cap under his arm. He walks towards the camera, his free arm swinging, and as he does so his face comes into sharp focus. It is a handsome face – beautiful, even. Dark-eyed, expressive, with high cheekbones and a perfect mouth. He looks straight into the camera; I could swear he is looking at *us*.

A prickle of unease. How did Lillian do this? It's uncanny. He looks exactly – *exactly* – like...

"Hugh," breathes Mary Arden beside me.

I wait for him to speak the first lines, to say *It's ten to six; another ten minutes.*

Instead, he says: "Good evening, Mary."

My fingers clutch the blue velvet armrests. My eyes widen; my heart accelerates. I draw in a shuddering breath, like a person on the brink of a terrifying leap.

This is simply *not possible*.

I close my eyes; open them again. From the screen, Hugh Mason is looking right at me. When I put a hand to my throat, fighting for the breath that seems to have been sucked right out of my lungs, those great dark eyes unmistakably follow the movement. I flounder, suffocating, my thoughts wheeling like panicked birds.

I love films – I have seen every type of special effect from Georges Méliès onwards – and I *know* this is not faked.

This is real.

It *cannot* be real.

My mouth opens and closes but no words come out.

There is a rustle of peach chiffon as Mary Arden reaches out, and one bejewelled claw lands on my hand, patting it.

"Hugh," I hear her say, "This is Theda Garrick."

Then I hear my own name in Hugh's mouth and I know I have passed some kind of frontier, slipped over the edge into the abyss of complete insanity.

No, I think. *No, no*. Tears of fright leak from the corners of my eyes. I drag my hand out of Mary Arden's grasp and try to cover my face, pressing myself back into my seat. I can't shut the blue light out. It seeps through my fingers and even when I squeeze my eyes tight shut it throbs behind my eyelids. I take my hands away, open my eyes against the glare, because not seeing is worse than seeing.

The blue light pulses, pumping out its brilliance in waves that drench me and Mary Arden, that turn our skin and her white hair and peach chiffon grey, so that we too might have been filmed in monochrome.

"Come," says Mary Arden. She gestures, and in the strobing light her movements are staccato, movements from an old film that jumps and flickers. "Come, Hugh," she says.

And Hugh Mason walks out of the film, into the room.

Chapter Forty-Nine

I watch Hugh Mason walk towards us, and behind him on the screen the young Mary Arden, the Lillian Velderkaust character, continues her role as though nothing has happened, as though he is still there. Her voice quietly rises and falls, speaking her lines.

I look at Hugh, I stare at him until it feels as though my eyes must burst from their sockets. This is the man I saw in the corridor, the man I had almost convinced myself was a hallucination – the result of too much obsessive thinking about Hugh Mason and Lillian Velderkaust. But I saw where he came from with my own eyes. He walked right out of that film.

I shrink back in my blue velvet seat. There is something hideously unnatural about him, and not just about his presence in the room with us, impossible though it is. My eyes cannot pick out what is wrong but my lizard brain can sense it. His smooth flawless beauty is a shell, a membrane stretched over something unspeakable. If he touches me I think I will go out of my mind. I remember the night my unseen visitor touched the pillow where my head had been, and I think I may actually vomit.

Mary Arden has no such fear – not anymore. She stretches out her gnarled hands towards him and he approaches, holding out his own hands to take hers. I can see the texture of his woollen uniform, the gleam of the buckles on his boots, each strand of carefully-clipped dark hair. His very *eyelashes*. His hands are like the rest of him: well-shaped, smooth-skinned, and somehow subtly horrible. But Mary Arden takes them without a moment's hesitation and brings them to her lips, kissing them with abandon; I see her tongue appear briefly and wetly before I look away, horrified.

"Soon," she says to him. "Soon, Hugh."

When she lets go of his hands he touches her cheek, her hair, a gesture that should radiate tenderness but which somehow strikes me as staged, as artificial as everything else about Hugh Mason. She closes her eyes for a moment, luxuriating in it. Then she opens them again, and shakes her head.

"Not long tonight," she says. "I simply wanted you to meet Theda, my dear, and she you. Theda has agreed to care for us. To become the new guardian."

Hugh half-turns and looks at me, and I cringe under the gaze of those dead eyes. Large, dark and limpid as they are, they are like holes punched into that perfect mask of a face. I see nothing human stirring in there. It is like gazing into the rancid depths of a well, the walls slimed and stinking.

He makes me a slight bow, sketching empty civility on the air between us.

I can say nothing, do nothing. *Don't touch me. Please, please, don't touch me.*

Beside me, Mary Arden sighs heavily. "Always too short a time," she says. "Enough for now. I see dear Theda is in no state to continue. Tomorrow will be longer. I promise, Hugh."

She raises one skinny claw, signing to Mrs Harris. The ghastly blue radiance slowly dies, running down as the film slows to a stop. Hugh steps back, and back, and with each step he becomes less substantial. I realise I can see the screen through him. Then he is gone. A moment of darkness, and then the lights in the sconces come on.

I shut my eyes, not wanting to see Mary Arden's avid old face, nor Mrs Harris's impassive one, nor the blue-and-charcoal room. I try to control my breathing, my hands curled into fists. I try to tell myself that this is all some grisly, horrible nightmare. I am hallucinating. I have lost my mind. I'm sick.

After a while, someone touches my arm gently and says my name. I open my eyes and find that Mrs Harris is standing over me, holding out a glass. I take it with both hands, like a child, and drink. Like a cliché, it's genuinely brandy. It makes a fiery trail down my throat.

"Don't wolf it," says Mary Arden in a bored voice. "That's a good Cognac."

I drain the glass, shivering. "I want to go home," I say plaintively. I don't understand what I have just seen. I simply want to get away, even if I have to walk out of here with just the clothes I am standing up in.

"Ridiculous girl," says Mary Arden. "Garthside is your home now. You can't *leave*."

I shake my head, hugging myself. "I can't do... whatever you want me to do. I just can't."

She laughs grimly. "Yes, you can. You're in shock at the moment. You'll get used to the idea."

"I can't. I can't have that... *thing* near me."

"His name is Hugh," says Mary Arden sharply. She looks at Mrs Harris. "Harris, fetch my cigarettes."

"I can do, Miss Arden, but you know the doctor said–"

"I don't care what the doctor said. I'm a hundred and four; not smoking won't keep me alive much longer. Fetch them."

"Yes, Miss Arden."

"Now–" says Mary Arden, turning back to me.

"Look," I say desperately, "I can't run the film for you, if that's what you want. I don't know how to."

"Harris will teach you."

"Can't Mrs Harris keep on with it?"

"No." Mary Arden shakes her head. "Harris is too old. And besides, the moment I'm dead she'll be out of here. It has to be you."

"I can't."

'I rather think you *can*. It's that or prison, after all." She sniffs. "For goodness' sake, stop crying. I'm offering you an enormous country house and a fortune. All you have to do is run the film every evening. If you don't want to watch it,

249

don't. You can stay in the projection room and read *War and Peace* for all I care."

The door opens; Mrs Harris has returned with the cigarettes, and a faint air of disapproval. She helps Mary Arden to light one using a gold lighter, and then she withdraws tactfully to a distance.

Mary Arden draws in great lungfuls of nicotine and exhales through her nostrils, so that she looks more than ever like an elderly dragon.

"Perhaps a slap *would* have done you more good than the brandy," she remarks. "What a very poor thing you are."

I look at her with savage dislike. "Why?" I ask her. "Why are you even doing this? What's the point? You'll be dead soon. You said it yourself. Why do you even care if anyone shows the film?"

"Oh, you're so desperately slow," she remarks. She takes another drag, blows out smoke. "Do you really want to hear this now? Very well.

"Lillian started this, as you know – poor dear, deluded Lillian – because she couldn't let Hugh go. She'd have given *anything* to have him back again, and indeed, I rather think I know what she *did* give." And the old wretch chuckles. "And she got him back, for as long as it took to capture him on film." She shrugs. "That's where he lives now, in the film – when we show it. As for the film stock – I told you it was singular. Keeping it in cold storage is more of a precaution than anything. It shows very little sign of decaying. And of course, when it's in the temperature-controlled store, it's protected against flooding, or fire in the house, or anything else that might occur.

"Anyway, Lillian got what she wanted. She watched the film every night, and worshipped Hugh. He is very beautiful, after all."

"He's hideous," I say in a low voice.

She eyes me. "Well, morally, perhaps. But aesthetically, he's perfect, don't you think?"

I say nothing.

"Well, well, you don't have to care for him." She waves a hand dismissively.

"How can *you*?" I ask her. "What even *is* he? A – a *ghost*?"

"An intelligent question at last," she remarks. "And not one I'm entirely sure I can answer. What Lillian did, so far as I can tell, was some kind of necromancy. What she summoned *looks* like Hugh and *sounds* like Hugh, but whether it is actually Hugh Mason in the sense that he originally was... well, that's another thing altogether."

"He's – he's–"

"An abomination? A horror?" she says, sounding bored.

"A *devil*," I blurt out.

"Oh come, come," says Mary Arden, examining her fingernails. "How dreadfully melodramatic. Besides," she continues, "what if he is? It's all very well to sit there in all your youth and health and say you'd never make a pact with one of them. Wait until you have five years left before oblivion, or six months, or one week. See how you feel then."

There is no point in telling her that nothing, nothing on *earth* would induce me to make any kind of arrangement with Hugh Mason, whatever he is. I hug myself, shivering, and glare at her.

When she sees that I am not going to say anything to this, she shrugs her skinny shoulders again.

"As you like. I may as well tell you the rest of it. Lillian never went to Hollywood, of course. She was as successful as she could possibly have been as a British director, but she could have been even bigger if she'd gone there. It wasn't for lack of offers, either. But she was tied to *The Simulacrum*; she couldn't have taken it with her to America.

"All the same," she adds, "It certainly helped her career. She never married, never had children, never did any of those things that get in the way of success. She made her

251

films by day, and at night she lost herself in adoring Hugh Mason.

"I didn't see much of her during that time, although she was as good as her word about helping me. My career took off – you don't need me to tell you about *that*. I made a mint of money; I was hugely popular in the '40s and I was still getting leading roles in 1960. This place – Garthside – I bought it early on. The parties I held here! You wouldn't believe them. There was one Scottish actor – incredibly debonair, marvellously drawling voice – who made love to me on the dining table; just swept all the plates and glasses onto the floor. Made a hell of a mess; it took the maids ages to sweep it all up. I daresay they hated me, but I didn't care."

I look at her with absolute loathing, but she is oblivious.

She continues, "I retired when I started being offered character parts all the time. Who wants to do those? Not I, anyway. It wasn't as though I needed any more money; I had plenty put away. So I came up here and recommenced my party lifestyle, though with somewhat younger men; that Scottish actor had died by then," she remarks.

"Well, that didn't last long. I suppose I was naive, or perhaps too preoccupied with living the high life; at any rate, suddenly all the money was gone. My accountant had swindled me out of the greater part of it, and absconded. I have since reflected," she adds, "that the timing was rather... convenient. Though I can't see how it can have been arranged.

"Anyway, it was at about that time that Lillian got back in touch with me. She was old then, and fabulously wealthy – no-one to leave it to, either. She said she had something she wanted me to do, and she'd leave everything to me if I'd promise to do it. I had to go and see her; she wouldn't come to see me. She wouldn't tell me what it was she wanted me to do, either, though you can guess."

I nod.

"So I went down there, to Lillian's home, which was a

big place in its own grounds on the outskirts of London. It had its own screening room, not dissimilar to the one here. I was not quite sure how to behave around Lillian. I wanted to play the *grande dame*; I was proud of my career, and how far I'd gone since *The Simulacrum*, and I was more of a household name than she was by that time. But on the other hand, she still had a deal of money, and I had none.

"Well, Lillian didn't ask me to keep showing the film. She asked me to destroy it."

Mary Arden sees me react to this, and her eyebrows go up.

"Ah, you thought she'd ask me to show it? Then you don't know very much about Lillian's type of love. It was very much of the *if I can't have him, then nobody can* variety. She wouldn't even let me watch the film. She showed me where it was stored, and asked me to destroy the reels, every single one of them, the same day she died. For all I knew, it was a regular film, though valuable because of what it was. But it was not worth as much to me as Lillian Velderkaust's fortune, so I agreed.

"I had to stay down there, of course; I couldn't have destroyed the film so quickly if I were up here, at Garthside. But looking at Lillian, I didn't think it would be all that long until the end. She advanced me some money, too, so I lived well, and I didn't have to sell Garthside either.

"She lasted longer than I expected – until 1980. Towards the end, I had to move into her house; she knew it would be soon, and she wanted to know I would be there. And still she would never let me see the film. I don't know how she ran it, by then; you would think it would be beyond a ninety-year-old woman to lift the reels and run the changeover.

"The day before she died, she made me promise all over again that I'd destroy the film; I had to take all the reels right outside the house, because they were so highly flammable, and burn them. Once again, I assured her I'd do it. It wasn't a lie; I really meant to."

253

"Why didn't you?" I grate out.

"I'm coming to that," she says. "That last night, she ran the film as usual. I had a room in another part of the building, but sometimes I would look out of the window and see a blue light in her part. So it was that night.

"I didn't go to bed; I paced my room and smoked cigarettes. I had the strangest feeling that Lillian was going to die. After a while, I couldn't stand it; I left the room and went to her part of the house. I didn't meet a single person in the corridors. Nobody challenged me. I felt a compulsion to take a look at the film, to watch a part of it if I could, before it was gone forever.

"I came to the screening room and my nerve failed me a little. What would Lillian say, if she saw me? I did not think that she would change her mind about the arrangement, not after all that time, but all the same...

"So I pushed open the door, a very little, just to peep inside, but not so much that someone looking at the film, instead of the door, would notice it.

"The whole room was lit up with that eerie blue light. That was the first thing I saw. The second was Lillian's foot. She was lying on the floor, stone dead. She'd changed the reels, I suppose, and her heart had given out. I pushed the door right open then, and went in.

"Right away I saw that there was someone else there. He was standing over her and I knew him at once. It was as though the years rolled back like a great tide, and I stood there with ice in my heart as his name drifted from my lips like breath on freezing air.

"*Hugh Mason.*

"And then I said, 'Have you come to take her with you?'

"He looked at me and said, 'No. What have you come to do?'

"I said, 'Lillian told me to destroy the film when she died.'

"'If you do that,' he said, 'I shall die too.'

"I didn't understand him, not then, but I said, 'She's paying me to do it. She's giving me her whole fortune.'

"And he said, 'I will give you something better. I will make you immortal.'

"So I listened to him, because although it was over forty years ago, and I was much younger than I am now, already I could feel the hand of Time on my shoulder. There was silver in my hair and there were lines on my face, and those things are hard, very hard, when you have been beautiful. Hugh promised me youth, and life – he said the power of the film could encompass me too, because I was part of it. He spoke to me in his terrible, impossible beauty, until I began to see that it would be a strange and exquisite thing to live with him forever. A compulsion came over me that was more than love had ever been. The Scottish actor was nothing next to him. No man was anything next to him."

The expression on her wrinkled face is rapt. It makes me queasy, not because she is old but because I do not believe that the thing that looks like Hugh Mason is human.

"But," I say, "Why didn't he offer this to Lillian? She was the one who summoned him."

"He couldn't," says Mary Arden. "She wasn't in the film. She couldn't be. *The heart that wishes must be the eyes that see* – remember? Lillian had to be *behind* the camera, not in front of it. The power, or whatever you want to call it, is in the film itself."

She smiles, and the smile is unpleasant to see, sly and self-congratulatory.

"I was the only one he could offer it to. So don't imagine that he will ever make the same offer to you, Theda Garrick. He has no promises for you – only threats."

"I'd rather die," I say under my breath. Mary Arden ignores this.

"There's very little left to tell," she says. "The reel ran to the end and Hugh vanished. I took the reel from the projector, and I took it and all the others back to the store.

I took a different film out and took it into the garden, away from the house, as Lillian had told me. I set fire to it, and while the flames were leaping up towards the sky I went and called an ambulance.

"The film I burned was just insurance, in case anyone asked whether I had carried out Lillian's wishes, but they never did. I suppose Lillian trusted me to do what she wanted, without writing it into the terms of her will.

"So I inherited the money, and the film, and I returned here. And soon, when I am dead, I shall be with Hugh – forever."

"How can you be sure?" I ask her.

"I know it," she says. "I can feel it, the nearer to death I get. Some nights, when I fall asleep in front of the film, my old heart slows down; I get close to the brink of death. And then I open my eyes and I'm in there."

"In the film?" I say, horribly fascinated in spite of myself.

She nods. "I see that poster on the wall, *Your chums are fighting – why aren't YOU?* And I know that somewhere, a little way away, there is something that used to belong to me, slumped in a chair. But I look down at my hands and they are a young woman's hands. I turn them over and over, looking at them, the smooth skin, the perfect nails. Who wouldn't want that – to be young again?"

"But... Is that even *life*? Being in there with that... with Hugh Mason?"

She looks at me with real distaste, smoke drifting out of her nostrils.

"It's better than death," she says.

Chapter Fifty

Mary Arden lets me go back to my room after that. There are questions I have to ask – so many questions – but those can keep. I need to be alone. I need to think what to do.

I look at my phone, at the texts I exchanged with Angus. I said I'd be leaving the day after tomorrow. I won't be, not now.

I can't help it – I start crying then. Not loudly, just quietly and hopelessly. I wish I could reach back into the past and change everything that's happened. Why was I so determined to get my hands on that film? I'd give anything now never to have heard of it. And why in heaven's name did I let Mary Arden talk me into telling her what happened to Max?

I killed Max. That's the plain truth of it, the bald statement that Mrs Harris has on tape. The one that could put me in prison.

Maybe, I think, *that's where I ought to be.* I don't know. Thinking about it makes me feel like an animal pacing mindlessly in a confined space. I *did* kill Max. I pushed him. He fell, and I saw his brains all over the flagstones. For a long time after he died, whenever I closed my eyes I saw that. The blood, the brain matter. Its red rivulets ran through my dreams. The shock, that was real enough. I was stunned by the sheer enormity of what had happened. What I had *done*. But what other people took for grief was guilt. I actually think that was worse. If Max's death had been an accident, I would have felt sorrow, in spite of everything. A clean emotion. But it wasn't an accident. I pushed him. I pushed him. *I pushed him.*

I've tried to tell myself that it *was* an accident, really. From that height, you won't necessarily die. You might break some bones, but you can survive it. That Max didn't was pure bad luck for him. If a friend, someone I loved, told me they had done this, under those circumstances, I would have tried to comfort them, to let them off the hook.

I can't let myself off.

I remember I called an ambulance, dialling 999 and stumbling over the explanation, while the woman at the other end tried patiently to coax it out of me. And then I seemed to drop down into a dark well. When the paramedics arrived, they were more concerned about me than Max; there was nothing to be done for him, that was obvious from the moment they saw him, but I was sitting there like a stone. I was so pale and bloodless they thought I might be injured in some way too, and then they thought I was having a heart episode. A young woman, seeing what had happened to her handsome husband...

And that was how it went. The police came too, and they were kind in their questions. Simon came, and Celia. Everyone saw a young wife, terribly traumatised by her husband's sudden death. I am smaller and slighter than Max was, after all; perhaps it didn't seem probable that I could have shoved him from the window. And none of them knew how Max had been. None of them knew it could very easily have been me lying there on the paving stones in a pool of congealing blood.

I didn't tell them then, because it was too enormous, like a great stone I had swallowed and couldn't sick up. And then it became impossible to tell them, because I hadn't done so at once. Where was my proof that Max had lunged at me, meaning to push me out? I couldn't clearly remember the circumstances of the fall down the stairs, and Max had put on a great show of caring for me at the time. And as for the rest of it – it would have sounded so thin and implausible, saying he tried to control things. Asking me to wear a particular outfit – that might just have been a sentimental thing...

So I pushed it all down, under the surface. I tried to go

on living. The obsession with *The Simulacrum* became a way to stop thinking about Max, to build something new, and for a while it worked, at least a little bit. But now I am face to face with it again.

I killed Max.

And now two other people know. If I say no to them, or anger them, or fail to do what they want, they will use the information. Perhaps they may even do worse – I don't believe for a moment that the others they shared their own secrets with just walked away, promising not to tell.

I have to co-operate.

Then I think about *what* I will have to do, and I feel as though I am unravelling. A tear falls onto the screen of my phone, blurring Angus' name. I think briefly about texting him. Or even phoning. The comfort of hearing him speak from his house by the ford, with Jess snuffling in the background.

Sanity, I think.

But what would I say?

I'm going to have to say *something*, because the alternative is saying nothing, and risking Angus turning up here, checking I'm alright. I have to think of some way of putting him off, without alarming him.

It's too much to think about tonight, so I switch off my phone and go to bed, first checking that the door is locked. I open the curtains too, so that the room is not entirely dark; I don't think my nerves could take that.

For a long time I lie awake under the pink satin coverlet, a broad stripe of moonlight across it. I think about Hugh Mason walking out of *The Simulacrum*, and about Mary Arden slobbering all over his well-shaped hands. I think about Mrs Harris, impassively running the film and holding out a glass of brandy to me. And I think about Max. Handsome, golden, dead Max. Sometimes I used to think it would have been better if it had been the other way around, if he had pushed *me* out. Now I wonder about that again.

There is no Theda-shaped hole anywhere in the world. There won't even be a book with my name on it.

I roll onto my side, curling into a ball, and although I'm not aware of it, at some point wakefulness dissolves into sleep, and when I next open my eyes it's a cold grey dawn.

Chapter Fifty-One

I breakfast late, and alone. I push the food around the plate, faintly nauseated by the glistening fat, and at last abandon it altogether in favour of strong sweet tea. Then I grasp the nettle and text Angus, keeping it brief.

Change of plan! Staying for a while longer.

After a moment's pause I add:

BTW they've mended the back fence, so I might not be visiting...

When the messages have been sent, I keep the phone out on the tablecloth but there is no reply. I suppose Angus is out in the Range Rover, with Jess riding shotgun. The battery is at 35%, I notice. I forgot to charge it last night; I'd better do it when I get upstairs.

I am draining my second cup of tea when the door opens and Mrs Harris comes in.

"Good morning, Ms Garrick."

"Mrs Harris," I say flatly, sitting back and folding my arms. I watch her advance into the room. "Mrs Harris, you *knew*. You knew what was going on here, and you let me walk into it."

She pauses. "Ms Garrick," she says eventually, "Do not forget that Miss Arden is my employer; you are not. And besides," she adds, "I do not think you are entirely blameless, are you?"

I scowl, and then something occurs to me.

"What has Mary Arden got on *you*, Mrs Harris? What did *you* do wrong?"

Something – some small reaction – momentarily flickers through those grey eyes. But she says, "I have no idea what you mean."

Of course. She wouldn't just *tell* me.

"Besides," she adds, "I didn't interrupt your breakfast to

261

discuss myself. I came to give you your new schedule. Miss Arden wishes me to begin teaching you how to operate the projectors today."

"*Today*? But Mrs Harris, there are so many other things I have to do." I snatch one out of the air. "She said I'd have to sell my house. I need to find an estate agent, and instruct them–"

Mrs Harris is shaking her head. "Miss Arden particularly wishes you to begin learning immediately. These other things can be done afterwards. She is one hundred and four, you know. There is no knowing how much time is available."

Personally, I wish the old witch would drop dead today. Now. This minute. I do not say this.

"Look," I say pleadingly, "I know what Mary Arden wants me to do. But I'm really not the person to do it. I have no idea how to handle a film that old without damaging it–"

"That is why you have to learn."

I stare at her helplessly. "Can't you stay on and do it? Please, please–"

"No," says Mrs Harris firmly, cutting me off. "When Miss Arden dies, I am free to go. And go I shall." She puts her head back, inhaling deeply through her nostrils. "You cannot imagine that I *like* running that film, or watching that – that *abomination* coming out of it. No. My time is nearly finished, and you must be ready when yours begins."

"*Damn it!*" Anger and misery overwhelm me. I slam my fist on the table, making the cutlery jump. My tea cup falls onto its side, spilling brown dregs onto the snowy tablecloth.

"Temper," says Mrs Harris, but she takes a step back. She adds, "When you have finished breakfast, perhaps you would like to compose yourself in your room for a few minutes, and then join me in the upper west wing. I assume you can find your way back to the screening room by yourself?"

"Yes," I say, nearly shouting. As the door closes behind

her, I burst into tears again. If I could keep a cool head, perhaps I could think of some way out of this, but panic makes my thoughts run around like rats in a trap.

I stand up, pick up my phone, and head back to my room.

Just a few minutes – a few minutes to clear my head–

The sight of my things mostly packed for leaving only makes things worse. I am not going anywhere. I stalk into the bathroom and splash cold water on my face, not wanting anyone else to see the traces of tears. Then I look for my charger so that I can plug my phone in. There is no sign of it.

I search in a desultory way for a few minutes, and then more carefully, feeling a little unsettled. No charger. I start to unpack my bags, thinking that it must have found its way into the bottom of one of them, though I am pretty sure I can remember where it was – plugged into a socket near the escritoire. If it's in my luggage, I must have done it automatically, without thinking, because I don't recall moving it. I suppose that's possible; I've been preoccupied. So I take everything out, until the floor is covered with folded and then increasingly tossed-about clothing, but I still cannot find the charger.

I look at my phone. 34%. It's a newish phone and the battery holds a charge reasonably well. With luck, it will last the day. Later, when I've finished with Mrs Harris, I will look for the charger again. Perhaps it's under the furniture, or one of the cleaners has put it in a drawer. It must be here *somewhere.*

Am I composed now, as Mrs Harris suggested I should make myself? No. I am a hideous jumble of emotions. But there is nothing I can do right now except conform to Mary Arden's wishes. So I pocket my dying phone, leave my room, shutting the door firmly, and set off down the corridor.

The double doors to the upper west wing are not closed anymore. They are propped open with wooden wedges. No place is forbidden to me now, because I have become one of the staff.

263

Chapter Fifty–Two

I spend the whole of the rest of the morning with Mrs Harris, in the projection room. There are two projectors, so that the entire film can be shown without breaking off to change reels, and cues to watch for which indicate when a reel is coming to an end. After each showing, the reels have to be rewound.

While she is instructing me, I think about trying to destroy the film. That is one possible way out of this mess. Not now – the moment Mary Arden is dead. If I did that, would Mrs Harris really turn me in to the police? That is a question I can't answer.

There's no chance of doing anything to the film while Mary Arden is still alive because I won't have any time alone with it. While Mrs Harris is teaching me how to operate the projectors, we run another film altogether, a different one of Mary Arden's. Self-obsessed to the last.

After lunch we go through it all again. And again. Mrs Harris starts explaining how the reels have to be kept, and later she takes me to the cold room to see them. She makes me look away when she enters the code, which she assures me is changed regularly. I wonder if that is true, given that it was an easily-guessed *9999* when I tried it, but perhaps they *wanted* me to see the film then. Knowing they really had it, I'd be more likely to stay. To talk. I decide to come back later and try the door again, but I'm not optimistic.

At dinner there is no wine. I ask for some and Mrs Harris shakes her head.

"You need a clear head this evening."

I stare at her.

"I've been learning all day."

"Nevertheless."

"I'm exhausted."

"It's Miss Arden's express wish that you come and run the film with me this evening – and every evening."

"No," I tell her. "I won't."

"It isn't really a matter of choice, Ms Garrick."

"I can't." I look at her desperately. "I can't watch... *that* every night."

Surprisingly, her expression softens a little. "Don't watch the film," she says. "Concentrate on the projectors. That's what I do. Don't look at what's happening in the screening room. They won't trouble you in any way – they need to keep the film running, after all. Just don't look."

"Mrs Harris," I say, "*Please*. Isn't there some way out of this?"

"No," she says simply. "Don't you think I'd have found it, if there were?"

There is nothing I can say. I stare at her, feeling the woe graven into my face.

"Well," she says, "Finish your dinner. I'll come and collect you from your room in – shall we say half an hour?"

I nod, and then I sit there, not eating, and watch her cross the room and leave, closing the door behind her. The big Art Deco dining room, done out in shades of champagne and dove, is marvellously luxurious, but I feel like an insect trapped inside a jewelled box. The opulence is nothing without the freedom to come and go. I look down at my plate too, at the expensive cut of venison, with no desire to eat it. I force myself to swallow a few bites, but it might as well be ashes. The crème caramel that arrives afterwards is no better: perfect but unappetising.

I wonder what will happen when Mary Arden dies. Will whoever prepares these dishes agree to stay on? Do I want them to? I imagine myself as mistress of this huge white elephant of a house, ordering this or that according to whim. There is no pleasure in the thought. I'd rather be round at Angus's, drinking tea from a chipped mug in front of the old range.

Angus. I told him it was too soon. He thought that meant, too soon since Max died, and in a way it did, but it was too soon for me to let go of my role of grieving widow, not too soon to love someone again. And now it is too late. Twist it and turn it as I can, I cannot think of any way I could start something with him while I am tied to Garthside and the need to run *The Simulacrum* every night. All the same, I think to check my phone in case he has replied to my message, and I see at once with a lurch in my stomach that it is down to 10% charge.

There is a reply from Angus: *Good about the change of plans. Not so good about the fence.* A break, and then: *Could drop by the house one evening? Unless the old lady objects...*

While I am thinking about how to reply to this, the charge drops to 9%. The phone is going to die soon, unless I can find the charger. Now I'm really anxious. I push back my chair, leaving the remains of the crème caramel, and head upstairs to hunt through my things again.

Nobody has been into my room since I left it last; clothes are still strewn everywhere. I go around picking things up, feeling them with my fingers, shaking them out in case the charger has become tangled in the folds of something. No sign of it. Then I get down on my hands and knees and look underneath all the furniture; I run a hand under anything too low to the floor for me to see properly. I turn up an old size 10p piece and a lot of fluff, but nothing else. I sit back on my heels and think.

A nagging little voice is telling me the charger isn't here at all, which means someone has removed it, because I have never taken it out of the room since I got here.

No, I think. *Surely they wouldn't do that. Why would they?*

The suspicion grows on me horribly quickly; I can feel my isolation at Garthside spreading like an impenetrable moat all around me. All of a sudden I can think of people

I'd really like to call to ask for advice or help or even just to hear a friendly voice. Angus. Susie. Ellie. Sam. Anyone. And now I can't. Panic rises up within me.

I scrabble for my phone. 3%. I open the text conversation with Angus and start typing, as fast as I can.

I don't think she'd like you coming here

In my haste I press send by accident, but no matter; I start typing *but too bad* and then the screen goes dark as the phone runs out of charge. I stare at it. *No.* Then I press the *on* button, willing the phone to hold that tiny bit of charge, just for a few instants, just long enough to send. *Please, please.*

No dice. The thing is absolutely dead in my hands. I stare at it for a few seconds. I'd like to fling it across the room, but I have enough self-control left not to do that; if I break it, it won't matter if I find the charger or not. Then I start hunting all over again, frantically. I try all the places I've already tried, and some others – lunatic places where it can't possibly be, like the top of the wardrobe and under the pillows on the bed. The room begins to look as though it has been ransacked by vandals.

Calm down, I tell myself. *It must be here somewhere.* But I don't really believe it is. Nothing else is missing – not the pretty aquamarine earrings nor the Montblanc pen, either of them more easily pocketed. Just the charger.

I slump down onto the bed in the middle of all the mess, and put my hands in my hair. I'm still there, staring at the ceiling and wondering how in heaven's name I got myself into this mess, when there is a quiet knock on the door. Mrs Harris has come to get me.

Chapter Fifty-Three

We run the film. Mrs Harris does most of it; she handles *The Simulacrum* as if it were solid gold or cut glass. She loads the first reel, watches to make sure it is running correctly, and after that she looks away, busying herself loading the second one on the other projector. Occasionally she glances at her wristwatch; she has the changeover times off by heart and down to the second. The door to the viewing area remains shut. As far as she can, she insulates herself from what is happening in there.

I tell myself not to look either – but I do. I can't help it. What I saw last time was so aberrant, so *impossible*, that I have to know if it was really true and not some kind of monstrous hallucination. My whole future life hangs on it. So when Mrs Harris turns her face away, I stare straight through the glass.

In the glare of the projector I see Mary Arden in the right hand seat, the ripples of her fine white hair almost glowing in the bluish light. On screen her younger self appears in the waiting room, poised and beautiful. And then Hugh Mason appears – so very handsome, so very *wrong*. He steps out of the film and I blink hard and blink again, my hands balling into fists, and he is still there, looking as real as me or Mrs Harris as he walks across the screening room. I cannot hear anything, but it seems to me that he exchanges some words with Mary Arden; she is as animated as she ever is, her head wagging and her gnarled hands reaching out for him. He does not take her hands, though. Instead, he steps past her and approaches the projection booth. He does not try to come in through the door. He simply stands there and looks up at the window for a long time. The light of the running film silvers him, and he is absolutely still, looking.

I am standing next to a brilliant light source. It should

not be possible for him to see me, but I know that he can. The gaze of those great dark eyes is fixed on me; his face is a pale mask hanging in the darkness. Without words, without expression, it says: *It is you now. You, Theda Garrick, as long as you live.*

No, I want to scream. *I can't. I won't.* But I say nothing. The future is as inevitable as tomorrow's screening, and the one after that, and the next and the next. Mrs Harris moves about the projection room behind me, handling the reels with careful efficiency, and I know that one day soon it will not be her doing it, it will be me, alone.

Mrs Harris calls me to help change the next reel, and afterwards, when I go back to the window, Hugh Mason is no longer standing there. He is sitting beside Mary Arden, in the other seat, and they are conversing. Sometimes she raises her old hand with trembling effort, and caresses his perfect face. I shudder then, not for him, but for her. That she can bear to touch him.

Once, Hugh Mason's head turns and he looks back towards me, his gaze as flat as a searchlight. After that, I don't look out of the window anymore. I keep my eyes on the job, on the turning wheels and the running strips of film. On my future.

And so it goes on, night after night. One evening, Mary Arden slides into sleep while Hugh is there. I see her sag low in her padded seat, her head nodding. And Hugh leaves the screening room. I know where he is going: out into the house, to explore the corridors and chambers.

I do not think that he can leave the house; I think he is chained to the film. But he can roam through it, feeling his way down the darkened hallways. He can go into the rooms, if they are unlocked.

I remember the night the unseen person came into my room, and ran their hands over the bed, exploring it while

I cowered beside the escritoire, my hand to my mouth. My gorge rises. I will never get over my horror of Hugh, the feeling that I would die rather than let him touch me.

Another night, Mrs Harris leaves the projection room for a little while. She trusts me now – she has confidence in my ability to keep the film running, to change a reel if need be. Nobody thinks that I will damage the film. They know their hold over me is too strong.

Alone in the room, I find my gaze sliding towards the window. I know I shouldn't look. I do look. Mary Arden and Hugh Mason are close together, holding hands, talking. I wonder what they can possibly find to talk about, after all these decades. I creep over to the door, and open it a little way, very softly. I put my head through and listen.

Their words are indistinct at first, particularly with the whirring of the projector and the murmur of Mary's words onscreen. But after a while, speech begins to coalesce more clearly. Words, phrases, at last whole sentences become audible.

What are they saying? Horrible things, unspeakable things. Ancient horrors, and atrocities yet to come, things so foul and filthy I could never tell them to anyone else. Their words contaminate the listener: I want to put my hands over my ears, to slam the door to cut out the sound, but I am frozen there, the poison seeping into me, moving sluggishly through my veins.

Someone leans past me, and quietly closes the door. Mrs Harris has returned, slipping in through the door at the back. I do not move at first. I lean against the doorframe, my mouth dry, straining to hear, not wanting to hear.

She shakes me gently by the shoulder.

"Ms Garrick? Theda? Don't listen. It does no good."

I turn my face to her, and I see from her expression that the look of me shocks her.

"Don't listen," she says again.

"Mrs Harris," I say in a low voice, "What is he?"

She shakes her head.

"He's not Hugh Mason," I tell her. "Not the real Hugh Mason."

"What does it matter?"

"He's a devil." I nearly choke on the word. "The things he says..."

She opens her mouth to say something, and then looks at her watch. Without another word, she leaves me and goes over to one of the projectors, working quickly to load the next reel. When it is running, she comes back. She is a little breathless, I notice.

"Look," she says. "As long as you run the film, they won't bother you. I've been doing this for a long time, and as long as you never slip up, he won't come into this room, not ever. Why would he? It's not in their interests to scare you to death. Just run the film, every night. And *don't listen.*"

I stare at her. "You've listened though, haven't you?"

"Once. Not anymore."

"What did you hear?"

"The same as you did, I expect." She compresses her lips into a hard line. I can see nothing else is forthcoming.

I say nothing for a while. I watch the projector running and squeeze my hands together restlessly.

Then I step closer to her, close enough to speak directly into her ear.

"What if I destroy the film?" I say in a low voice. "I could do it, when Hugh isn't... when he isn't here."

Mrs Harris shakes her head. "Don't think of doing that," she says.

"Why not? It would be the end of all this – this–"

"Because it will be the end of *you*, too." She turns to look directly at me. "If you destroy the film, you will let Hugh out. Do you understand? He will go back to – wherever he came from, but he will kill you first."

Her words strike me cold, but I persist.

"How do you know that?"

"He told Miss Arden a long time ago that that was what would happen if she ever destroyed the film."

I dig my nails into my palms. "Then I won't run the film," I say. "When Mary Arden is dead, and you've left, I won't run the film."

"You *will* run it," she says. Her voice is tired, as if this is something she has gone over in her own head time and time again. "You won't be able to help yourself. You'll see. But if you're strong enough to resist it, at least at first, and you try to leave here, I'll know. And then I'll give the recording to the police."

"Mrs Harris." I'm almost in tears. "I'll be rich. I'll give you money. All the money you want."

"Miss Arden has already promised to give me all the money I want," she says.

"I'll give you more."

"I don't need more." She looks at me almost sympathetically. "You were right when you said she has something on me. Well, she does. And when she dies, that – something – dies too. That's enough for me. That, and being free."

"But Mrs Harris–"

She waits.

"What can I *do*?"

"Run the film, Ms Garrick," she says crisply. "Run the film – and never ever listen."

Chapter Fifty-Four

Angus comes to the house.

I am upstairs in the library, listlessly browsing the books, when I hear the roar of an ill-tuned engine followed by the crunch of gravel. When I go to the window and peer out, I see the Range Rover on the drive outside. Angus gets out and stands for a moment on the drive, staring up at the house. Without really thinking about why, I shrink back behind the curtain. What would I say to him? I don't know. I wish I could run downstairs and out of the front door – I wish I could throw myself into his arms and beg him to take me away from here, to drive anywhere, to just go. But I can't do that. So instead I look down from my hiding place and bite my lip.

He does not see me. After a few moments he drops his gaze, and then he walks towards the front door. I see wariness in his gait, but also determination. There is movement in the Range Rover: Jess, her front paws on the dashboard, is watching him go.

I walk out of the library, down the hallway and through the double doors. Just as the doorbell sounds, I stop at the top of the stairs. It shrills out again, and again.

Footsteps on the parquet: Mrs Harris is going to open the door. My fingers close on the top bannister. I wait, listening.

From here, it is quite hard to make out individual words, although I am pretty sure I hear my name at least once. Angus speaks softly, patiently at first. Mrs Harris answers him in a smooth professional tone. Their voices rise and fall, and after a little while the conversation becomes more heated. Then there is an actual shout from one of them, a short bark of surprise. I suspect that Mrs Harris has tried to shut the door in Angus's face and he has put his foot into the gap, or something like that.

There is a brief skirmish, and then Angus wins. I hear the front door close and he is on the inside, because I can still hear his voice in the lobby. *Theda*, he keeps saying.

Eventually I hear Mrs Harris coming up the stairs. She looks up as she reaches the last stretch and sees me standing at the top. Her face is lined with disapproval but she waits until she is on the same level as I am before saying anything.

"There is an Angus Fraser downstairs, demanding to see you." Her tone is accusatory.

"I didn't ask him to come," I say.

"That's as may be, but you need to get rid of him – and make sure he doesn't come back."

"But... he's a friend."

"You can't have friends," Mrs Harris says, shaking her head. "You must know that. Especially not *that* sort of friend. You can't tell me he isn't."

"But–"

"It's simply impossible. Do you think he'd never ask questions? Never want to stay the night here, or for you to go out?"

"Mrs Harris," I say, feeling myself turning pink, "It's really not like that."

"It would be, though, eventually. Wouldn't it? No. You have to make him go, and you have to make sure he'll stay away."

"I don't see how I can."

"You have to." She eyes me. "It's for his own good, you know. It isn't safe for him here. They won't tolerate anyone interfering."

It isn't safe for him. That gives me a cold feeling in the pit of my stomach.

"Alright," I say slowly. "I'll try."

"He's down in the lobby."

"Okay." I brush past her and start down the stairs. I don't hurry; I am thinking hard about what to say. As I descend, Angus comes into view, his angular face turned up to look for me, his wavy hair dishevelled as usual. His hazel eyes widen as he sees me.

"Theda." He comes forward to meet me and I see concern on his face.

"Angus," I say. "What are you doing here?" I inject as much polite disbelief as I can manage into my voice and for a moment he hesitates.

"I told you Miss Arden wouldn't like it," I add.

"I know," he says. "I just wanted... to be sure you're okay."

I spread out my hands. "Perfectly okay, as you can see."

"It's just..."

I wait.

"I haven't heard from you for a while."

I shrug. "A few days."

"A couple of weeks," he says, looking at me.

I hope he doesn't see me flinch. *A couple of weeks? Has it been that long?*

"Well," I say, "I've been engrossed in working. I guess more time's passed than I thought."

He's still looking at me, very closely. After a while, he says, "I guess it's not my place to–"

"No, it really isn't," I say, interrupting him more curtly than I intended. "I'm fine. You can see I'm fine. Not," I add, "that it's really your business whether I'm fine or not."

He lets out a long breath. "Okay."

I draw myself up. "I'm sorry about what happened–" I'm about to say, *the other day*, and then I realise it's been far longer than that. "–that other time," I say. "I gave the wrong impression."

Unconsciously, he straightens up too. "Forget about that. I came here as a – a concerned friend."

"Well, thank you for your concern, but as you can see, it's really not needed."

He glances upwards, swiftly and I suspect he is looking

for Mrs Harris, wondering whether I know we are being overheard.

"Theda–"

"Angus," I say very firmly, "I'm sorry to be blunt, but I don't want you to come here again, and I don't want to see you again. I'm–" I dredge up an expression so clichéd and crass that it makes me wince to use it. "–just not that into you, you know?"

Silence. "Alright," he says slowly. He stands there for a moment, looking down at the floor. Then he says, "Goodbye, Theda," and turns away.

I watch him walk towards the front door and something twists painfully inside me.

"Angus," I say.

He pauses.

I can almost *feel* Mrs Harris straining to hear my words. All I can come up with is another horrible cliché.

"Really, it's not you," I say. "It's me."

His head turns slightly as if he intends to glance back at me and then thinks better of it. Then he lets himself out of the front door – not slamming it, closing it gently – and his footsteps fade as he goes down the steps.

Perhaps twenty seconds after that, I hear the Range Rover's engine starting up and the crunch of gravel as it moves away. Then nothing.

I thought I would cry after that. I felt like crying the entire time I was telling Angus to go away and not come back, that I didn't care about him. But I don't cry. I am frozen inside. I walk slowly back up the curving staircase to where Mrs Harris is standing. She starts to say something to me but I ignore her completely and walk back through the double doors, on my way back to the library.

Once inside, with the door closed, I run to the window, but of course the Range Rover is long gone.

Chapter Fifty-Five

It happens at last.

Mrs Harris and I are in the projection room. I am running the film, checking the time and changing the reels. Mrs Harris has given me her wristwatch to use, and I occupy myself watching the second hand going round and round. Anything rather than look through the window into the screening room.

Mrs Harris is looking, though. Generally she tries to avoid this, just as she never listens to what Mary and Hugh are saying, but today something has changed; her employer's usual tartness has been blunted and she seems indefinably under the weather. Mrs Harris suspects that the end is coming; she detects it the way we smell autumn on the air. She has hinted as much to me. There is no indication that she intends to try to prevent it, even assuming she could. She will be free as soon as Mary Arden has gone, after all.

I hear her exclamation and look up to see her beckoning energetically. With reluctance I go and stand by her, peering into the room beyond.

Mary Arden is slumped in one of the padded chairs. A skinny claw protruding from a lacy sleeve hangs at the side of it, motionless. There is something very inert about that hand; it does not look as though it belongs to someone who is merely asleep.

Hugh Mason stands beside her, looking down. I cannot read his expression; the light fluctuates so that shadows dance on his face. Then he turns to look at the screen.

On it, Mary Arden is looking towards the right, her image performing as always its preordained movements and gestures. A tremor seems to pass across the screen: a barely perceptible hitch in the film. Slowly she looks down, at her own hands. She turns them over. Then she looks directly out, at Hugh. At us.

"Holy Mother of God," says Mrs Harris under her breath.

I clutch at her arm, stunned into silence. We watch as Mary Arden's young self looks all about her, and performs a pirouette.

Hugh holds out his hands to her. And she comes to him, in all her youthful, beautiful, poised *wrongness*. She steps carefully out of the film, her feet dainty in their Cuban heeled shoes as they touch the thick blue carpet, her hands outspread as though balancing herself; she is relearning this youth, this flexibility. This life.

I watch her cross the room to Hugh and take his hands; I watch him kiss her, lingeringly. My skin prickles all over. My mouth is dry.

This is wrong. We have to stop this...

But I can't imagine how. Could I burst into the screening room and try to revive Mary Arden – press my lips to her sunken old mouth and try to breathe life back into her?

No. I can't do it, and besides, it's too late – I can see that in the slender young figure in Hugh Mason's arms. There is no going back.

Mrs Harris pulls at my shoulder, white-faced. "Don't look," she says. "Don't listen. Just keep the film running."

I turn to her. "Mrs Harris," I say, "What if they stop being happy with running the film once a day? What if they want me to run it all the time?" I can feel my jaw juddering with the effort of not bursting into tears of fright. "I can't do it," I tell her. "I really can't."

"They won't," she says. "They never have."

"That doesn't mean they won't want it now."

She shakes her head. "They can't run you into the ground. They *need* you."

"I can't do it."

"You *have* to."

She glances through the projection room window. "Dear God," she mutters. "I will be glad to leave this behind."

"But – but – what am *I* supposed to do?"

She looks at me. "You could try to find someone else to do it. Someone younger. The money, the house – someone might be tempted."

I don't reply; I don't think either of us believes this will happen.

Eyes averted, I busy myself with the projectors. Mrs Harris doesn't interfere or offer to help; the job is mine now. The seconds tick by, the projector whirrs, the light of the film flickers.

At long last, the film ends. I do not look through the window again while it is running, so I do not know how it ends for Hugh and Mary – whether they go willingly, or are drawn back in. I stop the projectors and Mrs Harris and I go out into the screening room.

We do not expect to find any signs of life in Mary Arden. All the same, it is appalling to see her slumped there, stone dead. One shoulder is hunched, the arm dangling lifeless. Her head lolls against it. Her mouth sags open and the perfect teeth, the dentures, protrude slightly. Her eyes, though – those are the worst, turned up so that the whites show. They are the colour of old ivory, the surface moisture slowly congealing.

I hate Mary Arden, but this is horrible. I cannot stop staring but I do not think I could bear to touch her.

Mrs Harris has no such compunction. With dispassionate briskness she speaks to Mary Arden, saying her name, although neither of us anticipates a reply. Then she leans in close to listen for breathing or to feel the merest exhalation against her cheek. Finally she takes the limp hand in hers and feels for a pulse under the papery skin.

Nothing.

For a moment her eyes slide closed and I hear her inhale, pause, and then let out a long sigh.

Freedom.

But not for me. No, not for me.

She opens her eyes.

"We'll have to move her."

"*What?*"

"She can't be found in here. Too many questions. Not enough time to put the film safely back in storage. And they'd want to know why nobody noticed she was dying while the film was running." She shakes her head. "We'll get her into bed, and then you'd better go to your own room. There's no reason for you to be in this wing, especially not at this time of night."

I shudder.

"Can't – can't someone else do it?"

She eyes me. "No. It has to be us, and now. She's been dead at least thirty minutes. There will be changes. Eventually, rigor mortis. I don't think they'll look too hard, because she was a hundred and four. But there's no point in risking anything too suspicious."

She makes it sound as if *we* killed Mary Arden. I know she's right, though. There's nothing else for it, though it turns my stomach to think of handling the body. She fetches the wheelchair from the side of the room, applies the brake, and then with great care we transfer Mary Arden from the padded seat into it. Mary Arden does not weigh very much; at her vast age she is mostly skin and bones. But she is a dead weight, which makes the job a little more difficult. As we lift her, her head lolls back so that her face is turned to mine, showing those dreadful half-shut eyes, and I have to fight down hysteria.

Mrs Harris puts the lifeless hands into Mary Arden's lap, and then she tucks in the trailing ends of the nightdress and the bed jacket so that they won't catch in anything when she wheels the old lady back to her room. The prospect of that happening, and Mary Arden being spilled onto the floor, is too grisly to contemplate. Then she wheels her employer's mortal remains to her powder blue bedroom. I have to go too, to help lift her into the bed.

To my relief, Mrs Harris takes the head end; I lift Mary Arden's feet. Mrs Harris nods at me to remove the old lady's marabou trimmed slippers, so I do, trying my best not to touch her at all. Her toes are gnarled but each nail is carefully lacquered a subtle shade of apricot, and I have a fleeting image of some unfortunate person – Mrs Harris? – having to kneel in front of her, applying the varnish.

Once the old lady has been artistically arranged in the bed, Mrs Harris turns to me.

"Go. Go to bed, and stay in your room until I come to get you. Understood?"

I nod. As I leave the room, I glance back once, and Mrs Harris is standing over the bed, gazing down at her employer. Her face is expressionless.

Chapter Fifty-Six

Back in my room, I quickly change into my night things, get into bed and switch out the bedside light. A little later the on-call doctor arrives; through a chink in the curtains I see the flash of headlights. Shortly afterwards, there are voices in the stairwell. It is very quiet after that. Eventually, exhausted, I drift off to sleep.

I wake at 8 a.m. to Mrs Harris's knocking on the bedroom door. Then she tries the door, but I've locked it out of sheer habit.

"Theda," she calls, not trying to be polite.

I get up, pulling my dressing gown on and tying the belt. Then I open the door.

"The funeral home took her away last night," she tells me without preamble. "It's official: she's gone."

I stick my head out of the doorway and glance down the corridor, thinking we may be overheard, but she shakes her head.

"No-one's listening. The night nurse has gone, and I've telephoned the morning shift and told them not to bother coming in. There's the cook, but she's down in the kitchen."

"What did the doctor...? I mean..."

She shrugs. "It was entirely expected. It was more surprising that she lasted this long." She raises her eyebrows. "You'd better come down and have breakfast. I can't say how long the cook will be working this morning."

"I'm not hungry."

Mrs Harris eyes me with disapproval. "All the same, you'd better have something. There may not be anything later. Not now Miss Arden has gone."

"Fine."

"I'll be telephoning Miss Arden's solicitors at nine. The doctor has provided the medical certificate, but as her executors they will have to register the death. They will also begin the process of making an inventory of her estate and applying for confirmation, and they will advise the beneficiaries." She pauses. "I have also telephoned Mr Foster, and left a message."

For a moment there is silence.

"I'll remain until the solicitors have everything they need," says Mrs Harris eventually. "The cook might be prepared to stay on, if you agree the right terms."

"Why on earth would I want a cook?"

"For company," she says.

I stare at her for a moment. Then I say, "I'll be down," and shut the door in her face.

I go over to the bed and sit down, rubbing my face with my hands.

"Oh God," I say aloud. "Oh God, oh God."

The solicitor wants to meet me. I watch from an upstairs window as he parks the Jaguar outside the house and approaches the front door, his leather document case tucked under his arm.

I go downstairs and find Mrs Harris already opening the door. She is eager to get this over with, eager to leave. The lawyer exchanges a few words with her in a low voice, and then he looks up and sees me standing on the staircase.

"Miss Garrick?" he says, coming forward with his hand outstretched. "Simon Murray, Murray Hawkes."

Reluctantly, I hold out my hand too, and he envelops it firmly, extending the moment so that he can take a close look at me. His face is well-fed under the beard, shrewd, and not unkind. I wonder what he makes of me – whether I am what he was expecting: a gold digger, probably; someone on the make, radiating superficial charm. I am aware I am thin and a little haggard, my clothes wrinkled. I don't look like someone who has just come into a fortune.

Mrs Harris ushers us into the Eau de Nil sitting room, says, "I will bring tea in a few minutes," and leaves, closing the door behind her.

Simon Murray puts his document case on the coffee table. He says, "May I offer my very sincere condolences?"

I stare at him for a moment. I don't need condolences, unless it's for the hideous situation Mary Arden's death has left me in, but there is no explanation I can give that won't lead to further and more complicated explanations. In the end I just say, "Thank you."

"Miss Arden was a valued client of ours for many years," he says. "We were honoured to handle her affairs."

There is a pause.

"That's... good," I say.

"The recent changes to her will were quite..." He pauses. "...marked."

"I suppose they would be."

"She'd never mentioned you before, Miss Garrick."

"No," I say. "We met fairly... recently."

Again, I have that feeling that he is assessing me.

"She must have liked you a great deal."

I look him in the eyes. "I don't think Miss Arden liked anyone that much."

He smiles briefly. "I wonder why, then...?"

I can see I shall have to say *something*.

"I love films. Old films. Classics. Miss Arden has – had – a collection of them. I think she wanted a – well, a sort of custodian for them."

"She didn't think of leaving them to the British Film Institute archive, for example?"

"I really can't say. But I know she asked one or two other people to do it, and nobody was keen." That's true, anyway. "But Mr Murray, didn't she discuss any of this with you when she made her new will?"

"We didn't really discuss her motivation," he says. "She was very direct – very clear about what she wanted to do."

He eyes me. "I should say she was very much in her right mind and I am doubtful that anyone could have put her under any kind of duress. She was a strong character."

"She was."

"What I am saying, Miss Garrick, is that I don't believe that anyone could successfully make a case that the will was created while Miss Arden was not in her right mind, nor that she was constrained by anyone."

"Is anyone likely to claim that?" I ask.

He ignores the question, instead reaching for the document case. "You may or may not be aware, Miss Garrick, that under Scottish law, a person may not disinherit their spouse, their civil partner or their children. This includes adopted or illegitimate children. However, distant relatives do not share these legal rights."

"You mean people like Richard Foster," I say.

"He would be an example of such a person," says Simon Murray. He removes a sheaf of papers from the document case. "As it happens, Mr Foster is a beneficiary under the terms of the will, and so is Mrs Harris. Mr Foster inherits one hundred thousand pounds, and Mrs Harris three hundred thousand. Everything else goes to you."

He talks for a long while after that, about the processes that have to be gone through before the money and the property actually become mine. This will take a minimum of six months and perhaps longer, given the extent and complexity of Mary Arden's assets. Funds can be made available from the estate in the meantime, to keep things running at Garthside.

Blah blah blah, I think, my mind drifting away from Simon Murray and the sitting room and the tea that eventually comes in the delicate green tea set that matches the walls. The main thing, the one thing, is that Mary Arden has done what she said she would; she has left very nearly everything to me. It doesn't matter if I shall get it now or in six months' time, or ten; it is mine. And so is *The Simulacrum*. Dear God.

I wonder whether Murray Hawkes have contacted Richard yet, and how he has reacted to the news. One hundred thousand, that's still a lot of money, though it's not what he was expecting. I can't really find it in myself to feel sorry for Richard though – him and his Foster charm. Then my mind flits to Angus, and I try to pull it away. There is no use in it.

"There's one other thing," says Simon Murray, when we are nearly at the end of our meeting. "Miss Arden left specific instructions for her funeral: an unattended cremation, with no service."

That is not a surprise; I imagine Mary Arden thought – or thinks – of her aged body as little more than a discarded suit of clothes. And I can't imagine she would want to draw attention to her demise with a big funeral – celebrities offering memories, and perhaps even journalists at the gates. No, she would want to avoid that.

Simon Murray is looking at me, waiting for a response.

"If that's what she wanted," I say uselessly.

"It seems she did," he says.

Eventually, Simon Murray has finished with me and drunk his tea from a green china cup that looks fragile in his large square hands. He shakes hands with me again and then he goes upstairs with Mrs Harris to examine Mary Arden's papers, carefully filed in some distant room. Later still, the sleek Jaguar purrs away.

The shadows are lengthening. Mrs Harris is still in the house, but tonight for the first time, I run the film by myself.

Chapter Fifty-Seven

The next morning I wake at nine thirty and something seems subtly different. I don't usually sleep this late, not here, and Mrs Harris has not knocked. I lie in bed for a few minutes, listening. This is a very big house, and quite often you can't hear anyone else moving about. There's a stillness today though: not so much as the creak of a board or the distant sound of a door closing, however long I listen.

I get up and dress, and go downstairs, my footsteps echoing in the stairwell.

"Mrs Harris?" I say, when I get to the bottom of the flight. "Anyone?"

There is no reply. I turn left, and with a little difficulty I find my way to the house's big kitchen. The door is ajar, but I knock on the panel anyway.

"Hello?"

No reply. I go inside. The room is cold; none of the appliances, not even the coffee maker, have been used in recent hours. The surfaces are all clean and bare; there is a faint smell of bleach on the air. I open a huge fridge and then the freezer and find that they are well stocked with food. That's something, anyway – no starvation in the short term.

I can find nobody in any of the adjoining rooms. Eventually I give up and go back to the hallway. The house keys are lying on a console near the door. When I try the door, I find that it is locked – so either someone is still in the house with me, or they let themselves out another way.

It does not seem very likely that there will be anyone in the Eau de Nil sitting room or any of the other rooms on this floor, but I look anyway. Then I go back upstairs. Hunger is beginning to gnaw at my stomach, but I have to know, first.

I try all the rooms in the east wing. Most of them don't appear to have been used for a very long time; a smell of dust and stale air hangs over them. Then I go into the west wing and work my way along the corridor, room by room. Nowhere do I find anybody. In Mary Arden's powder blue bedroom, the memory of Chanel No. 5 lingers on the air.

Eventually I open a door and find myself in a home office. There is a large leather-topped desk and on it a number of items, carefully laid out. A wristwatch, which must be Mrs Harris's: I know what that is for. My car keys, with a note attached. I pick them up and read: *Car is in outbuildings behind the house.* A whole file of notes about the running of the house: where to find the fuse box and the inside stop valve, details of the utility providers and local maintenance companies, and so on. And an envelope with *Theda Garrick* written on the front. I look at that for a moment, and then I pick it up and open it.

Dear Theda, it says. *Everything you need to run the house is here. If anything is missing, I can be contacted via Murray Hawkes, but in no other way. I will not be returning under any circumstances.*

For what it is worth, I am sorry it had to be you.

Run the film every night. I will know if you don't, and so will they.

Yours,

Verity Harris.

I crumple the letter in my fist. *I will know if you don't.* How can she possibly know? Common sense says she can't, unless the house has CCTV or something. All the same, I feel uneasy, as though I have been caught contemplating a crime as yet uncommitted. As for *them*... I shudder.

I pick up the car keys and the watch. Then I leave the room, the sound of the door closing very loud in the silence, and make my way downstairs.

It's a relief to get outdoors and feel the wind against my face – to feel anything moving other than myself. I go down the steps and crunch my way round the side of the house to the outbuildings. I have never entered these before; I've never had any reason to. There is a large door, through which vehicles can be driven in and out, and a smaller one, which I open.

Inside it's cool and dim, and in the pale light slanting through the high windows I see the faintly gleaming bulk of the car. Max's car. I press the button on the car key and yellow lights blink as the doors unlock with a solid clunking sound. I open the driver's door and climb in, smelling leather and air freshener. Then I pull the door closed, and just sit there. There is no sign of damp, no smell of river water or green weeds that I can detect. There is no rubbish either, and I am pretty sure that there were food wrappers in it from the journey when I drove it into the ford. Perhaps they really did take it to the garage.

After a while I put the key in the ignition and start the engine. It starts without a hitch, settling into an almost inaudible purr. I close my eyes and listen to it, to the familiar sound. I close my fingers around the padded steering wheel and I can almost believe I could just put the car in gear and drive away: to Angus's cottage, or to the road south.

Then I turn the engine off again, thinking of fumes building up in the enclosed space. I sit for a while with my hands on the wheel, my mind seeming to freewheel, not settling on anything. At last I get out of the car again.

My eyes have adjusted to the dim light now. I see that I am in a large space; Max's car only occupies the front part of it. Behind it there is another bulky shape, camouflaged by the tarpaulin over it. The tarp is old and discoloured with mildew; it does not invite further investigation. All the same, I go closer, knowing what it is concealing. I reach down and grasp a corner, pulling it back so I can look underneath.

A car. An older model of Ford with dusty red bodywork, sitting on four flat tyres. There is no number plate. Curious now, I let the tarp drop, go around the back of the car and look there too. The light is very faint here, but I can tell that the rear number plate has been removed too. I try one of the doors, but it is locked.

I look at that tarp, chewing my lip. There might be a perfectly innocent explanation for the presence of the red car. Perhaps it was Mary Arden's, back in the days when she could still get about, although it doesn't look expensive enough for her tastes. Or perhaps it belonged to someone who worked at Garthside, though it's hard to see why they would abandon it like this. I think about those probable explanations.

I also think about the little pot of face cream I found in the ensuite, and those other people who apparently agreed to write nothing about Mary Arden and *The Simulacrum*, and simply drove away. The more I think about them, and the longer I look at that tarp, the more it looks like a shroud.

In the end I go outside again, carefully closing the door. Then I wander back to the front door, take a last look at the overgrown gardens, and go back into Garthside House.

Chapter Fifty-Eight

As the sun sinks in the sky, I start to feel... restless.

I try to shrug the feeling off. It's the natural consequence of being all alone, of having only one thing to do, that's what I tell myself. It's too easy to start focusing on that one thing. Far healthier to thrust it to the back of my mind – to concentrate on the here and now.

I go to the big cold empty kitchen and make myself a bowl of pasta, something quick and bland. Then I sit on one of the vast unused sections of worktop and fork it mechanically into my mouth. There is the big dining room, the one where I ate with Richard, but I can't imagine carrying my food through there and eating it in solitary state. When I've finished the pasta I have a glass of orange juice, and then I put all the dirty things in the sink.

Through the kitchen window I see trees and a glowing sky that is fading from blue into pink. The sunset will be beautiful. I imagine it reflected in the glossy surface of the river as it runs past the little stone built house where Angus lives. Perhaps by this time of day he is already in the warm untidy kitchen with Jess snorting softly in her bed. I think about kissing him, about the way my hands made fists in his woollen jersey. I wish I hadn't pulled away now; I wish I'd done *everything*. Perhaps I would have stayed down there at the house then, and never made my fatal confession to Mary Arden. At the very least, I'd have some human contact to remember now, to clutch to myself as I face the darkness alone.

It's still there, that strange restless feeling, like a slow and turbid current flowing through me. It's not a compulsion, nor even a definite itch. It's just a faint sense of unease. I find I am very aware of the physical distance between myself and the film, safely in its upstairs store; it snags my consciousness, dragging at it gently. It is not time to go upstairs yet – not time to carry the cannisters through to the projection room and begin the work of loading them onto the projectors – but I can feel the future need throbbing like a tiny warning light.

Will it grow, this feeling? Will it bloom like a dark flower, sinking its roots into the crevices of my mind? I am very much afraid it will. *You won't be able to resist it*, Mrs Harris said. I shiver, hugging myself.

After a while I go upstairs and spend some time in my room, turning over the pages of *Moonfleet* without really reading them. It occurs to me that I could have any room now; I could have the green room Richard used, or the powder blue one that belonged to Mary Arden, or any other room in the house. But part of me wants to stay here, clinging to the idea that I am a guest, recently arrived – that I may actually leave again soon.

Still that feeling grows, a slowly, slowly increasing pressure. As darkness falls, I pace the room, rubbing my hands together. I can't settle to anything; I've stopped even pretending to read.

At last the urge takes me out of the room, drifting down the corridor towards the west wing, through the double doors, past Richard's room and the library. I come to the door that leads into the temperature-controlled store, and my fingers move over the key pad before I'm even conscious of thinking about the code. Part of me seems to be watching from a great distance as I work, loading the film cannisters onto a trolley, pushing them out of the store and down the corridor to the projection room; putting the first reel onto one of the projectors, the second onto the other. There is a strange comfort in these actions. The pressure inside my head seems to lessen; the restlessness recedes, replaced with quiet calm. My hands are deft and efficient, the desire to rub my palms together gone.

I start the film. That eerie blue light flows out of the

projector, flooding the screening room with its brilliance. I watch for long enough to see the waiting room appear, and then I turn my back. I sit down on the floor with my back to the projection window, in a spot where I can see the projectors running, but not what is happening in the next room, and hug my knees. I have Mrs Harris's watch on my wrist and it marks the passing minutes.

I say to myself that this is only a little time out of every day, that there is so much more time when I shall *not* be doing this, when I can wander about the house and grounds and amuse myself however I like. I will not crumble, I will not break, I will not scream because if I start screaming I don't know if I will ever stop. My hands press my face, dragging the flesh into strange grimaces.

I will not break.

The end of the reel is approaching. I stand up, ready for the switchover, and when it is done, after the second projector is running and I have changed the reel on the first, I forget my resolve and look through the projection window.

The screening room is empty. The blue light flickers, darkness flitting swiftly across the room like the beating of a wing, and for a moment I think I am mistaken. But no; they have gone, the two of them, out into the house. The room in the film is empty, the screening room is also empty, and if I crane to look around, I can see that the door leading out into the corridor is open.

A cold horror comes over me. Swiftly, I go to the door at the back of the projection room. The key is in the lock, and I turn it with trembling hands.

They won't trouble you in any way – that was what Mrs Harris said. And logically, sensibly, it ought to be true. Why should they? But somehow I cannot bear the thought of them roaming about the corridors and rooms – passing the black windows, probing, exploring together, making the house theirs. What will they do? What *can* they do? Will they go into the east wing, into *my* room? The thought makes my skin crawl; it is like imagining my things crawled over by snakes and spiders.

I am afraid, too, that this will not be enough. Won't it occur to them that they could have twice as much time together – three times, four times? Mrs Harris said they wouldn't do *that* either, but how could she possibly know that? I can't help it – I imagine myself trapped in this room all night, every night, while those creatures disport themselves outside. Awake all night, sleeping all day, until I'm creeping about Garthside like a vampire myself, thin, pallid, hollow-eyed from lack of sunlight.

I go back to my place by the wall and sit on the floor again, hugging myself. And all the time I am conscious of the seconds ticking past, of time unravelling until the next reel change.

Chapter Fifty-Nine

The days slide past. Sometimes rain patters against Garthside's big windows; sometimes cold bright sunshine slants through them. Outside, the trees are in blossom, later than it would be in England, and new greenery is pushing up in the gardens. Darkness falls later, but the itch is *worse*; it infects me more as time goes by. I can't keep the film out of my head as the sun descends the sky, and by the time I actually load it onto the projectors, the relief is so overwhelming it is like vomiting up a toxin.

I know that Hugh and Mary go out into the house every night. Sometimes I find things they have disturbed, or doors which were closed standing open. Occasionally they smash things, seemingly for their own amusement. Once, I go down in the morning and find that the front door is open; they went out into the neglected gardens the night before. Their range is extending. They feel freer all the time. The conviction grows on me that soon one showing will not be long enough.

In the daytime I try to distract myself. I drive into the town to fetch supplies, thinking that it will be good to surround myself with real, living people. It doesn't work. As I move about the little supermarket, filling my trolley with short shelf life items and loveless single portions, I am aware of the unseen membrane that exists between me and everyone else. To go further than the tight smile as I squeeze past someone, or a brief greeting, is to risk being asked questions I cannot answer.

Sometimes I think about Angus, and then the dragging ache inside me sharpens into actual pain. Once, I walk through the woods to the fence and stand with my fingers hooked into the links, my face turned towards the ford. It's no use – I know that. The wind shivers droplets of water from the trees onto my face, and I blink, the field beyond the fence softening to a blur. Then I turn back to Garthside, and I don't go again.

The task of selling my own house down in England still hangs over me. I have done nothing about that yet: I know it must be done, but it feels too horribly final. I wonder whether the mat is covered with piles of unopened letters, and the windowsills with dead potted plants, but it doesn't seem quite real; it is like the memory of a place, a dog-eared photograph in a wallet.

Sometimes the telephone rings – not my mobile, which remains uncharged, dead, but the landline. There are several extensions in the house; Garthside is a huge place, after all. The first time it rings, it is distant, and I think my ears have mistaken me: I've spent so long alone that I am hearing things. The second time, I am on the staircase and I hear it ringing in the lobby. Irresolute, I debate whether to answer it and eventually I start downstairs, but by the time I reach the bottom it has stopped. It occurs to me that perhaps Murray Hawkes are trying to get hold of me – that I should make more of an effort to pick up. So the next time it rings, I run to the nearest extension, which happens to be the one in the lobby, and snatch up the receiver.

"Hello?"

For a moment there is no sound except the faint hiss of an open line. Then:

"Theda."

It only takes me a moment to place the voice.

"Richard."

"You never pick up the phone, Theda."

"I couldn't think of anyone who'd want to call me," I say.

"Couldn't you?" His voice is silky but somehow unpleasant.

"No."

"That's disingenuous of you," he says.

"Is it?"

"We have rather a lot to talk about, don't we?"

I say nothing, thinking about putting down the phone.

"One hundred thousand," he says. "That's what Aunt Mary left me. One hundred thousand."

"That's... well, that's a lot of money," I say.

"It's chickenfeed. It wouldn't even buy a house in that one horse town along the road from Garthside. It wouldn't even buy a decent *car*."

"I don't know what to say," I offer, which is true.

"I suppose you wouldn't. Because you've got what's rightfully mine, Theda. The house, and all the rest of the money." His voice is rising. "What did you do, Theda? How did you persuade Aunt Mary to leave the whole bloody lot to *you* when you'd only just met her?"

"I didn't," I say quietly. "She chose me, and I really wish she hadn't."

"Bollocks. You're a gold digger, Theda. Might as well come out and say it, because that's what you are. A fucking gold digger."

"Richard," I say evenly, "She made the whole thing dependent on my agreeing to – to look after that film, *The Simulacrum*. That means living here, full time, and – maintaining the film. Do you want to do that? Because if–"

"Live in that white elephant? You must be joking. And Aunt Mary must have been out of her mind."

"She wasn't."

"She must have been, if she was prepared to disinherit her only blood relative and leave the lot to some–" With an effort he controls himself, probably thinking that this isn't helping his cause.

There is silence on the line for a moment.

"Theda, you must see that this isn't right."

I think about that.

"Yes, I suppose I do."

"Then do the bloody right thing and give it up."

"I can't," I say helplessly.

"You won't, you mean."

My knuckles are tight on the receiver. "I really – I can't unless you–"

"Bitch. You fucking–"

I put the phone down abruptly, cutting him off. His anger alarms me: he feels so *wronged*.

I look out of the window. It's still broad daylight. There is no reason to think that Richard is calling from anywhere nearer than his office in Edinburgh; no reason to think that he will threaten me with anything more than words. All the same, I feel vulnerable. I check that the front door is locked, and then I go upstairs to the library and gaze out of the window. There is no sign of life outside. The wind moves the trees and a couple of crows burst out of them, but there is no sign of anyone on the drive or in the garden.

I rest my forehead against the cool glass. I am tired, so tired. Under the exhaustion, like a sluggish current flowing under ice, the *itch* tugs at me.

After Richard's call, I am wary of the telephone. All the same, I try to answer it during daylight hours because it may be Murray Hawkes, and once it is – not Simon Murray himself but someone else, asking me to look for a piece of paper in the office upstairs. Most of the time there is seemingly nobody on the line. I pick up the receiver and hear the faint crackle of an open line but no words. It stretches on and on until I put down the phone. Once I say, "Richard?" and after a second or two there is a click as the person at the other end hangs up.

I remind myself that I do not know for sure it is Richard phoning. Perhaps it is a glitch, a wrong number. Perhaps someone has their eye on Garthside, thinking of a big empty house full of valuables; if that is the case, they will be disappointed if they think they will ever find it unoccupied.

Sometimes it rings at night too, long after I have finished running the film and staggered to my bed. I lie there in the darkness, under the pink satin coverlet, and hear the distant trilling travelling to me down the deserted corridors. I never answer it at night.

Chapter Sixty

It is evening, and here I am again, wandering the corridors of Garthside House, drifting slowly and inevitably towards the projection room; it is not yet time but it will be time soon. I pass a shell-shaped mirror and I turn my head away from it, not wanting to see the pale wraith I have become reflected in the glass.

In that instant of distraction I almost miss it – a small, brittle, distant sound. I pause near the double doors on the upstairs landing, and listen. A slate may have fallen from the roof. A bird may have flown into a window. Or someone may be trying to break in.

I wait. Nothing. The pull of the projection room, the need to get there and start loading the film, plucks at me. All the same, I decide that I had better do a brief check – the main doors, the front windows. I can go over the whole house properly later.

I descend the curving staircase making as little noise as possible, always listening. Still nothing. The front door is closed and locked, the keys projecting from the inside of the lock. Outside, it is nearly dark, so I go to the bank of switches and turn on the ones that illuminate the front of the house. Then I go and stand by one of the big windows and stare out.

Outside, there is barely any movement – just the gentle swaying of the more extravagantly overgrown plants and the trees that fringe the gardens. The expanse of gravel in front of the house is empty; there are weeds sprouting here and there, but no vehicle, no person. The thought of the film is like a tug on my arm, but I stay where I am for several minutes, watching. When I am satisfied that there is really nobody there, I turn and go back upstairs. I leave the outside lights on.

It is getting harder to resist the lure of the film but I take time to go into the library. I don't put the lights on in here. I go over to the window, standing at the side, by the curtain, not in the middle where I can be seen, and I look down at the floodlit gardens.

A fox in the bins, I think. *A deer crossing the gravel.*

I go back out onto the landing. I pause there, and it seems to me that the faintest of drafts can be felt around my ankles.

A window left open, I say to myself. I may well have done that; sometimes patches of time escape me, things go unremembered. But the doors are all locked; I went round before nightfall and checked them all.

The familiar compulsion to go towards the room where the film is stored is fully upon me now. I am at the door of the store room before I have even thought about it, entering the code. I load the film onto the trolley, push it out onto the landing. As I make my way to the projection room, the cannisters gently rattle on the trolley, and the wheels make a soft sound on the carpet, and everywhere else there is silence.

I go into the projection room and get to work, as I have dozens of times before, going through the familiar motions automatically. The effect is engrossing, soothing; it blunts that terrible sense of urgency that torments me when it is time to do this. When the first two reels are threaded into the projectors I switch on the lamp on the first and blue light haemorrhages out. The reels turn, the ribbon of film streaks between them; in the next room the screen is brightly illuminated. After a moment the image of the railway waiting room appears and I turn away. The next moment I almost jump out of my skin.

The rear door of the projection room is half-open, and leaning against the doorframe is – Richard. I know him instantly, though the lights are down and only that ghastly blue radiance shows his features.

"Hello, Theda," he says, and his tone of faux bonhomie sends me cold.

"Richard," I say. "What are you doing here?"

"What am I doing here?" he says. "That's hardly welcoming, is it? Considering this place is more or less a home from home to me."

His tone is light, bantering, but I know this mood – I remember Max being like this. It's dangerously unstable, just waiting to tip over into something else altogether.

"Nothing to say?" says Richard. "Well, no surprise there, since you wouldn't talk on the phone."

"You called me a gold digger and a bitch," I point out.

He shakes his head. "Just telling it how it is, dear Theda."

"I didn't ask for any of this," I say.

"You got it all the same though, didn't you? Every last penny." He steps right into the room.

The film is running, running while we speak; the reels turn, the blue light throbs. Involuntarily my gaze slides to the projector, and Richard notices my head turn.

"That fucking film. It's the one, isn't it? The one Aunt Mary was so obsessed with. The one she disinherited me for."

I nod, my throat dry.

"Why are you showing it, Theda? The old witch is dead." He steps closer. "You could be spending your evenings rolling in money instead. *My* money."

I do not think it would be safe to point out that the money has never been his money. As for why I am running the film...

I shake my head. I cannot explain it.

"You're obsessed with it too, I suppose," Richard says with disgust. "You're as sick as she was. A mile of crappy celluloid and Aunt Mary threw over her only relative for it."

I find my voice. "What do you want, Richard?"

"What do I want? I want my inheritance. I'm not going to get that though, whatever I do. I could strangle you with

302

a length of that bloody film and it wouldn't make the money mine."

Strangle you. I make a tiny choking sound, as though Richard's hands are already around my throat. My back is against the far wall now; there is nowhere else to go. Adrenaline fires inside me like an emergency flare. I put out my hands, trying to ward him off, but I do not say anything because there are no words, there is nothing I can tell him that won't make things worse.

Richard is close now, close enough that he can see through the projection window behind me.

He says: "Who the fuck are *they*?"

"It's Hugh," I say in an unsteady voice. "Hugh and Mary."

Richard pauses, his brow furrowed.

"*What?*"

"Hugh Mason," I say. "And Mary Arden."

This time there is an even longer pause.

"You're fucking kidding me. That guy Aunt Mary used to go on about? You..." He tries to make sense of it. "You got *actors* in to play them? Jesus, Theda. I knew you were a bitch, a *gold digging* bitch, but this is... insane. This is *off the scale* insane."

He takes another look and this time I follow his gaze. My heart is thudding. I *hate* looking at them.

They have seen Richard looking in. The pair of them, Hugh and Mary, are standing just below the projection window, looking up at us. Silent, side by side, their beautiful, horrible, unnatural faces lit blue by the running film. Watching.

"Fuck," says Richard. "That's creepy."

He grabs me by the arm, digging his fingers in until it hurts.

"What is it with you and her and that film? You're as obsessed with it as she was. This is sick, Theda."

I try to drag my arm out of his grip. "Let go. You're hurting me."

Let her go, Richard.

I hear it too, although it shouldn't be possible – you can't hear anything from the screening room unless you put your head through the doorway – not with the film running.

Richard's head turns from side to side, trying to identify the source of the voice. His grip on my arm slackens, but then it tightens again.

"Who's that?" he snaps.

Leave, Richard. Leave now.

Recognition seeps into his face.

"Aunt... *Mary*?"

For a second he looks grotesquely frightened, but then his natural bravado reasserts itself.

"The hell I will," he says to the world at large. "I don't know how you've done this – this *trick* – but I'm not leaving until I've done what I came here to do."

And with his free hand he starts to reach inside his jacket.

Knife, I think, and in my mind's eye the gleaming blade is already unsheathed – blue light flashing from it as Richard plunges it into me, stabbing again and again, until the walls are splattered with blood.

I grab his wrist, knowing it's hopeless, he's stronger than I am, but fighting anyway, fighting for my life.

Richard wrenches his arm out of my grasp with ease but at least he has his hand away from his pocket.

I know what he is capable of. I look at him and I see Max – Max yelling at the top of the staircase. Max's face in the bedroom, that horrible expression as he went to push me. Richard will kill me.

I yank up my right arm and sink my teeth into Richard's fingers. I bite as hard as I can, until my teeth meet something hard, and Richard shrieks. A coppery taste floods my mouth. I let go and Richard shoves me away. He is holding his left

304

hand and swearing, calling me a fucking bitch again, and red is dripping onto the floor.

I back away, putting as much space between us as I can. If I can edge far enough around the wall, I can make a break for the door.

Richard's shadow looms large against the wall, monstrous, bent over his bleeding hand. Then he straightens, lets go of his left hand, and thrusts his right inside his jacket again.

The projector is still whirring. The film runs between the spools, racing towards the end of the reel, and time is running out for me too.

I'm not leaving until I've done what I came here to do, he said.

The hand emerges from the jacket and it isn't a knife he's holding. It's a cigarette lighter.

For a moment I think Richard intends to burn *me* and the adrenaline ignites again; I tense, calculating which way gives me the best chance of escape.

Then I hear Hugh and Mary in my head again, and they are both screaming *No! No!* and I realise what Richard means to do.

I shake my head. "Don't," I croak. I don't know what Hugh will do to either of us if Richard carries out his intention. But my voice is drowned out by the screeching negative in my head; I see that Richard hears it too because he is shaking his head as though warding off stinging insects.

"Don't do it," I tell him.

And then Hugh and Mary are in the room with us and they are beautiful – beautiful in the way only filmstars can be: flawless, smooth-skinned, elegant – but terrible. There is a quality about them like that of a scorpion poised to sting; the air about them seems to shimmer with menace.

Richard stares at them for a moment, his mouth agape,

knowing that there is something dangerous here, but not understanding it.

"Don't," I beg him.

No, they tell him, closing in.

He does it anyway.

"Fuck your film."

He steps up to the projector, flips open the lighter and snaps the wheel. The flame flares up, very clear and bright in the dimness of the projection room. Very deliberately he thrusts it under the strip of film as it runs between the spools.

The film ignites with an instant and shocking brilliance, lighting up the room. Dazzling fire shoots from spool to spool – in a split second they are blazing Catherine wheels. The projector is engulfed in flames. Richard is swearing and beating at the sleeve of his jacket, which is on fire.

The high, piercing shriek which drills through my skull comes from Mary Arden. She stretches out her hands towards the expanding bonfire and rage and desolation stream out of her. The answering howl of fury from Hugh Mason is wild, inhuman. He steps towards the burning projector as though he can somehow contain the blaze, but it is too late. The fire has leapt to the second projector and that too is alight. The other reels are close by, the cannister lids off, and once those go up the inferno will be unstoppable.

Already the room is filling with smoke. Cellulose nitrate film is not only hideously inflammable, it gives off toxic fumes as it burns. I try to hold my breath, choking, coughing, and follow the wall with my hands, knowing that soon it will be impossible to see or breathe in here – impossible to do anything but die.

It feels like a miracle when the doorframe is suddenly under my hands. I stumble through it, and then I look back. What I see will be graven on my memory forever.

As *The Simulacrum* burns, Mary Arden burns too. Like wax under a blowtorch she melts and runs; her features lengthen, drooping, dissolving. With a scorching flare the carefully-dressed hair ignites, blazes, shrivels. Her old-fashioned clothing burns with savage brightness. The outstretched arms are consumed, worn down to nubs, gone. She shrivels, collapsing in on herself, and even after all recognisable attributes have gone, even when she has no mouth, I can still hear her screaming out her rage and frustration. Cheated, after all her efforts.

Hugh burns so brightly that I can barely look at him. Great gouts of crackling flame burst from his broad shoulders, his uniform, his sleek hair. Heat rolls across the room in shimmering waves. His beautiful face seems lit from within, glowing white hot. He does not scream – he opens his mouth impossibly wide and *roars*, emitting a plume of fire, extending arms which blaze a trail through the air. Then he steps forward and enfolds Richard in a fiery embrace.

Richard's clothing, his very flesh ignites, as though he has fallen into a furnace. His hair goes up in an explosion of flame, his clothes catch, flare and blacken; his face is a molten pit of fire. He writhes and screams and the sound he makes is like nothing on earth; it is the shrieking of a soul in the inferno and it goes on and on until at last it is subsumed in the roar of burning. He burns so fiercely that his body sizzles greasily, with great pops and crackles that bring the bile into the back of my throat.

The sound of that shrieking will follow me for the rest of my life, which will not be long if I stay here; the smoke that roils out of the projection room sears my eyes. I stumble away, coughing, my eyes burning, and the smoke follows me. Soon it will fill the corridor. If I draw those fumes down into my lungs there will be no escape: I will burn with the house. Some long-remembered advice about surviving a fire comes back to me and I drop to my hands and knees, trying to keep my head below the level of that toxic cloud. The carpet is soft underneath my fingers. I crawl, and crawl.

Chapter Sixty-One

When I come to the turn in the corridor, the air clears a little. Not for long: soon the smoke and flames will follow me, eating up the carpet and the walnut console table and the paintings on the walls with insatiable hunger. But for now there is enough respite for me to stand up. I don't run; I have no energy for that, after what I have just witnessed. I stumble along with one hand pressed to my mouth.

I am afraid to look behind me. I do not think that Hugh will pursue me – I was not the one who destroyed the film. Still, I do not want to look back. If I thought he was coming for me I would not be able to go on; I would stand right here and let him take me.

I pass the temperature-controlled store, the library, Richard's room. Behind me I hear a muffled thud – something has cracked or exploded. I keep going. It seems to take a very long time to reach the double doors that lead out of the west wing, and by the time I get there, tendrils of black smoke are reaching out for me. I go through the double doors and when they have shut behind me I take a long breath of clean air.

It flits through my head that I should go to my room and salvage what I can, because I do not believe that the fire can be contained. So many things are in there: not just my own possessions but all the papers relating to *The Simulacrum*, including possibly the only photograph of Hugh Mason in existence. For a moment I really waver, thinking about that, about the irreplaceable things that might be saved. But then I look over the bannisters, down the stairwell, and my heart fails me. The stairs look endless, curving round and down. It will be a miracle if I can find my way down to the ground floor before the smoke and fumes overtake me, even without stopping to collect things from my room. I decide to leave it all.

I start down the stairs, clinging to the bannister rail. My legs will barely support me – I go slowly, slowly, and it seems as if I am making no progress; I will never get to the bottom. Perhaps a third of the way down I realise that I am crying: the stairs below me are a blur and my face is wet. I do not know whom I am crying for – for Richard or myself, from sorrow or terror or relief.

Down, down I go, and somewhere up above and to the right of me I hear another distant sound of something smashing or falling in. Inconsequentially, I think of the copy of *The Hound of the Baskervilles* sitting by Richard's bed with the strip of paper hanging out of it to mark the place. He will never finish the book, and soon it, and the room, and perhaps the whole house will be gone. I force myself to keep moving.

When at last I reach the bottom of the stairs I stand for a moment, still holding onto the bannister rail. The expanse of polished floor between the spot where I am standing and the front door seems enormous; I feel like a polar explorer stepping out onto an ice floe. I let go of the rail and start to stumble across it, hugging myself and coughing. I find I am limping, but I don't know when I hurt myself. I taste salt and smoke on my lips.

It seems to take an eternity to get to the front door, and when I do I can't turn the key in the lock at first; my hands shake and I cannot get a purchase. But I manage it at last. The door opens and I stagger outside.

The air is cold – it is night time, after all, and Scotland. I draw it down into my lungs. It is clean and icy and it has the restorative effect of a brisk slap: I find the energy to go down the steps and away from the house. There is nowhere particular to go, so I make my way to the dried-up fountain and sink down on the stone coping. Then I look up at Garthside House.

The lights illuminating the front are still on, but abruptly they go out; some critical piece of wiring has burned through or melted. The house is not dark though. The fire has a fierce hold on the west wing. Glass shatters as windows blow out, smoke and flames belching out into the night air, shards pattering onto the terrace below. The blaze is running east, consuming everything in its path; soon the whole house will be burning.

Everything I brought with me is somewhere inside the conflagration. My wallet is in there, and my keys, and all my other stuff. I have nothing except the clothes I am wearing, and those are inadequate to keep out the cold which seeps into me from the stone coping and the freezing air. I hug myself, shivering, but I do not move. I have no idea where I would go, or how I would get there. I cannot call the fire brigade nor anyone else. It's a long walk to the town. So I sit and watch Garthside burning, and listen to the roar of the flames. I think about Mary Arden and Hugh Mason and Richard Foster, and watch sparks fly up into the night sky, chasing each other like fireflies.

Some time passes – it might be half an hour, or an hour, or two hours even – and I hear something. Footsteps on gravel, then someone calling my name.

"*Theda!*"

I don't look around. The flames are so beautiful. I keep watching them. I can feel warmth on my face now. The fire has reached the end of the east wing, and the whole of Garthside is one great conflagration.

Whoever it is keeps shouting out my name. He sounds desperate, and briefly I wonder why. I'm not in there; I'm out here, still sitting on the edge of the fountain. He doesn't stop shouting though, so after a while I turn my head.

Angus.

He stands there on the gravel in front of the house, his

fists clenched, and it occurs to me that he may try to go inside, thinking that that is where I am, although it is very plain that there is nobody alive inside Garthside. So I get up, very slowly and painfully because I am stiff from sitting here, and I limp over to where he is standing.

He doesn't hear me at first, because he is shouting and because I am moving so slowly.

"Angus," I say. "Angus, I'm here."

He turns around.

"*Theda?*"

He pulls me into his arms, holding me so tightly I can hardly breathe. "Thank God," he says. "Thank God. I thought you were in there."

I shake my head against his shoulder.

For a while he just holds me. Then he says, "Is there anyone in there?"

"Richard," I say. "Richard Foster, Mary Arden's relative. He's dead."

"Nobody could survive that." I feel Angus's head turn as he surveys the blaze.

"No," I tell him. "I mean, before."

"I don't understand."

"He broke in. He wanted to destroy the film – the one I went to talk to Mary Arden about. And..." I hesitate. "I think maybe to hurt me too."

"My God. What happened? Did you have to...?"

"No. I didn't do anything to him. He set fire to the film. I guess he didn't know how flammable those old films are. His... his sleeve caught fire."

Then it occurs to me that people may think I killed Richard in self-defence, or otherwise. All those months hiding what happened to Max, whom I did kill, and now they may think I killed Richard, when I didn't lay a finger on him. I could go to prison after all – for the wrong death.

I start laughing then. I can't control it. I know none of it is really funny but I laugh anyway, hysterically, and I keep laughing until I am crying, big ugly tears and sobs that scour my throat. And all the time Angus holds me and says nothing at all.

After a while, other people come up the drive: a fireman, a couple of paramedics. All of them are on foot: Richard's electric blue car is blocking the drive and the emergency vehicles can't get through until it's been moved.

The fireman looks at Garthside and swears under his breath. Then he comes up to us and says, "Did you call this in?"

"Yes," says Angus. "I could see it from outside my house. The whole sky's lit up."

"You don't live here, then?"

"No."

I find my voice. "I do."

"Right. Is there anyone inside, so far as you know?"

"Yes," I say. "One person."

The fireman looks very grim when I say this. "Do you know where this person is?"

"Upstairs in the west... in that part of house." I point. "His name is Richard Foster. But I think – I think he's dead."

This is stating the obvious considering the inferno that is the west wing. The fireman looks at me for a moment but he says nothing. I suppose this is out of concern for my feelings; for all he knows, Richard Foster is a close relative. A friend. A lover. He gives us an almost imperceptible nod and then he sets off at a jog, back down the drive.

After that, the paramedics close in.

Chapter Sixty-Two – Six Months Later

There was frost this morning; the blades of grass and the fallen leaves were rimed with it. In spite of the sun, there is a biting coldness to the air. I am sitting here in a thick winter coat, a woolly hat and fingerless gloves. Proper gloves would be better for this temperature, but I wanted to be able to use my phone – my new phone, since the old one is probably a smear of melted plastic and metal somewhere under the remains of Garthside. Same number though.

The winter sun is so bright and so low in the sky that I can hardly look to the east: it blazes, leaving bright afterimages on my eyes. I wonder if that was what Garthside looked like from here, the night it burned.

I have been back several times since that night. I was a little afraid the first time, as though Hugh Mason would somehow rise from the cold ashes to revenge himself on me. But I could tell immediately that he wouldn't. That strange compulsion that I thought of as an *itch* has entirely gone, dissolved into smoke along with *The Simulacrum*.

The house looks very sad. Only a stump of the ground floor remains, and that is full of charred beams that fell from above. In one or two places, odd things have survived: a tiny section of Eau de Nil wall, a panel from the staircase balustrade, warped by heat at one end.

The garden is the same as ever: dead, overgrown, neglected.

The insurers are still arguing about Garthside. I think everyone has agreed that it was Richard who burned it down, not me, but they don't want to pay out such an immense claim – not without a fight, anyway. There have been a lot of questions about the conditions under which Mary Arden's collection of cellulose nitrate films were kept, and whether anything could be considered negligent. I expect this will go on for a long time, but I don't really care. It will make a lot of difference to how much money I have in the end, of course, but I still feel largely indifferent. I survived Max and I survived Richard, and to my eternal thankfulness I survived Hugh Mason and Mary Arden too, and that is enough.

Richard's death troubled me for a long time. Would people believe that he came there with evil intent, and that his death was not on my hands? Or indeed that we did not conspire together to burn Garthside down for the money?

Fortunately, there was a lot of evidence to support my story. Simon Hawkes of Murray Hawkes confirmed Richard's reaction when he discovered that I had inherited most of Mary Arden's estate. In spite of the careful lawyer-speak it became apparent that Richard was so incandescently angry about it that he had to be escorted off Murray Hawkes's premises. The term "gold digging bitch" that Richard flung at me was bandied about in front of two of his colleagues as well. And of course there was the fact that he left his electric blue monster of a car parked well down the driveway, away from the house – blocking the fire engine and the ambulance when they arrived. There could have been no reason for that, other than the intention to approach the house by stealth.

I told the investigators from the Procurator Fiscal Service that Richard came to the house with the intention of destroying an old film which he believed was the cause of Mary Arden's leaving the house and most of the money to me. I described how he set fire to the film, not realising how very combustible cellulose nitrate film stock is, how toxic the fumes when it burns. His clothing caught fire. Such was the heat and the smoke that I could do nothing. He burned to death and I barely escaped with my life.

All of this is the truth, and nothing but the truth. It is not the *whole* truth, but I don't think anyone would believe that. Sometimes I think about it, and I can hardly believe it myself.

While I am sitting here, my mind on all these things, something enthusiastic and damp pushes its way into my free hand: Jess's nose. Automatically, I scratch the ruff of fur at her neck, just where she likes it. And then I look around.

Angus is coming out of the house with two steaming tin mugs. He looks as untidy as ever: he is wearing one of his more disreputable waxed jackets, and I'm pretty sure that is the sweater with the hole in it underneath. The dazzling sunshine makes him blink.

"Tea," he says, handing me one of the mugs.

I look up at him, and I want to say: *I love you*. I want to say – again – how much I regret those cruel things I said to him that day.

Angus has forgotten them already, or so he says. I told him I was afraid for him, that I knew Richard was angry enough to strike at anyone I cared about, and Angus said I should have shared it; I shouldn't have tried to handle it alone. We didn't argue about it, though. I told him I didn't mean any of it, and then I told him I loved him, and it ended the way it generally does.

So I don't say it again now, because he knows it. I take the tea and say "Thank you," and for a while we both just stay there, me sitting and him standing, looking east. From here you can't actually see the remains of Garthside, only the river and the fields sloping up from it. But it's there, that blackened ruin.

After a while Jess gets frisky and Angus collects the mugs and goes back into the house. He has things to do, and Jess will go with him. He kisses me before he goes, lingeringly, in a way that makes me think about later.

Me, I don't have anything I *have* to do. I think I'll just sit here for a while, watching the river flowing past and holding my new phone.

Mrs Harris. She was the one thing still bothering me. Mary Arden and Hugh Mason are gone now, because the film is nothing but ash. Even Garthside, where I made my confession, is gone. But Mrs Harris had a recording of it, carefully uploaded to a Dropbox. Would she use it? There was no particular reason for her to do that, because it wouldn't help Mary Arden's cause now. She might have done it out of spite though, or out of a sense of duty to her former employer, the one who left her three hundred thousand pounds. On the whole I thought she *probably* wouldn't, especially as time passed, but it was impossible to be entirely sure. It is not pleasant to live your life in that way, thinking that there is something hanging over you – that your future happiness is at the mercy of someone else's whim.

This morning, a little after four-thirty a.m., my phone buzzed quietly on the night stand. It didn't wake Angus – he always sleeps well, the way people do when they work outdoors most of the day. I do not sleep well.

I recognised the sound as a text coming in. I could have ignored it – I couldn't think of a single person who would need to text me at that time of the morning – but I picked the phone up anyway. I lay on my back next to Angus, the phone lighting up my face, and read the message while he slumbered on.

I switch the phone on now and read that same message again.

Ms Garrick, with regret, I must let you know something. I had a memento of yours – do you remember? I think perhaps you do.

Unfortunately, I seem to have destroyed it. Accidents happen, do they not?

I wish you well.

VH

I look at that message for a long time. My thumb hovers over the delete button, but in the end I decide not to; I want to read it again later. Then I turn my back on Garthside, and go into the house.

Acknowledgements

I would like to thank Clare Cain and Fledgling Press for publishing *Jump Cut*, and Graeme Clarke for the wonderful cover design.

Thanks are also due to Lindsey Fraser of Fraser Ross Associates, who represents me.

In addition, I would like to thank my daughter Iona, to whom this book is dedicated, and who shares with me a boundless love for cinema. Much of the inspiration and research information for this book sprang from her dissertation on early film.

Finally, as ever, thanks to Gordon.

BV - #0104 - 090823 - C0 - 198/129/18 - PB - 9781912280643 - Matt Lamination